WILDSTAR

"You make it sound . . . like I'm a child. I'm not. I'm a full-grown woman."

Devlin smiled as his gaze drifted lower to her breasts. "Full-grown, perhaps . . . but not entirely a woman."

The implied insult stung. "What is that supposed to mean?"

Have you ever bedded a man, angel? "Just that you're inexperienced."

Jess wanted to deny it, but when she frowned up at him, she was trapped by his gaze. His eyes were dangerous, the gray deep and subtle like smoke from a wildfire. But then he was a dangerous man. Dangerous as sin.

Other AVON ROMANCES

SCARLET KISSES by Patricia Camden
BELOVED INTRUDER by Joan Van Nuys
SURRENDER TO THE FURY by Cara Miles
THE LION'S DAUGHTER by Loretta Chase
CAPTAIN OF MY HEART by Danelle Harmon
SILVER FLAME by Hannah Howell
TAMING KATE by Eugenia Riley

Coming Soon

HEART OF THE WILD by Donna Stephens
TRAITOR'S KISS by Joy Tucker

And Don't Miss These
ROMANTIC TREASURES
from Avon Books

MIDNIGHT AND MAGNOLIAS by Rebecca Paisley
MY WILD ROSE by Deborah Camp
ONLY WITH YOUR LOVE by Lisa Kleypas

WILDSTAR

NICOLE JORDAN

AVON BOOKS ◆ NEW YORK

To Jay, of course; my own bright star.
This one's all for you.

WILDSTAR is an original publication of Avon Books. This work has never before appeared in book form. This work is a novel. Any similarity to actual persons or events is purely coincidental.

AVON BOOKS
A division of
The Hearst Corporation
1350 Avenue of the Americas
New York, New York 10019

First Avon Books Printing: December 1992

AVON TRADEMARK REG. U.S. PAT. OFF. AND IN OTHER COUNTRIES, MARCA REGISTRADA, HECHO EN U.S.A.

Printed in the U.S.A.

RA 10 9 8 7 6 5 4 3 2 1

          . . .'Twere all one
That I should love a bright particular star
And think to wed it, he is so above me.

                —WILLIAM SHAKESPEARE

Chapter 1

Silver Plume, Colorado; 1884

L ean and naked, the gambler lounged at the window of his second-floor hotel room, his attention drawn by the commotion on the street below. The thud of galloping hooves had shattered the peace of the lazy summer morning and startled the few brave souls who were out and about after a wild night's revelry. It was Sunday, the one day of the week that a rowdy mining town like Silver Plume slowed down. Except for the occasional rig or pack mule tied to the hitching rails, Main Street was nearly deserted.

The fury riding hell for leather up the dirt street— bareback, no less—seemed oblivious to the peace.

Garrett Devlin watched curiously from his hotel window. Ordinarily such a disturbance wouldn't concern him, but he'd come to this town for a reason. Everything that happened in Silver Plume interested him. And this sight downright intrigued him.

The rider wore skirts. Four inches of lace-edged drawers showing beneath blue sateen proclaimed her to be a woman, as did the long mane of honey-blond hair streaming wildly in the wind.

"Marshal!" Devlin heard her cry. She was targeting the man with the badge on his vest as he walked past the general store opposite the hotel. "Marshal Lockwood!"

She drew her horse to a plunging stop before the marshal in a spurt of dust, with a gasped plea of "Wait!" She was breathing hard, Devlin could see, while her tone was frantic.

The marshal touched his hat politely but remained on the boardwalk, safely out of range of the snorting horse. "Mornin', Miss Jess. What can I do for you?"

She had trouble catching her breath, and her full breasts rose and fell with the effort. Devlin studied the effect appreciatively, with the eye of a connoisseur.

She was wearing a wrapper—the kind of loose gown intended to be worn only at home—made of lustrous, dark blue sateen, without a bustle. Her tresses were tumbled enticingly as if she'd only just risen from her bed. Which perhaps she had, Devlin thought, enchanted by the provocative sight. She looked a bit younger than he'd first assumed from her luscious curves. Maybe twenty. From so far away, he couldn't make out the color of her eyes, but he could see well enough that her face was flushed with anger, or perhaps fear.

"Riley's been shot!" she gasped out finally.

"What in thunder?" The blank look on the marshal's face turned to a startled frown. "Your pa's been shot?"

She managed to nod but her voice shook when she answered, "Shot in the back. He was up at the mine . . . going over the books."

She pointed frantically up at the rugged mountains behind the store, making Devlin momentarily lift his gaze. The spectacular granite peaks dominated the earth and sky, towering over the townsite and the deep canyon where Silver Plume nestled. From his vantage point, Devlin could see the numerous mine dumps that littered the slopes, as well as the tortuous trails that zigzagged up the steep sides and seemed to disappear in the vast vault of blue sky.

"A guard from the Silver Queen found him and brought him home," Devlin heard her say. "He's in a bad way. If he hadn't been found when he was, he might be dead by now. The bleeding's stopped, but he's still not out of danger. I'm afraid . . . he may still die." Her voice caught on a sob, but then she swallowed hard. "I've already fetched the doc. He's on his way."

The marshal apparently was still trying to take in the events. "Who in tarnation would do such a thing?"

"You know very well who! Burke's hirelings, that's who."

"Now, Miss Jess, you don't know that—"

"I do so know it! And I want to hear what you're going to do about it."

"I'll go up to the Wildstar and take a look around."

She clenched a slender fist in a gesture of frustration. "Whoever did it will be long gone by now. Why don't you arrest Ashton Burke? He's behind the attack, I know it."

Ashton Burke. Devlin recognized the name. Burke was a rich English capitalist who owned this hotel, a dozen saloons and gaming halls in three towns, and any number of mining interests.

"You got any proof of that?"

"He threatened us last week when Riley wouldn't sell him the Wildstar. What more proof do you need?"

"Now, Miss Jess, you know I can't just go around arrestin' people without proof. Besides, an upstanding figure such as Mr. Burke would never resort to such violent means."

Her scoffed answer was drowned out by a petulant, seductive voice behind Devlin.

"Garrett, honey, I'm gettin' mighty lonesome. Why don't you come back to bed?"

He didn't glance at the sultry, ebony-haired beauty in his bed. Lena was a dealer for the Diamond Dust Saloon next door. She was also occasionally a lady of pleasure, with emphasis on the word *pleasure*. She chose her clients with discrimination, and she'd latched onto Devlin the first night he'd sat at her faro table.

Devlin was accustomed to such immediate attention. With his sable hair, smoke-gray eyes, and stunning dark looks, he'd always attracted women without the slightest effort. Sometimes it was a nuisance, the way women ran after him. But in this case it worked to his advantage. His suave, sophisticated appearance allowed him to pass for a gambler, while furthering his acquaintance with Lena Thorpe allowed him to find out more about the town without drawing undue attention to himself.

For the moment, though, he ignored Lena's seductive plea, more interested in hearing the conversation across the street.

"Did Riley see who did it?" Marshal Lockwood was asking.

"No, I told you," the young woman he'd addressed as "Miss Jess" snapped. "Some lily-livered coward shot him in the back. How could he possibly see who did it? All I know is what the guard said. There was a stranger nosing around up there this morning. He had a scar over one eye and he was riding a roan."

Devlin's interest shot up ten degrees. *A scar above his eye. Riding a roan.* He leaned forward, his gray eyes narrowing. In the three days since his arrival, he'd made little progress in locating the man he'd come to find. This was the first good lead he'd had since the train robbery two weeks ago.

"You should be arming a posse," the blond beauty accused. "Preventing law-abiding citizens from being shot down in cold blood, instead of standing here defending Burke and his hired guns. But then maybe you're on his payroll, too."

Marshal Lockwood turned red in the face—whether from anger or guilt Devlin wasn't sure—and made a blustering denial. "There's no call to say such things, ma'am. I was elected law officer fair and square, and I don't cotton to insults about my integrity."

Miss Jess squared her shoulders. "And I don't cotton to seeing my father shot while the culprit goes scot-free. I'm warning you, Marshal, if you won't do something about Ashton Burke, I will. I mean to fight back. I'll hire my own gunslingers, if necessary. Burke will never get the Wildstar, as long as there's a breath left in my body! Now, I've got to get home to Riley. The doctor may be there by now."

She wheeled her mount to leave, but as she turned, her gaze raked the hotel window where Devlin stood. For an instant as she looked up, her eyes locked with his, then took in his sleek muscular frame, exposed to her view. Her reaction to his nudity amused and charmed him: she flushed and ducked her head before kneeing her horse into a gallop.

"Miss Jess, don't you go doing anything foolish!" Marshal Lockwood hollered after her, plainly alarmed by her threat to take matters into her own hands. "You hear me?"

"What's all the ruckus about?" Lena asked as she came up behind Devlin. The scent of expensive perfume and the pure smell of woman enveloped him as she slid her arms around his lean waist.

Devlin gestured with his head at the street below.

Lena glanced out the window as the blond rider galloped off. "What's she in such an all-fired hurry for?"

"You know her?"

Lena shrugged and yawned, the fingers of one hand teasing the dark, curling hair on his chest. "Name's Jessica Sommers. Runs a boardinghouse for miners to keep food on the table and her pa outfitted with gear. Riley Sommers always did have his head in the clouds. He's been working his claim for nigh on six years, but it never amounted to much."

"He was shot this morning."

"You don't say."

She didn't seem surprised by the violence, Devlin noted. But then, here violence was a part of life. Silver Plume was a typical Western mining town: rowdy, lusty, and raw around the edges. Here men lived and hustled and hoped, scrounging for dreams in the hardrock earth, sometimes discovering wealth beyond their imaginations, sometimes finding death.

"How is Sommers connected to Ashton Burke?"

"Oh, Riley's been feudin' with Ash since time began."

Suddenly feeling a tickling sensation below his waist, Devlin glanced down to see Lena drawing a vivid red

feather boa across his taut abdomen, through the crisp
black hair of his groin.

"Sugar," she whispered huskily in his ear, "don't we
have better things to do than talk about some old mine
feud?" Pressing her nude voluptuous body against his bare
back, she moved suggestively against him.

He felt himself hardening in response. Lena made a sensual sound of approval deep in her throat, while unerringly
her fingers found the shaft that was swiftly becoming long
and swollen and thick. Intimately caressing, she explored
and fondled his burgeoning erection. "I do declare, you're
a magnificent fella."

His laugh was low and very male, but he remained still,
enjoying her play and the feel of warm, stroking fingers
curling around him.

Pressing harder against his buttocks, Lena rotated her
hips in invitation. "I want you to take me again, darlin'
man."

Fully aroused now, he turned with a virile, wicked
smile. "My pleasure, ma'am. I'm always willing to ac-
commodate a beautiful lady."

"My, what a smooth-talkin' fella you are."

"Who's talking?" he murmured as he slid his hands
down her back, beneath the smooth mounds of her buttocks. Unhurriedly he lifted her, in one easy motion wrapping her open legs about his flanks and angling so her
back was pressed against the wall.

Lena cooed and clutched at his naked shoulders, the
feather boa forgotten. When she arched against him, he
bent his knees and glided into her slick warm flesh, thrusting deep. Her throaty gasp turned into a hot little whimper.

Lifting her hips high and hard against his, Devlin took
her for the third time that morning, but part of his mind remained divorced from the pleasure. That part contemplated
the conversation he'd overheard just now about a stranger
with a scar over one eye—and planned what he would do
about it.

He had every intention of making the acquaintance of

Miss Jessica Sommers. In the meantime, though, he might as well enjoy what was left of the morning.

Six blocks away, in the kitchen of a small miner's cottage, Jess clenched her fingers till they ached as she watched Doc Wheeler dig the .44-caliber bullet from her father's back. At least he couldn't feel the pain. Unconscious, Riley Sommers lay on his stomach on the hard supper table, his blood dripping onto the yellow hand-woven cotton rug. The crimson splotches looked obscenely vivid in the bright pool of sunshine streaming through the window.

Jess didn't realize that the strangled sob she heard belonged to her until her father's partner and best friend, Clem Haverty, patted her arm in clumsy affection.

"He's bad hurt," the wizened old mule skinner said in a hoarse whisper, "but I ain't never seen Riley give up without a fight. He'll make it, Jess."

"Oh, Clem," she said shakily, then swallowed, trying to get hold of herself. Going to pieces wouldn't help her father keep his tenuous hold on life, or help her face this horrible situation any better.

How had it come to this? Riley had worked so hard to get where he was, and look what he had to show for it. A bullet in the back. She couldn't bear to see it.

Feeling Clem squeeze her arm in sympathy, she glanced up at him through her tears. The deep lines creasing his forehead beneath his shaggy gray hair showed how worried he was. He was fighting the same fear she was, she knew: a stark, gnawing dread in the pit of the stomach that felt like acid.

"Somebody tried to kill him a-purpose," Clem muttered unnecessarily, tugging on his long beard.

Jess nodded, not trusting herself to make a reply.

"I find the bastard what done it, I'll hold me a necktie party."

It was a measure of how shook up he was that he'd let the profanity slip out. Clem had a vocabulary that could set a prairie afire, but he always made an effort to curb his tongue around her. Normally, Jess didn't allow cussing in the home she shared with her father, or in her boarding-house a block away, where Clem and a dozen other miners lived. She was willing to make an exception this time, though. In this case, she shared Clem's sentiments exactly.

Silently she added her own oath to his, and the resultant surge of anger she felt was a welcome respite from her fear. Purposefully she hoarded that anger, directing it to-ward the man she knew was responsible for such treach-ery. Ashton Burke. Just the thought of him filled her with an icy cold rage. Wealthy, powerful, manipulative men like Burke deserved such fates as this, not Riley. All the rich men in the world, all the silver kings and railroad mag-nates, the financiers and industrialists and their greedy agents, all the money-grubbing parasites who lived off other men's hard work and honest sweat.

Just then Doc Wheeler made a sound of satisfaction as he extracted a flattened slug of lead from his patient's back. Jess hastened to hold out a basin to catch it.

"You better save that, young lady. Riley will want to see it."

"He gonna make it, Doc?" Clem demanded fearfully.

The doc grinned. "Sure he's gonna make it. Bullet missed the lung by a good quarter inch, lucky for him. Be-sides, Riley's tougher'n an old boot. Take a lot more than this to kill him."

Jess felt her knees go weak. Murmuring a prayer of re-lief, she sank into a kitchen chair and pressed a hand to her mouth, while Clem unashamedly wiped his eyes.

After Doc Wheeler had cleaned the raw flesh with car-bolic and scrubbed the blood off his hands, he carefully bandaged Riley's back. Then together he and Clem carried the unconscious man into the small blue-and-white master bedroom and laid him face down on the bed whose covers Jess had already turned back.

"He'll likely be out for a while," the doctor said to her. "I'll leave you a bottle of morphine to give him when he wakes. Sleep will be the best thing for him. Keep an eye out for fever and send for me if it gets too high tonight. Otherwise, I'll be back tomorrow to change the bandage."

Jess thanked the doctor and, too concerned to leave her father alone, asked Clem to show him out. She was sitting beside the bed when Clem returned. At her invitation, he claimed the other rocking chair beside hers, hooking his thumbs around the suspenders of his blue duck overalls.

They watched in silence for a while, until Jess finally spoke. "Burke had to be behind it," she said in a low tone.

"More 'n likely."

"Marshal Lockwood didn't believe me."

"Reckon he wouldn't."

"Darn it, it isn't fair!"

"Nope, that it ain't."

"Burke has everything money can buy. Everything any man could possibly want. Why does he have to have the one thing that Riley has worked so hard for?"

"I dunno. Don't seem right that Burke can do anythin' he's wishful of."

"Well, he won't get away with it this time!" Jess vowed.

"What you aimin' to do?"

"Make him think twice about sending his hired guns to do his dirty work."

Stroking his grizzled beard, Clem eyed her warily. "Maybe you best steer clear of Burke, Jessie. If he did this to Riley, he's liable to do jest about anythin'."

Jess looked away, her jaw set with determination. "You've got it all wrong, Clem. Ashton Burke had best steer clear of me. He's not laying claim to the Wildstar, and he's not going to hurt Riley. Ever again."

It was a vow she intended to keep. All her life Jess had watched her father struggle to eke out a living from the Colorado silver mines, first as a prospector, then as the owner of a low-grade ore mine. He'd been toiling unsuccessfully far longer than her twenty-one years, and had endured the pain of lost dreams and savaged hopes for all that time.

Gambling on what might be a worthless mine, he'd spent every penny of his life savings to work his claim. No one could make him see reason, not even Jess's mother.

The siren song of silver had gotten into Riley's blood. Always the bonanza was just around the corner, just a few more feet along a tunnel. That rich vein that would make him instantly wealthy.

He'd never found it.

And now Ashton Burke wanted to take away even that pitiful dream. Burke's Lady J mine was adjacent to Riley's Wildstar up in Cherokee Gulch. Just last week Burke had stopped by the house and offered to take the mine off Riley's hands for a goodly sum of hard cash. Not only wouldn't Riley sell, but he'd seen a hidden significance in the timing of the offer.

"Don't you see, Jess?" he'd told her excitedly. "If Burke struck a vein in the Lady J, then maybe there's rich ore in the Wildstar. I just have to find it."

She hadn't had the heart to crush his hopes. She hadn't insisted on making him see the truth—that Burke was acting out of pure vindictiveness. He wanted the mine simply to hurt her father by putting him out of business.

It was plain as day to Jess. The bitter rivalry had been going on since before she was born, ever since Riley had dared to marry the girl Burke had laid claim to. And Ashton Burke was a man who hated to be thwarted, who hated anybody who didn't sidestep for him. In fact, it seemed clear to Jess that Burke *enjoyed* crushing little people in his drive to accumulate wealth and power, particularly self-made men like her father.

But she wouldn't let him succeed. If she had to go up against a powerful silver baron like Burke to protect her father, she would.

It was a good three hours before Riley stirred. When his eyelids fluttered open, Jess bolted upright in her chair.

"What . . . happened?" her father rasped before suddenly flinching and groaning in pain.

Hurriedly, Jess knelt beside his bed and gently clasped his hand. "Don't try to talk, Riley. You've been hurt."

"Feels like . . . somebody shoved . . . a stick o' dynamite in my shoulder."

Clem, hovering over the bed, grunted. "Near enough. You was backshot."

"Who . . .?"

"Riley, please," Jess pleaded. "Come on now, you've got to take your medicine."

She directed Clem to help raise her father's head while she spoon-fed him a heavy dose of morphine. Riley grimaced in pain, but swallowed dutifully. When she was done, though, Riley clutched at her hand and wouldn't let go of it or the subject.

"Was it Burke?"

"Do you know anyone else who would want you dead?" Jess answered with no little asperity.

"Always knew . . . Burke wanted my hide, but I . . . never figured he'd stoop to shooting me in the back."

Lovingly, Jess smoothed her father's sweat-dampened brown hair that was sprinkled with gray. "I didn't either."

"Jess?. . . Got to tell you something . . . about your ma. . . ."

"Riley, don't talk, please."

"In case I pass on."

"You aren't going to die!" she cried furiously, then caught herself and took a calming breath. "Now, you hush and go to sleep like the doctor said."

"You don't understand. . . . Burke . . . doesn't know about you. . . . Got to tell him . . . so he won't hurt you."

"No one's going to hurt me. You just quit worrying and concentrate on getting better. When you're well enough, I'll make you a whole pan of strawberry biscuits."

"Strawberry?" The smile Riley gave was wan and drowsy. "All . . . for me?"

"Yes, all for you." She bent and tenderly kissed his temple. "Now you go to sleep."

It took a while, but eventually the morphine took effect. Squeezing her father's hand one last time, Jess tucked the covers around his waist, mindful of the bandage, then headed directly for the kitchen pantry where Riley kept his weapons.

From a shelf, she took down his double-barreled ten-gauge shotgun and a box of cartridges, and began to load.

Chapter 2

There were any number of ways to die in the Wild West, and Devlin had faced his share of near misses in his checkered career. He'd nearly been crushed by a shifting load of railroad ties while supervising the addition of a line spur for one of his father's many railroads; almost gored by a longhorn on a trail drive back in '74; barely missed being shot by an outraged, less-than-sober husband who never would've had the courage to draw on an acknowledged gunhand had he drunk a few less whiskeys; and come close to being speared by a Sioux brave's lance in the Dakota Territory during the Black Hills gold rush.

But he'd never before been confronted by a tawny-haired, avenging fury with fire in her eyes. She stormed into Burke's private gaming parlor like a desert whirlwind, bringing with her the fresh scent of life and carrying the threat of death.

The shotgun in her hands looked plain and lethal amid the gleaming walnut woodwork and polished crystal chandeliers. She had changed out of her morning robe, Devlin noted, while her fabulous hair was pinned up sedately beneath a small hat. Her gray skirts sported a modest bustle, and the high-necked jacket-bodice molded her firm, generous bosom to flattering perfection. Still, her sensible clothing looked dowdy compared to the fine feathers of the few sporting women present and the elegant evening attire of the male guests.

The Diamond Dust Saloon was closed to the public, it

being Sunday, but the private parlor boasted a good crowd. Devlin had accepted Ashton Burke's invitation to a friendly game of faro, lured more by the prospect of information than by the promise of high stakes, limitless champagne, and a distinguished clientele.

He was seated next to Burke when Jessica Sommers made her startling appearance. Devlin watched with rapt attention as she forged a path through the crowd and the haze of cigar smoke. She paused halfway across the parlor, narrowed eyes scanning the company.

The entire room gradually went silent, except for the rapid click of the still-spinning roulette wheel.

"Burke!" she said through gritted teeth when she laid eyes on the fair-haired Englishman, her low tone one of savage anticipation.

Chairs began to scrape as men in the line of fire moved out of the way. Devlin, though, held his place as she advanced, fascinated by the sight of Jessica Sommers up close. *Gold*, he thought with an odd sense of pleasure. Her eyes were a tawny gold to match her hair. And right now they were flashing like pyrite in sunlight. She was spitting mad and looking for blood.

Beside Devlin the raven-haired Lena, vividly gowned in red satin with paste diamonds and bare shoulders, edged back from her place as dealer at the table. On his other side, Ashton Burke sat unmoving, the epitome of power and wealth in his cutaway tailcoat and opera hat, a thin cheroot clenched between his teeth.

Burke was apparently unconcerned by either his wrathful caller or the weapon she carried. He played another card on the green baize table before removing his cheroot, tipping his hat to her politely, and smiling with mocking civility.

"Miss Sommers," he said, his upper-class British accent cultured and clipped. "To what do we owe the honor of this unusual visit?"

"Don't patronize me, Burke. You know exactly why I'm here—because one of your hired guns shot my father in the back and left him for dead. I used to think a snake like you might have a few scruples, but that was low, even for you."

Ashton Burke's smile never wavered yet grew decidedly cooler. "Ah, yes, your father. I was indeed sorry to hear of his ... misfortune. How does Riley fare?"

"He's alive, no thanks to you!"

"But you are mistaken, my dear. I had nothing to do with his accident, nor did any of my employees."

"Accident ... ?" Jessica Sommers clenched her teeth, obviously struggling for control. "Don't disgust me. You'd like nothing more than to see Riley gone so you can get your hands on his claim."

"Merely because I offered to buy the Wildstar mine for an extremely generous price is no reason to make unsubstantiated allegations. Your father's property interests me only from a legal standpoint, to preclude the possibility of conflicting claims, but certainly not enough to cause him harm. I suggest you look elsewhere for your malefactor. Now ... this is a private party, Miss Sommers. If you're quite finished, I will have someone escort you out."

Her hot amber eyes growing hotter, she made no move to leave. "I'm only going to warn you once, Burke. You keep your hired guns away from my father, do you hear me? If Riley so much as stubs his toe without cause, I'm holding you responsible. I'll come after you with this"— she raised the shotgun—"and put so many holes in you that you'll look like a sieve. They'll be able to pan for gold nuggets with you."

Burke's smile faded entirely. "I suggest that you refrain from issuing such dire threats, Miss Sommers. I should hate to have Marshal Lockwood issue a warrant for your arrest."

A silent bystander, Devlin watched the interplay between the firebrand and the silver king with keen interest and perhaps a touch of sympathy. He could almost feel Jessica Sommers's impotent rage and Burke's cool superiority—and the loathing they each felt for the other. Animosity shimmered between them, ripe and dangerous.

It was intriguing, the way they'd squared off like two mountain lions battling over the same lair, claws bared—

Curiously, Devlin looked from one to the other, suddenly struck by the similarities between them. Both had refined features, hardened now by the stamp of determination. Burke's eyes were pale blue to Jess's gold, true, and he was perhaps thirty years older. But they could have been cut from the same cloth.

Devlin tucked away the interesting observation in a corner of his mind, just as he caught a movement at the edge of his vision. A man was moving up behind Jess, out of her range of sight. A lean, black-haired man by the name of Hank Purcell; Devlin had met him briefly an hour earlier. The Colt six-shooter in Purcell's hand was aimed directly between Jessica Sommers's shoulder blades.

Devlin hadn't planned on interfering, but that was before the odds had turned uneven. With a smooth movement of his arm, he let the gambler's hideout gun fall from his sleeve, into his palm. The snub-nosed derringer had little range, but had the power to launch two solid one-ounce balls. One, Devlin shot at the ceiling, raining plaster dust down on Purcell's head. The second he held in reserve as Purcell froze.

The report echoed loudly in the elegant parlor. Devlin saw Miss Sommers flinch, felt Burke tense beside him, but kept his attention on Purcell, behind the girl. "I'd give it another thought," he suggested with deceptive laziness, his thumb holding back the hammer of the small derringer.

Jess spun around to face her attacker, her expression first one of startlement, then disgust as she eyed the weapon in Purcell's hand. "This is how your employees stay neutral, Mr. Burke?"

"Drop the gun," Devlin said as if she hadn't spoken.

Purcell's savage expression turned mutinous.

"It's your funeral," Devlin added amiably. He could feel Ashton Burke's pale blue eyes boring a hole in him, but he wasn't surprised by the silver king's decision.

"Do as he says, Hank," Burke ordered.

Purcell, after another moment's futile delay, gingerly laid the revolver on the floor.

"Now back off, easy." Devlin waited until the man had edged away, hands raised, palms out, before directing a lazy smile at the angry young woman. "Miss Sommers, I imagine this might be a good time to take your leave."

She turned slowly to give him a long glance, those tawny eyes of hers wary and questioning. But she must have thought better of arguing, for her gaze shifted to the silver king. "Don't forget what I said, Burke," she warned softly before pivoting on her heel and making her way to the door.

The quiet crowd, which inched back to allow her a wide berth, gave a collective sigh of relief when she'd gone. It was a long moment, though, before the guests returned to their previous pursuits and the noise level rose again.

In contrast, the silence at Devlin's table was deafening. As he slipped the small gun up his sleeve, he could feel Burke's simmering anger.

"Did no one ever tell you, Mr. Devlin, that it is not wise for a stranger to choose sides in an argument that does not concern him?"

Devlin smiled pleasantly. "Call it a major failing of mine, Mr. Burke. I never have been able to abandon a lady in distress ... or watch someone get ambushed from behind. Just doesn't sit right. Under the circumstances, however, I can understand why you might not see it in the same light."

"You understand correctly. When I extend my hospitality to a man, I expect a certain degree of courtesy in return, if not loyalty."

"Well, then, I won't take advantage of your hospitality any longer." Devlin pushed the yellow pile of hundred-dollar chips he'd won to the center of the table. "Keep it," he said dryly, "as a token of my appreciation for an enjoyable evening and to cover the damage to your ceiling. Excuse me, will you?"

With a polite nod at Lena, who was hovering about in dismay, Devlin slid his chair back and rose. Pausing long enough to kick Purcell's six-shooter under a table, he followed the path Jessica Sommers had taken, feeling at least three pairs of eyes—Burke's, Purcell's, and Lena's—burning into his back all the while.

Outside in the darkness, Jess was leaning against the wooden hitching rail, trying to control her trembling. She heard the bat-wing doors swing open, then the leisurely tread of footsteps on the planks of the boardwalk. It was *him*, she knew without even looking. Not wanting to let him see her momentary weakness, she straightened and brushed the telltale dampness from her eyes before daring to glance over her shoulder at him.

He had stopped three, maybe four feet away. His hat brim was pulled low, hiding most of his mahogany-colored hair. Jess couldn't see his features, either, even in the golden glow from a nearby streetlamp. But she'd already seen his face, already been stunned by it. If a man could be called beautiful, this one was. Beautiful as sin. With nothing remotely effeminate about him. He was no Eastern dandy; he was raw, diamond-hard masculinity in a twenty-four-karat setting.

He was the kind of man who made sensible mothers want to keep their daughters locked out of sight, the kind her own mother had warned her about. Just now, in his quietly expensive suit, his thumbs hooked into the pockets of his brocade vest, he looked sleek and refined and ... dangerous.

A dark angel with a devil's smile.

Jess had seen that smile inside the saloon tonight. Even in the tension of the moment when he'd held a gun on Purcell, that sensual smile he'd given her had shot through her like an arrow, making her stomach feel quivery and her knees suddenly weak.

The remembrance of that smile and his sleek good looks put Jess on her guard, made her want to seek the safety of her home and family. Still, she owed him.

"I want to thank you, mister, for what you did," she said quietly.

He responded with a slight bow that would have looked

absurd and affected coming from any other man, but from him it seemed right. "Think nothing of it, Miss Sommers. I was glad to oblige."

His manners were those of a gentleman, his low, silk-smooth voice that of a ladies' man. That voice unnerved Jess. She was accustomed to hard men and hard language and knew how to hold her own with that kind. *His* kind, though, she didn't know how to deal with. This close to him, she felt inadequate, somewhat rustic even, despite her two years' training in a fancy Denver finishing school where she'd been sent to acquire the graces of a lady.

"I'm afraid you have the advantage of me," she said carefully, in her best boarding school manner.

"The name's Devlin. Garrett Devlin."

Moving a step closer, he used his thumb to tilt back the brim of his hat, and smiled gently down at her, a smile that took the wind out of her again. But it was his eyes that held her attention. His shrewd, intelligent eyes. Jess stared up at him, trying to fathom their color. Inside, in the bright light of the chandeliers, they had looked cool, crystal gray. Here in the shadows they were a smoked silver.

Oh, yes, definitely dangerous, she thought a bit helplessly, even as she mentally chided herself for letting him affect her so.

"And you're Jessica Sommers," she heard him say softly. " 'Miss Jess' to some. I overheard your conversation with the marshal this morning."

Her tawny brows drawing into a puzzled frown, she thought back over the events of the morning. As she remembered, she abruptly felt a surge of heat flood her face. The man at the window. The *naked* man at the window. She'd only seen the upper part of his body, his bare chest and sleek, muscled shoulders, and then only for an instant. But that one glimpse had been more than enough to make her aware of his masculinity, of his physical superiority to other men she knew.

Flustered and trying to hide it, Jess took a step back and came smack up against the hitching rail.

"Was your father badly injured?"

Grateful for the change of subject, Jess shook her head. "No . . . he's going to be all right. The doctor said he was lucky, the wound wasn't as bad as it looked. Riley's been sleeping all day and so far he doesn't even have a fever." She paused, wanting to thank this man for his concern. "It was kind of you to ask."

The slow curve of his beautiful mouth drew her total attention. Nearby in the street a horse nickered, reminding Jess where she was. "I'm sorry . . . that you had to get involved in my fight. I'm afraid you've made a formidable enemy in Burke."

Devlin shrugged, a lazy movement of those powerful, elegant shoulders. "I've made enemies before."

I can well believe that, Jess thought as she silently studied him. And he didn't seem the least bit concerned. But then, Garrett Devlin didn't look like a man who scared easily. In fact, he looked like the kind of man who would be accorded respect wherever he went, even by wealthy barons like Ashton Burke.

"How is it you're keeping company with sidewinders like Burke?" she asked curiously.

"I was in town looking for a good game, and he was able to provide it."

The slight grimace Jess made was accompanied by a note of disapproval in her tone when she spoke. "You're a gambler?"

Devlin gave another shrug, but this time his glance held amusement. "Among other things. You've got something against gamblers?"

In fact, she had a great deal against gamblers, almost as much as she had against wealthy silver barons. In her opinion, they were lazy no-accounts who lived off other men's misfortune and lack of skill. Garrett Devlin probably fit that bill, too—but it would be highly impolite to deride him for his profession after what he'd just done for her. Her confrontation with Burke could have been a disaster. If Hank Purcell had managed to sneak up on her and take away her only protection, she would have been made to look like a fool, instead of walking out of there with her

point made and her dignity intact. No, she was grateful to
Mr. Devlin, no matter what or who he was.

Jess turned to look out over the street. It was a quiet
night, and blessedly peaceful, with a big half moon shining overhead, bathing the town in a silver glow and casting the surrounding Rockies in rugged silhouette. The
mountains were beautiful at night, with a raw majesty that
vanished in the stark light of day. At night you couldn't
see the ugly mine dumps that scarred the rocky slopes, or
hear the loud milling operations on the outskirts of town.

At the moment, the saloons and dance halls along Main
Street were mostly silent. The only noise was the low hum
of the crowd inside the Diamond Dust. Jess herself remained silent, even when Devlin moved to stand beside
her at the rail.

"I have no objections," he admitted, "to sitting at a table
with a man, as long as he's honest."

"Oh, Ashton Burke is honest at cards," she said bitterly.
"A man like him has no reason to cheat when he has so
many other ways to get rich."

"I take it Burke has made a practice of getting wealthy
off men like your father?"

"You take it right, Mr. Devlin. Burke has always
grabbed whatever he's wanted from this town, never mind
who got hurt. Everybody knows he's unscrupulous, but no
one's ever been able to prove it. But he won't get away
with it this time!"

At her quiet vehemence, she felt Devlin's gray gaze
drift down her body to the shotgun she still held. "You
think your warning will make him hold off?"

"Maybe not. But he wouldn't take any threat from me
seriously unless it was backed with lead."

Devlin slanted a glance of sympathy tinged with admiration at the young woman beside him. He had a pretty
good idea what she was feeling. Anger, frustration, concern for her father, fear. She hadn't wanted to march into
that saloon of gamblers and fancy women and face Burke
alone. But she'd done it. And it had shaken her, he was
certain. Not only had he heard the husky rasp of tears in

her voice when he'd followed her out here, but she'd been trembling, he would swear it. *You aren't as tough as you pretend, are you, sweetheart?*

He had the sudden, overwhelming urge to take her in his arms and tell her that she wasn't alone, that everything would be fine. But he knew precisely where such a damn fool action would lead. He would kiss her till she was limp and breathless, which would make him want her more than he already did, and then he'd be tempted to seduce her. . . . And he wasn't prepared to let things go so far between them. Lovely innocents like Jessica Sommers only spelled trouble for a man like him. Nor was he at all sure that he wanted to take on her battles for her.

"Do you know how to use that scattergun?" he asked, gesturing at the weapon she held.

"Well enough. My father taught me. I'm handy with a six-shooter, too, but one gun won't be enough against Burke and his gang. It would take an army." She sighed, then went on as if thinking aloud. "I'll at least have to hire an armed guard for the mine, find somebody who isn't beholden to Burke. That two-bit town marshal is too yellow to stand up to him—and the Clear Creek County sheriff is hardly any better. They both owe their jobs to Burke's support. As do half the men in this county—" She stopped suddenly, glancing up at Devlin with speculation.

Devlin's guard went up instinctively. He knew that look—the kind of calculating expression a woman got when she wanted something from a man and was figuring out the best way to get it. On the Sommers woman, the calculation wasn't as hard and mercenary as some he'd seen, but it was calculating all the same. *Ah, sweet Jessie, just what scheme do you have in that pretty head of yours?* He didn't have to wait long to find out.

"You aren't beholden to Burke," she said slowly.

"No," he agreed, his tone wary.

"I don't suppose you'd be interested in the job."

"Job?"

"Of armed guard for our mine. I could pay you"—she took a deep breath—"two hundred dollars a month."

Her offer surprised but didn't impress him. The wage was a staggering one around these parts, but Devlin often made more than that in a single day.

When he didn't answer, she went on quickly, the eagerness she tried to hide tugging at his heart. "The job would come with room and board, too. I serve the best meals you're likely to find this side of Denver."

Does the room come with you included, little firebrand? If so, I might be inclined to accept.

Devlin shook his head, disciplining his wayward thoughts. Miss Jessica Sommers was a respectable woman, he had no doubt about it. He'd known enough of her kind to recognize the signs and to steer clear. She was the marrying kind, the kind whose father came after a man with a shotgun if he thought his daughter's reputation had been besmirched. He wasn't about to get tangled up in a web like that. Besides, there was no sense in getting himself killed in a petty squabble.

On the other hand, he'd already made an enemy of Burke, so he had nothing to lose there. And hooking up with Jess Sommers would bring him a step closer to his goal. Putting himself squarely in the middle of the mine feud would give him ample reason to ask questions about a man with a bullet scar over his right eye. Wasn't that why he'd come here in the first place? To find an outlaw and the organized gang that had robbed the Colorado Central Railroad of sixty thousand dollars in cash and silver bullion and killed the engineer and fireman in the process?

Other than the description of the scar and the roan horse, Devlin's only lead was a snatch of conversation one of the wounded robbery victims had overheard: ". . . get back to the Plume."

He'd come here intending to lay low and sniff around, but had found the trail cold. That is, until Riley Sommers had been shot.

"It would be honest work," Jess added, obviously still intent on persuading him.

Devlin didn't misunderstand her insinuation. "Meaning that gambling isn't?"

"Well ... I ..."

Her stammer and the delicate flush on her face told him clearly that she wanted to be tactful, but that she included him in her low opinion of gamblers. Absurdly, her characterization of him stung his pride. Yet he didn't press the issue when she hurriedly returned to the subject of his possible employment.

"You would only have to work at night—stay up at the mine and make sure no one came around. You could still do ... whatever it is you do during the day. And it wouldn't be for long. Only till my father gets back on his feet. You weren't planning on leaving town just yet, were you?"

"Not just yet, no."

She hesitated, looking up at him with pleading amber eyes. "I could maybe go up to two-fifty a month. I'm afraid that's all I can afford."

Ah, darlin', don't look at me that way, unless you want to get more than you're bargaining for. "The salary isn't what concerns me," Devlin said.

"Well, if it's Burke you're worried about, working for me won't make a difference to him. There'll be hard feelings in any case, if you mean to stay in town. Burke won't forgive you for what you did tonight, and there's no telling what he might do in retaliation for your defying him. And Hank Purcell will no doubt try to cause trouble for you. But you're good enough with a gun to make him think twice about— You *are* good with a gun, aren't you?"

The anxious note in her voice almost made him smile. "Good enough for what you want."

"I thought so. Nobody would draw on a man the way you did unless he knew what he was doing. So you see, there's really no reason not to accept the job. That is ... unless, like the marshal, you're afraid to stand up to Burke."

Jess knew right then that she had pushed Mr. Devlin too far. Something bright and alive flashed in his eyes, something very much like anger, although when he spoke it was with hard-edged amusement. "Don't try to manipulate me,

Miss Sommers. Better schemers than you have tried and failed."

She flushed again, dropping her gaze. "I'm sorry. There was no call for me to say that. Whatever you are, you aren't a coward."

Whatever I am? You really know how to stroke a man's ego, don't you, love?

When he remained silent, she sighed. "Maybe it wasn't such a good idea after all. I'll find someone else, if I try hard enough. Thank you again for helping me in there, Mr. Devlin. Good night."

She started to turn away, but his hand on her arm forestalled her. "All right, Miss Sommers, I can spare a couple of weeks. I accept your offer. You've got yourself an armed guard."

Apparently not believing his answer, she stared up at him.

You don't trust me, do you, angel? That's good. I'm a dangerous man for an innocent like you. For your sake, keep away from me.

But Devlin didn't voice the thought aloud. Instead, he smiled. "Come on, Miss Sommers." He took hold of her elbow, turning her toward his hotel. "Let's go get my gear."

Chapter 3

"**W**ait a minute!" Jessica came to an abrupt halt and eyed him warily. "Just where are we going?"

With a casual pressure of his fingers on her elbow, Devlin urged her forward again, directing her along the wooden boardwalk. "Next door, to my hotel room."

"You're taking me to your hotel room?" The memory of seeing this man standing bare-chested at the window of his room only that morning assaulted Jess with disturbing force—and it wasn't helped by the masculine scent of sandlewood soap that emanated from Devlin. Both did strange things to her insides. In fact, she felt unnerved with him this close. "I'm afraid that wouldn't be at all proper," Jess said weakly, only to hear him give a quiet chuckle.

"No, I expect not, but it wouldn't be gentlemanly to leave you out here alone on the street at night, either."

"No one in this town would accost a lady, Mr. Devlin. And I *am* a lady, I assure you."

"I never doubted it, Miss Sommers." The grin he flashed her was sensual and mischievous and had all the power of a lightning bolt. Jess swallowed hard, scarcely hearing when he went on. "You'll be perfectly safe, I swear it. Especially armed the way you are."

When her expression remained uncertain, Devlin raised a black eyebrow. "You're not afraid of me, are you?"

She was a little, at that. But she was more afraid that if

25

she let him out of her sight he might change his mind about coming to work for her. And she had her shotgun, after all. "Very well, Mr. Devlin. I'll go with you."

"Call me Devlin. Or Garrett. 'Mister' is too formal if we're to have a relationship."

His choice of words didn't particularly reassure her, but it would be silly to argue with him over such a point. There was no harm in reminding him just what that relationship would entail, though. "All right . . . Devlin. And most of the men who work for me call me Miss Jess." She saw him raise one eyebrow, but he didn't reply.

They reached his floor by way of the outside stairs at the side of the hotel. The hallway was softly lit by crystal wall sconces, illuminating elegant carpeting and expensive flocked wallpaper. Jess, who had never been inside the Diamond Dust Hotel before, found herself calculating how much it must cost to run a place like this, and wondering about Devlin's success as a gambler. He had to be good if he could afford to put up here.

And the room. *Decadent*, was Jess's first thought when Devlin had lighted a lamp. The black walnut furniture gleamed, while the wine-colored tapestry drapes glowed. Gingerly she stepped inside, allowing Devlin to shut the door behind her. Above the bureau hung a smokey diamond dust mirror in an ornate gold frame, a color theme that was carried out in the trim of the washstand and the headboard of the huge feather bed.

Against her will, Jess found herself staring at that bed, where the wine-velvet counterpane and fine linen sheets had been left in a wild tangle. The image of Devlin sleeping there flashed in her mind before she could stop it. Thinking of him sprawled there, naked as he had been this morning, made her cheeks go hot.

When quickly she looked away, her gaze fell on a red feather boa carelessly draped over the arm of a leather chair. *That* feminine frippery didn't belong to Devlin, she was certain. And she seriously doubted it had slithered up here on its own. *Does he often invite women to his room?*

Promptly Jess squelched the thought, realizing she didn't want to know.

Devlin didn't seem at all self-conscious about the un-made bed, though, or the evidence left by his female com-panion. When he led Jess over to the chair, he merely picked up the boa and tossed it aside. "Sit down. I'll get you a drink."

"A drink?"

"Would you prefer whiskey or brandy?" he asked as he went to the bureau.

"I don't drink liquor."

"You do tonight. After what you faced today, you need it."

He had a point, Jess thought as she sank into the deep comfort of the chair, resting the shotgun across her lap. Her nerves did feel shaky, and it had *not* been one of her better days. First the terror of her father being shot. Then the tension of waiting all day to make sure Riley would be all right. Then the strain of standing up to Burke. And now the shock of being alone in a bedroom with a stunningly attractive stranger whom her memory persisted in keeping unclothed.

Blushing in spite of herself, Jess kept her gaze averted as Devlin poured a finger of brandy in a snifter and brought it to her. She had to look up then, which gave her a jolt. The soft, speculative way he was studying her made her feel like *she* was the one undressed. She wanted to reach up and see if the pins had come out of her hair.

"Here, drink it down," he said gently, offering her the glass.

Jess started to refuse, but there was a force in those gray-silver eyes that scattered her thoughts like chaff in a wind. What was it he'd said?

When she merely stared at him, Devlin smiled, a slow, lazy, sensual curving of his lips. "For medicinal purposes only."

Sweet glory, that lethal smile combined with that velvet-smooth voice could persuade a woman to forget her own name.

In something of a daze, Jess obediently accepted the snifter from him and felt the warm brush of his fingers against her own. Trying not to jump at the startling sensation his accidental touch aroused, she took a tentative sip. Her breath caught as the potent liquor went down, fiery and smooth. It was expensive stuff, even her inexperienced tongue could tell that. Nothing like the rotgut whiskey Clem was so fond of drinking. But then, no two men could be further apart than those two, in either tastes or appearance. Garrett Devlin obviously preferred the finer things in life and was willing to spend good money for them; Clem didn't have the money to spend. With his mules, Clem could have earned an excellent living with other outfits hauling ore down the mountainside to the stamp mills, but he had thrown in with her father instead.

"I'll only be a minute," she heard Devlin say. "Let me get my things together."

Nodding, Jess sipped her brandy and watched as he took some garments from the bureau and began filling a carpetbag. She knew better than to gape, and yet her gaze kept straying to his face. It was sinful, how a man could be that beautiful. His hair was a rich, thick sable—nearly black but with no trace of blue—and fell over a high forehead delineated by heavy, straight eyebrows. Smooth creases carved his face in several places, down the cheeks and around the sensuous mouth, giving his features the sculpted stamp of classical perfection.

He wasn't that old, Jess thought; maybe ten years older than she was. And yet those shrewd, smoke-hued eyes seemed as if they had seen a lot more of life than she had or ever would. Still, she would bet that life hadn't been the same struggle for Devlin it had been for her. There was a vital authority about him that suggested clearly he would succeed at most anything he attempted, and with relative ease.

Even as Jess made the observation, Devlin paused in his packing. Eyeing the small leather-covered trunk in the corner, he absently placed his hands at his hips, a gesture that called attention to the lean contours of his lower body.

Flustered that she should even notice such things, Jess cleared her throat and said hastily, "I'll send Mr. Kwan over in the morning to pick up your trunk."

"Mr. Kwan?"

"A Chinese man. He helps with the heavy work at my boardinghouse. His wife, Mei Lin, does laundry and cleaning." Jess hesitated. "You don't mind, do you?"

"Why should I mind?"

"Most everybody in Colorado hates the Chinese."

Devlin gave her a smile that was a bit grim. "When you get to know me better, *Miss Jess*, you'll find that I'm not 'most everybody.' "

Devlin went back to his packing then, leaving Jess to her contemplations. No, he was certainly was not "most everybody"; he was very little like the men of her acquaintance. He had the look of a man who knew the taste of power, and the confidence of someone accustomed to the best. A bit like Ashton Burke, perhaps, Jess thought with a grimace. And yet Devlin moved quietly, in the way of a man who *concealed* his power rather than flaunted it the way Burke did.

The reminder of Burke made Jess's mouth tighten. It was with grave satisfaction that she saw Devlin withdraw from the trunk a cartridge belt and a pair of Colt Frontier six-shooters with ivory grips and toss them on the bed. She was grateful he was so different from Burke. Unlike Burke, Devlin was kind. Coming to her rescue the way he had, agreeing to help her protect the Wildstar until her father got better . . .

He was also charming, smooth, and every bit a ladies' man. She had no business thinking about him in any way but a professional one—

The thought screeched to a halt as Jess suddenly realized what Devlin was doing. He had already taken off his elegant coat and vest and stored them in the trunk, and his long fingers were making rapid work of the buttons on his fancy shirt.

Her eyes widened as he pulled the garment off, baring his powerful shoulders and chest. Jess shot to her feet, nearly losing the shotgun that had been cradled in her lap. He was all lean muscle and rough curling hair, and the masculine sight made her pulse race.

Devlin merely gave her an amused glance, as casual about his nudity as he had been about threatening Hank Purcell. "You going to shoot me?"

"N-no, but ... I th-think I'll wait outside," Jess stammered as she edged toward the door.

"Maybe that would be a good idea," Devlin said with the teasing silver fire of devilment in his eyes. "I'll join you when I've changed."

Averting her gaze, she practically threw the brandy glass on the bureau top and got herself out of that room, closing the door firmly behind her. Devlin's whiskey-mellow laugh followed her down the hall, making her cheeks burn.

She waited outside on the stairs in the August night, grateful for the pleasant breeze off the mountains that cooled the heat of her embarrassment. How could she have shown so little dignity, running off like that? Devlin must think her green as grass after all the fancy women he'd known.

But then she *was* green about men like him, Jess reflected. She'd only just turned sixteen when her mother died. She hadn't minded in the least leaving that fancy school in Denver to take over running the Sommers Boardinghouse, nor had she minded the hard work; it only helped numb her grief over losing her mother. But having to look after Riley and two dozen other hungry miners had left her no time for pleasure or the pursuits other girls her age enjoyed. No time to think about marriage, either. There weren't enough hours left in the day to allow a man to pay her court, even if one had ever caught her eye, which hadn't happened. She'd scarcely ever noticed the opposite gender before, at least not in *that* way.

Certainly no man had ever affected her the way Garrett Devlin did. She'd seen bare male chests before, but none had ever hit her with a wallop like a kick from one of Clem's mules. Devlin's body was as perfect as his face, it seemed. But how had he gotten those muscles in his shoulders and arms? All the gamblers she knew of would have sold their mothers' souls before lifting a hand to do physical labor.

Trying to dismiss her improper thoughts, Jess glanced heavenward. From where she stood, she could see the dark outlines of Sherman and Republican mountains, whose mines provided the livelihood for most of Silver Plume's twelve hundred or so residents. Silver Plume was situated some fifty miles due west of Denver, at the bottom of a vast hollow, hemmed in by the towering Rockies. A wide, rushing stream called Clear Creek ran through the middle of town and continued down the canyon, channeling between high, precipitous walls of rock for two miles till it reached Georgetown, where Jess had been born.

Her father, Riley, had been lured there, along with thousands of other prospectors, during the Pikes Peak gold rush in '59. With its fabulous discoveries of silver ore, Georgetown had grown up almost overnight. Dubbed the Silver Queen of the Rockies, it was now the county seat, with a population of five thousand, making it the third largest city in Colorado.

A decade after the first rush, Silver Plume was established as a silver camp. Seeking greener pastures, Riley had moved his family there and played a small part in turning "The Plume" into a roaring, prosperous mining town.

The settlement had started with a single street and spread out in a ramshackle fashion, with hundreds of drab, hastily erected shacks crowded together on the valley floor of Clear Creek Canyon. Silver Plume now was no longer quite so shabby, though. Many of the shacks had been replaced by small clapboard houses, and the commercial district boasted numerous stores, a dozen saloons and hotels, several eating places, a lumberyard, three Chinese laundries, two churches, and an office for the town's own weekly newspaper, as well as the stamp mills that were the lifeblood of any Western mining town and boardinghouses like the one Jess ran, which lodged and fed the hundreds of hard-rock miners of the Plume.

Thinking about how tough those early days had been, Jess managed to get her pulse rate under control by the time Devlin came out, but it quickened again as soon as she saw him in the moonlight. He had buckled on his six-shooters, and with the dual Colts riding his hips and a black, low-crowned Stetson shadowing his face, he looked like one of those hard men who lived by the gun.

Jess found herself staring, despite her best intentions. Devlin had one thumb hooked in his gun belt, while the other hand carried his carpetbag and a Winchester rifle. Below that belt, the rough denim of his trousers stretched across masculine contours, calling attention to creases only a man would have. Unnerved again, she looked away. It wouldn't matter what he was wearing, Jess decided—or not wearing, for that matter. He would always make a woman think forbidden, dangerous thoughts.

"Did you come to town expecting a war?" she asked in an unsteady voice.

"Never hurts to be prepared. Where do we go from here?"

"Home. Afterward I can take you up to the mine—that is, if you don't mind starting right away?"

He thought of the comfortable hotel bed he'd just walked away from and sighed inwardly. "That's fine."

"Good. I'm afraid of leaving the mine unprotected. I should have thought of it before, but if Burke means to try something, it might be tonight, when he knows the Wildstar's unguarded. Do you have a horse?"

"No, I came in on the train."

"You can use my father's for a while, and maybe later on you could rent one of your own. There's a livery stable near our place."

Jess led the way down the stairs and along the street till she came to the mare she had borrowed from Carson's Livery.

"We can walk to the house," she told Devlin. "It isn't all that far. I only needed a mount because I had to look for Burke."

Devlin hooked his carpetbag over the horn of the lady's

sidesaddle and shoved the rifle in the boot. Politely taking the mare's reins from Jess, he fell into step beside her as she headed west, toward the residential side of town.

"Burke lives in Georgetown," Jess explained, "in a big fancy house, and I went there first. But his butler said he was here in Silver Plume. I had to go to two of Burke's other saloons before I finally tracked him down at the Diamond Dust."

"That must have been an interesting sight if you stormed into his other places the way you did here."

Hearing the amusement in Devlin's tone, Jess flushed and didn't answer.

"What precisely does Hank Purcell do for Burke, anyway?" Devlin asked a moment later.

"He's the mine superintendent for the Lady J. That's the claim next to ours, the one Burke wants to link up with the Wildstar."

They both fell silent then. A buggy went by in the street, its wheels rattling. Afterward, the only sounds were their footsteps and the gentle clop of the mare.

Jess cherished the quiet. Tomorrow Silver Plume would be teeming with buckboards and ore wagons and mules and rough men, but tonight the town slept in the dark shadow of the mountains. She found herself looking around her, trying to see it through Devlin's eyes. The double row of wood-frame stores and saloons, many of which had false fronts to make them appear two stories tall, looked like a hundred other main streets in the West. Nothing special, but it was home.

She would have liked to say Silver Plume was attractive, but it still held the raw simplicity of a frontier town. The hard-packed dirt streets turned to a sea of mud when it rained, and there were no trees to speak of—very few of the evergreens and quaking aspens and big cottonwoods that lined the residential streets of nearby Georgetown.

Silver Plume couldn't compare to Georgetown in size or sophistication, either. Miners and working-class folks lived here, while the wealthy silver barons and powerful railroad magnates built their mansions there. Georgetown boasted numerous attractive Victorian buildings, including an opera house and several first-class hotels, the premier one being the fancy French Hotel de Paris. The residential sections were filled with neat clapboard dwellings ringed by white picket fences and brightened by colorful flower gardens.

The entertainment in Georgetown was far more elegant as well—concerts and singing societies and theater performances, rather than the rock-drilling contests and wrestling matches Silver Plume usually offered. Jess wondered what had drawn Devlin here.

Oh, yes, gambling.

She stole a glance at him. What would Clem say when he learned she'd hired a smooth-talking stranger—a no-account gambler, at that? Clem would take one look at Devlin's sleek good looks and suave manner and dismiss him as a dude.

But Devlin *had* agreed to help her protect the mine. Even if she didn't think much of him personally, she was willing to overlook his faults—and Clem would just have to as well.

She turned south at the next corner and led Devlin down a quiet back street for two blocks, between dozens of small, closely packed miners' cottages of similar design. It was darker here, away from the few streetlamps Silver Plume possessed, but the moonlight was bright enough to outline the large, white, two-story frame building fifty yards down on the right.

"That's our boardinghouse," Jess said, directing Devlin's gaze. "My grandfather was a doctor who made a good living. Before he died, he had the place built for my mother so she would always have an income."

"I take it your father's mining ventures weren't too profitable?"

"Mining is a chancy business, Mr. Devlin."

"So I've heard."

At his wry drawl, Jess realized how defensive she must have sounded. His comment hadn't been an accusation against her father for being unable to support his family.

She softened her tone. "Taking in boarders provided my mother gainful employment. There aren't too many good jobs for women hereabouts, and she had me to raise."

"She seems to have made a success of it."

"She did well enough. She managed to put by a little for emergencies and to send me to school in Denver, even though I didn't want to go."

She could feel Devlin's gaze searching her face. "And you took your mother's place," he said finally, his tone oddly gentle.

Jess nodded. "I'm not as good a cook as she was—she was the best in all Colorado—but I'm still good. And at least we're always full up. I offer room and board to miners and pack a lunch for their shift."

"And you've been doing this for how long?"

"Five years."

Devlin came to a halt suddenly, which made Jess stop, too. She was a bit startled when he placed a finger under her chin and tilted her face up to his, studying her intently. "You couldn't have been more than a child. That's a large burden for a girl to handle alone."

She couldn't prevent the warm flush that seemed to flood her entire body. Devlin was regarding her with an admiring expression, as if she had done something special. But then running the boardinghouse *had* been a big responsibility back then. She was getting pretty good at it now, but some days she still felt like she had when she was sixteen—small and inadequate and scared. Scared of letting her father down. Riley depended on her to keep things going, and she couldn't fail him. Other times she felt annoyingly female. A man could do so much more than a mere woman could. Like walking into a saloon, or challenging a powerful silver baron like Burke.

It was odd how Devlin seemed to understand what she'd been up against. Odd and disconcerting.

"Oh . . . I don't do it all alone," Jess managed to say a bit breathlessly. "I have help. I told you about the Chinese couple, and there's a widow neighbor who waits on the tables and cooks on Sunday. That's my day off."

"Today."

"Yes."

He let her go and resumed walking. "Your day off didn't turn out too pleasantly."

"No." Quelling a shudder, Jess fell silent again, remembering the terror of this morning when they'd brought her father's bleeding body home. But he was going to be all right. And so would his mine, if she had anything to say about it. She *wouldn't* allow Burke to destroy everything Riley had worked for.

Her thoughts occupied, she almost didn't notice Devlin's surprise when they passed the boardinghouse.

"We're not going in?"

"No. Our home is just a bit farther." She'd done some fast thinking while she'd waited for Devlin to change clothes. Her original plan to put him up in her boardinghouse would never work, she realized now. A man like Devlin was accustomed to far fancier lodgings than a small plain room with a bed and a washstand, and a communal dining room shared by two dozen miners. He might even be insulted, maybe enough to quit. But she could take him home with her. Not only were the accommodations nicer, but he could sleep there during the day and keep an eye on Riley if she wasn't there to look after him. "I thought maybe you would be more comfortable at our home."

They turned right at the next corner, then walked for another block, before Jess came to a halt in front of a small dwelling. It was a typical miner's house—one story with a clapboard exterior—but had been spruced up a bit. The fresh coat of white paint boasted blue trim, while potted geraniums adorned the front porch and bay window.

"We don't live high on the hog," Jess said apologetically as she tied the horse.

"I'm not too choosy."

The smile he gave her in response to her skeptical glance took Jess aback. She didn't believe for one minute that Devlin wouldn't mind the lack of luxury, but it was kind of him to say so.

She held a finger to her lips as she led Devlin inside. "I don't want to wake Riley," she whispered.

The front part of the house was dark, but a light shone from somewhere down the narrow hall. Jess lit a lamp and gestured at the darkened room on the left as she passed. "That's the parlor, if you want to read or . . . my mother never let anyone smoke in the house, but you can if you want. The bathroom is at the end of the hall, the privy's out back, through the kitchen. I'm afraid the only running water we have is cold, but I'll be glad to heat some whenever you need it."

As she spoke, she moved down the hall, past a tiny sitting room, to the third door on the right. Obediently, Devlin followed her into the small bedroom. The furniture was plain, consisting of a brass bed, an iron washstand, a pine bureau and clothespress, and a rocking chair. But an obvious effort had been made at relieving the starkness. A thickly quilted yellow cotton spread covered the bed, lace curtains hung at the window, and a colorful braided rug decorated the wood floor. In all, the effect was comfortable, cheerful, and quite feminine, Devlin noted with chagrin.

"Will you be okay in here?" Jess asked.

He heard the uncertain note in her voice and turned to meet her anxious gaze. "This is your room, isn't it?"

"It's yours now."

"Where will you sleep?"

"Don't worry about me." She flashed him a bright smile as she whisked the hairbrush and comb off the bureau. "There's a pull-out cot in the sitting room next door. It will do fine for me. And it's closer to Riley. I can hear him better if he should wake in the night. Now, I'm sure you'll want to get settled, and I have to go check on my father. I'll see you in a few minutes." She backed out of the doorway before he could argue, leaving him the lamp.

Devlin looked around in disgust. If there was a cot in that closet next door, it could only be a mattress on the hard floor. But Jess Sommers was willing to sacrifice her own comfort—and even let him smoke in her house—so he'd have no reason to leave her employ. Clearly she desperately wanted to please him. But it grated against every chivalrous instinct he possessed to turn her out of her room. He had been raised a gentleman, and despite his rough living the past ten years, he still maintained a pretense of good breeding. And to sleep in her bed . . . Devlin's gray gaze strayed to that bed. How soft and feminine and virginal it looked. The sheets probably smelled sweet like her, too—

Get your mind on business, Devlin. He shook his head sternly. He had a job to do.

He dumped his carpetbag on the bed and began arranging shaving gear and clothes. A few minutes later, he heard light footsteps pass his room, then the murmur of voices. After waiting a bit longer, Devlin followed the sound.

He found Jess in the kitchen, sitting at the table and arguing in low tones with a grizzled, bearded old fellow who looked like he'd spent the last half century out of doors being weathered by the elements. The old man wore the loose woolen shirt and overalls of a miner.

Both of them glanced up at Devlin's entrance.

"Clem," Jessica said carefully, "this is the man I was telling you about. Mr. Devlin, this is Clem Haverty. He's my father's partner in the Wildstar Mine. Clem handles all the pack mules and drives the ore wagon."

Clem's black-eyed glare could have shriveled a rattlesnake. When Devlin touched his hat in polite acknowledgment, the mule skinner leaned over and spat a stream of tobacco juice in the spittoon at his feet. "Jessie ain't never brung a fella home afore, not even fer supper."

"Clem!" She threw an embarrassed glance of apology at Devlin. "I didn't bring him home for supper. I mean, of course I mean to feed him supper, but that's just in exchange for his acting as guard. We have a business deal."

The older man's fierce expression didn't let up one bit. "I hear tell Jess got herself into a shooting scrape with Hank Purcell and you pulled her out."

Devlin shrugged. "I merely impressed him with the necessity of dropping the gun he had aimed at her back."

For the first time, Clem took his eyes off Devlin to look at Jess. The mouth half buried in the shaggy gray beard twisted in a sneer. "Fancy talker, ain't he?"

"Yes, but he's a good man with a gun, Clem," Jess answered. "We need him."

Clem ignored her claim. "You a stranger in town?"

The smile Devlin gave him could have charmed a grizzly. "Do you know me?"

"Cain't say as I do."

"Then I guess that makes me a stranger."

For a minute, the mule skinner's scowl only deepened. Jess held her breath. Clem was a rough-talking, ornery old devil who lacked an education, but he was like family, and she didn't want to take sides against him. Devlin didn't exactly seem intimidated, though, or even offended. He stood there calmly taking Clem's deliberate insults, regarding the old man with a shrewd, unwavering gaze.

A hint of respect slowly dawned on the mule skinner's face, although he didn't drop his guard. "You from anyplace hereabouts?"

"Chicago originally, but I've been here and there."

"Chicagy, eh? One of them Eastern dudes."

"Chicago isn't that far east." Devlin indicated the straight-backed chair across from Jess. "Mind if I join you?"

A short silence was followed by a grudging headshake from Clem. With a hobnailed boot, he even nudged the chair back from the table in an invitation of sorts. "Town's full o' drifters, nowdays. Cain't be too careful."

"Devlin isn't a drifter," Jess interjected. "He's a—" She bit back the word *gambler*, not wanting to divulge Devlin's profession.

"Businessman," he finished smoothly for her as he seated himself.

"He figuring on camping out up yonder at the mine?" Clem asked Jess. Not giving her time to reply, he shook his shaggy gray head. "That's a crack-brained notion if I ever heard o' one, Jessie. Burke ain't gonna be afeared of no city slicker. And Hank Purcell, neither."

"Burke will think twice about taking on Devlin, believe me. You didn't see what happened tonight. I did. Devlin's no tinhorn. He knows what he's doing."

"It's you what worries me, Jess. I always thought you had a good head atop your shoulders, but it seems you ain't got a lick o' sense!"

"Clem, you're wrong. Hiring Devlin makes perfect sense. The Wildstar miners are scared, you know that. If we don't do something to protect them from Burke, they'll up and quit. Who's going to work our claim then? Riley won't be well enough for weeks."

When the old man didn't answer right away, she pressed her point. "And what about guarding the mine? Who will do that? You? Me? The marshal? I didn't see anybody rushing to volunteer—and never will, if it means going against Burke." She sent Devlin an encouraging smile. "We need him, Clem. He can sleep here during the day and be here for Riley while I'm at the boardinghouse."

"He's gonna stay *here*?"

"In the daytime. At night he'll be up at the mine. I'll take Devlin up there tonight and show him around—"

"Now just a dad-blamed minute! You ain't goin' up there at night, with or without no citified pretty boy!"

"Hush, or you'll wake up Riley!"

"I ain't gonna wake up Riley! He's out like a grizzly in winter. But he'd have my hide if I was to let you pull a damn-fool stunt like that."

"It isn't a stunt. We need to get up there tonight. The mine's unguarded right now, and if Burke means to try to sabotage it, now would be the perfect time."

"She's right, you know," Devlin said objectively, entering the argument for the first time.

Clem turned his fierce scowl back on Devlin. "If Riley was dry-gulched, who's to say you won't be, too?"

"I'll be ready for it."

"Yes," Jess agreed eagerly, "now that we know what to expect, we can take precautions."

"How you gonna ride back down alone in the dark, gal? That's jest askin' for grief."

Jess hesitated; she hadn't considered that problem. "I'll stay up there tonight with Devlin—"

"You sure as hell won't!"

"Don't cuss in the house."

His face red with frustration, Clem held back the retort he was plainly itching to make. "*I'll* go up yonder with him," he said finally.

"You can't. You need your sleep so you can be fresh for work in the morning. And you have to be at the boarding-house to convince the crew to go with you and make them see there's nothing to be afraid of. They'll take it better coming from you."

Clem's expression turned mutinous, but Jess's tone went soft and pleading. "You have to keep working the mine, Clem. If you don't, then Burke will have won, don't you see?"

He grunted, obviously unhappy with the corner he was being pushed into. "What about mealtime? You cain't just leave us to Mei Lin. She's liable to fix us a mess o' fric-asseed cat, like she did that one time afore we all knew it."

"Mei Lin won't do any cooking, I promise. Flo can make breakfast in the morning and fill the lunch pails." Jess paused to say to Devlin, "Florence O'Malley is the neighbor I told you about. She's almost as good a cook as I am."

"Hah!" Clem's grunt was followed by a muttered, "Thought your pa taught you better'n to tell tall tales."

"Clem . . . please?"

He gave her a hard, fuming look before throwing a narrow-eyed glance at Devlin. "Just fer one night?" he asked Jess. "You ain't going up there after tonight?"

"No, I'll stay right here, I promise."

"Well . . . I ought to have Doc take a look at my head. Must be loco for lettin' you rope me into this."

"Good, then it's settled." She turned to Devlin. "Are you hungry? I could make you something to eat before we go."

He shook his head, his lips quivering in amusement. "I ate earlier."

"All right. I'll just fix lunch in case you get hungry later on." Jess took a deep breath. "Clem, there's just one more thing. I want to take Nellie and Gus up to the mine with us."

Clem came up out of his chair like an erupting volcano. "Now wait a durn minute! Nobody touches them mules without my say-so!"

"I know. That's why I'm asking you."

"No! And that's *final!*"

"You don't even know why I want them."

He crossed his arms over his chest, glaring down at her. "You gonna tell me?"

"I just thought they would make good watchdogs. You know how they kick up a fuss whenever a stranger comes near. We can tie Nellie and Gus just outside the mine so they'll alert us to anybody who doesn't belong there."

"And jest who's gonna take care of 'em?"

"I'm sure Devlin will give them the best of care."

"I'll guard them with my life," he said soberly enough, though when Jess looked to him for confirmation, she had the distinct impression he was trying not to laugh.

"See? I know they're your favorite mules, Clem, but it won't hurt them to spend the night up at the mine for a few weeks. It's not as if this was winter."

"Damitall, Jess!"

Though frowning at the cuss word, she remained silent, waiting for him to relent.

Clem muttered under his breath, uncrossed his arms, crossed them again, tugged on his beard, and finally gave in with a sigh of frustration. "I reckon it won't hurt them much."

Jess gave the mule skinner a brilliant smile. "Thank you, Clem. Would you get them ready? And show Devlin to the livery stable? He's going to use Riley's horse. I'll be along in a minute, when I get a lunch packed."

With one last shake of his gray head, Clem turned and retrieved his rough jacket and coarse felt hat from a peg on the wall, then stomped out the back door, muttering about muleheaded womenfolk.

Jess let out her breath on a sigh before glancing at Devlin. The look he was giving her held laughter and something more . . . admiration, perhaps. Whatever it was made color rise to her cheeks.

"I'm sorry Clem was rude to you. He didn't mean anything by it. He treats all strangers that way."

"I didn't mind," Devlin said with a lazy grin. "I had a front-row seat for the entertainment. It was better than a ticket to a vaudeville show."

With that, he tipped his hat and rose from the table. Not knowing how to answer, Jess watched him go, her blush deepening. It wasn't much of a compliment to be told she had provided amusement for a man like that.

Devlin followed Clem outside and found the mule skinner kicking at the back step and swearing a blue streak.

"Dad-blister her! That bullheaded female can get me so riled!" He punctuated his opinion by spitting a stream of tobacco juice on the ground and administering another kick at the hapless step. "That durned gal is gonna land herself in a heap of trouble and there's not a blamed thing I kin do about it. Her pa would skin her alive if'n he knew she was going up to the Wildstar with you—"

Clem stopped and turned suddenly, balling his fists as he glared at Devlin. "Jessie's a proper lady, young fella, you best remember that. Don't you go and try nothin', or I'll turn you into a steer so fast you won't know what hit you."

"I wouldn't dream of treating her as anything but a lady," Devlin said dryly.

His answer seemed to defuse Clem's anger somewhat. "She ain't always this stubborn. Where her pa's concerned, Jess is like a she-wolf with her pup."

"So I gathered."

"Well, come on, then. We got work to do."

"Let me fetch my rifle."

After retrieving Devlin's Winchester from Jess's saddle, they walked the block to Carson's Livery Stable. There, amid considerable cussing, Clem got his mules ready and Devlin saddled Riley's horse.

Jess rode up just as they were leading the animals out.

She had brought her shotgun with her, Devlin saw, and was riding sidesaddle, as every lady in the West did, but she'd changed her gray suit for a plainer one of brown patterned calico. Thinking the outfit a shameful waste of a gorgeous figure, Devlin found himself re-dressing Jessica in a gown of satin and lace, her milk-white shoulders bare, her swelling breasts barely hidden by the low-cut bodice. It was an image he regretted, since it had the predictable effect of arousing him, a condition which held little immediate prospect of fulfillment.

Clem brought him back to earth with a gruff warning. "You'd best take good care of them mules or you'll have me to answer to."

Brusquely, Devlin nodded and mounted up. Jess, holding the lead ropes of the two mules, led the way.

"Don't pay Clem any mind," she said when they were out of hearing distance. "He's an ornery old codger, but he has a heart of gold."

"I'd say he thinks you're a bit ornery yourself. Do you always get your way?"

"When I have to." Wondering if Devlin's remark had been meant as a criticism, Jess fell silent, but the warmth that had afflicted her cheeks ever since meeting him rose again when she felt him watching her. "Maybe you'd better pay attention to the road, Mr. Devlin. In the dark, a lot of the mine shafts look alike, and you'll have to find your way alone from now on."

His beautiful mouth kicked up at the corner. "Yes, ma'am, Miss Jess. Whatever you say."

Jess gave him a sharp glance. Devlin's answer had been docile enough, but the lazy, provoking edge of amusement in his tone warned her it was going to be a long night.

Chapter 4

It was a scene ripe for seduction. A clear, cool, summer evening . . . stars blazing overhead in the heavens . . . the sweetness of pure, dry mountain air . . . a man alone at night with a beautiful young woman . . .

Devlin grinned wryly at the image. He wasn't alone with Jessica Sommers. He was in the company of two cantankerous lop-eared mules who objected to having to climb a mountain at this time of night. And the precipitous drop-off on his right was no gentle slope. One slip in the dark and a man could plunge hundreds of feet to his death—hardly conducive to seduction or even romance. It was also doubtful the young woman in question would be receptive to amorous advances from a stranger, especially one she considered to be her new employee. Plus, Devlin thought with a grimace, he had to face the disagreeable task of staying up all night to guard a hole in the ground and maybe get shot in the back in the process. Whatever had possessed him to agree to get involved in a miners' feud?

With a mental sigh, he checked the action of his guns and waited for Jess to cajole Nellie and Gus past a dangerous shadow in the road. Far below, the lights of Silver Plume twinkled on the canyon floor, beckoning, taunting him.

Shortly they resumed the laborious climb. The rocky wagon road made several switchbacks up the steep mountainside, scissoring past numerous tunnel mouths and the scars of barely passable trails. Wild berry patches grew here and there—raspberries, currants, snowberries, and chokecherries—but the rugged slopes were denuded of trees. All the lush natural forests of pine and spruce and aspen had been cleared for use as lumber or fuel or mine timbers—although Devlin did see the dark outline of one sole, brave ponderosa pine which clung in a crevice, too inaccessible to be cut down.

Beside every mine and shaft house stood huge dumps of waste rock that despoiled the rough landscape further. At least, though, it was Sunday and they were spared the terrible noise that reverberated through the mountains all the other days of the week—the thunder of blasting and the hammering of mechanical rock drills.

There were lights at the portals of some of the mines, illuminating the timber-frame chutes that were used to load ore. Jess pointed out the various workings along the way, calling them by name.

A half hour later, she finally brought the mules to a halt.

"That's it," she said quietly. "That's the Wildstar."

Devlin could make out a timber-framed opening in the wall of rock some dozen yards ahead that looked like every other mine they had passed. The shack nearest the entrance was probably the tool shed, and the one just beyond was likely the office.

"Burke's Lady J mine is just up the road, over the rise," Jess added.

Devlin hefted his Winchester and scanned the rocky terrain, finding nothing moving in the darkness. "Wait here. I'll take a look around."

When she nodded, he left her with the horses and scouted the area, entering the dark mouth of tunnel, climbing the slope above, circling the first shack, pushing open the door and peering inside. From what he could make out in the darkness, it was filled with mining tools—hammers, picks, shovels, explosives, and drill steel.

Shutting the door, he inspected the miner's hut next, stepping inside briefly to make certain no one was lying in ambush.

"All clear," he said as he walked back to her.

Before he could offer to help her dismount, Jess slid down from her horse and proceeded to picket the ornery Clem's two ornerier mules in front of the tunnel, her movements efficient and determined.

"You'd better let Nellie and Gus smell you," she warned, "so they won't set up a ruckus every time you go by."

Devlin bit back a crude remark at the suggestion, but after hobbling and unsaddling the horses, he did as she asked. Then he followed Jess to the hut and stood aside while she entered.

She fumbled for a minute in the dark, then struck a match against the door frame and lit the coal oil fixture hanging from the ceiling. The place was stuffed with the miscellaneous trappings of the mining trade, Devlin saw, and yet there was little actual furniture, only a rickety pine table and two chairs, and a narrow rope bed. The thin mattress was covered with a blanket but no pillow or sheets.

He shut the door behind them as Jess carried the knapsack of food she'd packed over to the table. When he heard her give a sudden soft gasp, Devlin swung his rifle up. She had come to an abrupt halt, staring down at the large black stain that darkened the raw pine floor.

"Riley's blood," she said faintly.

Devlin felt his heart soften at the tremble in her voice. "Looks like it," he said gently. Relaxing his rigid stance, he took the knapsack from her, laid it and his rifle on the table, and pulled out one of the chairs. "Sit down. You look worn out."

"No, I couldn't sit still just now."

Backing away from the stain as if it frightened her, she ignored his advice and went to stand at the small window whose shutter had been left open, restlessly peering out. "Do you suppose he was shot through the window?"

Devlin eyed the distance from there to the bloodstain. "The angle's right. Whoever did it must have figured him for dead."

"He nearly was." She shuddered, which made Devlin

feel the urge to go to her and put his arms around her—
and not just to offer her comfort. "I don't know what I
would have done if Riley had died," she whispered.

"Yes you do. You would have gone on without him."
He was certain of that. Jess Sommers was a strong woman
inside, for all her curvaceous softness outside. Devlin hesitated. "This stranger I heard you describing to the marshal
. . . you said he had a scar and was riding a roan. That's
all you know?"

"Yes."

"You've never heard of him before this?"

"No. But maybe some of the miners have. I could ask
around."

"That would be good. Any lead might help us find
him."

Wanting to give her something else to think about besides the attack on her father and his near murder, Devlin
joined her at the window and closed the shutter firmly.
"Why don't you show me the mine and tell me about this
feud with Burke? If you're paying me to guard this place,
I might as well know what I'm getting into."

Jess looked up to find Devlin smiling a teasing wayward
smile that unnerved her. "All right." She didn't really like
going into the mine, especially at night. It gave her chills
to be deep underground in the darkness. But even that was
preferable to the helpless, shivery feeling she got when
Devlin looked at her so intimately.

Moving away uneasily, she took down from a shelf a
miners' lantern and lit it, then led the way back outside.
Both mules set up a raucous braying the minute Devlin
came near. Jess scolded them both and made Devlin go
through the sniffing procedure again. Then, holding the
lantern aloft, she led him into the Wildstar tunnel.

The air immediately felt cooler, he noted, while the lantern light sent giant shadows leaping around the rock walls
that were braced by thick timbers. There was not much
room to move in a hewn passage that was approximately
seven feet high by four feet wide. Ahead of him, Jess care-

fully skirted an empty ore car and sidestepped the narrow rail tracks that ran along the tunnel floor.

"Be careful," she warned Devlin needlessly. "Accidents happen all the time underground. Just about every week you hear of somebody getting hurt. I always worry that Riley will be next, but he's been lucky. . . . That is, until today.

"This used to be the old Wilson claim," Jess added a minute later in explanation. "Back in '78, Riley used every penny he could scrape together to buy it and sink a prospect hole. He's been trying to develop the property ever since. It isn't much, but it's all he has. There are only two levels, this one and the one below. We should be working it two ten-hour shifts a day, but Riley can only afford a small crew for one shift."

She fell silent, not wanting to be disloyal to her father. Yet she had to admit Riley had no business trying to work a mine on this small of a scale. Mining operations were usually the ventures—or playthings—of wealthy entrepreneurs who'd made money elsewhere and had it to invest. An independent miner like Riley had little chance of success going up against the huge consolidated mines, which had the means to buy the latest technology and best equipment.

"How much capital would he need to work it properly?" Devlin asked in a musing tone.

Jess sighed. "Lots. Too much. There's an old saying . . . to work a silver mine, you have to have a gold mine."

"And your father doesn't have a gold mine."

"Nothing close. We can't even afford any compressed-air drills—we still use hand steels."

"What about Haverty? You said he was a partner?"

"Oh, he doesn't really own any of our claim. He gets twenty percent of the profits, if there are any—which isn't often."

They kept moving, past two side tunnels that Devlin could see played out quickly. Some thirty feet into the mountainside, the main tunnel ended in a vertical shaft that accessed the lower level. There Jess came to a halt.

Overhead was a hoist—a pulley-and-cable system—attached to an iron bucket the size of a large barrel. The bucket would carry ore up and men and tools down. Devlin recognized the setup from experience, since he'd once worked a gold mine in the Black Hills not so different from this one. And yet these conditions were much more primitive. The hoist was a hand-crank operation, for example, instead of steam-driven. And riding the bucket was far more dangerous than the more advanced metal cage designed to hold men.

"Do you want to go down?" Jess asked as she leaned over to peer down the shaft. She sounded reluctant, perhaps a bit afraid.

Devlin moved closer to inspect the shaft. Along the right side metal rungs had been driven into the rock at intervals to form a ladder, but he had no interest in exploring further. "No, not tonight. Where does Burke come in?"

"Right after my father started the Wildstar, Burke bought the adjacent claim at a sheriff's sale, just to spite us. That had to be the reason. None of the rock around here ever yielded anything but low-grade ore. Yet two years ago Burke began expanding the Lady J, and he's already developed three levels and blasted a dozen crosscuts. It's a waste of good money, if you ask me, but he has enough to throw away."

She straightened just then, only to collide with a hard male body. "Oh!" Her soft exclamation was one of dismay and nervous awareness as she found her breasts thrust against Devlin's chest, her thighs pressing fully against his.

Flinching, her senses screaming at the sudden shock, Jess tried to back away and nearly dropped the lantern. Reflexively Devlin reached up to steady her, which only prolonged the potent contact. Jess suddenly could think of nothing but the feel of him . . . the heat, the hardness, the vital maleness.

He must have felt something, too, for his grip on her arms tightened momentarily, as if he found it difficult to let her go, and he swore softly.

"Ex-excuse me," Jess stammered.

"My fault," Devlin replied in a voice huskier than he would have liked. The feel of her lush female form pressing against him had elicited an instant reaction in his body, but this was a hell of an inappropriate place to become aroused.

Gritting his teeth, he untangled himself and stepped a safe distance back. Gratefully, Jess turned away and unsteadily retraced her steps along the tunnel, not caring at the moment if Devlin followed her. She couldn't stop thinking of their accidental embrace, or the weak, feminine way it had made her feel.

She was still shaken when she entered the cabin. To think she had to spend the entire night with this man. . . .

"You can have the bed," Devlin said from behind her as he shut the door.

Jess's glance involuntarily went to the narrow cot and she froze. She would be alone with this man and that bed. Nervousness made her tone sharp when she retorted, "I suppose an Eastern dandy wouldn't deign to sleep on poor furniture like that."

"An Eastern dandy would never have come up here in the first place," he replied mildly as he lifted one of the chairs and placed its back against the far wall, so it faced the door.

Jess wished she could bite back the words. She hadn't forgotten what she owed Devlin. It was just that his masculine self-assurance disturbed her; *he* disturbed her. She'd never been tempted by a man before him. Never wanted a man to tighten his arms around her and hold her close. Never wondered what it would be like if he bent his head and kissed her. Back there in the mine she'd wanted Devlin to do just that.

In agitation, she clasped her hands in front of her and went to the shuttered window, feeling trapped and uneasy. Maybe she had made a mistake in hiring Devlin. Certainly she had made a mistake in planning to stay up here with him.

Behind her she could hear him settling into the chair.

When she ventured a glance, she saw that he'd stretched his long legs out in front of him, with his Winchester resting easily across his thighs. His Stetson was lying on the table, and his black hair shone softly in the glow from the lamp. He was watching her with something that looked like amusement in his eyes.

"I'm sorry about the poor accommodations," Jess said in a tentative apology.

"I'm not complaining . . . though I do admit having a preference for softer mattresses than that one. I'll be magnanimous and let you have it all to yourself."

His tone was lazy, disarming, with a hint of teasing humor in it. It only made Jess more nervous.

"Why don't you go to sleep?" he asked. "There's no use in us both staying awake."

Jess glanced again at the small bed. She was not about to lie down with Devlin so near. She wouldn't be able to sleep a wink.

"I'm not going to attack you, Miss Jess."

"I didn't think you would," she lied hastily.

"I won't even touch you . . . unless, of course, you want me to."

His glib, suggestive remark made color rise to her cheeks, and when she gave him a sharp glance, she found a bold and blatant mischievousness gleaming in his eyes.

"I am not at all sleepy," Jess said, trying to sound unconcerned but only managing to sound stiff and formal. It was, she knew, the result of her training at Miss Grater's Academy in Denver, where she'd had all the social graces and refined manners of a lady drummed into her head. Her speech often became more polished when she felt vulnerable—like she was feeling just now.

Trying to ignore the handsome devil who was making her feel that way, Jess turned away. For the next half hour, she wandered around the small hut, straightening the shelves that were already neat as a pin, closing the ledger that Riley must have been working on that morning when he was shot, generally pacing the floor with a restlessness that only seemed to grow stronger the longer she kept at it. With each pass, she sidestepped the large stain that vividly reminded her of how close she'd come to losing her father. She knew she ought to try to clean that dark blotch of dried blood off the wooden planks, yet she couldn't bring herself to touch it; simply looking at it brought back all the horror of that morning.

Devlin watched her every movement, the soft sway of her hips beneath her skirts, the delicious curve of her breasts, the slender, work-reddened hands. . . . Seeing the condition of her hands aroused a tender urge inside him, in addition to the natural male feelings of lust that were flaring through his senses at the sight of a beautiful woman expending all that pent-up energy on walking the floor. He could think of a dozen ways for her to channel that energy, most of them in bed. Tenderness for a woman was not a usual emotion for him, but with this woman he felt protective as well as possessive.

His mouth twisted wryly at the thought. He'd never known a woman who needed protection less, or possession more. Miss Jessica Sommers needed a man to show her how to relax, how to enjoy life, how to let her glorious hair down. And he wished he could be that man, the one to set her free.

I want you, lady, he thought, surprised at the depth of his hunger. *Oh yes, I want you.*

Devlin shook his head, trying to remember the last time merely thinking about a woman in his bed had caused such a strong reaction. He wanted Jessica in the most elemental way possible, groin-ache elemental. But she wasn't a woman he could bed and leave alone. She was almost certainly a virgin, one who wouldn't know the first thing about how to protect herself from unwanted pregnancies, one who probably didn't even know much about men. And while life in the West had roughened him around the edges, he was still enough of a gentleman to draw the line at seducing virgins.

"You really should get some sleep," he said finally. "After the day you've had, you must be on your last legs."

"I told you, I'm not sleepy."

"Well, then, at least sit down. You're making me jumpy."

She gave him a long look, but didn't respond.

"See that chair, Miss Jess? Go sit down there. Now. Before," Devlin threatened amicably, "I have to go to the trouble of carrying you there."

Jessica had the distinct impression he meant what he said. He was giving her one of those charming smiles that could melt rock, but he'd spoken with the cool assurance of a man who inevitably got his way.

"I am a bit tired," she admitted, preferring to give in graciously rather than press the issue. Crossing to the chair, she sank down and folded her hands on the table. "I'm not usually this fidgety."

"You have good reason to be."

"Next time I come up here," she said after another minute, "I'm going to scrub that bloodstain out."

"Quit thinking about it."

"I can't."

In answer she heard the scrape of Devlin's chair. Quizzically, she watched him rise and lay the rifle on the table. Jess tensed as he moved around behind her, and nearly jumped when she felt his fingers gently squeeze her shoulders.

"Hold still. I'm just going to give you a shoulder rub. You're as taut as a bowstring."

"I don't . . . need . . . a . . ."

She ought to complete the protest, Jess knew, but the magical feeling of Devlin's hands made the words die on her lips. The slow, gentle stroking of his fingers was compelling and soothing and entirely irresistible. He had no right showing her such kindness, now, when she was at her most vulnerable, but she didn't want him to stop.

She could feel the tension and aches draining away as he massaged the tight, weary muscles of her shoulders and neck, molding his long male fingers in a languid motion that was warm and rhythmic and sensual. She had no defenses against such gentleness, such tenderness. Closing her eyes, Jess gave a deep sigh. No one had ever taken care of her like this.

"You should relax more," Devlin said softly after a moment. "Not work so hard."

"I can't," she murmured. "I have too many things that need doing."

He smiled faintly at the conviction in her tone. She'd probably spent a lifetime denying her own needs, a lifetime of self-sacrifice, doing for others. He let his stroking hands move lower, along her spine, in an intimate caress. In response, Jessica arched her back, while a soft groan was dredged from deep in her throat.

Devlin felt a sharp, insistent sting of desire at the primal sound. He wanted to have her groaning for him as she wrapped her long legs around his waist, as she bucked wildly beneath him in the throes of passion, as she melted in his arms. His fingers tightened involuntarily at the image of this woman melting for him.

Jess, dazed by his sensual touch, did feel like she was melting. The seductive promise in his fingertips, his palms, the heels of his hands, no longer resembled the impersonal, soothing magic of his initial touch. This was skilled and expertly arousing. She shivered with each stroke of his fingers.

Somewhere in a dim corner of her mind a small voice was shouting a warning at her, but she couldn't heed it. Helplessly, she let her head fall back.

Standing above her, Devlin had an intimate view of the lush swell of her breasts bound repressively by the dark fabric of her bodice. His hands ached to reach around and caress her there, yet he knew that territory of her body was off-limits.

But he could do the next best thing. With one hand he slowly reached up and drew the hat pin from the small, severe felt construction on her head. Tossing it on the table, he proceeded to take down her hair, removing the pins, one by leisurely one, from the mass of twists and knots.

The woman beneath his hands didn't even seem aware of his unusual ministrations. In fact, she seemed half asleep. Gratified to be meeting no resistance, Devlin indulged his pleasure, combing his fingers in the thick mane till it streamed down her back in a flowing river of honey.

"You have beautiful hair," Devlin couldn't help but murmur, his voice rusty and low.

His observation brought no response from Jess.

"I should put you to bed."

The mention of the bed was an unwelcome intrusion into Jess's drowsy senses. She opened her eyes and looked up at him in confusion. "You make it sound . . . like I'm a child. I'm not. I'm a full-grown woman."

He smiled one of those beautiful smiles as his gaze drifted lower to her breasts. "Full-grown, perhaps . . . but not entirely a woman."

The implied insult stung. "What is that supposed to mean?

Have you ever bedded a man, angel? "Just that you're inexperienced."

She wanted to deny it, but when she frowned up at him, she found herself trapped by his gaze. They were dangerous eyes, the gray deep and subtle like smoke from a wildfire. But then he was a dangerous man. Dangerous as sin.

Sin. . . .

Her gaze dropped to his mouth, but it was a moment before she became aware just where his face was in relation to hers. Devlin had moved subtly, positioning himself beside her chair, angling his body as he leaned over her. His fingers were still twined in her hair, and when he bent even closer, she could feel his warm breath against her lips.

He was going to kiss her, Jess thought dazedly an instant before their lips met.

A dozen physical sensations shuddered through her. His mouth was cool and yet burned her. His touch was featherlight and yet more powerful than a blow. His masculine scent, his heat, made her senses swim. She felt excited and breathless, as if she'd run a great distance, and yet she hadn't moved. How could she when he had wrapped his hands in her hair, anchoring her head and holding her face still for his kiss?

Jess trembled. It was erotic, being this helpless while a hard, beautiful man made love to her mouth. She had never experienced anything like it. His tongue, warm and wet, traced the outline of her lips, sending a starburst of fiery pleasure spreading through her. She couldn't believe she was actually letting him do this to her. In a minute she would make him stop. In a minute . . .

His touch was so intoxicating, so tantalizing, that she ached to touch him in return. Hesitantly she reached up to place her hand along the side of his warm neck. His black hair felt thick and silky where the ends caressed her fingers.

At her tentative gesture, Devlin deepened his kiss. Every nerve in Jess's body flared and tightened when his tongue slid inside her mouth, coaxing, arousing.

Did he know what he was doing to her? she wondered dizzily. He had to be aware of the slow thudding of her heart, the sudden throbbing of her body.

Devlin felt a surge of triumph at the soft whimper he coaxed from her. Arousal, hot and heavy, flooded through him. Deliberately he loosened his hold on her hair, untangling one hand from the tawny silken tresses so he could touch her more intimately. His fingers stroked her collarbone, then slowly descended, to find and cup her breast.

He felt her stiffen, heard her soft startled gasp, yet he took advantage of her parted lips to drive his tongue deeper inside her mouth.

It was with a sense of surprise and pleasure that he felt her hand clutching at his left thigh. Her fingers climbed upward uncertainly. Her movement was awkward and fumbling, showing her innocence and inexperience, but no practiced woman's touch had ever excited him more.

With a guttural sound of satisfaction, Devlin slanted his head to attain a better angle, his tongue gently forcing her mouth to open farther so he could assuage his hunger. It took a minute for him to recognize the feel of cold steel jammed into his midriff.

The barrel of his Colt revolver.

She had drawn his own gun on him.

The realization was like ice water splashing over his heated senses. His muffled curse was loud in the sudden silence as he pulled back to stare down at her. Her golden hazel eyes were on him, soft, self-conscious, wary, full of distrust, but her grip on the revolver was entirely steady.

Devlin swore again under his breath. He couldn't believe he had gotten so carried away by a simple kiss that he'd never guessed what Jessica was doing. He hadn't even heard the gun clear leather. Hell, he hadn't been that careless since his first visit to a Chicago parlor house, when he was fourteen.

Or that aroused. He hadn't expected that kind of weakness from himself. He hadn't expected to lose all awareness of who she was and who he was. He hadn't expected to be left this hungry for more of her.

"I'm paying you," she said a bit breathlessly, "to guard our mine, Devlin. Not to kiss me."

He inhaled, striving for control. "A good thing, angel. It wouldn't be worth the price. You kiss like a child." He had tried to deliver the insult in a cool, languid drawl but it came out in a husky rasp that proclaimed his still-acute state of arousal.

His accusation seemed to startle her at first. Then her cheeks colored with a flush of embarrassment and anger. "How am I supposed to kiss then?" she demanded, perhaps before realizing what she was saying.

"With your mouth open. With your tongue. With your hands and body. A little passion wouldn't hurt, either."

Her flush deepened.

His rough chuckle softly mocked her discomposure. "It's obvious why no one's ever shown you how to kiss." His gaze dropped to the revolver still aimed at him. "Do you threaten to shoot every man who tries?"

"No, of course not!"

"Just if he gets too close, then? You know what I think? You're afraid to let yourself enjoy being a woman."

"That isn't true! I don't have *time* to enjoy being a

woman. I don't have time to primp and preen and deck myself out in fancy clothes."

"Oh yes, you're afraid, sweetheart. You're afraid to feel a woman's passion."

Jess stared at Devlin in dismay, realizing there was some truth to his accusation. She *was* afraid . . . of him, of the sinful promise in his eyes, of the way he made her feel. He stood there, arrogant and self-assured, his denim-covered legs spread slightly, his right thumb hooked over his gun belt. He looked more strikingly handsome than a man had any right to look.

"Oh yes, Miss Jess." His voice dropped to a husky murmur that sent tingles of physical awareness running along her skin. "Some man ought to take you in hand and show you the kind of desire a woman can feel . . . make you a complete woman."

"I suppose you think you're that man."

His grin slowly became tantalizing. "I could be."

Her breath seemed to stop at the notion.

"But not tonight. As you said, you're paying me to guard your mine, not teach you about womanhood. Do you intend to give me my gun back?"

"I don't know."

"Your virtue's safe . . . for tonight."

He held out his hand, waiting with apparent patience but with a glint of maddening amusement in his eyes. After a moment's hesitation, Jessica lowered the revolver and handed it to him, butt first.

He holstered it, then turned to the table and retrieved his hat. "I'll stay outside for the rest of the night. You can put a chair under the door handle if you're afraid of me."

Not answering, Jess watched as Devlin picked up his Winchester and crossed the small room. Reaching overhead for the lamp, he turned down the flame till it gave off only a faint glow. "Get some sleep," he ordered softly, before leaving the cabin solely to her.

When the door shut behind him, Jess let out the breath she'd been holding. The urge to shove a chair under the door handle, as he'd suggested, made her palms itch, but she refused to let that provoking devil think she was afraid of him. Determinedly she made herself get up from the table and walk over to the bed.

Sitting on the lumpy mattress, she struggled to unfasten her slim-heeled, high-button shoes. Then crawling beneath the blanket, she pulled it up to her chin and lay staring at the rough pine ceiling, trying unsuccessfully not to think of Garrett Devlin. It was a long, long while before her eyes drifted closed.

Outside, Devlin settled himself on the rocky ground near the hut, with his back to a boulder, and tried unsuccessfully not to think of Jessica Sommers. It was a novelty for him, being held off at gunpoint by a woman. For that matter it was a novelty that a woman had refused his advances. Females usually tripped over themselves trying to please him and win his attention. That Jessica hadn't was doubtless because she didn't yet know the size of his bank account.

What would she say if he told her that he owned mines, ranches, and railroad stocks worth millions? That he could claim two newspapers, seven banks, a dozen factories, a racing stable, and his own private railroad car? Her attitude toward him would change quickly enough then. She needed money badly—to get her father back on his feet and their mine operating in the black. If what he suspected was true, she would have to use her life savings simply to pay him the salary she'd offered.

Devlin hunched his shoulders as a cool night breeze blew off the mountain and swept across his overheated body; this high up the air was thin and pure and bracing. Yes, Jessica would change. While he might be intrigued by her courage, while he might admire her fierce loyalty to her father, he had little faith that she was any different from other women. As soon as she learned his net worth, she would prove to be just as mercenary as all the other money-hungry females in his past. . . . His mother, who had married his father for money and position. The married socialite who'd seduced him when he was fifteen in order to gain an introduction to his father. His one-time fiancée, who'd taught him that the lure of wealth and power could poison simple feelings like love.

It had been a hard lesson, one that had changed his life.

As the only son of wealthy Chicago railroad magnate C. E. Devlin, Garrett had grown up in the lap of luxury and been groomed to take over his father's empire. But the transition had never occurred. In fact, he'd scarcely spoken to his father in the past ten years, since their bitter estrangement when they'd quarreled over his future.

C.E. had always been a hard, exacting, aloof man who drove his son to meet impossibly high standards—until Garrett finally rebelled. He was twenty-one and fresh out of Harvard when he'd fallen head over heels in love with a young woman and asked her to marry him. His father, though, objected to her lower social status and threatened to cut Garrett off without a penny if he went through with the marriage. Declaring he could live without his father's money, he asked his fiancée to leave town with him.

Never once had he considered that she might turn him down. But her reaction quickly revealed her horror at the prospect of a life other than the wealthy one she'd bargained for.

"Go west? Garrett, darling, you don't honestly expect me to sacrifice my entire future simply so you can defy your father. Why don't you make up with him, tell him you're sorry?"

Garrett felt a sickening sense of disillusionment knotting in his stomach. "I don't think you understand. He means to disinherit me if we marry."

She gave him a coaxing, purely female smile that said such an obstacle was only a minor one. "Then we'll wait until we can bring him around."

"You don't know my father. He can't be persuaded from a course once he makes up his mind. And I've had enough of living under his thumb. I mean to go out west, and I want you to come with me."

"But where will we live, how will we afford a house, a

carriage, clothes? How will I entertain your guests? How will you support me?"

"I can earn enough to support you without being tied to my father's money bags."

"How, darling?"

"I'm familiar enough with the rail business to get a position with a railroad."

"But you would have to start at the bottom."

"I've always been skilled at cards. I could make extra money gambling if necessary."

"*Gambling?* Garrett, you know I love you, but you *can't* expect me to give up my life, all my dreams, so you can throw away your future. I have to think about my own future, too."

Which was all she cared about, he realized with a rising ache in his throat.

He'd pleaded with her to reconsider, hoping desperately that he'd misunderstood, that money and position didn't really mean so much more to her than he did. When she'd abruptly ended the engagement, it had felt like a knife being shoved in his gut. He had loved her—ardently, mindlessly, as only a young man of one and twenty can love. He'd believed she loved him. Her avowals had seemed so genuine. But what kind of love was it that couldn't pass even the first test of loyalty, of commitment?

Devlin restlessly shifted the Winchester on his lap as memories intruded. He had cried that night. Broken down and sobbed like a baby for his lost love, his lost innocence. And when his tears had dried, his disillusionment had stayed with him.

He'd gotten over her eventually. What had meant so much to him then now seemed like an unsavory dream. He could barely recall what she looked like now. Her name . . . her name didn't matter. There had been too many women since then to remember only one. But he'd never forgotten the pain she'd caused him, or the lesson she'd taught him. And he was determined he would never be used that way again.

He had gone west alone, without her, without his father's money, vowing to make enough on his own that she would regret refusing him, and determined to prove to his father he could be successful without his help.

Those had been tough years, since he was a greenhorn at nearly everything that mattered in the West. He'd had to grow up fast, had to learn new skills. He worked on the railroad for a time, drove cattle, tried his hand at panning for gold. He discovered a kind of pleasure in earning his livelihood by his own honest sweat, but the pay was poor for menial jobs. So he honed his talent for gambling—well enough to make a decent living at it. And then, because he wanted to continue living, he learned to draw fast. He achieved a reputation for being good with a gun, and was once a deputy sheriff in a small town in Kansas. He even hired on as an extra gun with a big cattle outfit in Wyoming during a range war.

All the while, he was investing his earnings and gambling winnings in ranches, mills, mines, and railroads throughout the West. It wasn't until the Black Hills gold rush, though, that he finally began to make money on a large scale. He lucked into a big strike while working his claim, and used the proceeds to buy an interest in the now fabulously rich Homestake Mine. By the time he finally returned to Chicago four years ago for his mother's funeral, he was well on his way to becoming a rich man.

He stayed there in Chicago, making it his home, and proceeded to increase his wealth significantly. Not only did he prove to be a shrewd investor, but he managed to charm, outwit, seduce, or slay any dragons barring his way to achieving his ultimate goal—being wealthy and powerful enough to thumb his nose at his father. At last, after ten years, he could claim success.

Not that his father noticed.

C.E. had kept his word, disowning Garrett as his son, never writing or speaking until Irene Devlin's funeral, and then only tersely. He'd never forgiven Garrett for bucking his command, or escaping his control. Devlin was certain his father at least knew of his achievements; any man of C. E. Devlin's consequence and shrewdness would be aware of events of even minor significance to the business community. But no acknowledgment had ever been made.

They'd crossed paths several times in Chicago since the funeral, twice at social functions within the past year. A cool nod was the only recognition C.E. ever gave him. Devlin found it a bitter absurdity that despite their ten-year estrangement, his father's snubs still bothered him. Dammit, he was thirty-one years old and he still hadn't outgrown his need for C.E.'s approval. He still craved his father's good opinion.

And without that approval, success seemed a hollow victory. Money hadn't satisfied him, nor had power. He could afford the best in life—the finest houses, the best entertainment, the most beautiful women—but he couldn't suppress the feeling of discontent that had plagued him lately, a weariness bordering on ennui, a hollowness of the soul that could only be called loneliness, despite his active social life. He was rich enough and good-looking enough to buy most any woman he wanted, but he stuck with fancy women and occasionally married ladies—only those sophisticated and worldly enough to know that an affair with him wouldn't lead to marriage.

The young woman who'd started it all had married a banker, borne three children, and was now a plump society matron lording over her dwindling coterie of Chicago's *nouveau riche*. Devlin had only learned about her because he'd bought her husband's bank shortly after his return to Chicago, and because she'd shown up at his doorstep, professing a willingness to share his bed in exchange for her husband's advancement. He'd sent her away with a strong feeling of disgust and only a vague feeling of regret for the loss of the love he'd once felt for her.

He felt a much greater regret for the loss of his father's respect and affection.

No one could have been more amazed than Devlin when C.E. had voluntarily paid him a visit during the week just past. For a full minute he'd stared at the calling card that bore his father's name, thinking there had to be some mistake, before finally directing his housekeeper to show the visitor into his study.

It was definitely his father. They stood eyeing each other like two strangers, until C.E. finally broke the silence.

"You're looking well, Garrett," he said gruffly.

Devlin could have returned the remark. At sixty, his father was still tall and attractive and sharp-eyed, though his black hair was liberally streaked with gray. Devlin found himself wondering if his father might not be a lonely man. C.E. hadn't remarried after his wife's death, and even during her life, Irene Devlin had been a cold, selfish woman, more concerned with the state of her social calendar than with her husband's or son's welfare. And if the string of mistresses his father was reported to have had since then was any indication, C.E. hadn't been satisfied with any of the women he'd had in keeping. But not for one minute did Devlin believe his father was interested in exchanging banalities or discussing the past.

"To what do I owe the honor of this visit, sir? I don't presume this is a social call."

"No, I've come on business," C.E. responded cooly.

Devlin invited his father to sit down in a wing chair, then settled himself behind his desk. There was another long pause before the elder man cleared his throat. "I hear you've done well for yourself."

"Did you doubt I would?"

"No. You're my son, after all."

My son. How sweet those words sounded. How bitter. Devlin couldn't stem the surge of anger welling up in him. Odd that C.E. should remember he had a son now. There had to be a reason, and whatever it was doubtlessly stemmed from his own self-interest. C. E. Devlin had been the son of a poor Irish immigrant, but he'd pulled himself up by his bootstraps and risen out of poverty to become one of the most powerful men in the country. And he hadn't done it by espousing sweetness and light. *Tycoon* was too kind a word for his style of management. Devlin knew; a strong streak of his father's aggressiveness ran in his own veins. But the old man was a controlling, manipulative bastard of the first order. It had taken Devlin twenty-one years to realize that, to understand that his father had always withheld his love and approval until he received whatever it was he wanted. Love had been a reward for obedience, purely that. Remembering, Devlin clenched his jaw and sat waiting for his father to come to the purpose of his visit.

"You've heard about the trouble with the Colorado Central by now?" C.E. asked finally.

"I've heard of it, yes." Three robberies in four months. It was a record anyone in the rail business had to be concerned with.

"And you know my position with that railroad?"

"I know." His father was both a major stockholder and on the board of directors of the Union Pacific, which had leased the Colorado Central for its own use back in '78.

"So you understand why I'm anxious to get to the bottom of this."

"I can imagine," Devlin said dryly.

"I want the robberies stopped. *Now.*"

Devlin managed to repress a hard smile. Of course his father would want immediate action. Not because he wanted justice. Not because he wanted to recover the stolen money. Not even because he felt remorse for the two men who'd been killed in the last robbery. But because C. E. Devlin hated to be thwarted.

"I expect you've already tried?" Garrett remarked.

"We've hired a half dozen of Pinkerton's detectives, but all we've gotten are worthless reports."

And of course he would not be willing to wait till the detective firm achieved any results. "So . . . what do you want from me?"

"You've lived out west. I hoped you might be able to recommend a reliable man who could be counted on to track down these outlaws, to put an end to these robberies. I'm willing to offer a substantial reward for apprehension and conviction of the criminals."

A dozen thoughts ran through Devlin's mind at once,

but the chief one was disbelief. His father had hundreds of contacts throughout the country, many of whom could have given him the information he sought. So why had C.E. come here, of all places? Could he possibly be using this as an excuse simply to see *him*? As an opening to renew their acquaintance, if not their relationship as father and son?

The surge of hope that possibility engendered made Devlin sit up. If that were true, he was willing to meet his father halfway.

"I know of someone, yes," he said slowly.

"Who?"

"Myself."

"You?" The skepticism on his father's face was not very heartening. "You can trace a gang of outlaws and bring them in?"

"You don't sound as if you have much faith in me." The comment was meant to be dry, but his tone sounded more bitter than sarcastic.

C.E. hesitated, eyeing his son for a long moment. "Faith is not the question."

"No?"

"No. I've always believed you could do anything you set your mind to. I just can't imagine why you would want to involve yourself in this. It could be dangerous. These men have already killed once."

Devlin had his reasons, some of them not so high-minded. To put his father in his debt. To show that for once C.E. needed him. To regain his father's respect by succeeding where others had failed. But more than that, this opportunity to prove himself might just possibly be a first step toward reconciliation.

Unwilling to voice any of those thoughts, Devlin shrugged his shoulders noncommittally. "Maybe I'm just bored. Sitting here running an empire isn't the challenge I thought it would be. I could use an adventure. I'd like to try."

"Very well, then. I would be grateful for your help."

I'm counting on it. Aloud, Devlin said, "Let me see those reports so I can get started."

He rose when his father did, and accompanied him to the front door. C.E. accepted his bowler and walking stick, but then hesitated.

"Garrett . . . perhaps you won't believe this, but ten years ago . . . my intentions were good. I wanted to spare you the kind of marriage I had to endure with your mother."

Devlin found himself clenching his teeth. He had wanted his father to admit that he'd been wrong all those years ago. Not wrong in denying his blessing for a marriage that would have been a disaster, but wrong in the methods he'd employed to gain his son's compliance. But this was the closest thing to an apology he would ever get from his father, Devlin knew. He could either accept it or reject it.

"As much as I'm loath to admit it," he replied with effort, "you were right. She would have made me an abominable wife."

C.E. gave him another long searching look, as if seeking reassurance, before he finally turned and quit the house. Devlin shut the door softly behind him, more determined than ever to live up to his father's expectations.

The reports from the Pinkerton detectives had suggested Silver Plume, Colorado, as a starting point for his search. It would be foolish, though, to advertise his millionaire status if he meant to quietly hunt the outlaws, so he'd decided to pose as a gambler.

The trail to Silver Plume had led him here to this mountain, to this mine, to a tawny-haired hellion who went for a gun every time she felt threatened by a man.

Recalling the incident in the mine shack just now when he'd kissed Jessica, Devlin shook his head in self-disgust. He couldn't deny that he wanted her, but the attraction was purely physical. She was too strong-willed and self-sufficient for a woman. Too tough. Too capable. Too intense. A man wanted a woman to be soft and feminine, to look up to him, to *need* him.

Devlin's mouth curved sardonically. Jessica Sommers needed a man all right. She was crying out for some hot-blooded male to take her in hand and soften her tough edges, to teach her about passion, to show her how to enjoy being a woman. He was tempted to take on the task himself. Oh, how he was tempted. Her rejection of his kisses had piqued his male vanity like nothing else had in a long while.

Devlin shifted his body uncomfortably. Just the thought of being the man to awaken her to pleasure was arousing enough to make him grow hard again.

Resigned to a long night, he resettled his shoulders against the boulder and turned his thoughts to the delightful prospect of avenging his wounded pride, indulging in forbidden fantasies that resulted in Jessica Sommers's conversion to full womanhood.

In the darkness, a slow grin of anticipation claimed his mouth.

He would protect Jessica from anyone who threatened her and her mine with harm. The question was, who would protect her from *him*?

Chapter 5

"Y ou did *what*?" Riley Sommers bellowed at his daughter. He tried to raise himself on his elbows and then promptly groaned as the raw flesh in his back stretched and pulled.

"Riley, please!" Jess said urgently. "You'll aggravate your wound. There's no reason to get so upset."

Riley had regained his senses around mid-morning, hungry and crotchety and anxious about his mine. Because of his bullet wound, Jess wouldn't feed him anything heavier than chicken broth and soda crackers, but she was able to reassure her father about the Wildstar. Clem had managed to convince the crew to carry on without their boss, and they'd gone to work that morning as usual.

It was only after she'd spoon-fed Riley half the bowl of broth that Jess told him about hiring Devlin to guard the Wildstar and about staying up there with him the previous night.

"No reason?" Riley repeated incredulously. "My daughter spends the night with a hired gun, alone, up on a mountaintop, and I have no reason to get upset?"

"Please, Riley, calm down."

"I don't want to calm down! I want to know who in thunderation this Devlin fellow is and what in blazes he was doing up there at the mine with you!"

Jess bit her lip. She hadn't expected her father to be happy about her actions, but neither had she expected him to be so furious. His stewing had caused a fresh crimson

70

stain to blossom over the dressing on his wounded back. "Lie still. You're bleeding through your bandage."

Quickly she grabbed a towel and began swabbing gently around the edges of the gauze, trying to stem the flow of blood. "I thought you would be pleased that I tried to protect the Wildstar," she said lamely.

The fight seemed to go out of her father. "Of course I am, Jess, but you had no business going up there with a strange man, even if it was for a good cause. What in tarnation were you thinking of? You don't know this man from Adam, and you spend the night with him alone? You were risking your life, not to mention your reputation."

She collected herself enough to protest. "I'm not *that* bad a judge of character. You'll see when you meet him that Devlin isn't the kind of man who would hurt a woman."

"Well . . . maybe," Riley grumbled. Awkwardly he reached for her hand and squeezed it in his large, calloused one. "I'd rather lose the mine altogether than have something happen to you."

His avowal warmed Jess's heart. "Well, nothing happened to me."

At least almost nothing. Devlin had kissed her half senseless last night, but he hadn't taken it any further after she'd pulled his gun on him. The speculative gleam in his smokey eyes when he'd woken her early this morning didn't count.

It had startled Jess to open her eyes and find Devlin sitting beside her on the small bed, his hip pressed intimately against hers through the blanket, his hands on her shoulders. He'd looked disreputable and dangerous with that shadow of stubble darkening his cheeks and jaw, though not a whit less handsome. But he'd behaved like a gentleman this morning . . . almost. His teasing threat to crawl into bed with her if she didn't get up had been delivered with so much charm and with such a dazzling male smile that she'd blinked in stupefaction. She'd only been the tiniest bit nervous until she was able to ride away, leaving

Devlin there to question the mine crew when they arrived for work.

"Where is this Devlin fellow?" her father's voice broke into her disturbing reflections. "I want to talk to him right now."

"I don't know. I thought he would be here by now. He stayed up at the Wildstar to talk to the men and see what he could find out about the coward who shot you."

"He's coming *here*?" Riley asked ominously.

Jess took a deep breath, preparing for another explosion. "Yes, here. He's going to sleep here during the day and look after you while I'm gone—"

She wasn't disappointed. Riley let loose a tirade that made Clem's rebuke the previous night seem tame. But Jess didn't back down. Determined to make her father see reason, she laid out all the logical arguments she'd formulated for letting Devlin stay with them instead of at the boardinghouse. The discussion turned into a shouting match, at least on her father's part.

"Goldarnit, I don't want you getting involved, Jess!" Riley said finally, his face twisted with pain. "If somebody tried to kill me, you could get hurt, too."

"I already am involved! You can't possibly expect me to do nothing while you go and get yourself murdered. Besides, I'm not about to let Burke win."

That was a potent argument Riley couldn't refute. He gave a weary sigh of resignation. "All right, I'll wait to meet this Devlin fellow before I decide to send him packing, but I don't want you going near the mine again, do you hear me?"

"I hear you."

"Promise me, Jess."

"All right. I promise." It shouldn't be a difficult promise to keep, she thought. From now on she intended to let Devlin guard the Wildstar alone. She didn't think she could go through another night with him like the last one.

Riley didn't seem satisfied with her capitulation, though, for his scowl merely deepened. "You're too much like your ma, Jess. You're liable to find out the hard way that some men aren't to be trusted."

His comment surprised her, but he didn't elaborate. He merely closed his eyes, grimacing in pain.

A frown gathered on her brow as she rearranged the covers to let him sleep. She already knew some men weren't to be trusted. What she didn't know was whether Garrett Devlin was one of those men.

Devlin spent his morning productively occupied, talking to the mine crew of the Wildstar and the guard from the Silver Queen who had found Riley just after the shooting.

Most of Riley's crew were Cousin Jacks—Cornishmen known for their colorful clothing and language. Like all hard-rock miners, they were rough as the ore they dug out of the earth and tough as oxen. Handling drill steel or swinging a four-pound hammer or a muck stick for ten hours a day built muscles and stamina and sheer grit. The Silver Queen guard was no miner, merely a kid who fancied himself a gunman.

He hadn't actually seen the shooting, but Devlin discovered several things of interest from him. First that the man with the scar who'd been poking around the area looked an awful lot like a rough character who once worked as an armed guard for Burke's Lady J Mine.

"His name was Zeke McRoy. 'Course I could be wrong," the young guard said. "I didn't get a close look yesterday. But that red scar above his eye stood out good enough. Don't know how he got that—didn't use to have it. Somebody musta shot him. 'Course Zeke was the kinda fella folks wanted to shoot."

"Any idea where he went?" Devlin asked.

"I dunno. When he saw me coming, he jumped on that roan of his and lit out over Republican Mountain, bound for the north. I figure he was headed to Middle Park or maybe Empire. There's some rough country up there, lots of places for a man to hide if he don't want to be found."

"You say this Zeke worked for the Lady J mine? Do you know why he left?"

"Nope. You better talk to the super over to the Lady J. His name's Hank Purcell. Or maybe the big boss, Mr. Burke, could tell you."

Burke probably *could* tell him, Devlin reflected, but it was doubtful that he *would*, especially if he'd employed Zeke as a hired gun.

Knowing he would have to get the information elsewhere, Devlin returned to the Wildstar to question Clem and his crew about Zeke McRoy. No one had seen Zeke around for perhaps six months, but everyone agreed he was mean enough to shoot a man in the back.

It was going on ten o'clock by the time Devlin rode down the mountain, accompanied by the echoing thunder of hammering and blasting. The purple haze that had wreathed the high range had burned off, leaving behind a brilliant blue sky.

Tired though he was, he headed toward the Diamond Dust Hotel, intending to settle his bill and make sure his trunk with the rest of his things had been collected by Jess's Chinaman.

This was the first day of a work week, and Silver Plume's Main Street looked entirely different from the sleepy place of yesterday. Hard-rock mining was an ugly, noisy business, and the hubbub and smoke had turned the town into an outdoor sweatshop. Ore wagons and buckboards jammed every corner, while numerous stamping and crushing mills ran full tilt, concentrating ore so it could be shipped by rail to the smelting works farther down the canyon for final processing. The street teemed with horses and mules and rugged men of every description and descent—Irishmen, Welshmen, Cornishmen, Italians, Mexicans, even a few Chinamen. Miners mixed with merchants, bankers, freighters, clerks, and occasionally women.

The hotel was quieter at least. Lena must have been watching out for him, though, for no sooner had Devlin gone up to his room than there was a soft knock on his door. When he opened it, Lena slipped inside.

"I missed you last night, sugar," she purred, wrapping

her arms around his neck and enveloping him in a heady perfume.

When she lifted her mouth to his, Devlin returned her kiss perfunctorily, with his eyes open, finding it impossible not to compare the kiss he'd taken from Jess last night to this one—with surprising results. Beautiful, sultry, seductive Lena, even with all her experience and skill, came in a distant second to the unpracticed, tawny-haired firebrand he'd ached to make love to last night. And, while Jessica had adamantly refused his advances, Lena's embrace was proprietary and clinging.

She was also apparently fishing for information. Drawing back slightly, Lena pouted prettily. "Where'd you go last night, sweetie? Not to some other woman, I hope."

He gave her an apologetic smile and a gallant answer. "What sane man would want another woman if he could have you?"

Somewhat mollified, Lena suggestively pressed her voluptuous body against his, which amazingly did nothing to arouse him.

"The truth is," Devlin prevaricated, "I spent last night alone, out in the open, on the cold hard ground, playing nursemaid to a mine shaft. *Not* an experience I relished."

Unwrapping her arms from around him, he poured Lena a shot of whiskey and sat her down in the leather armchair so he could explain about his involvement in the mine feud and ply her for his own information. Stretched out on the large bed, his hands behind his head, he told her about accepting the job guarding the Wildstar mine.

Lena wasn't at all pleased that he'd taken sides against Ashton Burke, or that he'd become involved with anything having to do with Jessica Sommers. But she told him everything she knew when he asked about Zeke McRoy— which wasn't a lot more than he'd already learned. Zeke was a trigger-happy drifter who'd ridden into town one day and hired on as a guard at the Lady J mine. He was on the payroll for almost a year before he'd disappeared about six months ago.

Lena did, however, have a lot to say about how the bitter feud between Ashton Burke and Riley Sommers had started. It was, naturally, over a woman.

"Mercy, but it was a big scandal at the time," Lena reflected. "Not that *I* recall it—I was only a baby back then. But I've heard a lot of talk since. Jenny Ann Elliot was a real pretty girl, not fancy or anything, just nice and a bit shy. Well, one summer Ash got smitten with her and began to pay her a lot of attention . . . dishonorable attention, you might say. Being British and all, Ash has these notions. He says he's the son of some esquire back in England, whatever an esquire is. Doesn't sound very important to me. Anyway, Jenny Ann wasn't good enough for him to marry. Her pa was well-to-do, but only a doctor, and Ash was a rich man even back then.

"It shocked everybody when one day she up and married Riley Sommers. Riley was only a miner, working for another outfit. But I guess Jenny Ann finally got wise to Ash and was willing to settle for being poor if she could have a respectable ring on her finger. Of course, she would *never* have become his mistress. Wasn't the type. But that was all Ash would have offered. Still, the way Ash saw it, it was like she'd jilted him."

Lena frowned down at her glass. "You know what I think, Garrett, honey? I think Ash named the Lady J mine after Jenny Ann. It was his way of causing talk and getting back at her for giving him the cold shoulder. Maybe he wanted to make her remember what she gave up. Not that she gave up much. He would have lost interest in her after a while, and then where would she have been? Ash only wants what he can't have."

She looked up and gave Devlin a half smile that held a bleakness that oddly touched his heart. "You know, I guess I ought to thank you, sugar. Ash has been a lot nicer to me since you came to town. Maybe it's the competition, you think?"

Devlin couldn't help the sympathetic urge he felt. Dragging his weary body off the bed, he crossed to Lena's chair, bent over her, traced her lips with a gentle finger, and gave her a chaste kiss that was more consoling than passionate. "I think Burke must be a blind man to over-look what you could offer him."

Lena's dark eyes grew moist. "You sure do know how to make a girl feel wanted, sugar." When Devlin smiled and tucked three gold double eagles into the pocket of her morning gown, her gaze turned solemn. "Jess Sommers ain't your type, any more than her ma was Ash's. You sure you want to get tangled up with her?"

He was already tangled up, but that wasn't an answer he could give. "After being up all night," he said instead, "the only thing I'm sure of right now is that I want a bath, a shave, a meal, and a soft bed—not necessarily in that order."

"I guess you want that soft bed all to your lonesome."

"If I had the energy, sweetheart, I would love the company, but I'm wrung out. And I was supposed to report for duty at the Sommers place several hours ago."

Lena gave him a sad little smile as she rose. "Well, you know where to find me if you change your mind."

Devlin didn't change his mind during the following week. In the first place he was too busy settling in to his new job and adjusting to his strange new schedule, not having slept during the day in years. In the second place, he remained distinctly uninterested in the notion of taking any woman to bed other than Jessica Sommers. Taking *her*, though, was out of the question. Besides the fact that she was a virginal young lady, having an irate father on his hands was not something Devlin wanted to deal with.

He was already under suspicion, it seemed. That first morning when he'd arrived at the Sommers home, bedridden Riley Sommers grilled him for a full half hour—about his name, his background, his previous occupations, and his current prospects—to make certain his intentions were honorable.

Devlin kept to the truth as far as possible, revealing that in the past he'd worked cattle, been involved in railroad construction, and served a stint as a law officer. But it was only when he admitted to having done some hard-rock mining in the Dakota Territory and that he could hold his own on a double jack team that Sommers reluctantly decided his character would pass muster. Double jacking was the old-fashioned method of breaking up rock. It required two or three skilled men, one to hold and rotate the drill steel, the others to pound the steel with a double-weight hammer. It was faster than single jacking—one man alone—but ten times slower than the new steam-driven pneumatic drills, which independent miners like Riley Sommers could rarely afford to own.

"Takes a good man to double jack," Riley conceded, his words slurred by pain. Obviously hurting from his back wound, he winced and shifted carefully on the mattress, as if trying to find a more comfortable position. "Still," he observed, "working a mine isn't the same as guarding one. You ever done that kind of duty before?"

"Not professionally," Devlin answered truthfully. "But I had a claim in the Black Hills that I couldn't leave unguarded for a minute, not if I wanted to protect it from claim jumpers. For three months I did nothing but camp there with a rifle, sleeping with one eye open."

Riley nodded wearily, discernibly beginning to tire but apparently not yet satisfied. "So why did you agree to hire on with us? If Burke wants the Wildstar bad enough to shoot me, he isn't likely to give up. It could get pretty rough."

"Your daughter persuaded me to take the job, Mr. Sommers. The salary she offered was generous, and I have nothing better to do at the moment."

"She's using the money she saved," Riley muttered, with a grimace of pain not entirely due to his bullet wound.

Devlin judiciously remained silent.

"It still doesn't set well," Riley said finally. "I don't like letting somebody else fight my battles for me. But I guess I'm in no position to be choosy." Giving in to exhaustion and pain, he closed his eyes. "Doc says I'm to lie on my stomach for a week, and then maybe I can get out of this blamed bed for short spells." He gave a sigh. "All right,

Mr. Devlin, you've got the job guarding the Wildstar. And I'm much obliged for your help."

To his surprise, Devlin found himself liking the older man. After the hardships Riley had apparently put his daughter through over the years, Devlin had expected to find a selfish son of a bitch who thought only of his mine and himself, but Riley obviously cared as deeply for Jessica as she did for him.

Another unexpected surprise, Devlin discovered during that first week, was the physical discomfort of being rejected by a beautiful woman. He'd never reacted to anyone with such immediate attraction—downright lust, actually—as he had with Jessica Sommers, nor had he ever been held at such arm's length. The frustration of being around her for several hours a day and not being able even to touch her, let alone make love to her, proved a severe exercise in self-restraint.

His schedule began to assume a routine. He spent each night from nine P.M. to seven A.M. up at the Wildstar, until Clem and the miners showed up for work. Then he rode down to the Sommerses' small house and ate the huge breakfast Jess had waiting for him—steak or ham, fried potatoes, hot biscuits with homemade jam, flapjacks with molasses or maple syrup, and anything else he wanted. Usually she served the meal in Riley's room so he could keep her invalid father company—or perhaps so Riley could keep an eye on *him*. Riley didn't quite trust him yet with his daughter, Devlin suspected, although he did seem resigned to the necessity of a guard for the Wildstar. Each morning when they discussed how the night had gone at the mine, Riley would always toss in some personal questions about Devlin's past. Devlin answered patiently and in most cases factually, withholding only the truth about his vast wealth. Afterward, Devlin turned in and slept until Jess woke him in time for supper.

To save her the trouble of carting his supper over to him like she did for her father each evening, Devlin usually walked the short block and a half to her boardinghouse at six o'clock and ate with the miners in the communal dining room. Jessica hadn't been boasting in the slightest when she'd claimed to be an excellent cook. She made fried chicken that was mouth-watering, a venison stew that was the best Devlin had ever tasted, a Cornish meat pastie that her boarders loved, and a rhubarb pie that the miners couldn't seem to get enough of.

He only wished she could afford to hire more help. The Chinese couple she employed worked like fiends, but the chores were never-ending and Jessica seemed always to shoulder the major burdens herself.

Devlin met Kwan Chi An and his wife, Mei Lin, the first night at supper. Like most other Chinese, they wore long plaited pigtails, straw hats, and shapeless wide-sleeved tunics over straight trousers. And, like most other Chinese, they were fiercely resented in the West, not as much for their differently shaped eyes and yellow skin as for their cheap labor and willingness to do the menial jobs no one else would touch. Having supervised gangs of Chinese laborers on his father's railroads, though, Devlin had learned to admire their dependability and capacity for hard work. He particularly appreciated the Kwans because of their devotion to Jessica.

It was because, Jess told him, years ago her mother had rescued Mei Lin from a life of prostitution in one of Silver Plume's illegal opium dens.

At that story, Devlin raised an eyebrow. "Mei Lin served in an opium den?"

Jess grimaced. "So I understand. And she was no more than a child. It must have been horrible. Places like that shouldn't be allowed to exist. But no matter how many times they get closed down, they always come back. Georgetown is rumored to have an opium den, too, although no one likes to admit it. I'm afraid we have as many vices as the big cities."

Devlin wasn't surprised that Mei Lin had once been condemned to such a squalid fate. The pretty young Chinese woman would no doubt have been in great demand, with her delicate Oriental features, flawless yellow-toned skin, and lustrous black eyes. The wonder, however, was

that Jenny Ann Sommers had been compassionate enough
to take in a wretched foreign prostitute at a time when the
rest of the citizens of the West were driving the Chinese
out by force, and when self-respecting ladies would go to
great lengths merely to avoid walking on the same side of
the street as a soiled dove.

Florence O'Malley was someone else Devlin found
himself liking. Jessica's buxom widowed neighbor drawled
with a pure Western twang, but she claimed Irish roots and
approved of Devlin because he was a countryman.

"Devlin is a good Irish name," Flo observed upon
meeting him. "My Paddy was Irish, God rest his soul, and
a better man you'll never find."

Florence was nearly as hard a worker as the Kwans
were, but the three combined couldn't provide Jessica the
help she needed. It disturbed Devlin that she scarcely had
a minute for herself. Between running her boardinghouse
and caring for her father, the only time she had a chance
to sit down was in the evening after the supper dishes
were done, when Clem visited and kept Riley occupied
playing cards. Even then Jessica would usually have to
referee their game. Riley wasn't allowed to sit up yet, and
Clem, who had to play the hands for both of them, tended
to cheat. More than once Jess had to put a halt to the
shouting matches that erupted between her father and the
ornery mule skinner.

Riley's growing frustration at being bedridden was another burden for Jess to bear. To relieve her, Devlin took
over reading to the invalid whenever he had a spare
minute. He managed to overlook Riley's grumpiness and
complaints about being helpless, and used his not-
inconsiderable charm to soothe the wounded man's ill temper. At the end of the week, when Devlin was invited to
join a card game, he correctly interpreted Jess's worried
look about his skill as a gambler and carefully lost his
stake of matchsticks. The smile of relief Jess gave him afterward made up for any affront his reputation might suffer.

Otherwise, for perhaps a half hour each evening Devlin

had Jessica alone. Usually he sat talking with her in the parlor until it was time to ride back up to the mine and relieve the evening guard. She'd employed a needy miner she trusted to take the four-hour shift from five to nine P.M. and Saturday nights as well, so Devlin could have some time off.

The only stylish room in the Sommers house, the parlor was small and modestly furnished, boasting two overstuffed velvet chairs with footrests, a matching settee, and a rocking chair. Lace and crocheted doilies decorated the two spindly tables, glass figurines and knicknacks covered all the flat surfaces, and sepia-toned photographs in oval gilt frames graced the plaster walls. Those parlor sessions were a strange, formal affair, with Devlin probing for personal details about her life and Jess politely keeping her distance. She wouldn't permit him close enough even to touch her. Certainly she refused to let him massage her shoulders again or take down her hair.

Jess thought she had good cause for wariness, though. Devlin seemed more interested in finding out about her and her father's long-standing feud with Ashton Burke than in guarding the Wildstar. And having him in the small house, in such intimate proximity, made her nervous as a cat. A novice at knowing how to handle a man like him, she frequently resorted to spouting the polite phrases for conversing with gentlemen that she'd been taught at finishing school—which immediately brought a teasing glint to Devlin's eye, as if he knew she was trying to erect defenses against him.

Flo liked Devlin, though, calling him a smooth charmer and "a gorgeous fella." Jess thought him smooth, all right. Smooth enough to charm the skin off a snake, which was too smooth, in her opinion. As for gorgeous, she thought Devlin altogether too handsome for his own good, with his almost patrician features and his lean, muscular physique. Flo, however, sighed with envy when she learned Jess had spent the entire night with Devlin up at the mine shack.

"Makes me wish I was thirty years younger," the widow said dreamily.

"Why?"

Flo left off peeling potatoes to stare at her. "Are you *serious,* Jess? I know you never think about men, but by now you gotta feel some kinda urge about love and courtin'."

"Devlin isn't the kind of man to come courting. Especially someone like me."

"Maybe not, but it sure would be fun seein' how far you could bring him."

"Flo!"

"Well, it would. And if anybody could use a bit of fun, it's you. Lord have mercy, gal, if I was your age, I'd be all over him like a tick on a bloodhound."

Jess sighed. She didn't doubt Flo meant it. No doubt other women found Devlin totally irresistible. And if she were honest with herself, she had to admit she did too. It was impossible to ignore Devlin's casual, disarming charm, or the blatantly suggestive spark in his gray eyes, or the maddening undertone of laughter in his rough-velvet voice. And he knew what kind of power he had over the members of the frailer sex, Jess was sure. For all his lazy seductiveness, there was a shrewdness, a cool intensity in his teasing gaze. She'd seen the amazement in those eyes when she'd used his gun to stop him from kissing her. She was probably the only woman who'd ever said no to him.

"If he thinks I'm going to fall all over him like every other woman," Jess returned as she picked up another spud, "he can just get that notion out of his head."

"Well, I think you're missing your big chance. You got a man like that right under your nose, you should take advantage of it. 'Course your pa might have something to say about it." Flo grinned. "I'll bet he cut up something fierce when he found out you were up at the mine all night with that gorgeous fella."

"He did," Jess replied wryly.

Jessica might not be willing to take advantage of the proximity, but Devlin certainly was. He did his best to break through her defenses, without success.

To his surprise, he actually enjoyed the novelty of the situation at first. After the clinging, cloying women in his past, Jessica's indifference was like a breath of fresh air. But as the week wore on, the novelty began to wear thin, and Devlin began to see her resistance as a challenge.

By week's end, he'd become determined to make Jessica admit her attraction to him. He would never let their relationship go so far as to compromise her virtue or claim her innocence, certainly, but a good dose of flirtation wouldn't do her any harm. She needed to loosen up, in any case. Jess was too rigid, too tough, too hard for a woman—although he had to admit there was nothing hard about her curves or lithe grace, or the motherly side that she showed to her rough boarders. Still, she needed to get more pleasure out of life, and he sure would like to be there when it happened.

As illusive as Jessica proved to be, Devlin's main goal in coming to Silver Plume was even more so. After the first morning, he made little progress toward finding the gunmen who had robbed the Colorado Central. During his tenure as night guard, no one attempted to sabotage the Wildstar mine. In fact, no one even came near. He seemed to have reached another dead end.

Riley appeared to view the lull as a victory. "Looks like Jess was right, Mr. Devlin. You acting as our guard is working—maybe even enough to scare Burke off. I'm much obliged to you."

Riley's appreciation, however, did little to relieve Devlin's frustration.

Hoping to stir things up, Devlin went into town Saturday night, purposefully seeking Ashton Burke. It seemed as if every miner in Silver Plume had flocked there with him. From the sounds of it, the saloons and dance halls along Main Street were doing a rip-roaring business. Plinking pianos and screeching fiddles and lusty songs were accompanied by laughter and shouts and hearty applause—the revelry of hardworking, hard-drinking men and the hard-living women who entertained them.

Devlin was at his third gambling hall, standing to one

side watching the action at the keno table, a drink in one hand, when, oddly, Burke found him.

"Good evening, Mr. Devlin," Burke said in his uppercrust British accent, adding when Devlin nodded politely, "You aren't playing. Is the company not to your liking?"

"Keno never has been my game."

Burke paused, evidently interested in holding a conversation. "I've been hearing some interesting tales about you, sir."

Devlin smiled blandly and took a sip of his bourbon. "Have you?"

"Rumor has it that you have joined forces with Riley Sommers in his mining enterprise."

"Rumor would be right."

Burke's smooth jaw tightened. "I took you for a smart man, Mr. Devlin, but that doesn't seem to be a particularly intelligent move on your part."

"No? And why not?"

Instead of answering, Burke asked, "How much is Sommers paying you?"

Devlin shrugged. "The pay's good enough."

"I can triple it."

He raised a black eyebrow and smiled. "I thought you told me you expected loyalty in a man. How loyal would it be if I were to leave Sommers's employ in favor of yours?"

The chill in Burke's blue eyes could have frozen molten metal. "It would not be wise to make an enemy of me, Mr. Devlin."

"I'm sure it wouldn't." He bit back a smile of satisfaction as Burke ground his teeth, obviously chafing at his impotence.

"Speaking of rumors," Devlin added pleasantly, "there's a substantial one going around that Zeke McRoy was the man who shot Riley Sommers. I understand McRoy used to work for you."

"I don't," Burke replied coldly, "care for your implication, Devlin. Not every misfortune that occurs to Riley

Sommers is the result of my disagreement with him. Perhaps McRoy had his own reasons for disliking him."

"Perhaps. McRoy did work for you, though?"

"He did. I fired him for disobedience six months ago and haven't seen him since."

Devlin expected that to be the end of the conversation, but Burke still wasn't finished probing, it seemed. "There is a railroad baron in Chicago by the name of Devlin . . . C. E. Devlin. Are you any relation?"

"I know of him. Devlin's a common enough name, though. I've met one in just about every state I've been in." He held Burke's gaze levelly, knowing that if the silver king was truly interested in finding out who he was, it could easily be done.

Burke let the noncommittal answer drop, however, and with a curt nod turned away.

Watching him go, Devlin felt marginally satisfied with his progress. They had danced around each other, but Burke's frustration in finding a man he couldn't sway was evident.

Clamping down on his own frustration, Devlin went in search of a good poker game. He could be patient if he had to, and it looked as if this job, like Jessica Sommers, would require an extraordinary amount of patience.

Chapter 6

Patience was not a quality Jess possessed much of Saturday night. She found it hard to sleep that night, although her restlessness had only a little to do with her concern over Ashton Burke. The Wildstar mine was well guarded, and things had been quiet during the past week since her father had been shot.

She *was* worried about Riley though. That afternoon he had stubbornly attempted to have Clem drive him up to the mine, but halfway up the mountain, all the jostling in the wagon had broken open the wound in Riley's back and started it bleeding again. Devlin had to be awakened to help Riley into the house, and Doc Wheeler had to be fetched. Doc had lit into Riley for his foolishness and railed about the danger of infection as he liberally applied carbolic to the raw flesh. Still muttering, Doc bandaged the wound tightly to stop the bleeding, then administered another dose of morphine to ease Riley's pain.

But what also bothered Jess, almost as much as her father's muleheadedness, was that Devlin stayed out most of Saturday night.

She heard him come in very late and quietly pass the door of the tiny sitting room where she slept on the floor. She wanted to ask where he'd been and what he'd been doing, but being his employer didn't give her the right to demand an accounting of his free time.

Irritably, she turned over on her lumpy mattress, trying to find a comfortable position. It really wasn't her business what Devlin did on his Saturday nights. He had probably been gambling, anyway, or, quite possibly, he'd found a woman to keep him company—

At the disturbing thought, Jess punched her pillow, then caught herself. She adamantly refused to admit she might be the least bit jealous of the saloon girls and fancy women who could attract Devlin's interest. In a determined effort to sleep, she forced her eyes shut.

It was later than usual when she woke Sunday morning, but the small house was quiet with both men still asleep. Jess lay there a minute, remembering the terror of last Sunday, when her father's bleeding body had been brought home. Shuddering, she threw back the covers and got up.

She ate a solitary breakfast of eggs and ham, and cleaned up after herself. Feeling at loose ends, with nothing to do till time for church, Jess heated water for a bath and washed her hair, then toweled and combed it dry. Remembering Devlin's hurtful comment about her being afraid to let herself be a woman, she spent nearly an hour arranging her hair, piling the tawny mass in a knot high on her head, with coils of braids down the back, feminine curls above her ears, and soft fringe of bangs on her forehead. Then she slipped into Devlin's room to retrieve her best Sunday outfit from the clothespress.

She risked only a single glance at him, finding the sight far too intimate in the dim light that filtered beneath the curtains. With his muscular shoulders and chest bare above the yellow quilt, his black hair and whisker-shadowed jaw a dark contrast against the white pillow, Devlin looked disturbingly, roughly masculine in the feminine surroundings.

Just then his eyelids with their thick black lashes lifted abruptly, and his gray gaze found hers with startling impact. His look was alert and piercing, as if he anticipated trouble and was eminently qualified to deal with it. Jess tensed, while her hand crept to her throat where her heart had lodged. She had forgotten Devlin was a hired gun . . . a stranger she'd found in a saloon barely a week ago. What did she really know about him, after all? At the moment he looked hard and dangerous, and just a little bit frightening.

He must have realized she was no threat to him, though, for he visibly relaxed, his features softening, his expression a striking counter to the previous moment.

"I didn't mean to wake you," Jess whispered when she had caught her breath.

Devlin smiled languidly, his eyes a tangled brush of dark lashes and pale smoke. "You can wake me anytime, angel," he replied in a voice raspy with sleep.

Fumbling in the clothespress for her garments, Jess dragged them out and clutched them to her breast. "Go back to sleep," she told Devlin when she realized he was watching her. His gaze was moving over her with an intensity that felt as physical as a stolen kiss. Instead of the blue sateen wrapper she wore, she might as well have had nothing on at all.

"I could think of better things to do than sleep if you would come to bed with me."

His outrageous remark brought a furious blush to Jess's cheeks. "I c-can't," she stammered. "I have to go to church. I mean . . . I wouldn't if I could."

"A pity," Devlin said with another sleepy smile. "You don't know what pleasure you're missing." Rolling over, he snuggled his face deeper into the pillows. "Call me when it's time to eat," he mumbled, and was breathing evenly in another instant.

More shaken than she cared to admit, Jess dragged her gaze away from the muscular splendor of Devlin's bare back and let herself out of the room. In her flustered state, she was thankful to have found an outfit that matched.

The fawn-colored skirt boasted a short train, and was covered by a wraparound overskirt of coffee-striped grenadine, drawn up behind to produce a bustle. After fussing with the skirts, Jess donned a white muslin waist that form-fitted her high, corseted bosom, then the basque jacket made of the same striped grenadine as the skirt. A lace collar fastened by a broach and a small feathered toque hat completed the ensemble. Critically eyeing herself in the cheval mirror in the sitting room, Jess thought she looked feminine and chic enough that not even Devlin could find fault with her appearance.

She attended the service at the Methodist church and remained afterward, talking with longtime friends, answering inquiries about last week's terrible shooting, receiving condolences, and accepting good wishes for Riley's swift recovery. She walked home, enjoying the quiet of the beautiful August morning. The stamp mills were blessedly silent, while far above her, lofty granite summits pierced the azure sky, flirting with puffs of snow-white clouds.

Jess was gazing up at the mountains when a carriage went bowling past her, driven by a groom attired in livery. She tensed when she recognized Ashton Burke. He might have been checking on his numerous properties in Silver Plume, or more likely, he'd spent last night gambling and then stayed at his Diamond Dust Hotel rather than return to his fancy home in Georgetown.

To Jess's surprise and immense wariness, he ordered the driver to pull over. She couldn't believe even the lordly Ashton Burke would have the audacity to stop and speak to her after what he'd done to her father, but he was obviously waiting for her, and she refused to be intimidated.

When she reached his carriage, Burke tipped his hat to her, his blond hair glinting in the sunlight like a new-minted gold piece. "Good morning, Miss Sommers. I trust your father is recovering."

His polite greeting, voiced in that clipped, haughty British accent, grated across her nerves. She was certain Burke didn't give a fig about her father. And although his tone oozed sympathy, she had the distinct feeling the silver king was taunting her. She managed a stiff "Good morning" in reply.

"I thought I might call on your father this afternoon, if he is free," Burke announced.

Jess bit back the urge to say, "Don't bother, you won't be welcome," not only because it was Sunday, when one was obliged at least to *try* to exhibit a Christian spirit, but because she wouldn't let this ruthless baron drag her down to his level.

"I regret that will not be possible," she returned in her best boarding school manner. "My father is not well enough to receive visitors."

"Oh? I had heard he was seen yesterday riding up to the mines."

Jess pressed her lips together. News traveled fast in a small mining town, but it was more likely Burke had spies in his employ who were instructed to report on her father's movements. "If you know that, then you know my father suffered a relapse yesterday."

His tawny eyebrows rose in concern. "Not a serious one, I hope."

His unctuous tone made Jess grit her teeth. "No. He could probably hold a gun if he needed to."

"There have been no more accidents to your mine?"

"I imagine you would know that better than I."

The maganate's blue eyes grew a shade cooler. "You wrong me."

"Do I?"

He smiled suddenly. "I don't wish there to be hard feelings between us, Miss Sommers. I would merely like your father to know my offer to purchase the Wildstar mine is still open. Please tell him for me, will you?" He inclined his head politely and motioned his driver to proceed. "Give my respects to Mr. Sommers."

Jess stared impotently after the retreating carriage, her beautiful morning spoiled.

Resentful, depressed, she returned home to find Riley awake and fretful, feeling more pain from his wound than he had in the entire past week. She fed him a bowl of soup, gave him another spoonful of morphine, and stayed with him till he fell asleep. Then she proceeded to fix Sunday dinner—roast beef, mashed potatoes, vegetables, biscuits, and raspberry pie.

Normally she would have changed out of her Sunday clothes, but after her run-in with Burke, she defiantly succumbed to feminine vanity and left on most of her finery so Devlin could see it when he woke up. Shedding only the basque jacket and hat, Jess covered the striped skirt and lawn blouse with a bibbed, white gingham tea apron so they wouldn't get soiled.

She felt oddly nervous when she went in to wake him for dinner—or breakfast, as it was in his case. "Devlin?" she murmured, setting a cup of coffee on the bureau for him. When he didn't answer, she moved to the side of the bed where he lay on his side with his back to her. "Devlin? It's time to get up."

Still he didn't stir. Jess leaned over him, gently touching his bare shoulder. "Devlin . . ."

Before she could finish the word, he reached up and trapped her hand in a light grip, pulling it down against his naked chest. The feel of hard, hair-dusted masculine flesh still warm from sleep made her pulse leap. "Devlin!" Jess gave a jerk and dragged her hand free.

As he rolled over to face her, she backed away, clasping her fingers, which were still tingling from his touch. She suspected that he'd been lying in wait for her, and the self-satisfied smile on his lips convinced her of it.

"Dinner," Jess said tersely, "will be ready in less than an hour. Your bathwater's heated so you can bathe and shave first."

Devlin yawned and stretched languidly, looking as sleek and relaxed as a well-fed cat. His hair was tousled in a endearingly boyish way that did anything but make her think of boys.

"I'd rather you join me here first," he said with a husky undertone of laughter that raked across her aroused nerves.

"Only a city slicker would laze around all day," Jess snapped.

"What's turned you into such a crosspatch?"

She could have answered that with one word. Him. His unkempt masculine beauty had affected her far more than she liked. But then having a stunningly handsome, half-naked man in her bed would make any woman feel urges that she shouldn't feel.

The gray eyes surveyed her intimately, traveling slowly

upward. He was staring at her bold as brass, and yet there was something warm and exciting and flattering in the way he was looking at her.

"You've done something different with your hair," he commented, his tone lazy and deeply sensual. "I like it." Jess was inordinately pleased that he had noticed, but her pleasure tempered at his next comment. "I'd like it better loose and wild around your shoulders. Come to think of it, it would look even better spread across this pillow—"

"Mr. *Devlin*!"

"Yes, ma'am?" His innocent smile was not the least convincing.

"If you don't want your bathwater dumped on your head, you will please keep your lascivious comments to yourself!"

"I'm surprised you even know what the word *lascivious* means, darlin'."

"Well, I do. And I don't appreciate your teasing."

"It isn't teasing. I'm totally serious about wanting you in my bed." He patted the mattress beside him. "You're sure you won't reconsider?"

"Yes, I'm sure! I will not go to bed with you! I don't care what pleasure I'm missing. Now will you please get up so I can serve dinner?"

Obediently, Devlin pushed aside the yellow quilt and moved in an easy uncoiling motion, dropping his bare feet to the floor. Expecting him to be naked, Jess felt a gasp catch in her throat, but thankfully, he wore long johns.

Even so, it was not a sight for a lady. The red flannel hugged all the masculine contours of his lower body—his lean hips . . . his long, muscled legs . . . and one undeniable bulge evidencing gender. Jess's gaze flew to Devlin's, the gold of dismay colliding with the impassioned glow of gray. He smiled his devil's smile.

As she stood there frozen, his hands went to the waistband of his underwear and hesitated. "You're welcome to stay and watch me undress if you like."

Alarmed, Jess beat a hasty retreat, while the self-satisfied, totally masculine chuckle Devlin gave made her ears burn.

She filled the tub in the bathroom with the hot water she'd had heating on the stove, and added another bucket of cold from the hand pump at the sink. Devlin came in just as she was straightening up. Jess was glad to see that he was dressed—if one could call hip-hugging denim trousers, bare feet, and no shirt or undershirt "dressed." She was also glad to see him carrying a straight razor and shaving brush so he could get rid of the disreputable shadow of whiskers on his jaw that made him look dangerous and far too masculine.

"How is Riley?" Devlin asked.

"He's asleep. I had to give him more medicine for the pain."

"You mean I have you all alone?"

Jess didn't dignify his suggestive remark with an answer. Instead she left Devlin to his bath, shutting the connecting door to the kitchen behind her.

She was putting the biscuits in the oven when he called to her through the door. "Miss Jess, I could use someone to scrub my back."

"I'm your employer, Devlin, not your personal servant."

"I'll scrub yours in exchange, if you like."

Jess gave an unladylike snort and refused to reply. She listened to him splashing in the tub for another minute, before he called to her again.

"Jessica, would you mind bringing me some fresh water? I have soap in my eyes."

She turned to stare at the bathroom door. She absolutely did not want to enter that small room with Devlin in there naked, even if he was telling the truth about the soap instead of trying to lure her into a compromising situation.

"Jess, please? I promise I won't ravish you."

Hearing the husky cajolery in his tone, she gave a sigh of disgust. No matter how she liked to pretend, she was no different from Flo or any other woman when it came to withstanding Devlin's charm. She filled another bucket and kept her eyes averted as she entered the bathroom.

"Pour it over me, will you?"

"You can't do it yourself?" she asked warily.

"How can I when I can't see?"

Summoning her courage, Jess made herself look at him, although not allowing her gaze to drop below the level of his head. Devlin had his eyes shut tightly, and there were soap suds all over his face. Yielding, she lifted the bucket and tipped it over, pouring a stream of water on his dark head.

"Ahhh," he said in relief, "thank you, angel." Wiping the water from his eyes, he flashed her another one of his sinful smiles. "I'll return the favor anytime you like."

"You know, Devlin," she said in exasperation, "you really missed your calling. Instead of a gambler you should have been a snake oil salesman."

His grin blossomed into appreciative laughter.

Blushing in spite of her determination not to, Jess returned to the kitchen. Fifteen minutes later, Devlin joined her. He was dressed in a three-piece gray suit and string tie, looking elegant and as stunningly attractive as she'd ever seen him.

"Dinner smells great," he said genially as he came to stand at the cast-iron stove and sniff the roast. "I'm starved."

"I'm not surprised. You stayed out late enough last night."

He gave her an amused glance. "Jealous, sweeting?"

"Of course not," she replied with too much conviction. "I don't care what you do on your time off."

"You should have come with me. I won."

"You were gambling?"

The teasing light in his eyes intensified. "What else?" He picked up a spoon, tasted the rich gravy she had made for the roast, and made an approving sound of pleasure deep in his throat.

"Will you please go sit down?" Jess exclaimed, nervous with him so near. "I can't work with you hovering over me."

He settled himself at the kitchen table while Jess finished preparing the meal. Watching her labor at the hot stove with her pots and pans, Devlin decided he'd never seen her looking lovelier than she did just now, with her face flushed and damp tendrils wisping around her face. That was how she would look in the throes of passion, he decided. Except that she had on far too many clothes. The lace collar at her throat, though, gave her a touch of feminine fragileness, while the apron she wore did little to hide her curvaceous figure.

Just then, Jessica bit her lower lip as she pulled the pan of biscuits from the oven, making him suddenly remember the taste of her mouth and skin. Devlin shifted uncomfortably in the chair. No matter how virtuous or genteel or sexually inexperienced she was, he couldn't help imagining how Jess would feel in his arms, naked beneath his hands.

His voice came out huskier than he intended when he took his flirtation a step further. "You know, sweetheart, it isn't often that I've had to apologize for depriving a lady of her bed. I feel guilty as sin for kicking you out of yours. You'd be doing my conscience a kindness if you would return. It's just large enough for both of us, and I'm perfectly willing to share."

Jess stiffened at his provoking remark, treating it with the disdainful silence it deserved. She might have to put up with his scandalous teasing because she needed his help at the moment, but she didn't have to respond or encourage him.

"Aren't you going to answer, Jessica?"

The laughter in his voice grated on her nerves. "Do you ever have anything else on your mind besides bed?" she retorted with her usual forthright manner.

Devlin countered with his most disarming manner. "Can you fault me? Taking you to bed is what any red-blooded male would want to do with a beautiful girl. Actually, you should be flattered."

"Well, I'm not."

"I think you are. I think you wonder what it would feel like to let your hair down with a man ... with me."

She gave him a quelling look, only to find him watching her with a lazy lift to his brows. "You have a mighty high opinion of yourself if you think that."

"Do you honestly expect me to believe you didn't enjoy kissing me the other night?"

That she couldn't say, since it wouldn't be true. She *had* enjoyed kissing Devlin—far more than was proper. But she wasn't about to admit it. As it was, his swollen ego was probably twice the size of any normal man's.

Refusing to answer, Jess busied herself with setting serving dishes on the table and tried to ignore him. It was like trying to ignore a lazing wolf. She could feel Devlin watching her every move, and as she took off her apron and hung it on a wall hook, she felt as if she had undressed for him.

His eyes continued their indolent scrutiny, coming to rest on her lawn blouse and her high, generous bosom. "You have a gorgeous figure," he remarked in a voice as soft as a purring cat padding across satin. "It's a shame you cover it up with those high-necked outfits."

"If you're trying to seduce me, Devlin, it won't work," Jess replied irritably as she carried the platter of meat to the table.

"No?"

"No. I realize you're used to women falling obligingly at your feet, but I'm not about to add myself to their numbers."

"But then, we've already established you're not a normal woman."

Jess put her hands on her hips. "We've established nothing of the kind. I am so a normal woman!"

"No, you aren't, love. Just about the only feminine thing I've seen you do is cry." He followed up his silver-tongued attack with a deliberately provoking observation. "I think I was right. You're afraid of being a woman."

"I am not!"

"So prove it."

She gave him a questioning look, her amber eyes wide and uncertain.

"Come here and put your arms around me and kiss me."

"You must be joking."

His slow, beautiful smile told her very clearly that he was not. "You're afraid you won't be able to resist me."

"That isn't true."

"Coward," he taunted lightly, his voice suddenly becoming soft and whispery.

His smug arrogance was too much to ignore. Setting her teeth, Jess marched over to his chair. How she would like to shatter his confidence! He was certain he could seduce any woman to willing compliance, but she would show him she wasn't about to succumb to his practiced charm.

When she reached Devlin, though, he slipped an arm around her narrow waist and, to her surprise, gently pulled her down on his lap. His thighs felt hard and uncompromisingly male beneath her skirts, and the shocking contact discomfited Jess. She hadn't planned on letting things get so out of hand.

She was about to change her mind about accepting his challenge when Devlin reached toward the table and set his dinner knife beyond her reach. "I'm not taking any chances," he replied to her inquiring look with a dancing light in his eyes. "I suppose it's a good thing I'm not wearing my guns."

Jess felt heat rising to her cheeks at his teasing. Before she could retort, though, Devlin said softly, "All right, I'm ready now. Put your arms around my neck and kiss me."

When she hesitated, his beautiful mouth curved in a very male smile. "Come on, 'fraidy cat, it won't hurt you. You might even find you like it."

Jess hardened her resolve. She couldn't stand the idea of him questioning her courage, but more than her pride was at stake. She needed to prove to herself, even more than to him, that she could resist his seductive advances.

She took a deep breath. Since she was sitting on his lap, her face was at the same level as Devlin's. All she had to do was lean forward.

She did, slowly, and touched her mouth to his. His lips

were soft and warm and somehow luxurious. It made her think of savoring rich chocolate.

Involuntarily, Jess shut her eyes, while her arms stole around his neck almost of their own accord.

She heard the throaty sound of approval Devlin made as he wrapped his arms around her waist and pulled her closer. Drawing her breasts against his chest, he forced her to increase the pressure of the kiss. Tentatively, almost shyly, Jess's lips fluttered beneath Devlin's in unwilling surrender. She didn't know how to deal with the physical sensations overwhelming her. He made her feel hot and quivery and weak, as if she were no longer in control of her senses. When he used his tongue to paint her bottom lip with dampness, she almost gasped at the erotic ripple of heat that surged through her body.

Eventually, he pulled away, and she saw that his smoky eyes had darkened to charcoal. "Not bad for a first time," Devlin said in a low, husky voice. "Try it again with more passion this time."

"But . . .dinner's . . . getting cold. . . ."

"Let it. Open your mouth to me, Jess," he whispered against her lips.

"But—"

"Don't think, angel, just feel."

Unbelievably, Jess wanted to obey him. She wanted just once not to think about everyone else first. Just once to give in to pure lush sensation. And that was what his kiss was . . . sensation. Exquisite and arousing. Delicious and intense. She felt as if her bones were melting as Devlin tasted and sipped at her mouth, irresistibly blending tenderness and demand, intimacy and boldness. His tongue was like slow fire as it took the deepest corners of her mouth, spreading and stroking, leaving her without a breath to call her own. He was a highly experienced man with a masterful touch, she knew that. But it didn't matter. Not when she was so stunned by the wildly primitive urges beating in her blood.

She clung to him, wanting his incredible kiss to last forever, desperate for it to end before she dissolved into a pool of liquid heat.

Devlin felt her trembling acquiescence. He had known too many women not to recognize need when he saw it, held it in his arms. She was so needy for everything a man could give her. And he ached to be that man.

He made his kisses deliberately provocative, stroking and sensual, using every skill he possessed to heighten her pleasure. It was an art he had been practicing for a very long time. And Jessica responded with blind desire, pressing closer and giving a hushed little moan from deep in her throat.

Her eager hunger entranced him, inflaming his own hunger. He wanted to throw away the pins in her hair and plunge his fingers into her glorious tresses. He wanted to unbutton that high-necked blouse of hers and lavish attention on her beautiful, full breasts. He wanted ... But he knew very well that once he began such intimacy, he wouldn't be able to stop himself from going further.

With agonizing reluctance, Devlin summoned all his willpower and forced himself to end their embrace. When slowly he drew back, Jessica opened her eyes with a dazed look of pleasure.

Devlin drew a ragged breath and gave her a smile of blatant male satisfaction mingled with frustrated desire. "I think that's enough of a lesson in passion for one afternoon. Any more and I won't be able to let you go."

When he tucked an errant tendril behind her ear and eased her off his lap onto her feet, Jessica stood there unsteadily for a moment, looking around blankly, trying to remember what she'd been doing before she'd so foolishly accepted Devlin's challenge to prove her womanhood, before his devastating kiss had left her aroused and flustered and shaken to her very core.

Oh, yes, dinner. She had been about to sit down and eat.

Moving slowly around the table, Jessica lowered herself into her seat. Somehow, after Devlin's kiss, she knew it would be impossible to keep her mind on roast beef and mashed potatoes.

Chapter 7

Monday morning dawned bright and clear, with none of the smoky blue haze that usually hung over the mountains. Up at the mine, Devlin watched the Colorado sky turn from ebony to pale gray to cloudless cobalt, but he made no effort to saddle his horse. The Wildstar crew tramped up the mountain road and reported for work, and the endless toil of hard-rock mining began . . . drilling and blasting, shoring tunnel and shaft walls, shoveling rock and tramming it to the surface in buckets, to be loaded into ore cars. But still Devlin hesitated to leave. He wasn't sure he trusted himself alone with Jess.

He'd gone too far yesterday with her, he knew. The game he'd been playing had turned dangerous. It had been easy—too easy—to awaken her passion and make her respond to him, but his plan had nearly backfired. He was an experienced man taking advantage of an innocent, yet he'd come close to losing control himself.

His reaction had surprised the hell out of him . . . and scared him, too, if he were honest. Jessica Sommers wasn't his usual kind of woman, the only kind he ever allowed himself to get involved with. The sophisticated, worldly kind who could share his bed and indulge in sexual intimacies without thinking it meant a lifetime commitment. The kind who lacked the power to ensnare his heart and then savage it, the way his one-time fiancée had done.

Jessica likely was the kind to take his flirtation seriously, or at least convince herself he was serious. If he continued in the same vein, she'd doubtless be looking for a ring on her finger. He didn't want to lead her on. Certainly he didn't want her to get hurt by his careless games.

It had taken him a restless night of guard duty and prowling the mountainside to come to a decision. From now on he would quit teasing her, quit trying to prod her into some kind of reaction. From now on he would keep their relationship strictly business.

Devlin still had made no move to leave when he heard the rumble of an ore wagon, accompanied by the crack of the skinner's whip and the genial sound of bells. Ore wagons belonging to various hauling outfits passed the Wildstar regularly, carrying supplies up to the highest mines and loads of ore down, but Devlin had no trouble recognizing Clem Haverty's distinctive voice and colorful language.

Shortly Clem appeared around the distant hairpin turn, driving his ten-mule team up the steep grade, applying his whip with utmost precision. Devlin had once seen a bullwhip expert knock a fly off the ear of an ox at twenty feet without drawing a drop of blood, and Clem's skill was better than that.

"Haw! Steady, Milo, George! Milo, you got mush for brains, you lop-eared excuse for buzzard bait," the ornery mulewhacker yelled. "Whoa!"

Having reached the mouth of the Wildstar and turned the narrow, high-sided ore wagon around, Clem positioned it beneath the loading chute, then hauled back on the reins and set the brake. As he climbed down from the wagon seat, he was still cussing Milo with relish. "That mule is just too indegodampendant! I want my Nellie back!"

Clem gave Devlin a glare that had all the charm of a riled grizzly. The mule skinner still wasn't happy that his usual leaders, Nellie and Gus, had been appropriated to act as sentries for the Wildstar each night.

Repressing a grin, Devlin pushed himself to his feet and went to fetch the two mules that he'd come to know rather well over the past week. They no longer brayed in his presence, and had actually provided welcome company during the long nights alone.

He led the mules to the head of the team, and decided to use the opportunity to ask the old-timer about the conflict between Riley Sommers and Ashton Burke.

"Why do you suppose Burke only recently developed an interest in buying the Wildstar?" Devlin inquired as he helped Clem with the harnesses.

"Don't rightly know."

"I can think of at least one good reason. If Burke discovered a rich vein in the Lady J next door, he might suspect the Wildstar of holding good pay ore. Have there been any rumors about the Lady J hitting a big strike?"

Clem grunted. "Not so's I've heard."

"Well, if that *is* the case, then Burke would certainly want to keep the news quiet until he had the deal locked up. I wouldn't be surprised if he's planning something else to force Riley to sell the Wildstar, would you?"

"How the goddamn hell am I s'posed to know what Burke is plannin'? You gonna keep pestering me with your dang-fool questions?"

Devlin gave him a cool glance from his gray eyes. "I'm on your side, Haverty."

"Mebbe you are. But jest because Riley's taken a shine to you don't mean I got to. And you ain't gonna turn me up sweet, neither, by bein' nice to my mule," Clem added with a suspicious look when Devlin scratched a grateful Nellie behind her ears.

"I wouldn't dream of even trying. An ornery old cuss like you could sour a lemon."

Clem harrumphed loudly. Pulling a pouch from his shirt pocket, he drew out a plug of chewing tobacco, cut a fresh quid, and stuffed it in his mouth. Devlin turned and joined two other men who were pushing an ore car from the mine up the timbered ramp to the loading chute.

When that load was dumped, Devlin picked up a shovel and climbed into the wagon himself. As he spread the heap of ore more evenly over the bottom of the wagon, he eyed the mule skinner narrowly. "What is it you have against me, anyway?"

Clem finished buckling a leather cheek strap before answering. "Nothin', I guess."

"You want me to leave, is that it?"

He spat a stream of tobacco juice on the ground. "Naw. The boys've been right edgy since Riley got shot, but it's only 'cause you hired on that they're even working. What I got no notion of is why you was game to hire on in the first place."

"The pay's good."

"There's lot easier ways to make money."

"Maybe it's because Jessica asked me."

Clem gave that a long consideration. "Yep, that's a good reason. It ain't easy turning that gal down when her mind's made up."

Devlin made another trip to the ramp to help dump a load. "What makes you think Riley has taken a shine to me?" he asked when he returned.

" 'Cause he said so. 'Course he didn't take kindly to Jessie staying up here that night, jest like I warned you, but he's right glad you hooked up with us." Suddenly losing his sour look, Clem grinned broadly through his beard. "I reckon Ash Burke was madder than a new-made steer when he found out."

Devlin grinned as well. "He was indeed."

"How come you always talk so highfalutin', young fella?"

"It's the way I was raised, I expect. Do you intend to hold it against me?"

Clem tipped back his hat and shook his shaggy gray head. "I guess not."

"Then why don't you tell me why Burke would want the Wildstar enough to kill Riley for it?"

Relenting in his fierce attitude somewhat, the mule skinner squeezed his weathered face into frown. "I dunno. I still ain't so sure that's what Burke meant to do. Ash Burke is snake-mean, but I never figured him for a killer.

I reckon maybe he jest wanted to scare Riley a bit. Nothin's happened since the shootin'.''

"You think hitting Riley was a mistake?"

"Could be. 'Course you could be right 'bout a strike at the Lady J. This here hill's full 'o silver, and me 'n Riley always did think this was the best place to find it. I'll get the boys to see what they can sniff out about a Lady J strike down to town."

It took another half hour to load the rest of the ore into the heavy wagon. When it was done, Devlin saddled up his horse and reluctantly headed down the mountain. With any luck Jess would be occupied with her father.

Behind him, Devlin heard Clem climb aboard the driver's seat in order to drive the ore down to the stamp mill in town.

"Up, Nellie! Up, Gus! Gee up thar!"

The heavy wagon wheels began to turn just as a faint noise like the echo of thunder sounded from beyond the crest of the hill at Devlin's back. Because of the wagon's rumble, it was a minute before he recognized the sound as the drumming of horse's hooves, and by then it was too late. The pounding hoofbeats crested the hill in a thunderous wave, accompanied by men yelling and the explosions of rapid gunfire.

Wheeling his horse even as he reached for his gun, Devlin mouthed an expletive at having been caught unprepared. Above him, at the mouth of the mine, riders were attacking the Wildstar—whooping and racing their horses in circles and firing pistols in the air. Devlin couldn't make out exactly how many raiders there were, or who they were; their faces were masked by bandannas. But he spied the distinctive red coloring of a roan horse.

His curse drowned out by the chaos, Devlin rammed his heels into his mount's barrel and started up the steep road at a gallop, his revolver raised. He had taken a sight on one of the riders when he recognized a new danger. The ore wagon, with Clem on board, was headed pell-mell down the mountainside, dragged by a dozen galloping, panic-stricken mules.

The skinner was wildly hauling on the bunch of reins with his left hand, shoving on the brake lever with his right foot, and bracing his wiry body against the footboard in a desperate effort to hold back the racing vehicle. The hold-back chains that locked the rear wheels in place did little to check the momentum.

With the heavy wagon bearing down on him like an avalanche, Devlin had only an instant to decide. Ignoring the bullet that whined past his head, he abandoned the chase and pulled up his horse. Spinning around, he started back down the road, trying to match speed with the wagon.

"Hellfire and thunderation!" he heard Clem yell above the screech of brake blocks as the wagon shot past. "Whoooooa!" He had planted both feet on the brake, pushing for all he was worth, but it was like trying to stop a bullet with a feather. Galloping alongside, Devlin saw the brakes smoking as the wheels spun faster and faster.

"Jump, man!" he shouted as he drew even with the driver's box. He extended his right arm, gesturing for Clem to abandon his attempt to save the wagon.

Just then the left forewheel struck a rock and the brake pole snapped. Clem was nearly pulled off the seat and thrown headfirst into the galloping team, while Devlin barely missed colliding with the wagon body as it veered toward him. He swerved his horse on the narrow road and almost went over the edge. Throwing his weight to the right, Devlin used the reflexes honed by long months of punching cows in order to aid his mount. The horse stumbled but somehow regained balance and galloped on.

In another four strides they made up the ground they'd lost and again reached the front of the wagon. Clem was still clinging to his seat and trying ineffectually to halt his uncontrollable team.

Looming before them was the hairpin turn of the road. Beyond that was a rocky ledge and a drop of several hundred feet.

"Clem, dammit!" Devlin shouted again. "Let it go!"

Still desperately clutching the reins, Clem held on to the wagon seat and inched his way to the left.

"Clem!"

Devlin knew he had to pull up now or risk going over himself. He'd just started to draw back when the old mule skinner finally decided the situation was hopeless. Lunging to his feet, Clem jumped free an instant before the mules, the wagon, and a ton of silver ore plunged over the ridge in a cacophony of splintering wood and screaming animals.

With one arm clutching the mule skinner's waist, Devlin savagely hauled back on the reins, bringing his horse to its haunches. They slithered to a halt a scant two yards from the edge. His blood hammering in his ears, Devlin let Clem drop to the ground.

For another instant, neither of them moved. They were both breathing hard, and Clem was staring up the steep road in shock.

"They were fixin' to kill me," he gasped in disbelief. Then he raised his fist and shouted furiously, "You goddamned yellow-bellied buncha sidewinders!"

His cry echoed over the range. The gunfire had stopped and the mountainside was now ominously silent.

Devlin felt a surge of pure rage streaking through him. The disaster had erupted so suddenly that he'd had no time to consider how to deal with it, but it could only have been a few minutes at most since the shooting had started. The gunmen couldn't have gained that much of a head start.

"Are you okay?" he asked Clem. "I ought to ride after them."

Still looking dazed, the mule skinner nodded. "I'm beholden to you. You saved my bacon."

Devlin turned his sweating horse up the steep slope and spurred it into a lumbering gallop—then promptly swore. After the punishing ride and gallant effort, the animal had gone lame and was limping badly, favoring its off rear leg.

Devlin had drawn rein and swung down from the saddle, intending to inspect his lame mount, when he heard a plaintive wail.

"My mules!" Clem cried. Devlin turned to see him staring down over the rocky slope, and had to grab the old mule skinner's arm to prevent him from rushing over the edge.

A look of shock and devastation gripped Clem's face. "My Nellie . . ." he said hoarsely.

The thud of booted feet interrupted them as a score of miners dressed in grime-coated overalls, shapeless jackets, and coarse felt hats came running down the road from the various mines along the way. Devlin suspected some were from the Lady J, but their supervisor, Hank Purcell was not among them. They slowed to a halt beside Clem and Devlin and took in the scene of wreckage below.

They were followed by several men of the Wildstar's crew. One of them looked at Devlin helplessly and shook his head. "There was three of 'em this time," he said in a hushed voice. "They made for tall timber."

Devlin's jaw hardened. He couldn't take off after them now, with a lame horse and without the proper gear or adequate weapons. He would have to go down the mountain to get another saddle horse. And before that, he would have to see to Clem. Tears were streaming down the old man's grizzled face, disappearing into his shaggy gray beard.

Without warning, Clem lurched forward drunkenly, intending to climb over the rock ledge, but Devlin tightened his grip on the mule skinner's arm, dragging him back.

"I g-got to see to my mules," Clem protested in a choked voice.

The wagon had burst apart, scattering ore and splintered planks over the sleep slope. Of the dozen mules lying tangled in harness and debris, one or two were thrashing in pain. Someone would have to climb down and put the poor beasts out of their misery.

"I'll do it," Devlin said grimly. He looked around at the dazed, dirt-streaked faces of the silent miners. "If someone will fetch me a rope?"

Someone turned and started the long trek back up the road.

His old knees giving way, Clem sank down in a palsied heap. "My Nellie . . . my poor Nellie. . . ."

Jessica was in the kitchen of her boardinghouse with Flo as usual when Clem and Devlin came in.

The mule skinner poked his grizzled head into the large room for barely an instant. "I don't want you saying nothin' about it, Jessie, so I'm givin' you fair warnin'. I'm aiming to get likkered up in private." Then he turned and stomped up to his room, leaving Devlin to tell her about the tragedy.

Jessica's reaction was predictable; her face turned white with shock and horror. "Dear God, was Clem hurt?"

"No, he's all right, but he's upset. His favorite mules were among the ones killed."

"Not Nellie and Gus? Oh, no!"

"I'm afraid so."

Flo had a few pithy words of her own to say, while Jess stared at Devlin with growing fury. "You say the gunmen got away? We have to go after them!"

"I intend to. I'm riding out in a minute to search the mountains for them. I only came back to hire another horse and pick up a bedroll and more ammunition."

"I'm going with you," Jess declared, already tugging off her apron.

Devlin's grim expression turned flint-eyed. "No, you're not, Jess. I'm riding alone. This is no job for a woman."

"This is no job for a lone man, either. You need help— and I can shoot. You'll need an extra gun if you have to go up against three of them. And there's no one else you can ask on such short notice, at least not anyone we could trust."

"Maybe, but you'll only be more trouble for me. I don't want to have to worry about you."

"You won't. I can take care of myself."

"Not in a situation like this," Devlin declared. "It's far too dangerous."

"What about the danger to you? It wouldn't be right to

ask you to risk your life for us and not give you all the help I can."

"It's my risk to take."

"Well, it's our mine. You work for me and I'm going!"

He shook his head adamantly. "I'm riding alone, Jess."

Taking a deep breath, she tried another tack. "You can't succeed alone. You need me. You don't know the mountains north of here, and I do. I've ridden over them before and I know the terrain."

That gave Devlin pause, but only for an instant. "I'll ask the marshall to accompany me."

"That lily-livered coward? You must be joking. Even if we could trust him, he wouldn't lift a finger to help us. Besides, you don't have the time to waste looking for him."

"True. But that's all the more reason why you can't come. I don't have time to wait for you."

"I can be ready to leave in ten minutes."

Devlin eyed her grimly. He'd never known a woman who could get ready for anything in ten minutes, but then he'd never met a woman like Jessica Sommers, either. "I'm not going to argue with you, Jess. You're not going, and that's final."

"And I won't try and change your mind. If you ride without me, I'll just follow you."

She didn't wait for him to reply, but turned to Florence O'Malley. "Flo, you're in charge here. I'm counting on you to take care of Riley and Clem while I'm gone. I've got to get home and pack," she added as she marched from the room.

Devlin looked after her with a narrow-eyed expression that was half scowl, half exasperation. He did *not* want Jess tagging along with him as he tracked three gunmen who'd already proven they weren't above killing indiscriminately. Besides the fact that he didn't want her anywhere near that kind of danger, he *absolutely* did not want to be alone on the trail with her. He'd already demonstrated that his usual legendary control vanished whenever he had Jessica to himself. But short of tying her down, he had little choice but to accept her company.

"How do you stop a hellion in full march?" he murmured to no one in particular.

Flo grinned broadly at him. "I've always admired pluck in a girl, haven't you?"

His mouth twisted in a rueful glance. "Pluck? Is that what Jess has? That's like calling a Kansas twister a summer breeze."

Reluctantly he followed Jess outside, catching up to her on the street just before she entered the small house she shared with her father. He was counting on Riley to forbid her to go.

Jess wisely saved that announcement for last, however, first telling her father about the disaster up on the mountain. Still bedridden, Riley wasn't prepared to withstand this new blow.

Wearily, with an air of defeat, he closed his eyes. "Maybe it might be wise to consider selling out to Burke, Jess."

"Over my dead body!" she vowed. The thought of meekly letting Burke drive her father to capitulate stuck in her craw. She wasn't a quitter, and neither was Riley.

She turned to Devlin, a look of entreaty on her face. "Tell him he shouldn't sell out."

Devlin nodded. "I think it's too early to give up just yet," he observed dispassionately. "Let me see what I can do to find the men who were behind the attack."

"What do you mean to do then?"

"If I can catch them, I'll bring them back to town for the marshal to arrest."

"I'm riding with him, Riley," Jess interjected. She knew her father would try to stop her, but she didn't intend to give him a choice in the matter. She couldn't stand any longer to live with the threat of death hanging over their heads without even lifting a finger to prevent it.

As she expected, Riley did not take kindly to the idea. "Jess, that's plumb crazy!" he exclaimed.

"No it's not. Devlin needs help. One man alone won't

stand much of a chance against three hired guns. And you're certainly in no condition to go with him."

"Then let Clem do it!"

"By now Clem will have already downed half a bottle. You know how worthless he is when he's been drinking."

"Well, find somebody else!"

"There's no one else to ask. Even if we could find anyone with the gumption to ride after a gang of gunmen, it would be too late. We'll lose their tracks if we wait much longer. I have to go, Riley. We're wasting time. Flo will look after you while I'm gone."

She didn't stick around to finish the argument, but left the room.

"Jess, I forbid it! Do you hear me?" Riley shouted after her. He couldn't leave his bed, but he struggled to sit up as he continued to complain loudly. Jess fetched her clothes from the wardrobe in Devlin's bedroom and carried them to the sitting room without interference. Through the connecting door, she heard Riley promising to blister her hide, but he hadn't paddled her since she was little, when she'd sassed her mother, so she wasn't worried.

She took three minutes to change into an outfit rugged enough to withstand a long trail ride—Spanish-style leather riding chaps worn over men's trousers, a white shirt and bolero. A flat-brimmed hat, a bandanna, gloves with flared gauntlets, and riding boots completed the costume. She took three more minutes to throw some food and cooking utensils into knapsacks and fetch her father's ten-gauge.

When Devlin entered the kitchen, she was almost ready. He eyed her attire with approval, even if he didn't condone her reason for wearing it. He didn't try to stop her, though. He wasn't fool enough to argue with a woman packing a shotgun. The weapon Jess carried would tear a hole in a man that was big enough to drive an ore wagon through.

He had belted on his guns, and now he checked the chambers of his pistols and the magazine of his Winchester. Then he set his black, flat-crowned hat on his head, slung the provisions over his shoulder, and followed Jess to Riley's room.

She bent over her father's bed, giving him a farewell kiss on the cheek.

"Jess, dadgummit, I don't want you doing this!" Riley declared, trying one last time.

"I know. But it has to be done. Don't give Flo too much trouble while I'm gone."

When she turned away, he looked after her helplessly, then gave Devlin a pleading look. "I'd be obliged if you'd take care of my girl," he said in a voice made rough by worry.

Devlin nodded soberly. Then, turning to follow, he and Jess set out.

Chapter 8

The high country to the north of Silver Plume was a maze of rocky peaks and rugged wooded slopes. Jess and Devlin rode over little-used tracks toward the distant mining town of Empire, asking at the scattering of mines along the way about three armed riders, especially one mounted on a roan horse. It would have been easier to take the stage route that ran from Georgetown through Empire to Central City, Jess knew, but then they would likely miss their quarry. A man could hide out for months in this rugged terrain.

It was a warm, glorious deep-summer day, at odds with the deadly purpose of their journey. Each time they topped a ridge, the wide expanse of the Colorado Rockies stretched before them . . . a majestic array of bold summits and windswept gulches and narrow mountain passes.

The golden air was sweet and pure, redolent with the scent of life. The slopes were cloaked in towering ponderosa pines and thickets of aspens, whose white trunks stood out in striking relief to the riot of deep greens surrounding them. The meadows were carpeted with the colorful wildflowers of late August—mountain pinks and lavender harebells and yellow paintbrush. In shaded places along the edge of the woods, vivid blue columbine swayed on slender, aristocratic stalks.

Both Jessica and Devlin scarcely noticed. They spoke little during the entire day, except to comment once or twice on their dispiriting lack of progress. Their quarry seemed to have eluded them. Around noon they came across a mine shack where the mine foreman remembered seeing a roan horse pass by earlier—only there had been two men, not three.

As the day wore on, a burning frustration filled Jess, eating at her stomach like acid. The same frustration seethed in Devlin; the knowledge of having failed in his responsibility to protect the Wildstar filled him with a desperate anger.

Matching Jess's mood, Devlin remained grimly silent. A few times as they rode along the rocky trail, he felt an itchy sensation between his shoulder blades, a sense of being watched. But each time the feeling passed quickly. He decided it must be wild animals, a cougar or a bear, maybe, but his vigilance increased.

They made camp at sunset, off the track near a black-green forest of pine. Devlin picketed the horses on a patch of grass and took care of the saddles and bedrolls, while Jess fried some bacon and warmed up some biscuits for supper. A curious whisky-jack flew down to investigate her preparations, but Jess shooed the fearless camp thief away.

The sun was flaming red, turning the mountain range crimson, as they settled down to eat. Jess merely picked at her food.

"Do you think we'll find them?" she said finally, asking the question that had preyed on her mind all day.

"It's becoming less likely."

There was another long silence.

"Devlin?"

"What?"

"You didn't deserve this, being dragged all over the mountains. I'm sorry I ever got you involved in our fight."

Devlin gave her hard glance. "It's my fight now."

Her gaze meeting his, Jess saw the cold determination in his gray eyes and realized he meant it. He wasn't in this just for the money anymore, or even for her. For him, the feud had turned personal the minute Burke's gunmen had attacked the Wildstar while it was under his protection.

Jess smiled faintly in gratitude. It gave her a welcome feeling of relief, knowing Devlin was truly on her side.

He turned to stare out at the distance and resumed his meal. Involuntarily, Jess's scrutiny increased. He didn't look like a city slicker just now. In his denims and leather vest and red-checkered bandanna, a chambray shirt that was well worn and faded, a full day's growth of black beard shadowing his face, he looked rough and capable and dangerous as sin.

The unbidden thought made Jess flush, while the memory of what had occurred between them yesterday—Devlin's stunning kisses in her kitchen—came flooding back to haunt her. No matter how firmly she'd resolved to remain unaffected, she hadn't been able to withstand his devastating charm; no flesh-and-blood woman could have. With scarcely any effort, Devlin had made her body hot and her blood race. After that intoxicating embrace, she should have felt nervous around him today, but what she felt instead was an intimacy of common purpose.

Still, she wasn't immune to him by any means, even when he wasn't putting himself out to be charming or seductive, or provoking her to lose her composure. At the moment his face looked as cold and hard as any stranger's, but it still had the power to make her think hot, forbidden thoughts.

Realizing how vulnerable she was to him, Jess fell awkwardly silent.

The long shadows of the pines enveloped them, while the rose-amber light of evening turned to blue gloom. After finishing her bacon sandwich, Jess wiped the plates and frying pan clean and set them aside for tomorrow's breakfast. Devlin had arranged their bedrolls side by side near the fire, with their saddles for pillows. Jess climbed into hers and lay there staring up at the darkening sky.

She listened while Devlin built up the fire and laid some sticks close to hand, then settled on his own bedroll. He had left on his gun belt and laid his Winchester within easy reach.

"Mind if I smoke?"

"No, go ahead."

He fished in his saddlebag for papers and tobacco, then rolled a cigarette. When he flicked a match on his boot heel, the golden flame lit up his handsome face for a moment. No, she wasn't immune to him, Jess thought with consternation. Nor was she unaware of the danger of spending the night alone with him, even if it was on the trail, out in the open.

The night closed in around them, bringing with it a soft breeze redolent with the sharp scents of wood smoke and wildflowers and pine. A full moon hung over the shoulder of a majestic peak in a radiant sphere, while overhead stars blazed in a cool, deep sky. Jess was trying to discipline her thoughts when Devlin quietly spoke.

"Why is Burke so determined to destroy your mining operation?"

"He wants to ruin my father," Jess said simply. "He's always hated Riley, ever since my mother . . ." She hesitated, embarrassed to be dredging up the vicious stories about something that had happened before she was born.

"Since your mother married another man," Devlin finished for her. At her discomfited look, he explained. "I've heard the rumors. I also heard that Burke named the Lady J mine after your mother."

Jess nodded. "I expect it's true. He never forgave her for choosing Riley over him."

"She wasn't interested in Burke?"

"No. Oh, maybe he turned her head for a little while. She was flattered that a man of Burke's consequence paid her attention. But he wasn't willing to marry her. Besides, my father is ten times the man Ashton Burke is."

"She could have pursued a relationship with Burke afterward. Marriage isn't synonymous with fidelity."

Jess flashed Devlin a startled look. "That's a disgusting thing to say! My mother would never have even thought of betraying my father that way."

Devlin tossed the stub of his cigarette into the fire. Few women in his experience would have been concerned over betraying their husbands if it meant getting something they wanted. "Not even for all Burke's wealth?" he said skeptically, not bothering to keep the sardonic edge from his tone.

Jess's amber eyes narrowed. "*Especially* not for that. She never put much store in wealth."

"She sounds like a paragon."

"She was!" Jess shot back, not liking his tone.

"Climb down, hellcat. I didn't mean to ruffle your fur."

When Devlin held her gaze levelly, Jess forced herself to relax, realizing she'd sounded a bit too defensive.

"What happened to her?"

"She died of pneumonia five years ago."

"And you still miss her," Devlin said softly, hearing the pain in Jess's voice.

"Very much. And I'm not the only one. All the miners around here just about worshiped the ground she walked on. Riley, especially. He took it awfully hard when she died." Jess sighed heavily. "I could never fill her shoes."

"I don't know about that. I think you do a pretty good job of it."

"That's because you didn't know her."

Restlessly Jess sat up and wrapped her arms around her knees, looking out at the distant peak.

"Why do you call your father 'Riley'?" Devlin asked finally.

The question surprised her. "I don't know, I just always have. What do you call your father?"

"I guess if I call him anything, I use his initials like everyone else does. But then he and I never have been close, not the way you are with Riley." He paused. "It must be satisfying, having such a special relationship with a parent."

Wondering if she'd actually heard a hint of wistfulness in Devlin's tone, Jess smiled softly. "It is."

She and Riley might not be rich in monetary terms, but they had a lot more than most families she knew, because they shared a wealth of love. Material things weren't important if you had that. Her mother had strongly believed in that philosophy. Jenny Ann had never once complained about their lack of luxuries or Riley's extravagant dreams. Riley had always done his best for his wife and daughter, and was always apologetic that he couldn't do more. Jess would have let herself be stampeded by wild horses before she allowed one reproachful word against him to pass her lips.

"Not all the money in the world," Jess said ardently, "is worth one ounce of real love. Burke could never understand that. His kind never has learned that you can't buy everything you want."

"What do you mean, 'his kind'?"

"Rich men like him."

Hearing her scornful tone, Devlin appraised her for a moment. Jess knew nothing of his vast wealth, he remembered. She still thought of him as a gambler.

He shifted uncomfortably on his bedroll. Now was probably the time to tell her about his background. She'd given him an opening. And he really had no good reason to hide the truth from her any longer ... nothing except long and bitter experience that told him what to expect. Once she knew his net worth, Jess would change toward him. It was inevitable.

He didn't want to watch it. He didn't want to see the same glint in her amber eyes that he saw in other women's: the calculation, the coy flirtation, the greed ... as if she were estimating the extent of his wealth, the size of his cock, and speculating how to turn both to her own advantage.

That was reason enough not to enlighten Jessica about his financial status.

"I take it you don't like rich men any more than you do gamblers?" Devlin said instead.

"I *despise* rich men. They're every bit as bad as gamblers. They both live off other men's honest sweat and blood—" She stopped, as if recalling his profession. "Present company excluded, of course."

"Of course," Devlin drawled. He didn't care at all for her characterization of "his kind," or being lumped in the same category as Burke, even if she wasn't aware she was doing it. "Not all rich men are alike," he said in his own defense.

"All the ones around here are. Burke just happens to be the worst. Not only is he greedy and heartless, he's made it his personal goal to use his power against my father. For the past twenty years, he's done everything he could to make it hard on Riley. The other silver kings aren't much better, though. They've made their money off all the poor people who work for them. You should see how the big mine owners treat their employees. They don't give a single thought about safety. If an accident occurs, it's your fault. If you get sick, you're out of a job. They let men die; they watch them get maimed all the time without raising a finger to help. They turn whole families out of their homes—"

Realizing how strident she sounded with her fervent argument, Jess took a calming breath and lowered her voice. "At least Riley doesn't run our mine that way. That's one of the reasons he never has been successful. Profit isn't the only thing he cares about."

Devlin drew his lips together in a frown. Unwilling to believe that she truly put so little value on wealth, he refused to let the subject drop. "What would you do if you were rich?"

"I'd make sure Riley had the capital to work the Wildstar until he made his big strike," she answered without hesitation. "And I'd fight Ashton Burke on his own terms—keep him from hurting all the little people around here."

"And after that, what then?" Devlin prodded, intent on proving she was no different from all the other women he'd known. "You wouldn't want anything for yourself?"

"Oh, yes. I'd pay off the mortgage on our boardinghouse."

"That's it? Is that all you want out of life? Just to run a boardinghouse?"

"No, that's not all. I'd like to have a family someday."

"Marriage and children." His tone held scorn.

"Yes." She glanced at him curiously. "You don't want a family of your own?"

He didn't answer right away. Once, naively, he'd wanted the same things she did, marriage and family. But he no longer was sure marriage was even possible for a man in his situation, at least not the kind of marriage he wanted, one that was strong and enduring, based on mutual love.

Enduring love. He'd never had that in his life. Not from his mother, or his fiancée, or any of the countless, nameless women in his past, either ladies or ladies of pleasure. A few might have been able to see past his bank account and the dazzling prospect of becoming Mrs. Garrett Devlin, millionaire, but he'd never given them a chance. Perhaps he was overly mistrustful, but the one time he'd given his heart openly, it had been sliced to ribbons. He wasn't about to lay himself open to that kind of pain again.

"I've never met the woman whom I'd want to bear my children," he said finally in answer to her question.

Jess was a bit surprised by his soft vehemence, and his lack of interest in having a family. But then the things a man put store in weren't the same as a woman's choices.

"You really don't want to be rich?" she heard him ask in a doubting tone.

"Well ..." She pursed her lips in thought. "It might be nice to have a fine house in Georgetown like Burke has ... and maybe go to the opera sometimes and keep a carriage. But I'd settle for hot running water in the kitchen and bathroom." She gave a small laugh. "I'd have a giant tub with a pound of perfumed bath salts and no interruptions and nothing to cook for an entire day. I swear I would sit and soak until I turned into a prune."

Giving her an odd look, Devlin suddenly leaned across the short stretch between them to capture her hand. When Jess would have drawn back in surprise, he refused to let go. Assessingly, he turned her hand over, palm up, tracing the calluses and rough lines in her skin.

"Your hands are red and raw. You should take better care of yourself."

Jess flushed in the darkness and pulled her hand from his grasp, linking her fingers in her lap to hide them from his critical gaze. "I don't have time to pamper myself."

"You should make the time. You could be quite beautiful."

"It doesn't matter to me how beautiful I look."

Devlin raised an eyebrow. "Do you mean to tell me you haven't a trace of feminine vanity?"

"Of course I do. Do you think I *like* having chapped hands? Not being able to afford beautiful dresses and perfumed baths? Cooking and caring for rough men who don't have the manners or morals of a jackass?"

"I think," Devlin said gently, "that you work far too hard."

"Well, some of us don't have the luxury of choosing our livelihood."

"I also think that running a boardinghouse isn't a job for a lady."

Misunderstanding his concern, Jess took offense. "I *know* how to act like a lady, Mr. Devlin! I went to finishing school for nearly two years to learn how. But knowing how to pour tea and to balance a book on your head doesn't put food on the table or pay wages for a mine crew. And the fact that I do what I do doesn't make me any less a lady!"

"I never said you weren't a lady, sweetheart. I said you didn't know how to enjoy being a woman, feeling a woman's passion. There's quite a difference."

His half-lidded gaze was amused, Jess saw. And this subject was becoming highly dangerous. Devlin's expression had lost that grim edge, and he was grinning with a slow laziness, looking more like the handsome devil she'd come to know over the past week.

Deliberately, she averted her gaze, and her attention was suddenly caught by a bright silver-red flame streaking across the sky.

"Look!" she exclaimed in a hushed voice, as much to provide a distraction as in awe. "A falling star. We should make a wish."

She was silent for a moment, watching until it plunged beyond the horizon. "My mother would have called it a wild star," Jess said, half to herself. "That was how the Wildstar mine was named. One fell over the mine the first time Riley took her to see it." Her voice dropped to a murmur, sounding distant and yet dreamy, as if she was recalling fond memories. "Mama said that sometimes love was like trying to catch a wild star . . . elusive . . . always too far away. And if you did somehow manage to get hold of it, maybe you'd find out it wasn't what you wanted after all."

Devlin could find more than a grain of truth in that theory. He'd once been in love, but it wasn't anything like what he'd wanted or hoped for. He'd known the hungry yearning that love aroused, the confusion, the excitement, the joy, the fierce ache . . . the desperate hurt of having his love rejected. The mortification of knowing his prospective inheritance was his prime attraction. The blind determination afterward never to repeat his folly.

He no longer believed so blindly in love. Love made a man a fool, sapped him of wits and pride—and he'd sworn never to be played for a fool again. If his life was sometimes barren and lonely, if at times he still dreamed about finding a woman who could fill the emptiness . . . well, his wealth might be cold comfort, but it was good for something at least. He usually was able to find consolation in a pair of scented arms, between a pair of soft thighs.

The silence lengthened.

"What did you wish for?" Devlin murmured finally.

The sensuous, whisky-rough quality of his voice stroked all the feminine nerve endings along Jess's spine, as provocatively as a lover's touch.

Against her will, she turned her head and her gaze tangled with his. His smoke-gray eyes were fastened on her with an impact that made Jess catch her breath. There was a primal quality of seduction in Devlin's gaze that left her utterly weak. He couldn't help it, she was certain. Looking at a woman that way, as if she were the most beautiful woman in the world, was as natural to him as breathing.

She didn't *want* to succumb to him, though. The man

who claimed her ought to be her husband and no one else. She had high standards for the man she would marry. She wanted a good man, someone kind and tender, one who was willing to work hard, who wasn't afraid to face tough odds. She wanted to be able to look up to him the way she did her father.

Garrett Devlin most certainly didn't fit that bill. Devlin was a gambler, a hired gun. The kind of man who lived off other men's sweat, whose loyalty could be bought ... Well, maybe that judgment was a bit harsh. Devlin had taken on her fight against Burke, Jess reminded herself, and he was helping her now, tracking the gunmen who'd shot up the Wildstar and nearly killed Clem. He'd proved he was better than most of his kind. Yet he was still too self-indulgent, too sophisticated, too attractive for her taste. And he certainly wasn't the marrying kind. She knew better than to fall for his practiced charm.

Still, that didn't help her find him any less appealing, or make it any easier to forget the devastating kisses he'd given her yesterday ... or allow her to resist his touch now. He had taken her hand again, and was holding her fingers firmly in his grasp while his thumb intimately traced the sensitive center of her palm. She couldn't have pulled away if her life depended on it.

"Wh-what did I wish for?" she repeated falteringly, her own voice sounding absurdly breathless. "The same thing I've wished for every day since this trouble started. That Burke would get his comeuppance."

Devlin looked down at her slender, work-worn hand with bemusement. He should have expected that answer; all she cared about was saving the Wildstar mine for her father. But it surprised him, the sting of envy he felt. What would it be like, being the object of such devotion? Having a woman care for him that much? A woman who put every ounce of energy and determination she possessed into seeing you fulfill your dream? A woman who wanted you for yourself, not for the depth of your pockets or your sexual prowess in bed? Someone to ease the loneliness—

"What did you wish for?" Jess asked, trying to sound normal.

He hadn't made a wish. He didn't believe in such foolish superstition. But if he had, Devlin thought silently, sentimentally, he would have wished for a woman who existed only in his deepest fantasies ... one who would love him for himself, one who would give her heart to him totally, without regard to wealth or position. He'd never known a woman like that. He'd thought she didn't exist. He still didn't believe it. Jessica Sommers was no fantasy; she was a flesh-and-blood firebrand who was too hard-headed, too independent, too capable to appeal to a man who wanted yielding softness and sensuality in a woman.

Who are you trying to fool, Devlin? He couldn't possibly deny he wanted her, regardless of all her toughness. He wanted to taste her again, wanted her moaning with pleasure beneath him, wanted her long legs wrapped around him as he drove himself into her. Just the thought of it had the power to arouse him.

Devlin felt himself tugging gently on her hand, drawing Jessica's wide-eyed face closer. He knew damn well he shouldn't touch her. Especially now, when he was alone with her in a dark wilderness, with a crackling fire casting a golden glow over her skin. Especially when Riley had pleaded with him to take care of his stubborn daughter. Especially when his control was so tenuous. It could easily get out of hand. . . .

And yet he knew damn well he *would* touch her. If only to make certain her kisses held the same sweet innocence they'd held yesterday. To see if her lips possessed the same bold honesty that her words had tonight when she'd professed to scorn riches and rich men.

With his free hand, he reached behind her neck, wrapping his fingers around her nape. She was acting just like a skittery mare, nervous and wary. But he could read past the uncertain light in her tawny eyes. He'd been on the receiving end of enough sultry looks and honeyed kisses to know when a woman was interested in him and ready to be aroused, and Jessica most definitely was ready. Just now her lips were parted, her breathing shallow. He was certain that if he placed his hand over her breast he would feel her heart racing in anticipation.

"Jessica?" His voice was low, muted, and sleekly velvet as the night.

"Wh-what?" she stammered. Her tongue flicked out to wet her dry lips, drawing his gaze to her mouth.

"You have the power to grant my wish, sweet Jessie."

Slowly Devlin lay back on his bedroll, gently pulling her with him. Jess felt herself being drawn down, down, into his arms, into his gaze. His eyes were a lazy, fathomless gray-black, and she wondered fleetingly if it were possible to drown in a man's eyes, to faint from just the wanton feel of him. She lay draped across Devlin's chest, hard against soft, soft against hard. Her breasts felt heavy and tight as they thrust against him, while the rest of her body felt weak and aroused.

"Sweet, sweet Jess," Devlin repeated in a husky whisper as he drew her lips completely down to his.

She thought she knew what to expect. He'd tutored her enough yesterday for her to be prepared for the devastating effect of his mouth ... his wet heat, his thrusting tongue, his sheer seductiveness.... It was all intimately familiar to her. What was new was the overpowering need to get closer to him. His kiss filled her with such a fierce yearning she couldn't begin to name all the sensations she felt. They all merged into a persistent hot ache deep inside her that somehow began and ended with Devlin.

Blindly Jess's hands sought his thick black hair, while her mouth feverishly tried to fuse with his. She couldn't remember ever feeling so alive, so reckless, so free. Her body quivered at the wild storm his kiss was causing. When finally he broke off and let her up for air, she didn't want to let go.

Her breath coming in soft gasps, she gazed down at him with dazed yearning. "Devlin?" she whispered, not knowing whether she was protesting the cessation of his kiss or pleading with him to fulfill the nameless longing.

"Hush, sweet," he replied, silencing her.

His eyes were hot and smoky, like haze from a wildfire,

as he rolled over with her, pressing her back against the thick yielding mat of pine needles between their bedrolls.

His mouth ate hers in small, tantalizingly brief nips as he pulled at the pins in her hair and freed the silken mass for his fingers to cherish. "Beautiful . . ." he murmured.

Jess stirred restlessly beneath him. She could feel his thigh pressing between her legs, making the ache there almost unbearable. Without volition she arched her hips, hardly aware that the soft whimper she'd heard came from her own throat.

Devlin took advantage of her dazed state; his dexterous fingers pushed aside the lapels of her bolero, working at the buttons of her shirt.

"Devlin," Jess said shakily when she felt his fingers brush against her breasts.

"Hush, darlin'. I won't do anything you don't want me to do."

His lips found hers again, driving away thoughts and fears. His tongue was like a hot brand in her mouth, marking her as his . . . demanding, possessing. She closed her eyes, unable to think about the danger of what he was doing to her, with her.

She had left off her restrictive boned corset but wore a camisole under her shirt. Carefully, with a gentleness bordering on reverence, he pushed up the soft fabric and bared her beautiful breasts to his gaze. They were high and full and taut, the pink nipples already budding with arousal.

Bending his head, he pressed his lips against one distended peak. A surprised gasp erupted from deep in Jessica's throat.

A grim smile of satisfaction curving his mouth, Devlin brought his hand up to cup the heavy underside of her breast and flicked his tongue over the swollen bud. Her gasp turned into a soft moan, while her fingers dug into the muscles of his shoulders.

Devlin took it as an invitation to continue. Both hands came up to hold her breasts prisoner to his pleasure.

His hot mouth showed no mercy, his velvet-rough tongue doing shocking, wanton things to her breasts that

Jess had never even dreamed about . . . licking, stroking, suckling. He seemed intent on driving her wild.

Even when her breath began coming in shallow gasps, Devlin wouldn't give her a moment's respite. His right hand moved downward over her body to close possessively beneath her buttocks and draw her tightly against him. Erotically he rocked her, making slow, lazy circles with his lean hips, letting her feel the hard length of his arousal.

His passion-edged voice came to her through a dim haze of sensation. "Jess . . . what do you want me to do, honey?" His tongue traced the aureole of her nipple with tantalizing slowness.

Jess tossed her head feverishly. She didn't know what she wanted. She only knew the hot ache inside her had grown till she felt she was on fire.

Devlin experienced no such ambivalence; he knew very well what he wanted. He wanted her passionate and writhing. He wanted to show her the meaning of pleasure. He wanted to be the man to awaken her, the one who would set her free.

Devlin groaned at the image. He could almost feel himself sinking into her hot welcoming flesh, feel the exquisite pleasure of her slick heat enveloping him.

The angry whip of a bullet at first didn't penetrate his overheated senses; it was sheer instinct for danger that made Devlin fumble for his rifle as the gunshot exploded in his ears. He felt Jess stiffen beneath him and fear clutched his heart. There was no time to ask if she'd been hit, though; in the golden light of the campfire, they made prime targets.

Grabbing desperately at the rifle with one hand, holding on to Jess with the other, Devlin prayed and started rolling . . . over and over, pulling her with him, toward the woods, away from the deadly light.

"Oh!" Jess's sharp exclamation told him at least she was alive—and she would stay that way, if he had anything to say about it.

They came to a bone-jarring halt at the base of a pine. Scarcely breaking momentum, Devlin twisted his body, half lunging, half crawling behind the shelter of the tree trunk, dragging Jess with him. An instant's glance showed him a dazed Jess trying to push herself up on her elbows.

Feeling a fierce surge of relief, he rose to a crouch, rifle ready to fire, and squeezed off a shot in the direction of the gunfire. A burst of flame shone in the darkness some twenty yards away, just before a gout of earth kicked up to his left.

Jess had managed to climb to her knees. "Give me a gun!" she cried.

The Colt leapt into Devlin's hand in a smooth motion and he tossed it at her, not daring to see if she caught it.

A bullet ricocheted off the stones of the campfire, then a chunk of bark flew from the tree next to his head.

A nearby gun spoke, and Devlin knew it was Jess. Keeping to cover while she let loose another shot, he edged his way forward, toward the gunmen. There were two of them, from what he could tell. During a lull in the shooting, he stepped from behind the sheltering pines and fired three fast shots in succession.

He was answered by another rifle blast. Raising his Winchester, he took a sight on a shadow and fired.

A rough cry told him he'd hit something.

Another spurt of gunfire exploded into the night, before the shots slowed.

"Zeke?" a panicked voice came from the darkness. "You hit? Zeke!"

Devlin held his fire, his finger hugging the trigger. His fifteen-shot repeating rifle had six bullets left.

He wasn't given the chance to use them. A few seconds later, he heard the snort of a horse, then the scuffling sounds of a man mounting up. Whoever it was rode off at a gallop, as if the very devil were on his heels.

The echo of hoofbeats was followed by an ominous silence.

A long moment passed while Devlin stood there, blood pumping in his ears.

"Jess, are you all right?" he said finally.

"Yes." Her voice was shaky, but held the same determined note of courage she'd shown during the gunfight.

"Stay where you are."

Cautiously, Devlin moved forward into the darkness. After a moment, he saw the body in the dim light of the campfire, lying facedown in the pine needles. With the toe of his boot, he rolled the man's body over.

Zeke McRoy. The livid scar above the right eye stood out clearly against a bloodless face.

Devlin went down on one knee to feel for a pulse, to check for a breath . . . praying for anything that would signify a sign of life. A full minute of fruitless searching put an end to his hope.

He swore softly, viciously.

"Is he dead?" he heard Jess ask in a small voice as she came up behind him.

"Yes."

He felt her shudder. Helpless anger and regret flooded him. Anger because Jessica's life had been endangered as well as his own. Regret because Zeke McRoy had been his only link to the outlaws who'd robbed his father's train.

He couldn't question McRoy about the robberies now, and without that, he was at a dead end. To continue the search would be futile. He had only a general description of the other outlaws, not enough to lead him to the gang's hideout. With nothing more definite to go on, he wouldn't know where to begin looking in this vast rocky maze of peaks and canyons. It was unlikely he would find any other promising leads, either. By now the stolen bars of bullion would probably have been melted down and stamped with a new serial number.

"The other one got clear," Jess said in a quiet voice.

"Did you get a look at him?" Devlin asked tonelessly.

"No. I'm sorry."

He bowed his head, squeezing his eyes shut. The enormity of his frustration felt like a lead weight in his gut.

He felt Jess's hand, tentative, protective, on his shoulder, offering comfort. He wanted to shrug it off, to strike out in his anger, and yet more powerful was the urge to take her hand and pull her down to him, to cover her lips with his and draw from her warmth, letting her drive away the hard chill that had seeped into him.

He set his jaw and did neither.

Eventually Jess drew her hand back. "What do we do now?"

"We take the body back to town."

Slowly Devlin rose to his feet, feeling ten years older than he had a few minutes ago. Jess was watching him in concern, he knew, but he hardened his resolve.

When she handed his Colt back to him, he accepted it without looking at her and holstered the weapon. The passionate embrace they'd shared might never have been—except for the disheveled state of Jess's clothing. As if recalling her near seduction at Devlin's hands, she turned her back on him and began buttoning her shirt.

A muscle tightened in his jaw as the awkward silence stretched between them. He ought to say something to relieve her embarrassment, he knew. Any man who called himself a man would have tried to reassure her, would have attempted to convince her that what had happened between them was natural and beautiful. But Devlin stopped himself. If she thought he was a callous bastard who only wanted to climb between her legs, then maybe she would try harder to keep away from him. And it was becoming obvious that Jess would have to be the one to keep away. He certainly didn't have the willpower to withstand the fierce desire that had raged through him when he kissed her, when he merely touched her.

Devlin's mouth twisted with bitter self-mockery. He'd never thought of himself as a weak man, but that was before he'd met a honey-haired avenging fury named Jessica Sommers. It was little comfort to know that only a hail of bullets from a desperate outlaw could have stopped him from taking her and destroying her innocence. Zeke McRoy's untimely appearance had saved her.

Devlin wasn't sure whether to view it as a blessing or a curse.

Chapter 9

H e didn't need this, Devlin thought with self-derision as he rode up the dark mountainside five days later, on Saturday evening. He couldn't afford to spend precious time worrying about a stubborn, tawny-haired miner's daughter who very obviously was capable of taking care of herself and her worthless mine if left to her own resources. He was wasting what might be his last opportunity, trapped here in Silver Plume while Zeke McRoy's gang doubtless planned another train holdup. He needed to be miles north of here, asking questions and trying to discover who McRoy had ridden with.

He liked even less what was happening between him and Jess ... the closeness that was developing between them. He was letting himself get far too involved with her, Devlin knew. Not just her problems, but with *her*.

He didn't like the tender feelings he was beginning to feel for Jess, the protectiveness, the desire. He didn't like leaving himself so vulnerable. He'd spent ten years successfully avoiding getting caught in a woman's clutches, and while Jessica Sommers's ambitions might not be as mercenary as most other females', his relationship with Jess was becoming too intimate for comfort.

Yet the only solution that would let him protect himself—keeping away from her entirely—was out of the question. He couldn't leave Jess to face Burke's hired gunmen alone, not with her father still down and her mine crew deserting her. The past five days had been hell for

Jess, beginning with the death of Zeke McRoy. Seeing a man die had shaken her, Devlin knew, though she'd tried to hide it. And then there'd been the craven marshal of Silver Plume to deal with.

When they'd returned to town at dawn with McRoy's body and roused the marshal out of bed, Lockwood had done absolutely nothing besides mutter about throwing Devlin in jail for killing a man. Clearly the marshal was not about to go hunting down the gunmen himself. He valued his own skin too much, not to mention his standing with Ashton Burke.

Furious almost to the point of hysteria, Jess had lit into him with a blistering tirade that should have taken a strip off his yellow hide. Devlin had his hands full calming her down enough to get her out of there. He wasn't concerned about the spineless marshal. Jess could testify that Devlin had acted in self-defense, and there'd been a dozen witnesses to the shooting spree at the Wildstar and the deliberate wrecking of Clem's ore wagon. Marshal Lockwood didn't have a case strong enough even to arrest him. Besides, Devlin had access to some of the best legal counsel in the country—although he did not tell Jess that.

She was still ranting when he got her home. "The nerve of that slimy little worm, accusing you of murder! He ought to be tossed in jail himself!"

But she was using anger, Devlin suspected, to cover up her horror at being involved, however unintentionally, in the death of a man.

Seeing the desperation in her eyes, he'd felt a fierce rush of tenderness, an overwhelming need to protect and comfort her, yet he had refrained from taking her in his arms as he longed to do, knowing where such an unwise action would lead. He'd allowed her father to comfort her instead.

After Jess had told the story to her father—Riley had been worried sick about her during their absence—Devlin had to physically force her to lie down in her own bed and threaten her with mayhem if she didn't drink the mug of warm milk he'd laced with laudanum. Even then, she only acquiesced because he promised to ride up to the mine right then and stay there for the rest of the day and that night as well. Playing guard for that damned mine was the absolute last thing Devlin wanted to do just then, but he had no choice, not with Jess's pain-filled eyes pleading with him. He'd never seen her so vulnerable, so helpless. Her last words before her eyes closed in exhausted slumber were about taking care of the Wildstar.

The next morning, though, she was up at the mine at dawn, packing a shotgun, with no trace of vulnerability showing in her eyes or her expression. Instead, Devlin saw fierce determination and sheer grit.

She needed every ounce of grit she possessed to get through the next few days. Clem was little help to her. The mule skinner was still mourning his dead critters, and although he showed up for work each morning, he moved like an old man in a daze. He had only four mules left, and Jess had to scrounge for the money to buy more. She ordered an ore wagon on credit, as well, to replace the one that had been destroyed in the accident, but until it came, Clem had to haul what little ore the crew took out of the earth down the mountain by jack train, the rawhide sacks of rock strapped securely to the mules' shaggy hides.

Production had suffered even further because of the rain that came down in torrents. For two incessant days, the heavens had opened up, rendering the mountain roads treacherous and submerging the town streets in knee-deep mud.

Jess herself took over guarding the mine during the day, against her father's fierce protests. Riley was beside himself with concern, but he was in no position to argue if he wanted to keep his mine crew going. Two of the miners had already quit, claiming they couldn't afford to continue working under such dangerous conditions when they had families to think about. Riley wasn't able do any mining himself, either. Although he was getting physically stronger each day, he still couldn't leave his bed for longer than a half hour at a time without tiring himself out. Nor could he make the long trek up to the mine without risking exhaustion and setting his recovery back even further.

Devlin didn't like the situation any more than Riley did. Jess had refused to allow him longer duty at the mine, saying it wouldn't be right to impose on him, but it galled him to feel both helpless and trapped.

He'd nearly reached the end of his restraint yesterday afternoon, when Burke had called at the Sommers's place. Devlin had been awakened from a fitful sleep by a knock at the front door, and when he'd dragged himself out of bed to answer it, he found Riley planted in the open doorway, blocking the entrance, one hand clutching his chest. Ashton Burke stood outside on the front step.

"I've told you before," Riley was saying, "I'm not interested in selling."

Barefooted, holding a revolver at the ready, Devlin came up behind Riley. Burke immediately raised his hands to show that he was unarmed.

"I merely wanted you to know I'm willing to increase my offer," the Englishman murmured pleasantly. "Ten thousand dollars more. Twenty-five thousand, total. That's a great deal of money, Mr. Sommers."

Riley shook his head.

"You heard him," Devlin interjected. "He's not interested."

Burke stretched his lips into a sour smile. "I hope you don't come to regret your decision. Good day to you, then."

They watched as Burke returned to his waiting carriage. As it drove away Riley slumped wearily against the door. "I've thought a lot lately about taking Burke's offer," he murmured. "Maybe it would be cowardly, but it might also be smarter. Trouble is, I don't think I could stand myself if I gave in to his threats. And Jess would have my head."

Running a hand down his stubbled face, Devlin nodded in agreement. After the violence of last week, Jess was more determined than ever that Burke would never win. It couldn't go on much longer, though. If her resolve didn't weaken, her dwindling resources would force her to cut back her efforts. And Burke would go for the jugular. One more incident like the ore wagon accident and the Wildstar would be out of business.

The thought made Devlin grit his teeth. Although he could feel the trail left by the gang who'd robbed his father's train grow colder every day, he didn't intend to quit and leave the victory to Burke. In fact, he'd almost decided to put up the money himself to bring in outside help.

And that was *before* Jess hadn't come home this evening.

She was supposed to have been relieved by the guard for the evening shift so she could return in time for supper, but supper had been over for a full hour. As worried as Riley, Devlin had gone after her.

He approached the Wildstar with caution, his Colt drawn. He saw her horse hobbled a few yards from the main entrance, but there was no sign of Jess. Nor was there any light shining from within the cabin.

"Jess?"

Devlin slowly dismounted, his eyes searching the moonlit mountain scene. He could hear little but the occasional distant thunder of dynamite as a charge was exploded somewhere, and the dull, hammering echo of drill steel as other mining operations carried on the endless task of cutting rock. Many of the large consolidated mines worked the Saturday night shift, not shutting down until Sunday morning for a day of rest.

The contrasting silence here at the Wildstar seemed highly disquieting.

Needles of fear began to crawl up Devlin's spine. If anything had happened to Jess—if she'd been hurt or shot the way her father had been—he would personally strangle Burke with his bare hands . . . very slowly . . . inflicting as much agony as possible.

Just then, he heard a small slide of rock scree, followed by quiet footsteps. He leveled his six-shooter, holding it steady as Jess came around the corner of the cabin.

She gasped and nearly dropped her shotgun. "Devlin! You scared the life out of me!"

You scared the daylights out of me, too, sweetheart. "Where the hell have you been?"

His demand came out harsher than he'd intended, and Jess's eyes widened in confusion. "I heard a noise. . . . I went to look. . . ."

Devlin's mouth tightened at her stammered explanation. "If you mean to continue this fool notion of guarding the Wildstar yourself, you'd better learn to use your head. *Never* leave your post, for any reason. A noise could be a decoy . . . to draw you away and leave the mine unprotected. Stay put and keep your eyes open for a trap." As he spoke, Devlin took her arm and steered her firmly toward her horse. "Why didn't you come home?"

Chastened, Jess pulled her arm from his grasp. "Because somebody had to be here for the evening shift."

"Llewelyn didn't show up?"

"Oh, he showed up. He came up here to tell me he was quitting."

The bitterness in her voice sliced at Devlin's heart. The need to put his arms around her and offer her comfort was like a burning knife in his gut, but he didn't trust himself to touch her and do nothing more than that.

Instead, he kept his hands off her and saddled her horse. "You should have ridden down to get me."

"This is Saturday night. I figured you would be in town living it up."

Devlin turned to eye her coldly, his gray gaze hard in the moonlight.

Jess was the first to look away. "I'm sorry. That was uncalled for. You've done more than I had any right to ask of you. I'm just tired."

"I know. You're driving yourself into the ground."

"I'll be all right."

Like hell. From the corner of his eye, he saw her raise a weary hand to rub her temple and he cursed under his breath. It was insupportable that she'd taken this entire burden on her shoulders. She was pushing herself to the brink of exhaustion and was going to break soon. No one was that strong.

He tightened the cinch around the horse's barrel with more force than necessary, making the animal dance. "You won't be all right if you keep up this pace."

He heard her sigh softly. "I can't give up. The crew will only work because I promised them protection."

"You don't have to do it all yourself. You've got no business staying up here every night, Jess. Dammit, you're not invincible."

She rallied at his attack, her chin coming up. "If you dare say one word about me not behaving like a woman should, I'll . . . I'll throw you down the mountain!"

Devlin took a deep breath and strove for patience. "Pull in your horns, angel. I wasn't maligning your femininity." When she simply stared at him numbly, he reached up and brushed her cheek with his knuckles. "Jess, go home and get some sleep. I'll handle this from now on."

Flinching from his touch, she shook her head. It would be too easy to let Devlin shoulder her problems. Too easy to lean on him and let him carry on the struggle for her. But it wouldn't be right. She couldn't allow him to keep risking his life for her while she walked away. One day his luck just might run out, and she couldn't live with herself if that happened. If he were hurt or killed because of her . . . She couldn't bear to think of it.

"I can't let you handle it by yourself," she replied quietly. "I can't leave you to fight them alone."

Refusing even his assistance in mounting, Jess dragged her weary body up into the saddle and straightened the skirts of her brown calico gown. She was so tired she was ready to drop, not only because of the grueling demands on her time during recent weeks, but because of the lack of sleep. She'd found it hard to live with herself the past five days. She had helped kill a man, and the memory made her sick to her stomach. Ever since then, she'd had nightmares about it—and about the rest of that night on the trail. It made her skin crawl, knowing she and Devlin had been stalked by the same gunmen they'd been trailing. And then there was Devlin himself. Every time she looked at him, at his hard sensuous mouth, she remembered the feel of him kissing her bare breasts and she flushed with humiliation. Dear Lord, she'd nearly allowed Devlin to seduce her.

Only the gravity of her other problems kept her from dwelling on that serious lapse in judgment. She was in big trouble. All her efforts at protecting the mine had been a failure. McRoy's death had ended their search for the gunmen, and now they were like sitting ducks, not knowing when the next attack would come.

In her weakest moments she allowed herself to hope that the shooting of McRoy would warn off the others, maybe even end the feud. Maybe, just maybe Burke's gunmen wouldn't be back. But it was far more likely that they would retaliate for the death of one of their members. They'd choose a time when the mine was most vulnerable, and then . . . They wouldn't have to destroy the operation entirely. Even minor sabotage could be enough to make Riley lose his crew and drive his business under.

She felt the ache of unshed tears clog her throat. Lately it felt like her entire world was crumbling around her.

She started to turn her horse and came up short.

"My God . . ." Jess breathed. "Look."

A red flickering light shone ominously from within the Wildstar, while a small crackling noise reached her ears.

The abrupt oath Devlin gave was low and vicious as he turned to run. Weariness gone, Jess was off her horse and following him in less than a second, reaching the mouth a few yards behind him. She didn't like entering the mine even under normal circumstances, and this was far from normal, with black and red shadows leaping on the walls. She stumbled more than once along the glowing tunnel, over rail tracks and rough floor.

Halfway along the narrow rockbound passage she came to the fire. It was a only a small blaze—apparently made of debris and ore bags, but the smoke it gave off was black and choking, and the stench of kerosene was almost overpowering.

Devlin had already scooped up a rawhide bag and was beating at the flames. Jess turned to fetch one of several buckets of water that were always kept in the mine for drinking and for emergencies like this.

"A trap ... Jess, get out of here!" Devlin shouted.

Jess halted in indecision, torn between common sense and loyalty. That fire hadn't started by itself, and was very likely the kind of decoy Devlin had warned her about. She wanted to obey him, but she couldn't bear to leave him here to fight the fire on his own.

Before she even had a chance to decide, the choice was taken from her; a sharp crack like a gunshot sounded from the mouth of the tunnel.

Devlin reached for his Colt.

"No!" Jess shrieked. "Don't shoot in here!" It would be insane to fire a gun in a mine tunnel; the danger from ricocheting bullets was too great.

Devlin apparently understood. Even as he nodded and started back toward the mouth of the tunnel, another spark lit up the entrance.

Then all hell broke loose. A jarring boom, a violent rush of air, a loud grinding rumble ... the tremendous explosion seemed to make the whole earth vibrate. The deafening sound of splintering timbers and crashing rocks drowned out Jess's scream. She felt herself being hurled back as her world erupted in a fusillade of flying stones, timbers, and dirt. Then pain exploded in her head and everything went black.

The stink of sulfur and smoke and suffocating dust greeted her when next she opened her eyes. Immediately Jess found herself gasping for breath. She must have been knocked out by the blast for a minute, she realized dizzily as she heard a man's agonized voice call her name.

"Jess! Answer me!"

"D-Devlin?"

Even that small attempt sent her into a spasm of coughing and choking.

"Are you hurt?"

Am I hurt? she wondered, forcing herself to take inventory. She was sprawled on the rock floor, her face pressed against the wall, that much she knew. Her ears were ringing, while her head ached abominably.

"I think so—ooh—" She broke off as another stabbing pain knifed into her left temple. Her groan echoed hollowly in the tunnel.

"Don't move! I'll come to you."

I'm not going anywhere, she thought dazedly. Helplessly, she waited, her body convulsing in another fit of coughing. When it was over, she tried to make out Devlin's outline, but she couldn't see a blessed thing. The darkness was absolute, the silence terrible. Her heart began to pound with raw fear as the horrible realization of their predicament began to dawn on her.

Then Devlin unearthed a still smoldering sliver of wood from the smothered fire and fanned the ember to life, chasing away the blackness with the tiny flame. Jess blinked at the sudden brightness and raised a hand to shield her eyes, but she couldn't block out the sight that met her gaze through the haze of dust. White-faced, with dread clutching at her heart, she stared at the wall of rubble that blocked the entrance to the tunnel.

They were trapped. Imprisoned in a rock-walled tomb. Buried alive!

"Dear God . . ." she croaked, her voice hoarse with panic.

She heard Devlin crawling toward her, and suddenly she couldn't seem to stop babbling. "It was my fault . . . all my fault. . . . I shouldn't have left to go check out that noise . . . they must have started the fire . . . Oh, God . . . we're trapped . . . we'll never get out—"

Her voice cracked on a rising note of hysteria as Devlin reached her and grabbed her arm. The small flame went out, leaving them surrounded by blackness again, and she gave a keening animal cry.

"Stop it, Jess! Dammit, get a hold of yourself!"

She felt his fingers dig into her flesh as he pulled her up from the rough floor and shook her. With a choked sob, Jess flung herself at Devlin's chest. Instantly, his arms

closed around her, holding her protectively while he muttered meaningless sounds in her ear.

"Don't fall apart on me, angel. . . . Take a deep
breath. . . . That's a good girl. . . . That's my sweet Jessie."

On his knees, he cradled her tightly, fiercely, his body
absorbing the tremors from her own. Gradually, her whim-
pers subsided. Devlin let out a deep breath.

"Jess, tell me where you're hurt. I have to know."

She swallowed hard, trying to force back the raw edge
of panic as she willed her mind to function. She felt
bruised and battered all over, but the worst pain was in her
head. "My . . . temple . . . the left . . ."

His fingers came up to gently feel her face, moving to
touch her hair. "I think you're bleeding. Let me up, sweetheart. I have to have a light. It should be safe now that the
worst dust has settled."

Her arms tightened in a stranglehold around his waist.
"Don't leave me!"

"I won't, I promise. I'm just going to stand up for a
minute. I'll be right back."

It was long moment before Jess felt brave enough to let
him go. Pulling away, Devlin struck a match on the heel
of his boot.

The box had come from his vest pocket, Jess saw.

"Lucky I came prepared." He flashed her a smile that
made her blink in confusion. How could he be so unconcerned? Didn't he know they might very well die?

She watched in bewilderment as he lit the candle in the
wrought iron sconce mounted on the tunnel wall. Then he
knelt beside her again and examined her temple in the
flickering light.

"Yep, you're bleeding . . . a nasty gash. Bet it hurts like
hell." Without warning, he bent over and raised her skirt to
her knee. "What fun. I get to undress you after all."

His mouth curving in a smug grin, he tore several strips
off her petticoat, then made a pad and pressed it against
the bleeding flesh at her temple. Ignoring her wince, he
wound another long strip around her head, fashioning a

headband to hold the bandage in place. Finally he pressed his lips gently against her forehead in a soothing kiss.

"If we only had a feather," Devlin teased, "you would look like an Indian brave. Now help me think, Jess. What should we do?"

"D-do?"

"You're the mine expert here. You'd better take charge or we'll wind up in a heap of trouble."

We already are in a heap of trouble, she wanted to reply, but she couldn't force the words past her dry throat.

"Jess?" Devlin repeated patiently.

Dazedly, she looked around her, peering through the haze of dust. What had happened? Someone had dynamited the entrance to the mine, that much was clear. The tunnel roof had caved in, spilling a deadly wall of dirt and rock some ten yards away, barricading the entrance. How thick the wall was, she couldn't guess. At least the heavy timbers propping up the ceiling adjacent to the entrance had held, keeping the mass of dirt and stone above their heads from crushing them. And the fire had been extinguished by the rubble.

Jess closed her eyes as she thought of how close they'd just come to death. Growing up in a mining town, she'd heard countless stories of cave-ins—called "caves" by anyone in the business—that buried miners under tons of rock. Few escaped alive, without terrible injuries. Her father worked daily with explosives, blasting rock into ore, and her greatest fear had always been that some day Riley would miscalculate in setting a giant powder charge and bring the mountain down on his head.

And now, here she and Devlin were, trapped in a rock-bound passage, four feet wide, seven feet high, without air or food. . . .

The blackness closed in on her again and she couldn't seem to breathe. . . .

"Jess!" Devlin's harsh voice prodded her sharply. "I never would have expected you to quit when the going gets tough."

"I can't—"

"Yes, you can! Think! Tell me what to do!"

She couldn't think. They were going to die here. They were going to suffocate from lack of air . . . unless they found some air first. Yes, that was it. They had to get away. Find someplace to wait till the choking dynamite fumes dissipated. A quiet place to recover from the blinding headache giant power always caused. Jess raised a hand to her aching temple. Her skull hurt so much just now she could barely speak.

"Maybe . . . we should move . . . to the lower tunnel. It's too hard to breathe here. The air will be better down there."

"Good idea. Come on, honey."

Putting an arm around her waist, he lifted Jess to her feet.

She didn't protest; she knew Devlin wouldn't allow it. She'd never been so scared in her life, but it was obvious that Devlin wasn't going to let her dwell on her fears.

He took one step forward, though, then stumbled and cursed roundly.

"Jess, I've twisted my ankle. You're going to have to help me."

"Is it bad?"

"Yes. Get the candle."

She obeyed automatically, moving to fetch the candle on its spike holder, then lending her shoulder for Devlin to lean on. The thought of him in pain was somehow harder for her to deal with than her own pain; it brought out all her motherly instincts and spurred her to action in a way all the other danger had failed to do.

Slowly, awkwardly, they made their way down the narrow tunnel, ducking frequently to avoid a beam or a jagged outcrop of rock, till they reached the end. The huge iron bucket that normally transported people and ore up and down the shaft could not be used without someone to operate the hand-crank, but steel pegs had been driven into the shaft walls at regular intervals to form a ladder of sorts. Jess went down first, awkwardly negotiating the rungs while holding the candle, splotches of dripping wax burning her hand.

The air was sweeter there, almost bearable. She took a deep breath as she set foot on solid ground, then called up to Devlin. "Can you make it?"

"Yes." His tone sounded grim but determined. Jess waited below for him, wincing each time he missed a peg of the ladder.

When finally he reached her, she moved into his embrace without speaking. Pressing her body against his lean-muscled frame, Jess wrapped her arms around his waist tightly, unsure whether she was offering support or drawing from his strength. Maybe both.

They stood there a minute, holding each other, savoring the feeling of being alive.

"Can you find a place for us to rest?" Devlin said at last.

Jess swallowed hard and summoned her courage. Nodding, she drew away.

"There's a good place over here," she said a moment later. Returning to his side, she helped him limp along the lower tunnel, moving deeper into the mountain, skirting several ore cars. Shortly this level came to an end and the iron rails stopped. Jess settled Devlin on the rock floor with his back to the wall, and sat down beside him, placing the candle safely out of reach. There was little space, but they had enough room to lie down if they chose.

"Ah, much better," Devlin said with a sigh that sounded almost like pleasure. When Jess didn't reply, he cast her a sidelong glance. "Are you all right?"

"No." Her body was shaking helplessly, and she couldn't control it. "We're going to die down here."

"No, we aren't. Don't sound so dour. We'll survive. We have plenty of drinking water and"—he fished in his vest pocket to pull out a small wrapped parcel—"biscuits and ham for supper. Flo packed a supper so I wouldn't starve, bless her heart. What will you give me for a biscuit, angel?"

His grin was teasing and altogether too irreverent for

their dire situation. Wrapping her arms around herself, Jess shook her head. "We can't live without air," she reminded him bleakly, her voice quivering.

"It won't come to that. We'll be rescued long before our air runs out. I wouldn't be surprised to hear a crew working with pickaxes and shovels in a little while."

"You really think we'll be rescued?"

"Absolutely."

"I can't see how. Even if anybody heard the explosion here, they wouldn't have paid it any mind, not with all the blasting going on in the other mines. The night shift is the best time to set charges, so the fumes will be gone when the crew shows up for work in the morning—"

"Perhaps," Devlin cut off her chatter. "But there's still a chance someone heard this one and became suspicious. It's common knowledge that you don't work a night shift in the Wildstar. And someone might pass by and notice the collapsed tunnel and go for help. In any case, when you don't come home right away, Riley will send Clem after you."

"You think so?"

"Most certainly. And after what I did for Clem last week, he damn well better hightail it up here or I'll have his ears." Devlin's adamancy surprised a faint, fleeting smile from Jess. "Until then," he added, "we sit tight. Come here."

Lifting his arm, he wrapped it around her shoulders and pulled her close. Willingly, wearily, Jess leaned against him, resting her cheek against his collarbone. Her head still throbbed savagely, but she felt calmer now, touching another person, touching *him*.

"Devlin . . . I'm so sorry . . . for ever dragging you into this mess."

"Don't be, angel. It was my decision."

She gave a ragged sigh as Devlin smoothed her hair gently back from her injured temple.

"Think you can do without a light?" he said after a while. "You were right . . . we'd do better to conserve air."

"I . . . can manage."

He leaned around her and blew out the candle, then settled back again. In the darkness she felt his hand cover hers, linking their fingers.

"This isn't so bad," he murmured. "I could use a good shot of bourbon just now, though."

"So could I."

Devlin chuckled softly. "I swear I'm going to corrupt you yet, Miss Jess."

She shuddered a little at his blithe attitude. "How can you sound so cheerful?"

"Why shouldn't I be? I can think of worse things than being stuck in the dark with a beautiful woman."

Amazingly Jess felt herself start to blush.

"I suppose I could try to dig our way out," Devlin remarked unenthusiastically.

"No, you couldn't!" she exclaimed. "You'd use up all the air before you cleared a foot."

"Good. I wasn't looking forward to moving a ton of earth." She felt him hunch his shoulders and roll them around slowly. "My muscles are out of shape after all the easy living I've done. You're in a lot better condition. Perhaps I should make you climb up there and dig."

Incredibly, she almost wanted to laugh at his teasing. How could she possibly think of laughing when they were in such danger? In all likelihood they wouldn't make it. She'd known of too many disasters like this to hold any false hope, known too many men who had been killed . . . crushed or suffocated in caves like this . . . friends, neighbors, her own boarders. She'd seen their cold, stiff bodies laid out for burial. She'd mourned their loss with the families they left behind, shared in the grief. And now that grief would be for her. Would her death devastate Riley the way his death would have done her?

Devlin, however, wasn't going to leave off trying to make her forget their terrible predicament, it seemed.

"Jess, you have a smudge of dirt on your nose."

"What? How can you tell . . . in the dark?"

"I peeked. When we get out of here, I'm going to give you a long bath, Miss Jess. I'll put a ton of bath salts in the water and make you stay there till you turn into a prune." His fingers squeezed her hand. "Then I'm going buy you some hand lotion and rub it all over you. . . . Now there's a thought."

"Do you ever have any thoughts besides lecherous ones?"

"Sometimes on Sundays."

She did laugh then—a reluctant, shaky ghost of a chuckle that made her head hurt. How could she not, with Devlin teasing her and trying to charm her? He'd kept up her spirits since the moment she'd realized they were trapped. She had nearly despaired up there, but Devlin had brought her back from the edge.

"Devlin, I'm sorry I went to pieces a while ago. I behaved like a ninny."

"No, you didn't. You behaved just the way a woman should." His tone was so smug that Jess pushed her elbow into his side. "Ouch!"

"I don't want to hear any more about my not acting feminine."

"I'm serious, sweetheart. It makes a man feel important, saving his woman. Can't you see how puffed out my chest is?"

An irrepressible snort escaped her. "I can see how puffed up your vanity is."

"You wound me."

"You aren't wounded—" A sudden suspicion struck her. "Your ankle isn't really hurt, is it?"

"It smarts a bit."

"I'll bet." She was now certain he'd only pretended to twist it in order to give her something else besides their predicament to worry about.

"Devlin?"

"What, angel?"

"Thank you."

"For what?"

"For being here with me." She was profoundly grateful he was here. She couldn't have held off the terror without him, couldn't have borne the long hours of uncertainty that stretched ahead of her, not knowing if they would be rescued in time, if she would even be alive tomorrow. The possibility that they might die was easier to bear with him holding her.

She felt his hand move to her cheek, gently stroking. "My pleasure."

It was a gentle gesture, one meant to reassure. And it did momentarily make her fear recede. More unaccountably, it made her remember the last time Devlin had touched her, had held her intimately. Her heart skipped a beat. She drew a shallow breath, waiting to see if he would take his caress any further. But he seemed content merely to hold her.

"Are you hungry?" he asked sometime later.

"Not much."

"We'll save the biscuits for breakfast, then."

"You should eat. You didn't get any supper."

"Don't mother me the way you do your boarders, Jess. It won't hurt me to skip a meal." He patted his stomach lazily. "I'm liable to get fat on your cooking as it is."

They were quiet for a time, and Jess managed to keep her most dreadful thoughts at bay. They weren't going to make it; she knew it. But she could face the terror more calmly now. And trying to stay calm was all she could do.

At least the piercing headache began to ease, and her skull quit pounding quite so fiercely.

"I am a bit thirsty," she said after a while.

"I'll go get some water. We can use it to wash with. And I'll find some of those rawhide bags to make us a bed. We might as well get some sleep as long as we can't go anywhere."

She didn't want him to go, but she didn't want to seem cowardly, either. She didn't protest when Devlin untangled himself from her. He lit the candle, then rose and made his way back along the tunnel. Without limping, Jess noticed, her mouth curving in a bleak smile.

He was gone for a long time. Jess began to miss not only his warmth but the reassurance of his presence. She hated being alone down here in this dark underground hole. It was too easy to believe the Wildstar mine was a tomb from which she would never escape. Without Devlin, she couldn't keep the specters at bay.

She could see the flickering light of his candle farther down the tunnel, but it seemed as if he had paused in his search.

"What is it?" she called out. Her voice echoed hollowly, holding an edge of fear.

"Nothing."

He returned a few minutes later carrying a dozen rawhide bags and a covered water bucket. While Devlin spread the bags on the floor, Jess drank gratefully from the dipper, then tore another strip from her petticoat to sponge off her face. Devlin followed suit, assuaging his thirst and washing the dust off. Finally settling beside her again, he carefully unwound the bandage from around Jess's head and examined the gash on her temple.

"The bleeding's stopped," he observed as he used the wet rag to wipe the dried blood from her cheek. "You'll live."

Her troubled gaze met his. "Are you sure about that?"

"Entirely."

He kept his tone light, she noticed. Rising to his knees on one edge of the makeshift bed then, he grinned and bowed from the waist. "Your pallet, milady." When she hesitated, he reached for her hand.

Uncertain but obedient, Jess lay down. Devlin took off his gun belt, then blew out the candle. Stretching out beside her, he pulled her gently into his arms, arranging her so that her head rested on his shoulder. The blackness enveloped them, but it wasn't quite the dreadful, suffocating inkiness of before. Instead it was cool and quiet, almost peaceful. Yet it wasn't in the least soothing. Jess couldn't relax. Her mind wouldn't let go of the haunting images of tombs and death.

"I never thought it would take such drastic measures to get you into my bed," Devlin murmured in the darkness.

Jess could almost see his lazy smile and knew he was still trying to cheer her. It didn't work. Devlin was holding her comfortingly, but she didn't feel comforted. Instead, she felt restless and edgy and frightened of what the morning would bring—if it even came.

"Go to sleep, Jess," he said a minute later, his tone patient.

"I don't want to sleep."

His hand came up to stroke her hair tenderly. Jess stirred in his arms. She didn't want tenderness from him. She wanted him to ease the terrible feeling of fear and urgency that was gnawing at her.

"Try to relax, sweetheart," he murmured against her hair. "You should know by now that I'm not going to attack you."

"I wish you would."

She felt his muscles tense perceptibly. "I beg your pardon?"

Jess felt her heart begin to beat heavily, its swift rhythm at odds with the conviction that was steadily building inside her.

"Jess? What did you mean, you wish I would?"

She took a slow, deep breath. "It means that if this is going to be my last night on earth, I don't want to spend it sleeping. I want to know what I've been missing all my life."

She heard his sharp inhalation and knew he understood what she was asking.

"I don't want to die like this, without knowing what it's like to feel passion . . . to be a complete woman," she said softly, so there would be no doubt.

"Jess, you aren't going to die."

"Can you promise me that?"

He was silent for a long moment.

Deliberately, she shifted her head, nestling her face in the naked hollow of his throat. "Devlin, please . . ." she whispered against his warm skin. "Show me what it's like to be a woman."

Chapter 10

"**Y**ou don't mean what you're saying, Jessica," Devlin replied, his tone as taut as his body.

"Yes, I do," she said quietly. "I want you to make love to me."

He lifted his head slightly, trying to look down at her, silently cursing the darkness that wouldn't let him see her face. His fingers reached up to touch her chin, curling around it with an unconscious pressure, while his thoughts raced.

A short time ago during his search of this level, he'd passed a crack in the rock and his candle flame had suddenly flickered. Unless his imagination had been playing tricks, there seemed to be a small stream of air blowing into the tunnel where he and Jess were trapped. If it really *was* air, then they might be able to survive for a while. He hadn't mentioned it to Jessica because he didn't want to falsely raise her hopes. Besides, he could be wrong. The odds were greater that they wouldn't make it through the night.

Devlin grimaced at the morbid thought.

"You're supposed to save your virginity for your husband," he finally said, his voice rough, husky.

"I may never have a husband."

"Yes, you will. We'll get out of here shortly, and sooner or later some man will come along and sweep you off your feet and give you that family you said you wanted."

Jess shook her head mutely. She didn't believe him.

And thinking about a future with some nameless man didn't help. She wanted Devlin, God help her.

But then a man like Devlin could have any woman he wanted. He could afford to be particular. Maybe he didn't want to make love to someone like her, an inexperienced virgin who had few of the feminine qualities he thought a woman should have.

She pressed her face harder against Devlin's shoulder, not knowing if she could bear the humiliation of being turned down by him just now, not with her nerves so raw and unstable.

"You don't want me?" she asked shakily.

His heart turned over. She was burrowing against him like a small animal seeking shelter, and he longed to comfort her, protect her, reassure her.

"Not want you?" He laughed harshly. "I've wanted you every day for the past two weeks . . . ever since I saw you galloping down the street in your morning robe."

"I thought . . . you were just playing a game with me, trying to prove you could charm me like you could every other woman."

"A man doesn't kiss a woman the way I kissed you if he doesn't want her, Jessica." His voice had thickened, and without his being aware of it, his grip had loosened on her chin, his fingers spreading lightly over the warm, silky texture of her cheek, stroking it soothingly.

"Will you kiss me again at least?"

Devlin inhaled sharply, striving for control. Her breath was warm and sweet against his face, while her fingers had curled into his shirt. Even that brief touch speared him with desire; need ground through his body, making his loins hot and heavy. God, how he wanted her. Yet he felt the urge to protect as well as the urge to take.

"Devlin, please?"

"Jess . . ." he said warningly. He let out a pent-up breath and forced himself to recall all the reasons why what she was asking was insane, impossible. He'd promised himself he wouldn't seduce her. He didn't want to hurt her, and hurt was all he would bring her. He wouldn't be staying

around once his mission was finished. He couldn't fulfill
Jess's dream of a marriage and kids. He wasn't the kind of
man she needed. He couldn't let her throw away her virginity on him. If they somehow lived through this, she
would regret her rashness. She might even come to hate
him for it. He didn't want her to hate him. . . .

"Devlin, please? Make love to me."

He thought of being inside her and a jolt of pure driving
lust swept through him.

"Jessica," he said again, but with an agonized note of
indecision in his voice. They might not make it. A man
shouldn't die without tasting a woman on his lips. A
woman shouldn't die without knowing the ecstasy a skillful lover could give her.

Jess waited, listening to the powerful beating of his
heart beneath her ear, feeling the tensely coiled muscles in
his body as he held her. She knew what she wanted him
to do was wicked, foolish. But right or wrong, foolish or
wise, she wasn't going to change her mind. Devlin was
something real and warm to cling to in the dark night. She
didn't want to spend what might her last moments on earth
being terrified. She wanted to forget that she was trapped
in this dark hole, waiting to die. Devlin could make her
forget her dire situation, her grim surroundings. He could
make a woman forget her very name if he tried. And that,
even more than simple comfort, was what she wanted. She
wanted to know what it really meant to be a woman . . .
Devlin's woman.

She lifted her head again. She could see nothing, not his
beautiful face, not even the gleam of his eyes. She wel-
comed the darkness, though; it hid embarrassment, fear,
nervousness. Yet it couldn't hide the feeling that ached in
the pit of her stomach, the breathless tightness of her
throat.

Cautiously, hardly daring to breathe, she raised her hand
to his face, letting her fingertips brush the hard edge of his
jaw.

"Jess, stop it."

She touched his mouth, his beautiful, sensuous mouth.

"Dammit, Jess. . . ."

"Please, kiss me. . . ."

"All right, I'll kiss you, but that's all I'll do."

"That's not all I want—"

His lips found hers abruptly as he rolled over her, pinning her down. Hard and determined, they covered her soft, dewy mouth in a kiss meant only to silence her. He didn't want to hear her pleading with him. There was no way in hell he could listen to her begging him to make love to her and not respond. He was only a man, with a man's weaknesses, a man's fierce desire.

At his sudden assault, Jess sighed and wrapped her arms around Devlin's neck, losing herself in the dark magic of his lips. *This* was what she wanted, what she needed. They could die tomorrow, but for now she would *live*. Their imminent danger only added a distinct urgency to the moment, to her need for him.

She returned his kiss almost desperately, with all the frustrated yearning he had aroused in her body during the past two weeks. She strained against him, the swollen tips of her breasts pressing against his hard chest, her hips seeking his instinctively and finding the hard tumescence that made him male.

By the time Devlin broke off the kiss and drew away, her breath was coming in soft pants, and so was his.

"That's enough," he said hoarsely.

"No . . . it's not."

"Jess. . . ." Almost of their own volition, his fingers moved to cradle her cheek. *Stop me, Jess, don't let this happen.* Against his will, he bent his head again.

He kissed her once more, knowing it was wrong. But he wouldn't, couldn't, deny her. He would give her what she wanted . . . at least some of what she wanted.

Praying he had the strength to stop with "some," he shifted his weight onto his elbow so that he had better freedom of movement. While he plundered her mouth with his tongue, his hand went under her skirt, pushing it up slowly, sliding along her cotton-covered legs to their juncture, to caress her feminine mound.

Jess made a soft choked sound deep in her throat, but she didn't pull away. Instead she arched her back, pressing up against his hand. Devlin felt his breath falter at the erotic movement, while the stiff bulge of his erection thickened and grew even harder. It was beguiling, her eagerness, her innocence, her untutored need.

"Part your legs a little, sweetheart . . . that's it."

His lips gently brushed her forehead as he slipped his fingers through the opening in her drawers, finding the triangle between her thighs, touching intimately.

Jess's gasp was loud in the dark tunnel, and then her breathing ceased altogether as his fingers tangled in the curls between her legs. He stroked the warm satin, making her quivering thighs open to him as he murmured soft, coaxing phrases against her temple.

"D-Devlin?" she rasped.

"Hush, sweet. Don't talk."

Purposefully, he continued his intimate ministrations, cupping her swollen, moist flesh, exploring the slick folds. Then his fingers sought out and found the damp, throbbing nubbin of flesh protected by the dense curls.

Jess thought she would die of the incredible sensations . . . but she didn't. Instead she whimpered and thrashed her head at the flaring pleasure that was spreading from his incredible touch to every throbbing point of her body.

Hearing her breathless little moans, Devlin closed his eyes and silently recited the litany that would be her salvation as well as his own. *She's a virgin, remember that. A sweet virgin. Not for you.*

He was glad of the darkness. Because of it, he wouldn't have to watch the flush of desire spread over her skin, the startled pleasure on her beautiful face when he brought her to climax. He could hardly bear it now. That slick, hot satin flesh was responding so erotically to his eager hand. She was unfolding before him like the petals of some rare flower. . . .

He stroked the tender morsel of flesh and clamped his teeth together against the savage need that was grinding through him. What he wouldn't give to bury himself inside her, to ride in the silky sheath that would be soft and wet and hot. He'd never known such sweet torment as this.

Moments later, he felt her wild clutching at his shoulders, and he increased the pressure, the rhythm, bringing her skillfully, sweetly, inescapably to fulfillment. Jess arched violently, crying out, clinging to Devlin as she experienced a fiery explosion so shattering that she felt herself coming apart.

"Easy . . . easy," he whispered in her ear as tenderly he gathered her close.

He held her shuddering body for long minutes, his breath fanning against her hair. Jess couldn't move. She lay limp and stunned in Devlin's arms, with her cheek on his chest, where she could hear the erratic beat of his heart. When eventually he kissed the top of her head softly and started to ease away from her body, she tightened her hold.

"Devlin," Jess said in a sweetly hoarse voice, "if you let me go now . . . you'll never find all the pieces."

He smiled in the darkness. His fingers stroked her neck lightly as he remained where he was, enduring the fierce ache of his own body.

"That's . . . what I've been missing?"

"That's what you've been missing."

She was silent for a moment. "That isn't all there is to it, is it?"

His chest shook as he laughed helplessly. "Sweet Jessie, did anyone never tell you that you shouldn't crush a man's ego?"

"Your ego doesn't crush, Devlin. Besides, you know perfectly well that what you did to me was . . . wonderful."

"Was it?"

"Yes."

"A man likes to be told when he's pleased a woman."

"Oh." There was a pause. "Devlin, you pleased me very much."

His chuckle whispered against her brow as he pressed his lips there. "Good."

"But I didn't please you."

"How do you know?"

"Flo told me . . . what's supposed to happen. I know there's more to it than what we just did, no matter how wonderful it was."

Devlin silently cursed Florence O'Malley; Jess silently blessed her. Because of Flo, at least she wasn't totally ignorant about men.

Her hand slid up from Devlin's shoulder and curled around the back of his neck. "Show me the rest," Jess whispered, drawing his head down to hers.

His kiss was slow, reluctant, as he tried to maintain some semblance of control, tried to remind himself that he had no right to do this. But her mouth was so soft and inviting. Her body so pliable. His mouth lingered and melted into hers, making Jess arch toward him.

His breath was harsh and uneven when he forced himself to draw away. "You're making it damn hard for me to be noble, angel."

"I don't want you to be noble. . . . I just want you to make love to me all the way. Are you supposed to keep all your clothes on?" Finding the lapel of his vest in the dark, she pushed it down over one shoulder.

"Confound it, Jess." Devlin grabbed her hand and held it tight as he raised himself up on one elbow. "You're determined to go through with this, aren't you?"

"Yes."

The word was soft, husky, unshakable.

Remembering how impossible it was to withstand Jess's determination when she'd made up her mind, Devlin clenched his jaw. He shouldn't listen to her. He had to be wise for the both of them.

And yet the thought of making her sexually responsive, of awakening all the exquisite, undiscovered passion in that lovely body was a hungry ache inside him, sharp and cutting.

His willpower fading, he let her draw his head down again, let her brush her pleading lips against his, let her beg him.

"I'm scared, Devlin," she whispered. "If we're going to die, I don't want to think about it. Help me forget. . . ."

All his fierce resolve melted. All his good intentions fled. This might be their last night on earth. He couldn't pass up not knowing what it was like to make love to this woman. He might be damned, but he couldn't do it.

His shaking fingers reached for her hairpins. He was a man who liked his woman's hair down, falling loose and free, and Jess's hair was magnificent. He didn't need the light to picture the glorious tawny mass. His fingers tangled in the silken tresses, a sensual experience that filled him with delight.

Then he reached for the buttons that ran down the front of her bodice. When she would have helped him, he bent to taste her lips briefly. "No, sweet . . . this is my pleasure. Just lie still and let me enjoy it. I intend to take my time."

Jess obeyed, trying to relax. Slowly, expertly, he began to remove the many layers of clothing that covered her lush body . . . the jacket-bodice of her gown . . . the over-skirt, gathered and looped up at the rear . . . the muslin waist . . . the underskirt . . . the wire-and-horsehair bustle that tied at her waist with tapes . . . the two petticoats . . . the camisole . . . the corset.

By the time he loosened the laces of her corset, Jess was stirring restlessly. "Devlin, do you have to go so slow?"

"Absolutely. It's called anticipation, Jess. It's half the pleasure."

"I want the other half."

Devlin gave a husky chuckle as he released her breasts from their tight confinement. "Don't be so impatient."

How could she not be impatient when he was driving her mad? She wanted him to hurry . . . she wanted *him*.

But she couldn't have him, not yet. He was determined to draw this out, to build the tension inside her to a fever pitch. She had asked him to make her forget her fear, and he meant to grant her wish. If this was their last night on earth, it would be beautiful. . . .

Disposing of the corset, he drew her chemise over her head. Jess gave a breathless murmur. The cool air felt incredibly arousing to her bare breasts. Then Devlin bent lazily to touch his lips to a throbbing nipple and Jess gasped.

"Luscious," he murmured with satisfaction. Deliberately, he licked a lean forefinger and languidly drew a wet teasing circle around each tight crest. Jess couldn't stifle a keening whimper.

She thought he would at least linger over her breasts, but his hands moved down to her legs, laboring over the myriad buttons on her high-topped shoes, drawing off her garters, and peeling down her stockings. Finally all that was left was her drawers.

He untied the drawstring slowly, provocatively. Jess held her breath. She didn't dare release it as he tugged the garment slowly over her hips and down her legs. She lay there tautly, naked in the darkness, her heart pounding. It was so decadent, so wanton, lying there with no clothes on when he was fully dressed.

Then he touched her, his hand moving in a lazy caress down her body.

"I've dreamed of this," Devlin said reverently, and Jess believed him. She had dreamed of this, too. She was still dreaming. She reached for him—

"No, lie still," he ordered. "I haven't even started."

In frustration, Jess dropped her arms. At a loss as to where her hands should go, she clenched them at her sides while he had his way. He took his time, his hands slowly, languorously learning her body . . . the lush breasts, the slender waist, the curvaceous hips, the long legs . . . the delicious stretches of silken skin in between.

"Devlin . . . you're tormenting me."

"That's the whole idea."

"I want to do it to you, too."

"Be my guest."

She hesitated, not knowing how to begin. "You have all your clothes on," she said finally.

"So what are you going to do about it?"

Her body throbbing, she sat up slowly. "I guess take them off?"

Rising to her knees, she leaned over him and tugged at

his garments, undressing him by feel, first his vest, then his shirt. She paused when it came to his trousers, though.

"Want me to do the rest?"

Her cheeks flushed. It was absurd to suddenly feel so shy, but she was. She was grateful that Devlin seemed to sense her uncertainty. "Yes, please."

She heard him move then. Heard his boots drop to the rock floor one by one. The soft rustle of socks and trousers and long johns as they left his body. Another rustle as he stretched out again on the makeshift bed. She knew he was waiting.

"Jess, you don't have to do this," he said tenderly.

"But I want to."

She reached out blindly, finding his shoulder with her trembling hand. His skin was warm, almost hot to the touch. Tentatively, she explored its smooth satiny texture, feeling the curve of bone and sinewy muscle beneath. Gathering courage, she moved slowly on to the bramble of dark hair on his chest. His masculine body was so different from hers, harder, rougher . . . fascinating.

"I wish I could see you," she said in frustration.

"See me with your hands."

Emboldened, Jess moved her hands lower, to the hard, flat planes of his abdomen. He tightened; she could feel the muscles of his stomach bunching beneath her palm. His reaction gave her a totally unexpected taste of feminine power. It was a heady feeling to know she could affect him with a mere touch.

She skipped a certain part of him and advanced to his legs next. His powerful horseman's thighs were corded with well-honed muscle and dusted with hair. She stopped there, not having the nerve to go on.

She was almost grateful for the hand that reached out to capture hers and gently guide her to the hard, pulsing length of him. Shock and excitement flooded her at the forbidden contact. His masculinity was thick and heavy with arousal. She trembled at the enormous size of him.

Then she felt him shudder against her.

"Did I hurt you?" Jess asked, her voice soft with alarm.

She tried to pull away, but Devlin held her palm pressed against him.

"You didn't hurt me in the least, love. It feels exquisite."

Jess frowned doubtfully. "You're so *large*."

Devlin caught his breath on a gasp of laughter. "Some women would say that's good."

"Why?"

"Because I can fill you better when I'm inside you."

Inside her? Just the thought of having that swollen rigid length inside her body set an ache throbbing in the feminine recess between her thighs. "I don't see how you can fit."

Again the choked laughter. "I will."

Timorously she traced the unfamiliar length, touching him, discovering him—the hard shaft that felt like hot satin over steel, the swollen sacs that fit in her hand like warm plums. With growing confidence, she learned the shape and texture and contours of his powerful, sleek body, while he encouraged her exploration in a rough-velvet voice that could woo a woman's heart from her breast.

Finally she drew her hand back and gave a short, embarrassed laugh. "I'm not very good at this."

"That's debatable," Devlin said in a raw voice. "But I'm glad you don't have much experience."

"I don't have *any* experience. Have you known a lot of women?"

"None like you."

It was a smooth, polished reply that really was no answer. Jess was certain he'd been with countless other women, but just now it didn't seem to matter. Not when Devlin was pulling her down to lie beside him. Not when the sensation of having his body, strong and muscled and unclothed, against hers was driving every conscious thought from her head.

The hot flesh of his broad chest pressing against her sensitive nipples, the probing heat of his maleness against her stomach, thrilled and aroused her. And his lips. . . . He kissed her throat, her collarbone, the rising swell of her breasts, his whiskered jaw warm and abrasive, making her skin prickle and tingle as he trailed a fiery path downward.

His hands came up to caress her naked back as his feathery kisses descended. She could feel his breath, hot and heavy on her breasts, on her nipples, now tight and hurting. Then his mouth closed over a taut bud. Desire pierced her, its depth and intensity shocking her. Heat centered itself, throbbing and moist, between her thighs, making her whimper with need.

Devlin heard the soft moaning sound with satisfaction and another feeling akin to relief. He had pleasured a lot of women in his life, but he couldn't remember the last time he'd wanted a woman like this, couldn't remember that he ever had. Just now he felt like a boy experiencing his first time—nervous, excited, incredibly aroused, afraid of doing the wrong thing. None of the women in his past had required such care. He wanted it to be good for Jessica. He wanted it to be much more than good.

Calling on every lover's skill he possessed, he suckled her nipples until Jess was arching her back wildly. And still he didn't stop. He caressed her breasts until they were tender and swollen and tingling from his kisses, taking intense pleasure from the pleasure he was giving her. Returning to her mouth then, he kissed her with more urgency this time, his tongue entering her warm depths with the same thrust he longed to use elsewhere.

The velvet rapier of his tongue met and tangled with hers as his arousing hand moved down to her stomach. The lean fingers spread there and stroked her taut flat belly, brushed downward along the smooth skin of her thighs, glided slowly upward again through the downy curls at the portal of her womanhood.

Jess caught her breath, expecting the same incredible ministrations that he'd performed earlier. But this time was totally different. Instead, he slid a finger inside her, *deep* inside her. Her breath spiraled away from her, out of pace with her body.

His fingers were dark magic.

"Dev-linnnnn. . . ." The word was a keening gasp.

"Hush, darlin'," he murmured seductively, caressingly. He nuzzled her neck, all the while continuing the slow deft movements of his fingers deep inside her, readying her for his invasion.

She bucked and writhed.

"Easy, baby."

His hand withdrew, to her immense dismay. But before she could protest, he fitted his knee between her legs, pressing against her fiercely aching feminine flesh.

His lips were velvety and hot as he lightly kissed her face, delicately feathering his lips across her chin, her flushed cheeks, her fevered brow. His erotic tenderness drove her wild.

"Devlin . . . I can't bear it."

"Yes, you can, love."

No, she *couldn't*. She felt as if she were suffocating with longing. She wanted him to ease the tight ache inside her, wanted things from him she couldn't even begin to imagine.

And he only seemed bent on making her longing worse. Purposefully, he worked his lips, his tongue, in a sensual accompaniment to the slow, rhythmic motion his hips initiated. The hot, hard knot of desire inside her tightened with each tantalizing, tormenting movement of his body.

Finally, when she thought she would go mad with the craving need, he shifted his weight, pulling away briefly.

"Devlin?" she said shakily.

"Don't you think it's about time you started calling me Garrett? I'd say we're a bit beyond the formality of last names."

"Garrett . . . I'll kill you if you stop now."

A melting tenderness infused his laughter. "I'm not about to stop." Bracing himself on his forearms, he covered her, spreading her thighs wide.

Jess ceased breathing.

He entered her with exquisite slowness, parting the fiery, aching folds between her legs. She felt her flesh stretching, then a brief moment of pain as the feminine barrier split.

She stiffened . . . but then Devlin was kissing her deeply, taking away the pain, taking away even her breath, making it a part of his own. Otherwise, he was completely still, holding himself inside her, content to wait until she grew accustomed to his spearing invasion.

"You okay, angel?" he whispered finally against her lips.

Jess exhaled in a soft, contented sigh. "Yes." It was so natural to be with him like this, to have him fill her. Yet it wasn't enough. The burning need had returned with devastating force.

"Please, Devlin . . ." she murmured, not even knowing what she was pleading for.

"Garrett."

"Garrett, please . . ."

His hips began to move then, with restrained passion and devastating tenderness. Slowly, slowly thrusting . . . slowly, slowly withdrawing. Again . . . again . . . until Jess instinctively caught his sure rhythm. Until the shy undulations of her body became a bolder demand for fulfillment. Until the pleasure became so exquisite it was a pain of its own.

Jess clung to him, her nails digging half-moons into his bare, sweat-dewed back, as a hot, bright feeling burgeoned inside her, heating every nerve, every pore, every sensate inch of her body. She couldn't bear it. This pleasure was too keen, too fierce to be borne.

"Noooo . . ." she whimpered in protest.

"Yes," Devlin demanded, "yes, love." He felt the tremors begin inside her, felt her shake with raw passion, and helplessly the spasms became his own. His body convulsed, a vast and wild sweetness exploding through him like fire. Shuddering, he poured himself into her, losing himself, his harsh, guttural moan mingling with her strangled cry, shattering the silence.

The echoes of their passion faded slowly, leaving behind only the erratic, rasping sounds of gasped breaths. Slowly in the darkness sanity returned and Devlin managed to shift his weight so that he was no longer crushing her. But that was all he was capable of doing.

Long moments later, he stirred again, lowering his lips to her swollen mouth, tasting it gently. "Are you all right?"

Not answering, Jess lay beneath him, numb, limp, and more complete than she'd ever been in her life. She'd never felt so *right*. Devlin had made her feel like a woman ... desirable, passionate, enticing. She'd never felt so deliciously feminine, so *wanted*. . . .

"Jessica?" His lips moved lightly over her flushed face, over her throat where the pulse still hammered wildly. "Jess, are you awake?"

"No ... I'm not even alive."

His hoarse chuckle reverberated softly in the darkness. When he rolled onto his side and gathered her in his arms, Jess went willingly, her face buried in the smooth, sweaty silk of his bare shoulder, her legs threaded with the long, corded length of his.

She had never known such passion existed. She'd never even *imagined* the possibility. She sighed with exhausted pleasure. She was safe in the arms of this potent, beautiful man. Safe and cherished.

It had been worth it, throwing away her innocence. If she died tomorrow, she would go content.

Chapter 11

S he didn't die, but neither did her contentment last.

At the first sounds of rescue, the pleasant dreams Jess had been having dissolved, and she came awake with a start. In the pitch-blackness she could hear the faint but unmistakable clink of metal on rock. *Men digging.*

Jessica stiffened.

"Ah, help is at hand," Devlin murmured in her ear with a sleepy yawn. "What did I tell you?"

Jess stirred uneasily. She'd slept for a time in Devlin's arms, her body pulled tightly against his, warm under the layers of petticoats and skirts. But their nakedness now seemed scandalous, wanton. The danger wasn't entirely over, but it was likely that they would live to see another sunrise. *And she would have to face Devlin.*

The realization of what she'd done, what they'd done together in the darkness, swept through her with humiliating force. Dear Lord, had she really thrown herself at him and begged him to make love to her?

Abruptly, Jess untangled herself from Devlin and sat up, clutching a petticoat to her bare breasts. The unfamiliar tenderness of her nipples made her wince. She shut her eyes. It had really happened. Last night she had lost her innocence. Devlin had awakened her body to passion, had made her fully a woman. The twinging ache between her thighs attested to that undeniable fact, while her mouth was swollen from his caresses.

167

"We have to get dressed," she blurted out, her voice unnaturally high and edged with panic.

"There's no hurry . . . it's still the middle of the night. And clearing away the rubble will likely take hours."

His hand reached out to stroke her naked back in reassurance, but Jess pulled away, her face flaming in embarrassment. She had been so bold, so brazen last night. Devlin must think her incredibly cheap, no better than the worst sort of saloon girl. She wanted to sink through the rock floor.

She heard Devlin stretch lazily, and glanced involuntarily over her shoulder just as he struck a match. The tunnel was flooded with flickering golden light. In alarm Jess averted her gaze, though not before she glimpsed a powerful male chest and shoulders rippling with lean muscle. Below the waist he was buried in petticoats—thank God—but that didn't detract one bit from his stunning masculinity.

He lit a candle, and then there was silence.

"Jess. . . ." His tone was soft, hesitant, regretful.

She didn't want to hear what he was going to say. She didn't want him telling her that what they'd done was wrong. She didn't want him to make light of it, either, or brush off with a laugh what had been the most incredible experience of her life. She didn't want him to say anything at all.

"I hope they get us out in time for breakfast," Jess forced herself to exclaim cheerfully. "I'm starving to death."

She felt Devlin's intent gaze burning into her back, but she couldn't look at him. Instead, she fumbled for her chemise.

He gave a soft sigh. Without speaking again, he rose and pulled on his trousers and left her alone, allowing her privacy to wash. When he returned, he helped her dress, making a game of finding their numerous articles of clothing that he'd strewn around the floor when he'd made love to her.

"This has to be," Devlin said with dry amusement as he

reached for her corset, "among my more unique experiences ... playing lady's maid in a mine cave."

Jess bit her lip. It was obvious Devlin had a good deal of experience playing with women's clothing, for he knew just how to tie the laces of her corset, and in just which order each garment went. He was proficient and casual about dressing her, just as he'd been proficient and casual about comforting a hysterical woman last night ... and making love to her. What had been unique and special for her—her introduction to womanhood—had been nothing in the least extraordinary for him.

When they were both dressed, and she had brought some semblance of order to her wild, sleep-tumbled hair, he snuffed the light again to save oxygen and fed her bites of biscuits and ham in the dark. He was tenderness itself, never once mentioning the intimacies they'd shared. But his discretion didn't assuage Jessica's conscience in the slightest, or relieve her acute embarrassment. Devlin had told her they'd be rescued. He'd also told her that one day she would find a man who would give her the family she wanted. He couldn't have made it plainer. *He* wasn't that man. Her face burned in remembrance.

She couldn't blame him for what had happened. He had tried to refuse her advances, but she hadn't heeded him. Now all she could do was pretend their lovemaking had never happened, and instead concentrate on stopping Burke and his hired killers.

She had a long while to contemplate her rashness, for it took even more time than Devlin had predicted for the debris to be cleared. The shouts of men outside the blocked tunnel grew louder as the long night wore on. After several hours, when they judged it to be near daybreak, Jess and Devlin moved to the upper level, a safe distance from the cave-in in case more rubble was loosened in the digging. There they waited, sitting quietly, not touching, not talking, simply hoping.

It was already morning before a hole was opened about the size of man's head. Jess blinked at the blinding daylight and nearly sobbed when she heard Clem's ragged voice calling to her.

"Jessie? Jessie, you in there?"

"Yes! We're here. Please, hurry and get us out!"

"Godamighty! She's alive!"

She heard the cheers that rose from outside, and the frantic digging that followed. Clem's litany of foul oaths as he cussed every boulder and piece of rock in his way was like angels' music to her ears.

It seemed like an eternity before the opening was large enough to permit a person to squeeze past the fallen timber that braced one wall. Finally the digging stopped. With Devlin helping push from behind, Jess crawled out into the open, skinning her palms and knees.

She was dragged the last few feet by a dozen masculine hands, and then pulled to her feet and crushed in a violent bear hug. Hardly able to stand, Jess gulped deep, urgent breaths of sweet air and clung to Clem.

She didn't realize she was crying until Clem drew back, his own grizzled face wet with tears. "Dammitall, Jess, you sceered ten years off my life."

"Mine, too." She angled her head frantically to regard what had been the entrance to the Wildstar mine. "Devlin's still in there . . . please, help him," she pleaded, unnecessarily. An army of grim-faced miners was already hard at work, rescuing the other survivor of the explosion.

"Jess . . ." Her father's choked voice sounded from a short distance away, making Jess whip her head around. He was trying to climb down from the back of a buckboard wagon, she saw in dismay, while Flo was trying just as hard to hold him back.

Shaking off Clem's hold, Jess stumbled over to her father. And then Riley was taking her face between his calloused hands and showering her with desperate kisses, and she was laughing and crying and babbling. "Riley, you shouldn't be out of bed. . . . Flo, you should have stopped him. . . . Riley, don't . . . your wound."

"Forget about my wound! I'll be fine. What about you? God, Jess, are you all right?"

"Yes . . . just shaken up a bit—"

"What in tarnation happened?" Clem interrupted as he lumbered up behind her.

"Somebody set a fire in the tunnel and then blew up the entrance while we were inside."

The mule skinner's curse was low and fluent, while Riley's face went paper-white.

"That does it," Riley muttered under his breath.

Before Jess could ask what he meant, Devlin came to stand beside her. She glanced up to find him searching her face, his gray eyes clouded with smoky intensity in the early morning sunlight.

She didn't know where to look. It had all seemed so clear to her last night in the dark. She had needed him so desperately. She'd wanted him to drive away her fear, wanted the simple reassurance that she was still alive, the comfort of his touch. But now . . . she didn't know how to act, or what to say.

As if he knew how confused and vulnerable she felt, he smiled a quick mercurial smile that held a bewitching masculine charm. Jess felt her heart jump to her throat. Dusty, unshaven, weary, he was still the most stunningly attractive man she'd ever known. She couldn't look at him without remembering the possession of that hard expert body, without a dozen shocking, vividly carnal images playing in her head. It was all she could do to drag her gaze away.

She had to get hold of herself. She had to at least try to give the appearance of normality around Devlin. *Devlin*. He'd asked her to call him Garrett, but she couldn't—wouldn't—do it. Being on a first-name basis with him would fairly shriek inpropriety, and she wanted nothing to suggest how familiar, how intimate, they'd been last night. Addressing him as "Devlin" was much wiser, especially if she was to keep up the pretense that nothing had happened between them. "Devlin" was safer, more distant—or at least it gave the illusion of distance.

Glad that her father had kept his arm wrapped tightly around her waist, Jess chose her words carefully. "Riley,

Devlin saved my life. I would have gone crazy in there if it hadn't been for him."

"Thank you, Mr. Devlin." The unashamed quaver in the older man's voice indicated how precious his daughter was to him. "I don't know how I can ever repay you."

"You don't have to," Devlin replied, his expression grim. "If I hadn't been careless, they never would have gotten close enough to use that dynamite."

"You mean if *I* hadn't been careless," Jess said quietly. "You don't have to take the blame for my mistakes, Devlin. You weren't even on duty yet."

An oppressive silence settled over the small group.

"Well," Flo exclaimed, breaking the sudden tension. "Give me a hug, Jess, and then let's get you back home and put to bed. There's a pile of work that sure isn't gettin' done on it's own."

Devlin's jaw tightened at Flo's insensitivity. Reminding Jess of unfinished work was like waving a red flag in front of a bull. She certainly didn't need to be burdened with the boardinghouse after she'd nearly lost her life. But going to sleep in the middle of the day was against her religion, it seemed, and she protested with automatic vehemence.

"Mebbe you should, Jessie," Clem observed. "You look plum wore out. Mebbe you oughta have that sawbones Wheeler take a look at you."

"I'll be all right! I don't need Doc Wheeler, and I don't need to be pampered."

You do, angel, Devlin thought. *I've never seen any woman who needed it more.*

"You'll go to bed, Jess," her father said in his sternest voice. "You've done enough. Clem's staying to shore up the mine entrance, and we're going home."

Wearily, looking as if she hadn't the energy to fight, Jess gave in. She helped Clem get Riley resettled in the back of the buckboard, while Flo climbed into the driver's seat.

Devlin collected the horses he and Jess had ridden last night and followed, feeling a smoldering rage at Burke and a disgust at his own unfamiliar helplessness. Despite all his experience with the opposite sex, he didn't quite know how to deal with this situation, with Jess. He'd felt her withdrawal the moment they'd awakened, but he hadn't known the right thing to say to ease the tension, the awkwardness. For once he'd been bereft of words. At a time when it had never seemed more important to strike just the right note.

In spite of all his past affairs and involvements, he had never experienced anything quite like the fierce ecstasy of helping Jess blossom from an innocent girl into a sensual, sexually responsive woman. He'd felt such an overwhelming rush of tenderness, his heart *ached* with it. He hadn't expected, either, the sweet languor of lying woven together afterward. Usually he merely tolerated such closeness from his lovers; women needed the reassurance of being held in the aftermath of passion, and he was nothing if not considerate of his bed partners. Yet he hadn't known how to handle Jess—her shyness, her uncertainty, her regret.

Nor had he known how to silence the warning bells clanging in his head. He was getting in too deep with Jess, Devlin realized with a feeling close to panic. He was running the risk of letting his heart get sliced up again, by a young woman who'd never given even the slightest hint that her affections might be engaged. In fact, Jess seemed determined to forget that last night had ever happened.

He couldn't forget, though. Not the sweetness of her passion, or his own guilt. He had taken her innocence, the innocence she should have saved for her husband. There was also the possibility that he had made her pregnant.

He tried to tell himself there had been extenuating circumstances last night. He'd warned Jess she would feel differently in the morning, and he'd done his best . . . almost his best . . . to refuse her. But she hadn't listened. Instead, she'd insisted she knew what she was doing. And he'd wanted to believe her. She was old enough to know what she wanted. . . .

There was no need for him to flay his conscience, really. He was blowing this out of proportion. Jess had been

terrified and had turned to him for human comfort and assurance, that was all. And he had offered it.

So why then did he feel guilty as hell? And why was he
running scared?

It took two hours for Flo to get Jess cleaned up and fed
and put to bed in her own bedroom. For the entire two
hours Devlin found himself fighting the urge to send Flo
away and take over. *He* wanted to be the one caring for
Jessica.

And that was the problem. He already cared too much.

His fierce possessiveness shouldn't have surprised him.
It was perfectly reasonable that he should feel protective
of Jess after all that had happened between them. But he
didn't have the right to perform such intimacies as bathing
her or tucking her into bed. Not unless he intended to
make it a lifetime commitment by offering to become her
husband—and he wasn't willing to risk suffering that kind
of pain again. And so he took his own bath and shaved
and dressed, and then joined Riley in the kitchen to eat the
breakfast Flo had prepared.

As soon as Jess had fallen asleep, Flo left for the boardinghouse. Jessica's father sat at the kitchen table, not
touching his food. He wasn't in dire *physical* pain, Devlin
was convinced. Riley could get around if he moved
slowly, and his injured body seemed to have held up under
the strain of trekking up the mountainside and the terrible
wait to find out if his daughter was alive. But his conscience was another story. He looked like a man at the end
of his rope.

Respecting the man's privacy, Devlin finished eating in
silence, then leaned back in his chair, nursing a cup of coffee.

"I nearly got her killed," Riley said finally, to no one in
particular. He dropped his head in his hands.

Devlin held his tongue, unwilling to argue the point.
Sommers's past determination to hold on to his mine at all
costs had led to a feud that was now out of control. Last
night he had nearly paid a dear price for his single-

mindedness. The question was whether he considered the price *too* dear.

Devlin had already decided what action he would take regarding Burke—he'd had a long time to think about it while trapped in the Wildstar with Jess—but he wanted to be certain he hadn't been mistaken in his judgment of Riley Sommers.

Sommers didn't let him down.

"I'm gonna sell out to Burke, like he wanted. I'll go down and file for a quit claim deed tomorrow morning."

"You're going to give up now?"

"I've got to," Riley said hoarsely, wearily. "I can't risk my daughter's life any longer. If it was just me . . . But Jess . . . I can't do it. I should never have let it drag on this long."

"What would you say if I could get Burke and his hired guns to back off?"

Riley raised his head sharply. "How?"

"Never mind how right now. What would you do?"

"Even then—" He shook his head. "It wouldn't matter now. This last trick of Burke's 'll break me. Do you know how much it'd take to dig out and rebuild?"

Devlin sipped his coffee before he answered thoughtfully, "Both tunnels are still standing and probably structurally sound. The major damage was done at the mouth. I'd say a few thousand should do it."

Riley snorted. "Might as well go wishing on stars. I couldn't even raise five hundred."

"I'd be willing to supply you the working capital to rebuild."

The other man's brows drew together in a frown. When he looked as if he was about to refuse, Devlin added casually, "And another fifty thousand to get your operation in a position where you can compete with the other consolidated mining outfits."

"Where," Riley said slowly, "in the name of Pete would you get that kind of money?"

He smiled at the suspicion in the older man's tone. "I

haven't robbed a bank, if that's what worries you. Have you heard of the Homestake Syndicate?"

"You mean the Black Hills' Homestake? Who hasn't heard of it?"

"I was in the Dakota Territory in '77 and bought into the Homestake. I own a small interest."

Riley simply stared. "You own part of the largest gold mine in the country?"

"A small part."

"How small?"

"Enough to make me a millionaire several times over."

Riley's slow exhalation was long and loud.

"I just have one question," he said finally. "If you're so blamed rich, then what on God's green earth are you doing here?"

"I followed a lead. The man I killed last week—Zeke McRoy—was rumored to be running with an outlaw gang from this territory."

Keeping the story short, Devlin told the older man about the robberies of the Colorado Central and his own determination to stop them.

Riley nodded. "I heard about those holdups. Had a lot of folks here real upset. But that still doesn't explain why you ever let Jess talk you into guarding our mine in the first place. You sure don't need the money, like I first thought."

"Have you ever tried to say no to your daughter? I don't think she understands the word."

Riley smiled briefly, for the first time that day. "I see your point."

"Besides, my hiring on with you gave me a good reason to ask around about McRoy without raising eyebrows."

"You sure picked the hard way to ask questions."

"I suppose so."

Draining the last of his coffee, Devlin went to the stove and poured himself another cup. When he held up the pot, Riley shook his head. He still looked somewhat dazed, as if he didn't know quite how to act after all the revelations he'd heard. Devlin decided now was the time to speak up.

Settling himself at the table again, he met Riley's gaze. "You have at least one other option I'd like you to consider. Instead of selling out to Burke, you could let me buy in."

"What," Riley said cautiously, "did you have in mind?"

"A simple transaction. I propose that you sell me a quarter interest of the Wildstar mine for say, fifty thousand dollars. That should give you the working capital to rebuild and to increase your crew size to two shifts, plus cover the expense of expanding your tunnels for the first year or so."

Riley looked uncomfortable. "Mr. Devlin, I won't be less than honest with you. You could buy the whole damed mine twice over for that much money."

"I don't want the whole mine. I merely want the leverage to deal with Burke. Part ownership will give me that."

"You don't even want controlling interest?" he asked in disbelief.

"No, I don't want that, either. I have too many investments to oversee as it is. I don't need another headache."

"Still . . . fifty thousand is a powerful lot of money. I don't know if I could stomach being that beholden to you."

Devlin flashed his most charming smile, determined to overcome any objections, even though he liked Sommers better for not jumping at such a lucrative deal. Integrity wasn't an abundant commodity these days, and it was refreshing every time he found it.

"Mr. Sommers, I already give to my favorite charities, and you aren't one of them. This is purely a business deal. And I don't do business halfway. If I become involved in your mining operation, I want it run correctly. With the right backing, I believe you can turn a good profit with the Wildstar. You can pay me twenty-five percent of net earnings after the first year, which will give me an adequate return on my investment."

Riley was still looking unhappy. "Those are mighty generous terms, Mr. Devlin. I just wish I understood why you're willing to offer them."

What could he say? Please, let me make amends for taking your daughter's virginity? Maybe that will help assuage my guilt?

At least it would keep Jess from having to scrub floors for the rest of her life. And it would provide for her if there should happen to be a child.

In any case, although Jessica was his main consideration, she wasn't the sole reason he was proposing to throw away good money on a possibly worthless mine, and pressing it on a man who was too proud to take anything he didn't earn by his own hard sweat. Given the choice between an honest underdog and a shady capitalist, he would back the underdog any day of the year.

"I don't like letting men like Burke win," Devlin replied instead. "He's already gone about two steps too far, and he won't go a third if I can help it."

Sommers wasn't buying it. "This never has been your fight. You'd do better to just walk away."

"Mr. Sommers, when people try to kill me, I get a bit upset. When I'm forced to go back on my word, I like it even less. I promised you I'd protect your daughter, and she nearly died. I'm not about to walk away now. I'm surprised you would consider it, either. I didn't think you were the kind of man to accept defeat."

"I told you, it's Jess I'm worried about."

"So am I. But I'll handle Burke and his hired guns, this time for good."

"You mind telling me how you plan to do that?"

"By making it in his best interest to leave the Wildstar alone." And he would fight this war on his own terms, using all the weapons at his disposal, not just the pitiful resources Riley Sommers possessed. "If it would make you more comfortable, we'll draw up a contract specifying that you can buy back my quarter interest a year from now for the same price, plus ten percent. Once the Wildstar has begun showing a profit, you shouldn't have any trouble with that financing."

Watching Devlin closely, Riley rubbed his whiskered jaw. "You look like an honest man."

"Thank you," he said with a wry twist of his lips.

"No offense meant. I just need to be sure I'm doing the right thing. It's my daughter's future, maybe her life we're talking about."

Devlin waited.

"You wouldn't maybe be doing this for Jess, would you?"

It was as close to asking for a declaration of intentions as a father could get without coming out and demanding one.

"That has something to do with it," Devlin said carefully. "I admire your daughter, Mr. Sommers. She has more determination than any woman I've ever known—and more courage as well—but sometimes hardheadedness isn't enough. She needs my help, whether she realizes it or not. And so do you. Selling me an interest in the Wildstar happens to be the easiest way to achieve our mutual goals. Either way, I'm involved for good. Burke has dynamited his last competitor."

"I guess I'd be a fool to turn down your offer then," Riley said finally.

Devlin flashed his slow smile. "You don't look like a fool."

"Well, then, maybe we should shake on it." Riley reached out his hand—gingerly, because of his wound—and Devlin took it.

"Think you could call me Garrett, partner?"

The older man grinned. "Sure, if you'll call me Riley."

"Good," Devlin said, satisfied. "If you're agreeable, we can go down to the claims office this afternoon and fill out the paperwork."

"Today's Sunday. The claims office will be closed."

"Then we'll have it opened. That's one of the advantages of having wealth. You can afford to do business on your own terms. I only have a few thousand cash on hand, but I can wire my bank in Chicago to transfer the rest of the money here."

"Lord, I forgot about the money." Riley suddenly looked a bit overwhelmed, like he couldn't believe his good fortune. "I don't know what I'll do with so much all at one time."

"You'll figure it out." Devlin took a sip of coffee. "In addition to increasing the size of the mine crew, I'd also like to hire some help for Jess at the boardinghouse. She's working herself into the ground."

Riley's wondering look vanished as he shook his head firmly. "That'll have to be between you and Jess. I don't interfere with her business." He paused. "Jess doesn't know about you, does she?"

"About my having money? No. I didn't see a compelling reason to tell her." He didn't explain *why* he hadn't wanted Jess to know about his wealth. But he doubted Riley would take kindly to hearing such suspicions voiced about his daughter. Especially when all the evidence suggested they might be unfounded. Jess had yet to respond like any other woman of Devlin's acquaintance—a trait he found both refreshing and quite often infuriating.

"She won't be too happy to learn she's been cottoning up to a rich fellow," Riley commented.

The memory of just how Jess had cottoned up to him last night gave Devlin a distinctly lustful surge of pleasure, a feeling that was immediately tempered by sobering reality. Last night had been a profound mistake. It would have been far better for both of them if she had stayed a million miles away from him. Just as it probably would have been better if he'd told her who he was. "What exactly does she have against rich fellows?"

"Well, you see, she hasn't had too many good experiences with them over the years. Burke especially hasn't set much of an example. And I guess maybe I encouraged her . . . I taught her to believe that having money doesn't mean as much as having an upstanding character. Plus, her ma told her watch out for—" Riley suddenly faltered, his face coloring.

"I've heard the stories," Devlin said gently. "From what I can tell, your wife was a wonderful woman."

"She was. And I was damned lucky to get her. She

might of been in love with Burke, but she married me," Riley added, his tone defensive.

Devlin remained silent. He had put some of the pieces together before now. Jenny Ann had chosen Sommers over Burke, not because of love but because of what Burke wouldn't offer her. Marriage and family. *Just what Jess wanted.* Devlin shied away from the thought. It seemed odd, though, that Jenny Ann was still the cause of this intense rivalry. Ashton Burke must have felt something stronger for her than simple lust to still be holding a grudge after all these years.

Apparently Riley was remembering those years, for his look grew distant. "I did my best for her, even if I couldn't give her any of the fancy things she deserved. If only I could've made that big strike before she died . . . I could've given her everything Burke was able to."

The pain in his voice made Devlin uncomfortable. Finishing his coffee, he rose, thinking it kinder to leave Riley alone with his memories.

"If you'll excuse me?" he said politely. "I'd like to catch up on some of the sleep I missed last night. Will you wake me in a few hours so we can take care of our business?"

"Sure." Riley looked up, his brow wrinkling. "Are you gonna tell me what you aim to do?"

Devlin's smile was not a pleasant one. "It's simple. First I'm going to get the legal right to carry on this war *my* way. Then I'm going to have a little talk with Ashton Burke."

Chapter 12

The darkness was quiet and soothing. When Devlin brought a cheroot to his lips, an orange glow faintly lit up the huge bedchamber. Burke should arrive home any time now.

Devlin was actually looking forward to the confrontation. Until now he'd been hampered in his actions, unable to use the vast wealth he'd accumulated over the past ten years, or the power he'd grown accustomed to wielding—because he'd wanted to keep his real purpose quiet. But now he had little to lose, with the outlaws' trail cold. And now he was every bit as determined as Jessica to terminate Burke's career of intimidation and destruction.

He glanced absently around the shadowed bedroom as he waited. Not ostentatious but certainly opulent, with its crystal globe hanging lamps, satin gilt wallpaper, thick patterned carpet, and forest-green tapestry drapes. The huge four-poster bed was a masterpiece of polished walnut and rich brocade, while the comfortable, overstuffed armchair that Devlin was sitting in was covered with fine leather. Ashton Burke had excellent taste.

The silver king also had no apparent qualms about displaying his wealth. His mansion was staffed with an army of liveried servants, including footmen and a butler.

Devlin had met the butler earlier tonight. It had been a simple matter to learn of Burke's plans for the evening from Lena, and then confirm them with a formal call at

Burke's residence in Georgetown. According to the butler, the Englishman was attending the opera.

It had been more simple still to wait an hour, then climb up to a second-story window under cover of darkness and let himself in. Much of the household was asleep now, for it was well after midnight.

Some ten minutes later Devlin heard the rattle of carriage wheels on the street below. Eventually the murmur of voices reached him, then the sound of footsteps climbing the stairs. Finally the bedroom door swung open.

The room suddenly brightened as a fair-haired gentleman in elegant evening dress entered carrying a lamp. He shut the door, set the lamp down on a small table, and began tugging at his cravat.

Devlin thumbed back the hammer of his Colt.

At the ominous click, Burke froze.

"No sudden moves," Devlin said softly.

Slowly the Englishman turned his head to stare into the shadows at the intruder. Gesturing with his revolver, Devlin indicated the adjacent chair. "Please join me for a moment, Mr. Burke."

"At gunpoint? Is that really necessary?"

"I have something to say to you, and I want to be certain I have your undivided attention."

After a slight hesitation, Burke moved to the other chair and sat down, crossing one elegantly clad leg over the other at the knee. "Very well, I'm listening."

Devlin had to admire the man's coolness, but it had the effect of raising his own blood temperature. He thought of Jess the night of the cave-in—her terror, her vulnerability, her surrender—and he wanted to rearrange Burke's face with his fists. Violently.

Resisting the temptation, Devlin lowered the revolver and laid it carefully on his lap. "I'm here to discuss the little accident at the Wildstar last night."

"I heard about that. Yes indeed, dangerous thing, dynamite. My condolences to you and Miss Sommers. It cannot have been pleasant, being trapped underground."

"Spare me the bullshit, Burke. You and I both know you arranged it."

There was a moment of silence.

"Very well, Mr. Devlin. Why don't you come to the point of your visit?"

"I'm here to issue a warning. I'm now a partner in the Wildstar mine."

There was another pause. "And this should concern me?"

"If you have half the intelligence I credit you with, yes. Fighting me will not be the same as fighting Riley Sommers and his daughter."

"No? And why not?"

"Because I can afford to be ruthless. And I've had a good teacher. You told me you knew a railroad baron in Chicago by the name of Devlin. C.E. has a reputation for being remorseless in his business dealings. In fact, he could put even you to shame. I know because he's my father."

"Indeed."

The remark was uttered without inflection, but Devlin could almost see Burke's sharp mind churning as he digested this new information and recalculated the odds of success against someone of C. E. Devlin's stature.

"My father taught me a great deal about winning regardless of the cost," Devlin said levelly. "And on this issue I intend to win."

"I suppose you intend to tell me what it is you think you'll be winning?"

"If you insist. I can think of only two reasons why you would want the Wildstar mine so badly that you would kill for it."

"I did not try to *kill* for it, Mr. Devlin."

Even as he issued the denial, Burke shifted in his chair—a gesture which, if made by any other man, would have been called squirming. He actually looked distressed, Devlin realized with surprise. Was it possible the mine explosion had been an accident after all?

"The first," he continued, "is that you suspect the Wildstar of bearing rich ore. If, let's say, you happened to deliberately conceal your knowledge at the time of purchase so you could acquire the property at a fraction of its real value—and if, furthermore, you used intimidation tactics to coerce the mine owner into selling to you . . . Well, you don't need me to tell you that any court in the country would consider that fraud."

"And the second reason?"

"Which is the most likely one, in my opinion. You've struck a rich vein in the Lady J mine which belongs to the Wildstar."

When Burke remained conspicuously silent, Devlin flashed a cool smile. "I keep a staff of expensive legal talent on retainer, and they tell me some interesting facts about Colorado mining law. Whoever owns the apex of a vein owns the silver. If a lode surfaces on a man's claim, he can follow it all the way to China if he chooses, even if it passes out of bounds of his claim. Even if it crosses several claims. No one else can legally touch it. I think the Wildstar owns the apex of a vein you struck, which makes it Wildstar silver you're mining. That's why you wanted to buy out Sommers."

Burke laced his fingers in his lap. "I suppose you have proof of these farfetched allegations?"

"No. But I don't imagine you're willing to let a reputable surveyor into the Lady J to inspect your workings in order to disprove my allegations, either."

When Burke didn't answer, Devlin relaxed back in his chair. "Perhaps I should mention what I intend to do about my suspicions if we can't reach an agreement tonight. My first step will be to get an injunction to prevent you from mining Wildstar property further. If I bring suit, all operations in the Lady J will have to halt. You won't be hauling ore out of the Lady J for a decade, if then. I'll see to it that the case is tied up in court for years. And I have the capital to withstand costly litigation, even if Sommers doesn't. My second step will be to hire my own army of gunmen and turn Silver Plume into an armed camp. As a pillar of this community, Mr. Burke, is that what you want?"

The Englishman stared coldly.

"Think of it, Burke ... all those court costs and law-yers' fees, not to mention the expense of equipping an army of guards. A half million dollars in lawsuits could prove to be a drain even on your vast resources. Even if you consider it worth the cost to break Riley Sommers, you won't succeed. Because I'll be there to stop you. And I'm warning you now, if anything more happens to either Jessica Sommers or her father, or their mine ... anything at all ... one more accident, big or small, you're a dead man. I'll take you out personally. And if I'm not around to do it, I'll hire it done." He paused to let his words sink in. "You can't win this one, Burke. You *won't* win this one."

A full minute went by while the Englishman considered his options. "What do you want from me, Mr. Devlin?" he said finally.

"I want you to back off."

"Very well. I agree."

"No more attacks on the Wildstar. No more attempts to buy Sommers out."

"I said I agree."

Devlin's eyebrow rose. Burke's capitulation had been al-most too easy. He wondered if there was a hidden catch. "You've made a wise decision."

The silver king's smile was dry. "When presented with unpleasant alternatives, I can be a very pragmatic man." He hesitated, looking uncomfortable again. "For what it's worth, I never meant this situation to get so out of hand. I certainly never intended anyone to be hurt."

Devlin narrowed his eyes skeptically. "You want me to believe you had nothing to do with dynamiting the Wildstar?"

"Yes, since it's the truth. I did instruct my mine foreman to pursue ownership of the Wildstar, but perhaps he was a bit too zealous. I have no proof that he engineered the ex-plosion, of course, but it's likely he had a hand in it."

"You're talking about Hank Purcell?"

"Yes."

It was Devlin's turn to remain silent. His jaw muscles clenched as he thought of what he would do to Purcell when he caught up with him. "I trust you intend to rein him in," he said with more casualness than he felt.

"Oh, indeed. I intend to fire him. I don't keep men in my employ who can't follow orders." The hard edge in the Englishman's clipped reply made it apparent he was quite, quite angry.

Holstering his revolver, Devlin stood up. "Then I think our future association will be quite amiable." He touched his hat with mock politeness. "It's been a pleasure doing business with you, Mr. Burke. No, don't trouble yourself to get up. I'll show myself out."

The sounds of men's voices raised in argument woke Jess from a drugged sleep. She rolled over with a groan, every muscle in her aching body feeling like it had been pounded with a drill hammer. Clem was shouting something, and occasionally her father's calmer tones would reply.

Annoyed, she dragged a pillow over her head in a vain attempt to drown out the harsh noise, and tried to hold on to the fleeting snatches of the disturbing dreams she'd been having. Erotic dreams about Devlin. He was kissing her and stroking her breasts and calling her his woman. Then he moved, settling his hard body between her thighs, and she opened to him, welcoming his deep thrusts with a joy that she'd never before felt—

The argument rose to a shout.

Unable to ignore the disturbance any longer, Jess lifted her head. She was in her own bedroom, and though the door was closed, the voices seemed to be coming from the kitchen. The room was dim.

It was barely light outside, she realized with dismay. It had to be early Monday morning. She had slept almost a full day.

That brought her scrambling out of bed in a hurry. Too much of a hurry, she discovered as blood rushed to her head. She stood there for a minute, swaying dizzily and seeing spots. Quite suddenly she remembered everything that had happened in the mine, and her cheeks flooded with scarlet. She hadn't been dreaming. Devlin's erotic caresses had been very, very real.

Almost frantically, she brushed her tumbled hair from her eyes. Was he here in the house now? If so, could she look him in the eyes after what had happened between them? How ever would she forget the wanton intimacies they had shared?

Getting a hold of herself, Jess straightened her shoulders. She'd never been a coward and wasn't about to act like one now. Besides, no one had ever died of embarrassment, as far as she knew. She would stick to her resolve and try to pretend that she'd never lain with Devlin in the dark, never had him moving inside her and bringing her to ecstasy, gifting her with the knowledge of what it meant to be fully a woman.

It was a tall order.

The argument was still going on. Hastily Jess pulled her wrapper over her nightgown and shoved her feet into her houseslippers. She had to go put an end to it before Riley and Clem came to blows.

Opening the bedroom door, she felt her pulse begin to speed in anticipation of seeing Devlin again.

As she made her way to the kitchen, she could hear Clem ranting. "Twenty-two years you and me been together, and this is what I got to show for it! A knife the back!"

"Quit carrying on so," her father returned. "It won't change anything between you and me. You'll still get your twenty percent of the profits, once we start seeing any."

"It ain't the money, goldammit! I don't give a flyin' hoot about the money! If I did, I wouldn't't've stuck by you all these years!"

"He's gonna help us fight," Riley said quietly.

"We done just fine by ourselves till now. We sure as hell don't need any two-bit—"

"We can't go it alone any longer, Clem. Do you think I would have trusted a near stranger with something this important if I didn't think he could do better than me at protecting my daugh—" Riley suddenly broke off and fell silent when he spied Jess standing at the door.

Her heartbeat slowed down. Her father and Clem were sitting at the kitchen table all alone, with no Devlin in sight. "I'm sorry I slept so late," she said uncertainly.

Clem glowered, while her father tried to smile. "You needed it, Jess"

She walked over to the stove to pour herself a cup of coffee. "Where's Devlin?" she asked casually, as if the answer held little importance to her.

"He said he was going to check into a hotel last night."

Jess turned with a startled look. "A hotel?"

"He didn't want to inconvenience us any longer, especially you. Said he didn't feel right, turning you out of your bed and all."

It had been something of an inconvenience, his staying here at the house, so why did she feel as if she had been slapped in the face? She'd been worried sick about how she would act toward Devlin, how he would act toward her. In fact, she would have given anything to avoid him today. But now that she was getting her wish, all she could think was *Why?* Why had he suddenly decided to move out? Was it something *she* had done? Had she scared him off by demanding he make love to her, by forcing him to do something he hadn't wanted to do? Had it been so distasteful to him?

"He said he'd be by later on to pick up his things."

He was actually leaving. As the realization sank in, Jess was shocked at the fierce knot of hurt that was gathering in her chest. She bit her lip to keep it from quivering and turned away, holding on to the towel rack at the end of the stove. Her face felt as if it were burning, while her mind wouldn't seem to function.

"What were you two arguing about?" she asked finally, surprised that her voice hardly shook.

"We weren't arguing," her father began.

"Yes we was!" Clem said with a growl. "I never thought I'd see the day, Jessie, but your pa done sold us out." Pushing back his chair, the old mule skinner stood up, jammed his hat on his head, and stomped past her, out the back door.

Turning, Jess stared white-faced at her father. "You didn't sell to Burke?" she demanded hoarsely.

"No, not to Burke."

Relief flooded through her, until she realized Riley wasn't meeting her eyes. "Then what did Clem mean about selling us out?"

"Your Mr. Devlin bought a quarter interest of the Wildstar."

"My Mr. Dev— You *sold* part of the Wildstar to him?"

"That's right," Riley replied irritably. "And I don't need you giving me any grief over it. Clem's already likened me to Judas."

Jess didn't know what to say. Like Clem, she felt betrayed. She had worked hard for years to make sure Riley could keep the Wildstar operating, and now ... It was more than giving up part ownership of the mine. It was selling out a dream. *How could you, Riley?*

"Why?" she asked in a raw voice. "Because we needed the money?"

"That, partly. We couldn't have afforded to dig out and shore up the timbers and make it safe to mine again without the cash Devlin's willing to put up."

"We would have found the money somehow."

"How?" He lifted a weary gaze to hers. "Jess, I'm tired of scraping by. I'm tired of having you scrimp and save and work your fingers raw so I can beat my head against a rock wall. You deserve better than that."

"But I don't mind! And anyway, it won't be forever. Just until you make a strike."

Riley sighed. "I don't know if I even believe that anymore. And even if I did, it's too dangerous to go on like we have been. We can't fight Burke alone—it was foolish to try. It nearly got you killed. If you had died in that explosion, I couldn't have lived with myself. . . ." His voice quavered and broke off.

"You're letting Burke win," Jess said tonelessly.

Her father shook his head. "I don't think so."

She didn't reply.

"Jess, I know what I'm doing."

When still she didn't respond, Riley carefully got up from the table, clutching his chest and avoiding his daughter's accusing gaze. "I'm going up to the mine."

That gave Jess a start. "Riley you can't, your wound—"

"My wound's fine. It only hurts like the devil. And it's about time I got back on my feet and did something for myself, instead of letting you and Devlin carry all the load. Somebody has to check out the damage and figure out how it can be fixed, and I'm still the best one to do it. It's still my mine."

His low tone held stubbornness and pride and left no room for argument. Jess knew better than to try.

He walked over to the wall by the door where coats and hats were hung on pegs. Taking down his hat, he put it on and let himself out quietly.

Hearing the door close, Jess felt the raw ache of tears prick her throat. Why did it suddenly feel like her whole world was collapsing around her?

When Jess showed up at the boardinghouse twenty-five minutes later, Flo scolded her for getting out of bed so soon after her ordeal. But she wasn't about to laze about all day, not when there was work to be done, and not when she had only her own despairing thoughts for company. The only way she could get through the day without dwelling on the past week's disturbing events, Jess figured, was by keeping busy.

There was a good deal of household work that had failed to get done in her absence. All the dusting, cleaning, dishwashing, laundering, airing bed linens, ironing, mending, baking, ordering supplies, carrying out stove ashes, trimming lamp wicks and filling the bases with kerosene— all the thousand and one chores that were required to care for two dozen rugged bachelors—were too much for Flo and Mei Lin and Mr. Kwan to handle alone. Jess plunged in with a vengeance, grateful for the occupation. At least here, in her own familiar domain, she could exercise a small amount of control over her life, something that was sorely lacking in the rest of her existence.

It was perhaps two hours later that a delivery wagon from Greene's Drugstore in Georgetown pulled up at the back door.

"Since when do you order from Greene's?" Flo demanded, peering out the kitchen window.

Jess pulled her hands out of the pie dough she'd been working and wiped them on a towel, a puzzled look on her face. Greene's was altogether too fancy and expensive a store for her to patronize. In fact, the last time she'd shopped there was seven years ago when she was hunting for a special Christmas present for her mother.

The delivery boy came to the door, carrying two packages, each tied up in a red bow. He couldn't, or wouldn't, say who had commissioned the purchases, but both were for Miss Jessica Sommers.

When the boy had gone, Jess sat down at the huge wooden table to open the packages. One turned out to be a large crystal jar of bath salts that smelled of lavender. The other was an elegant bottle of glycerin hand lotion scented with roses.

"Jess, you sly thing," Flo said, grinning. "You got you a new beau. That handsome devil Devlin is sweet on you."

"No, he isn't," Jess protested automatically, staring down at the gifts.

"A man doesn't give presents like this to a girl who's not his sweetheart."

"No, you don't understand. . . . He's only keeping a promise he made when we were trapped in the mine. He said if we got out alive, he would buy me something to put on my hands."

"Uh-huh." Flo's grin didn't waver one bit. "I understand all right. That gorgeous fella is courtin' you."

Jess didn't know how to answer that charge. She'd never felt more confused in her life. On the one hand, Devlin had walked out of her life without so much as a by your leave, and then gone behind her back to strike a deal with her father to buy into the mine. On the other hand, he'd given her these expensive presents. The crystal jar alone had to have cost at least ten dollars—enough to pay two full days' wages for a miner, or cover the cost of room and board at her place for nearly a week. He shouldn't have done it. It was sinful, spending that kind of money on something so frivolous. But still . . .

She touched the delicate crystal timorously. It gave her a strange, warm feeling inside to think Devlin cared enough to give her something so beautiful. She'd never had a present so lovely.

"I say he's taken a fancy to you," Flo declared again. "The question is, do you fancy him back?"

Could she answer that question? Did she fancy Devlin? Was she actually falling in love with him?

No, it was impossible. She would be a fool to follow that dangerous path. She had no business harboring such tender feelings for a gambler, a professional gamester who made his living wagering on men's ill luck. Besides, he wouldn't want her love. He'd already made that plain enough.

She didn't *want* to fall in love with a man like him, either. She wanted a man she could look up to, a man who was dependable and honest and hardworking.

And yet she couldn't deny the hot, flushed feeling she got every time she remembered Devlin's kisses, his caresses. Or the rapid quickening of her pulse when she recalled how it had felt to have him moving inside her. Or the soft glow in her heart when she thought of how protective and caring he'd been.

Warm, insistent memories tugged at her constantly . . . Devlin keeping her calm in that awful crushing darkness. Devlin making her laugh. Devlin turning her inside out with his magical touch. If she wasn't in love with him yet, she was dangerously close.

That gentle, bewildering feeling lasted only an hour. Jess was still trying to make sense of the turmoil in her heart when a small band of Chinese laborers showed up on her back doorstep—three women and two men, all dressed in wide-sleeved tunics and straight trousers, flat wide-brimmed straw hats, and glossy black pigtails.

None of them spoke much English, and the words they

could say didn't make a lick of sense. They seemed to think they were to be employed at the Sommers's boardinghouse.

"Maybe we should fetch Mei Lin," Flo said after Jess had tried for the third time to convince them she didn't need any hired help.

And so Mei Lin was called to interpret. The pretty Chinese woman had worked here at the boardinghouse since Jess's mother saved her from a life of prostitution in an opium den, but she lived with her husband in the small Chinese community at the edge of town, and apparently she knew these people.

Mei Lin held a discussion in rapid Cantonese with the newcomers, then turned to Jess. "They say they here to work for you, Missy Jessie."

"But I don't need them. Please tell them I'm sorry but I can't afford to take on any more workers."

Another conversation ensued.

"They already have payment, full month," Mei Lin relayed. "Salary very generous."

Jess stared. "That's impossible. Who would have paid them?"

"I can guess," Flo said with a satisfied smirk. "You still gonna try to convince me that gorgeous fella isn't sweet on you?"

Devlin. It had to be him. Rather than flatter Jess, however, the realization that he'd gone behind her back for the second time in one day only annoyed and frustrated her. "He may have bought part of the mine from my father," she said tightly, "but he has no right to interfere with my boardinghouse!"

"Now, Jess, don't you go gettin' on your high horse. You know we could use the help around here. What with you being gone so much lately, Mei Lin and I just haven't been able to keep up."

That sent a stab of guilt through Jess. "I know, Flo, and I'm sorry. But I can't let Devlin spend that kind of money on this place. I won't be able to repay him."

"Maybe he doesn't want to be repaid." The widow

looked at the eager Chinese laborers, who were smiling and nodding and making small respectful bows. "Me, I've never been one to look a gift horse in the mouth. I think we ought to put 'em to work. You can always argue with Devlin later."

Jess gave in grudgingly, with a silent promise to do more than argue with Devlin. She intended to give him a piece of her mind at the first opportunity. It was bad enough for him to make secret deals with Riley behind her back and to send her expensive presents as a result of a promise he'd made under duress. It was another thing entirely for him to blatantly meddle in the running of her boardinghouse.

What occurred next, however, made Devlin's interference in her business pale in comparison. Doc Wheeler stopped by to check the gash on her temple that she'd received in the mine explosion.

"I'm all right, Doc," Jess protested as he pushed her down in a chair. "Flo's already seen to it."

"Might as well look now that I'm here. That Devlin fella ordered me to get over here first thing, and I don't dare report back to him empty-handed."

Jess's lips tightened—and not in pain, even though Doc was poking and prodding at her scalp.

"Just where do you and that young fella stand, anyway? I thought he'd taken sides with you and Riley."

"He has," Jess said, puzzled.

"Didn't know he was so cozy with Ashton Burke."

"What do you mean, cozy?"

"Why, he was at Burke's house early last night. I had to drive into Georgetown and I saw him myself at the front door, talking to that fancy butler. Seemed mighty odd to me when you're in the middle of a mine feud."

Jess felt a sudden coldness start to creep over her skin and curl in her stomach. Devlin and Burke? There had to be some mistake. "I . . . don't know what he was doing there," she replied in a voice that didn't seem like her own.

"Well, it just seemed strange."

Yes, it did seem strange. The coldness inside her intensified as a horrible suspicion began to take root. She tried to dismiss it. It wasn't possible that she and her father had been betrayed, surely. Devlin and Burke hadn't been in league together all along. Devlin couldn't have been working for Burke and merely pretending to be on their side . . . could he?

Disbelief, shock, denial all screamed at her in warning. She couldn't accept that Devlin might be a traitor. It wasn't true. And yet there was no denying that Devlin had been keeping company with Ashton Burke. Doc had seen it with his own eyes.

No, what she was thinking wasn't possible. She *knew* Devlin. She had lived in the same house with him and ridden with him and faced death with him. She'd made love to him, for God's sake.

But did she really know him? Until two weeks ago, before she'd offered him a job as night guard, he'd been a total stranger.

And he had been with Burke the first time she'd met him.

He had followed her outside the saloon, and she'd convinced him to take the job. He had seemed so reluctant at the time. . . . Dear God, had she just played right into his hands?

"Yep . . . your head's okay," Doc pronounced, "but you oughta keep it dry for a few days. Miss Jess?" Doc waved a hand in front of her face.

Dazed, Jess turned to look at him. "I have to talk to Devlin."

Doc's forehead wrinkled in a frown. "I passed him on the road a while back. I think he was headed to your house."

Rising to her feet, she fumbled with her apron strings. "I have to see him," she murmured again.

Leaving Doc Wheeler to stare after her, she made her way blindly out the door, anger, dread, and anguish warring within her. She almost ran the block and a half to the house, hardly seeing her surroundings. Surely Devlin hadn't betrayed them. Surely she couldn't be that mistaken about someone. No one could be that good an actor, could he? No one could be that cruel, that low, that deceiving.

Devlin's horse was tied up out front when Jess arrived. She let herself into the house quietly, surprised to realize her hands were actually shaking. Devlin was in her bedroom, stowing his clothes and gear in a carpetbag.

He looked up to find her standing in the doorway. When he saw her, he pushed his hat back and smiled. "Riley wasn't here, so I let myself in."

"He's up at the mine," Jess replied absently, distracted as usual by the sheer masculine beauty of Devlin's face.

He looked different today. He was wearing a superbly tailored suit and waistcoat that fit his lean contours to perfection and gave him an added aura of sleek elegance and power—as if he needed any other advantage to enhance his striking physique. Her gaze slowly swept downward, drawn by a force more potent than she could resist. She could remember all too well how that hard body felt pressed against her own, how it felt moving over her, between her thighs, God help her.

Realizing she was staring, Jess forced herself to drag her gaze upward to meet Devlin's smoke-hued eyes. She wanted to demand that he tell her what he had been doing at Burke's house, but the words wouldn't come. She couldn't just come right out and accuse him of something so sinister. She didn't know what she would do if it were true. Desperately trying to maintain her composure, she clasped her fingers together.

"Were you just going to sneak out?" Her voice was raw, unsteady, and it seemed to take Devlin by surprise.

"I beg your pardon?"

"You heard me."

He frowned as he surveyed her pale face. "Jess, are you all right?"

"No . . . I'm not all right."

"I suppose you're angry about the laborers I sent over."

That had totally slipped her mind, but now that he'd brought it up, it gave her something else to focus on besides the terrible possibility that she'd been so wrong about him. "Yes, I'm angry about that. I've been running our boardinghouse on my own for five years. I can manage without your help—"

"Whoa, hold up there, angel. I never said you couldn't manage by yourself."

"Why didn't you *ask* me before you went and hired five people to work for me?"

"Because you would have refused to accept them if I'd offered first."

"Of course I would have refused! I don't need them!"

"You do. You just won't admit it." Devlin paused. "What are you so upset about? I'm paying their salary. If you don't want to use them, that's your affair, but you'll just be wasting a good money."

"I don't want you paying for my hired help—" Jess faltered, a burning ache in her throat. They were arguing over something that was totally trivial compared to the real issue. She swallowed hard. "You didn't bother to consult me or even let me know about any of the decisions you've made on my behalf recently. I'm wondering what else you haven't seen fit to mention."

His look suddenly became wary as he realized Jess must have learned about his vast wealth. Riley had warned him she wouldn't be happy about it. "Your father told you?"

"Yes, he told me. But I'm sure he didn't know we were harboring a traitor in our house."

"Harboring a *what*?"

"You were on Burke's side all along, weren't you?"

Devlin's eyes narrowed in a sudden scowl. "What are you talking about? I've never been on Burke's side."

"Then what were you doing visiting him last night?"

"Is that what this is all about?"

"Yes!" The word was high-pitched and ragged, since by now she's worked herself into a frenzy. "Doc Wheeler saw you in Georgetown at Burke's house, so don't deny it!"

It was a moment before full comprehension of her accusation finally sank in for Devlin. He looked at her in total disbelief for a minute, feeling like a knife was sliding into his gut. Could she really trust him so little, after all they'd been through together? Raw pain welled up in him, accompanied by bitterness at her evident lack of faith. With deceptive casualness, he crossed his arms over his muscular chest. "I won't even try."

Jess stared at him. She'd expected denials, maybe that Devlin would try to bluff his way out. She'd prayed that he would have a good reason for going to see Burke at his house, though she couldn't begin to imagine what that might be. She hadn't contemplated no explanation at all.

His voice was cold, deadly, when he finally spoke. "You honestly think I've been betraying you with Burke?"

"I don't know." Her tone held anguish. "You go behind my back, buying part of our mine from Riley and hiring servants that I don't want and ordering Doc to examine me when I'm fine—I don't know what to think anymore."

"You might," Devlin said carefully, not trusting himself to relax his rigid control, "try giving me the benefit of the doubt."

She didn't look as if she were willing to give him anything. Devlin found himself clenching his teeth. Sonovabitch—she ought to be grateful for his intervention. He was saving her precious mine, for Christ's sake. Instead she was actually standing there accusing him of treachery! The idea that she could believe such a thing of him filled him with a stabbing rage, and a pain so deep he didn't even want to acknowledge it.

In an abruptly vicious gesture, he jerked his hat off his head and threw it on the bed. She'd been spoiling for a fight ever since she'd shown up here, and he would give it to her.

"I had the impression," he said tightly, his hands going to his hips, "that you wanted to stop Burke from taking over your mine. Was I wrong?"

"No."

"Well, I did pay Burke a visit last night. First I threatened him with a half-million dollar lawsuit if he didn't give up his ambition to own the Wildstar. Then I told him I'd kill him if he or any of his men dared hurt you or your father again."

Her eyes searched Devlin's face. "Why should I believe

you? How do I know you weren't working for Burke all along? How do I know he didn't bribe you like he has most everyone else in this town?"

Devlin felt his hands curl into fists as he fought the urge to wring Jess's pretty neck. After all the risks he'd taken for her, the long tedious solitary hours spent up at that goddamned mine, the countless times he'd sacrificed his own pleasure on her behalf, she was actually calling him dishonest to his face. Some men would kill over such an insult.

Devlin's usual seductive charm deserted him totally. "I never set eyes on Burke until two weeks ago," he said with tight-lipped anger. "And even if I were the kind of man to accept bribes, why would I need his money? I have plenty of my own. I'll never miss the fifty thousand I gave your father. I spend more each year on my horses."

Her gasp was audible in the small room, though she comprehended only part of what Devlin had said. "You gave Riley fifty thousand *dollars*?"

"That's the usual currency exchange in America," Devlin snapped, his tone holding a slicing edge of mockery.

She was silent for a long time. "You're *rich*?" she finally said in a hoarse voice.

"That's the term for millionaires, yes." The hard light in his gray eyes pierced her. "You said Riley told you."

"He ... never ... told me *that*." She sounded breathless, as if she'd been running too long too fast. "*You* never told me. . . . You said you were a gambler."

"I said I was a gambler among other things."

"You lied to me. . . . You *lied*."

Devlin drew in a deep breath, struggling violently for patience. "I didn't lie to you, Jess. There was a time when I earned my living gambling—I still do to some extent. Only now I gamble on stocks instead of games of chance."

"How could you?" she whispered, her gaze agonized.

"How could I be wealthy?" His lips twisted in a cold smile. "Actually it took a lot of hard work. I made my money honestly, if that's what worries you. Mostly in mining stocks. Gold at first, until I diversified. I found I have a talent for playing the market. I can't give you a precise accounting, but I imagine I could buy Burke twice over."

"You're richer than Burke?"

The stricken look on her face gave him no satisfaction. She stood there staring at him in shock, her face drained of color.

"Look, what the hell difference does it make what size my bank account is?"

What difference did it make? Everything. If she had known how rich he was, she never would have hired him to help guard the mine, never would have trusted him or come to depend on him. *She never would have given herself to him that terrible night in the Wildstar.* Dear God, she had made love to a man who was just like Burke, maybe worse. At least she knew better than to trust Burke. Devlin had fooled her entirely. He had *lied* to her from the very first moment she'd set eyes on him. He had bought her father, and he had lied. . . .

The room started to spin; Devlin's face started to blur.

He was watching her intently, his expression skeptical. "You told me you didn't care about money. Are you saying now you didn't mean it?"

She took a deep, steadying breath, surprised to realize she was shaking. "No . . . I don't care about money. What I care about is honesty. I *trusted* you . . . but you've been lying to me the whole time. And now I find you sneaking behind my back, using your filthy money to take over our mine—"

"Sweet heaven, Jess, stop it! You're being ridiculous."

Her eyes burning with tears she wouldn't shed in front of him, Jess shook her head. She'd been more than ridiculous. She'd been a total fool, thinking she could love him. He was a wealthy mining baron, the kind of man she had always despised. He'd given her father more money than Riley could repay in a lifetime. He *owned* Riley. Just like Burke owned much of this town.

Struggling desperately for control, Jessica lifted a trembling hand and pointed at the door, her wild-eyed gaze fixed on Devlin. "Get out. Get out of here. I don't ever want to lay eyes on you again as long as I live!"

Chapter 13

Devlin stood staring at Jessica for a full thirty seconds, unable to fathom what had her so upset. *He* was the one whose honor had been impugned. *He* was the one who'd been accused of treachery and betrayal—when his only crime had been withholding the truth about his prosperity. He'd originally had good reasons for that, though. Reasons she knew nothing about. Now he would have to tell her what had brought him to Silver Plume and why he'd come in the guise of a gambler, instead of flashing his wealth and riding into town on his own private railroad car—

"I mean it!" Jess cried before he could decide where to begin. "I want you out of my house!"

Devlin strode angrily past her, but instead of obeying, he slammed the door shut and turned to face her, his expression tight. "I'm not leaving until we get this straightened out."

"There's nothing to straighten out!"

"Yes, there is! I owe you an explanation, and you're going to listen." He didn't give her a chance to argue, but launched in. "I didn't mean to lie to you, Jess. It was important that I retain some kind of anonymity if I hoped to find the outlaws who robbed my father's train."

At least that got her attention. "Your . . . father's train?"

"The Colorado Central. It was held up three times since the spring—the last one a month ago. The gang stole a silver bullion shipment and killed two people."

"Your father *owns* the Colorado Central Railroad?" she asked weakly.

"Not entirely. He's a major shareholder, though, and a member of the board of directors. He asked me to put a stop to the robberies if I could. I came here following a rumor. A man with a scar over his eye, riding a roan, was identified as one of the outlaws."

He let that sink in a minute. She watched him mutely, her breasts swiftly rising and falling with her ragged breaths.

"I was hunting down the rumor when I overheard you tell the sheriff about a man with a scar being seen up at the mine the day your father was shot. So I let you hire me as a guard. It seemed a good bargain at the time. You needed help, and I stood a lot better chance of finding the gang if I had a good reason for asking questions, if every move I made wasn't suspect. The man turned out to be Zeke McRoy, but my only lead dried up when I killed him. That's why I was so angry that night."

Jess heard his explanation, but only one crucial detail mattered. Devlin had used her to find McRoy. He had *used* her. It was almost worse than betrayal would have been. Not only was he filthy rich, not only had he lied to her from the beginning, but the only reason he had helped her was because he'd needed her for his *own* purposes.

"Get out," she said hoarsely. "Get out of here."

Devlin's temper started to soar again. "In the name of thunder—haven't you heard a word I've said?"

"Yes, I heard! Now, get out of my house! Get out of my life! You don't need to use me anymore. You got what you came for."

"I didn't get what I came for. I was too busy playing nursemaid to you and your goddamned mine."

"Don't cuss in my house, darnit!"

He gave a harsh bark of laughter. "Right. Saint Jessica's rules for boarders." His mouth curled as he eyed her disdainfully. "I'm not leaving until I'm good and ready. I still have unfinished business with your father. And technically I still work for you."

"No, you don't! You're fired!" Abruptly Jess recalled the salary she owned Devlin for guarding the mine. "I said I'd pay you two hundred and fifty dollars a month, but I'll give you every cent of that, even though the month is only half up. I'll send the money to your hotel."

He stared at her as if she'd lost her mind. "I don't want the damned money! You could give me a thousand times that sum and I'd never notice it. What I want is an apology."

"*You* want an apology!"

"Yes, for putting me in the same category as that bastard Burke."

"You *are* in the same category! You're no better than he is! In fact, you're worse, confound you! You're manipulative and heartless, just like he is!" Furious, hurting like she'd never hurt before, Jess stood there glaring at Devlin and unconsciously dashing tears from her eyes. "You *used* me, damn you!"

"Yes, I used you! Which is exactly what you did with me—used me to save your mine."

"No, it wasn't the same! I was honest with you from the start, but you . . . You're lower than a *rattlesnake*. At least a rattler gives a warning before it strikes."

Devlin clenched his fists to keep from hitting something. He couldn't ever remember being so livid. "So help me God, if you weren't a woman . . ." he said through his teeth.

Jess regarded him with loathing, her own fists balled in determination. "If you won't leave on your own, I'll get a gun and make you!"

She started to march past him, but his arm shot out and stopped her, lightning quick and hard. His eyes were like flint as his fingers dug into the soft flesh above her elbow.

"Let go of me!" she exclaimed, trying to break free of his grip.

The hot rise of desire within Devlin was swift and sudden. *I shouldn't have touched her*, was his abrupt thought. Touching her only made him recall too vividly what he should never have known about Jess, only brought to mind forbidden memories of taut silky breasts ... velvet warm skin ... a lush, supple body. ...

Devlin swore viciously under his breath. He'd promised himself he would keep away from her, that he wouldn't give in to his need to have her, to hold her. He'd been eaten up with guilt for two days, ever since the dark night when she'd exchanged her innocence for the simple human comfort the act of mating could bring her. But now ... anger and arousal made his blood surge hot, his body harden.

When Jess started to struggle, he gripped both her arms, wanting to shake some sense into her, wanting to make love to her again. Dammit, but this stubborn, beautiful hellcat aroused so many emotions in him—he'd never felt so many conflicting desires for a woman. He wanted to protect as well as to take. He felt the urge to throttle her at the same time he ached to bury himself so deeply inside her that he wouldn't know where either of them began or ended.

"Let—me—go!" Jess was half shouting, half sputtering, her golden eyes blazing with fire. "I don't want anything to do with you, you bastard! You lied to me and used me! You made love to me under false pretenses! I would never have let you touch me if I'd known what kind of man you are. *You're* the one who owes *me* the apology!"

That last charge cut more deeply than even her accusations of lying and betrayal. "The hell I do!" Devlin shot back, his voice icy with fury. "I won't apologize for being rich. I've worked hard for everything I own. I won't apologize for using you to find a gang of vicious killers! You were my best lead—and you got more than your money's worth in return for my services. Guarding your mine nearly got me killed. And I damn sure won't apologize for making love to you! You wanted it as much as I did. In fact, I recollect you *begging* me to take you."

"I did not!" Jess said fiercely, totally shamed by the truth.

"You did! You begged me to teach you about passion—and you're lying to yourself if you remember otherwise."

"No . . ."

All the while he'd been impelling her slowly backward across the small room. He stopped when he could go no farther, when they reached the pine bureau. Jess found her back pressed painfully against the upper edge of the chest, with Devlin crowding her in front, his hard thighs brushing up against her skirts. She winced and tried to shrink away. She didn't want him touching her. She'd been betrayed by him, even if it wasn't the kind of betrayal she had first thought.

But he wouldn't release her. He wouldn't even let her avoid his gaze. He was towering over her, his sculpted face hard with fury. She saw the fierce light moving in his eyes, in the storm-gray irises, and for the first time since meeting him, she felt a twinge of real fear. She didn't know this ruthless stranger, this dangerous man. But then she never had. The tender, caring lover she remembered from the mine had been nothing more than a figment of her distraught imagination.

Certainly there was no tenderness in him as his rough mouth crashed down on hers. The room reeled; the sudden dark seizure of his kiss made Jess's head spin. She tried to cry out, but Devlin lifted her hard into his kiss, smothering her angry protests.

Her fists doubled against his chest, trying to push him away, but his fingers clamped onto her chin and held it so he could enter her mouth with his tongue. He was punishing her, satisfying his anger, his tongue thrusting deep into her mouth to overwhelm any resistance. The hard sensual caress was detached, brutally lustful, the savage pressure subduing her, making her open wide for him.

She struggled, twisting and heaving, but he used his body to crush her up against the bureau. She couldn't move. Her mouth was filled with the hot searching stab of his tongue, her nostrils filled with his heat, his scent. She couldn't breathe. He assaulted her senses, pinning her with the length of his masculine frame, cradling her pelvis against the hard ridge of his manhood. All the feminine parts of her body so recently sensitized to his touch suddenly awakened to throbbing, pulsing life.

His mouth was still eating hers feverishly when she felt his rough hands in her hair, searching, pulling the pins out, tossing each one aside, finally loosening the tawny mass. Catching a silken skein, he tangled his fingers in it and held her still. When he lifted his head, his gray eyes were fierce.

Jess dragged a ragged breath of air into her lungs.

Then his free hand reached for the top button of her bodice and her eyes widened in shocked comprehension.

"No . . ." she repeated in a shaking voice.

"Yes, angel." The button tore free and clattered to the floor, making her gasp.

"What are you doing!" Jess squirmed, but the vise of his hand held her head still, his muscular thighs pressing hard against hers, while his fingers continued their purposeful work.

"What does it look like I'm doing?" he retorted, his voice going even lower and rougher. "I'm taking off your clothes." He finished with the fastenings on her basque bodice, and with uncompromising expertise, started on the small buttons of her camisole. "You wanted to know what you've been missing. I'm going to show you right now. That first time, I was gentle. Now I'm going to take you hard and fast, then real, real slow."

His gravelly voice held none of the teasing seduction he used with other women, none of the smooth sophistication or devastating charm Jess had come to know. "I'm going to make you feel so much you won't know your fingers from your toes. I'm going to make love to you, sweetheart."

"No, don't!" she protested, her heart starting to pound at his threat. "I don't want anything to do with you!"

"You do so, Jess. You want me."

"I do not. . . . I despise you!"

"You didn't despise me two nights ago. You enjoyed everything I did to you."

"Two nights ago I didn't know what a cad you are—"

Her retort ended in a sharp inhalation as he ripped the final buttons of her camisole, baring her corset and the chemise beneath.

"I'm going to prove you wrong, lady. You're going to eat your words before I'm done." He said it coldly, calculatingly, and with the supreme assurance of a man determined to win. "I can, you know."

"Realizing he was right, she pushed against his chest frantically. "Please, stop it. . . ."

"Stop undressing you, sweet?" He shoved aside the folds of the camisole, exposing the shadowy prelude to a luxurious cleavage. "We can leave your clothes on if you want. I'd rather have you naked, I'd rather see your beautiful body, but I can satisfy you just as well like this. I can take you right here, standing up."

Giving her no chance to respond, he tightened his grip on the veil of her hair and pulled her head back, exposing her bare throat to his mouth. His breath seared her skin as his lips found the vulnerable hollow at her throat where her pulse hammered wildly. Jess felt her head spinning, felt herself growing warm at his words, at his feather-light kisses.

"You want me, Jess." His husky voice vibrated against her throat and sent hot shivers of pleasure rippling over her.

"No . . ." She only wanted to demand that he leave her alone. She wanted to tell him to go to the devil and not come back. Trouble was, she couldn't find the strength to fight him. Her legs suddenly had gone weak. She reached for something to hold on to and found his upper arms, feeling the heavy cords of muscles beneath his tailored coat.

His mouth was hot and hungry on her throat. The scent of him surrounded her, the odor of soap and sandlewood and aroused male. He pressed hot kisses down the slender column, and lower, over her bosom, above the neckline of the corset-covered chemise which hid her creamy rose-pointed breasts. His hand joined his lips in the assault then, dipping beneath the soft cotton and rigid buckram to find an aching nipple.

Jess made a gasping sound, her body jerking convulsively. Refusing to release her, Devlin slid one hard arm around her waist, holding her prisoner, while the thumb of his other hand rubbed her nipple into a rigid peak. An involuntary moan escaped Jess as the buds of her breasts tightened unbearably. She couldn't believe this was happening. She had never imagined the brutal rush of feeling his rough caresses would kindle in her. His hard stroking fingers felt like fire on the sensitive, swollen tips of her breasts, echoed in the moist aching weakness that pulsed between her thighs.

As if he knew what effect his ministrations were having, he lifted his gaze, and his eyes held hers, hot and silver. "You want me, Jess."

Her lips parted to answer him, but no sound came out. His arm still held her tightly, and she could feel the pressure of his obvious arousal against her skirts, the suggestive movement of his hips thrusting against hers.

Then his hand left her aching breasts and he reached down, raising the layers of skirts and petticoats that enveloped her legs.

Realizing that he really meant to carry out his threat, Jess cast a frantic glance at the closed door. "Devlin, stop . . . we can't . . . my father . . ."

"Is up at the mine. We're all alone, honey."

"Devlin, please. . . ."

"That's right, beg me."

"No . . . I didn't mean—"

"No? You don't want my hands on you . . . my mouth on you?"

His hand moved up the shivering surface of her inner thigh, his probing fingers finding the opening in the soft cotton of her drawers. When he raked the tight curls between her legs, Jess jerked, gasping. "You don't want me to touch you here? You don't like this?" One finger eased into the slit of her soft folds, dredging a ragged whimper from her.

Helplessly Jess clung to him. She did want him to touch her there, God help her. Her damp trembling thighs opened wider for him.

Watching the quivering reaction in her startled eyes, Devlin pressed against the moist cleft. Jess's entire body clenched from the exquisite pleasure of it.

"Devlin, don't . . ."

"Shhh, I'm not going to hurt you." Raw desire darkened his husky voice. His lean fingers stroked her, gliding through the hot dew seeping like honey from between her legs. "Do you know how wet you are?" Devlin whispered roughly.

Jess closed her eyes and arched against his hand. She didn't think she could bear what he was doing to her.

"You want me, Jess."

She *did* want him, Jess realized helplessly. She'd had no notion how much until this moment. The fiery craving inside her was so insistent and sharp it frightened her.

Then his finger entered her. Slowly thrusting.

"Ohhhh . . ." She almost sobbed.

His narrowed look followed every shock, every startled reaction in her face, taking in the cloud of tawny hair, her flushed cheeks, her trembling mouth. He was flooded with fiercely masculine satisfaction and a desire so violent he ached. He wanted her so badly he thought he might explode just from touching her. All he could think about was how tight and hot and wet she would be on his throbbing shaft.

He lowered his head again, his hungry mouth covering hers, hard and compelling, kissing her with a fierceness that stopped her breath, while his bold fingers continued their determined arousal.

Jess lost the ability to speak, to reason. She felt the stroking thrusts of his tongue in the depths of her body, a carnal imitation of the stroking fingers between her thighs. The world was reduced to his hot mouth, his thrusting tongue, his erotic hand.

She moaned into his mouth, a panicky, anguished sound, which Devlin answered with a deep-throated mas-

culine growl. His fingers plied her weeping flesh merci-
lessly, back and forth, in and out, rubbing, probing, tormenting.

Jess squirmed wildly against him, seeking release from
the terrible, exquisite tension. Her nails frantically raked
his shoulders while her hips strained feverishly against the
imprisoning caress of his hand.

They seemed the acts of a stranger. This couldn't be her,
making these little whimpering sounds of feminine need,
feeling this desperate wanting, this raw frenzy. This wasn't
her. She couldn't be doing this.

A low sob rolled from her throat as she tore her lips
from Devlin's.

"I don't ... want this ..." Jess panted with a last attempt at sanity.

"No? You want it lying down? I can oblige, angel."

His brazen fingers left her abruptly, yet he didn't release
her. Instead, he bent and scooped her up in his arms. Jess
gave a startled cry, but the impatient heat of his mouth on
hers again silenced any possible protest.

She no longer wanted to protest, though. Her body had
caught fire. Every muscle and nerve she possessed trembled and ached with need. She wanted to scream with the
violence of it. Her fingers clenched in his thick sable hair,
anchoring Devlin's lips to hers.

Kissing her hard, he strode to the bed, laying her on the
yellow-patterned quilt. His eyes fiercely primitive, he covered her with his body, one powerful knee wedged between her thighs, pressing hard against her woman's
mound.

"I'm going to have you in a real bed," he promised
hoarsely, "the way it should have been the first time."

His lips were both tender and harsh as he assaulted her
mouth again, yet it was only a score of heartbeats before
the fierceness left him. His kisses turned hungry, needy.

Jess felt the difference, gloried in the difference. The
stranger was gone; her dark lover had returned. His lips
were the same lips that had offered her comfort and ecstasy in a night of darkness and fear, his kisses the same

devastating kisses. He was here with her, desiring her, needing her, loving her. She clutched at his hair, trying to get closer, trying to tell him with her body that she needed him, too.

In some distant corner of her mind, she felt Devlin shudder against her. Then he drew back with a sharp inhalation.

"Damn, I want you," he muttered raggedly.

"Devlin . . ." she breathed in return.

He shut his eyes tightly, fighting for control—but he knew he'd already lost it, the way he always did with her. Only Jess could stop him now.

She wasn't even trying. She lay with her eyes closed, her hands reaching for him, her wet, passion-bruised lips parted. She was hot and excited and oblivious to anything but their lovemaking, and the knowledge made him rigid with longing.

Fumbling with the buttons of his trousers and drawers, Devlin freed himself and shoved up her endless skirts. He felt near to bursting, and knew he *would* burst if he didn't have her now. Pushing apart the folds of cloth between her parted thighs, he thrust his burning shaft into her, groaning aloud with pleasure, with shattering relief, as her moist tightness swallowed him.

At his savage entrance, Jess gave a soft cry and arched wildly beneath him. He clutched her to him, drove deep inside her, hard and fast, taking her as if she were an experienced whore and not the innocent young virgin he'd taught to know passion just a few nights ago. Yet Jess met his every thrust, her hips moving in fervent response, hungry and unashamed. She hadn't known love could be so furious, that it could be like riding the edge of a dark, wild pleasure. He was all taut and fierce and driving. He was her world—mating, claiming, filling, surrendering, pumping into her with mindless, blinding need.

"Oh, God . . . Jess. . . ."

The sudden possessive explosion took them both by surprise. She sobbed his name as with one last strong plunge the peak burst on him helplessly, savagely. She heard his choked sounds against her ear, the side of her face, passion tearing from him in hoarse gasps. Then together they were convulsing and tumbling and falling into a dark chasm of ecstasy.

In the heated aftermath, the tortured sounds of their breathing filled the small room. Collapsing, Devlin buried his face in her damp throat and lay there panting, while the sweet, piercing pleasure slowly dissipated, leaving behind a glow of sated warmth.

He should regret what had happened just now. He should be cursing himself and giving Jess the apology he'd insisted he didn't owe her. He'd never behaved so savagely toward any woman. He couldn't remember a time when he'd lost control with a woman, wanting her so badly he'd buried himself inside her like a maddened kid. Always before he'd made it a practice to act the consummate lover, pleasing his bed partners as he expected to be pleased. He'd never been so angry that he'd lost every shred of civilized behavior and decency.

But then he'd never met a woman who questioned his integrity, his honor. He'd never met Jessica Sommers.

Just then she stirred beneath him with a small moan. Devlin froze at that slightest movement of her hips. It startled him, the sharp renewed hunger that surged through his body. He wanted her again, and he hadn't even recovered from the devastating climax he'd just shared with her. That was something else he'd never experienced with any other woman—that shattering explosion that left in its wake an even more shattering sense of completeness.

In response to her plaintive movement, though, he eased his weight onto his elbows, sparing her the crushing heaviness of his embrace, yet not relinquishing the hot, moist sheath that still enveloped him. He couldn't bring himself to be that noble.

That was another surprise, to learn he wasn't so gallant a lover, after all.

Pressing light apologetic kisses over her scented skin, he asked her in a voice still husky with passion, "Did I hurt you?"

Still half dazed with sensation, Jess pondered the question. He had hurt her, but not in the way he meant; not physically. What he had done was far worse. She felt the heat of his cheek against hers, the feathering of his breath as his mouth traced delicate patterns over her face and throat—and she wanted to cry.

"I've thought of sharing this bed with you since the day you turned it over to me," Devlin murmured.

Jess opened her eyes slowly. His look was intent, expectant, as if he were waiting for her to say something. A dark flush of passion stained his cheekbones, and his eyes were dark and smoky. And all her senses were gradually returning.

Appalled at what she had just done, allowed him to do, *wanted* him to do, she averted her face. She couldn't believe it.

"Get off me," she whispered.

The lips that had been moving upon her flushed face stilled. There was a long silence before he said, "Jess, look at me."

"No." She just wanted him to go away. It shamed her to realize how easily she'd been seduced, how disgracefully she'd behaved, mindlessly tumbling into bed with a man whose only interest in her was whatever use he could make of her at the moment. First he had used her to accomplish his secret schemes, now he had used her body—

"I'm sorry I was so rough." He reached up to catch her chin, but she flinched and shook off his grasp.

"Get out of my house."

Going rigid, Devlin stared down at her. He couldn't believe that after what had just happened between them, the explosive passion they'd shared, she was kicking him out of her bed. She'd felt the same powerful exaltation, the same keen joy he had, he was certain. In all his experience, he'd never felt anything quite like it. But then, she didn't have the experience to realize how special it had been.

A fierce wave of contrition swept over Devlin. He had wronged Jess. She wasn't a virgin any longer—thanks to him—but she was still very much an innocent. He should have taken more care, shown her more tenderness. She had wronged him, too, with her mistrust, but she hadn't meant what she'd said. She couldn't really believe he'd been in league with Burke. When she'd had time to consider, she would realize how absurd her accusations were.

Gently Devlin brushed back a disheveled tendril of blond hair that adorned her forehead, wanting to take back his harshness, wanting to make it up to her—

"Don't touch me." The command was low and raw and filled with self-loathing.

Devlin heard only the loathing—and thought it directed at himself.

"I can't believe I ever trusted you," Jess added almost to herself.

"Jesus, are we back to that again?" The fire of anger that had been momentarily banked in Devlin flamed to life again.

He was still joined to her in the most intimate way possible, still half hard inside her, but he withdrew from her at once, taking care only to be considerate of her tender flesh and to yank down her skirts. Then he rolled off the bed and stood up, rapidly buttoning his trousers.

Jess winced at the throbbing ache between her thighs and rolled onto her side, giving him her back. "We never left it. I can't forget how you lied to me."

"Goddammit, that's enough."

"Or how you used me. You did it then and again just now."

"What are you talking about?"

"You used me to slake your lust."

"Let me tell you something, angel." His voice was deadly. "If all I'd wanted was a piece of tail, I sure as hell wouldn't have come to you. I can find a lot better elsewhere, believe me."

His mockery cut deep. Jess drew her knees up to her chest, curling into herself. "Then why did you—" She faltered, unable to call what they'd just done "making love" when they'd rutted like savage animals. "Why did you take me to bed just now? What motive are you hiding this time? You can't expect me to believe you did it because you want me."

"You're damn right about that, I don't want you. A man wants a woman who's soft and feminine and delicate, one who needs his protection, not one with the balls to take on magnates like Burke—or one who's as bullheadedly blind as you are."

Wounded beyond measure, Jess retorted with a bitterness that she'd learned from years of struggling against Burke and all the wealthy, power-hungry, manipulative men like him. "Well, a woman wants someone she can trust not to lie to her. Not someone who's only interested in using her to further his empire."

Devlin swore. Viciously. He'd had enough of being called a liar, of being likened to that sonovabitch Burke. If he stayed one more second he was likely to do something he regretted even more than what he'd just done in bed with her.

Gritting his teeth, he turned and grabbed up his carpetbag, stalked across the room, and jerked open the door. He slammed it behind him with enough force to shake the small house.

Listening to his retreating footsteps, Jess shut her eyes. In agony, she turned and buried her face in the pillow that smelled hauntingly of Devlin.

She lay there curled on her side, hearing the reverberation of the slamming door echo the beat of her aching heart.

Chapter 14

J ess suffered from an overdose of self-condemnation
during the three days following her break with Devlin.
  She hated herself for being taken in by a smooth-talking
bounder with a bank account the size of the U.S. mint.
She'd compromised her deepest principles by even giving
him the time of day, let alone surrendering her body, but
at least then she'd had the excuse of ignorance. She hadn't
known then what kind of dandified polecat she was deal-
ing with.

But she'd known what Devlin was when he'd made
love to her that last time. She hated herself for falling into
bed with him the instant he'd kissed her. And she hated
herself for still wanting him. Her lips felt bruised from his
passion, her heart tattered, but she couldn't stop remembering the shattering ecstasy she'd found in his arms, or
the powerful way he'd made her feel—all weak and feminine and trembling and hungry for love.

She must be touched in the head to have fallen for him.
Her mother had warned her a hundred times against men
like Devlin. It was a cardinal rule. No matter how charming or handsome or glib of tongue a man was, no matter
what promises he made, never, *never* give him your trust
until after the ring was on your finger. Wealthy barons
weren't like normal folks. Success and power went to their
heads, until the only relationships they were capable of
were based on manipulation and lust. Love was the last
thing on their minds. They didn't even know how to love.

217

Her mother had discovered that the hard way with Ashton Burke.

Fiercely Jess tried to swallow the ache in her throat. Devlin would never love her. He wouldn't want marriage and a family—

The startling thought that flashed through her mind just then made Jess draw a sharp breath. Her hand stole to her stomach. What if she were pregnant? What if making love to Devlin resulted in a child? She would want the baby, but Devlin wouldn't. He'd told her as much that time on the trail when they'd talked about what they each wanted out of life.

It was a long moment before she decided there was no point in tormenting herself with such possibilities. She would just have to face it if it happened.

But the terrible ache in her heart wouldn't go away. She'd known Devlin didn't want a wife and family. What she hadn't realized was that their whole association was based on a lie. He had used her. For his own purposes, his own convenience. She couldn't forgive that or forget.

Confound it, she *would* forget it—and him! If she had to dose herself with laudanum for the next century, she would quit thinking about Devlin day and night and every minute in between.

Trouble was, she hated laudanum and the headachy sluggishness it always left behind. Trouble also was, everyone around her seemed to conspire against her. No one would let her forget Devlin. Riley was pushing ahead with the renovation of the Wildstar and the expansion of his operation, and he refused to hear a word against the man who'd made it possible. Clem, while still unhappy, had accepted the situation when Devlin's money financed *five* brand-spanking-new ore wagons and mule teams. That many would be needed just to keep up with the new steam-powered mechanical rock drills they'd ordered. Flo couldn't stop talking about how grand it was that that "gorgeous fella" was obscenely rich and that he was gonna give Burke his comeuppance.

Jess could hardly stand it. Could no one see what Devlin was doing with his filthy money? Pretty soon he would have total control of the Wildstar. Oh, maybe not legally, but her father would be under such a financial obligation that he couldn't dare refuse whatever Devlin wanted to do with it.

She nearly took Flo's head off one afternoon for merely mentioning Devlin's name, but it didn't seem to faze the widow one bit.

"What's got you so het up?" Flo demanded.

"Not a blessed thing," Jess returned resentfully. "I like seeing my father being taken in by a snake-in-the-grass."

"You talking about *Devlin*?"

Jess gritted her teeth, remembering what he had done yesterday. She'd gone to the bank to draw out the two hundred and fifty dollars she owed him, which put a huge hole in her savings. She'd sent Mr. Kwan over to Devlin's hotel with the money, but Devlin had sent back double the amount, with a note scrawled on the back of a gold-embossed calling card saying he carried more in pocket change and why didn't she buy herself a pretty gown with it, something soft and feminine? Reading the note brought back the red-hot shame Jess had felt when he'd last accused her of acting like a man. And then he'd had the gall to show up for dinner yesterday at the boardinghouse when she wasn't there. Not only had he weaseled Flo into serving him a three-course meal, he'd managed to sweet-talk her into swallowing his side of the story.

"Yes, I'm talking about Devlin," Jess ground out. "He lied to me from the start about who he was, pretending to be a tinhorn gambler when he was as rich as Croesus, and then—"

"Come on now, Jess, he explained all that."

"Okay, maybe he had cause for not telling the whole world who he was at first, but there was no good reason for not telling *us*. Especially after he found Zeke McRoy. All Devlin did was *use* us," she added bitterly. "And he had no call going behind my back to buy the mine from Riley. He didn't even have the gumption to tell me to my face." Jessica had more she could say about why she felt betrayed, but she wasn't about to tell Flo. Her seduction at Devlin's hands—or his seduction at hers, if she was perfectly honest—was not something she intended to discuss with anyone.

"Don't you think you're being a mite unfair?" Flo demanded. "Not every rich fella is like Mr. High-n'-mighty Burke."

"Devlin's like him. Worse, even. At least I knew better than to trust Burke. As far as I'm concerned, Devlin can take his fat bank account and ride out of town with it."

"I swear I don't understand what has you so riled."

"You don't *understand*? He's already started trying to run our boardinghouse, and he's changed everything up at the mine—how can you be so blind? If we keep taking his money, he'll be able to ride roughshod over us any time he takes a notion."

"Well, I think you're gettin' stirred up over nothing."

"I am not! And if he tries anything else . . . if he so much as looks crossways at me, I'll . . . I'll . . . box his ears."

"Us widows aren't so picky as you young gals," Flo said cheerfully. "That gorgeous fella can look at me any which way he wants, and I'll be right glad of it."

Jess shook her head, but she understood very well the appeal Devlin held for females of any age. She herself couldn't deny the fierce attraction, no matter how hard she tried. But it wasn't Devlin's stunning looks that she objected to. It was the way he *used* them to get his way.

Much worse, though, was the way wealthy men like him used their money, manipulating people and events to insure whatever outcome they wanted. Devlin had yet to prove that he was any different from all the other greedy, power-hungry magnates she'd known all her life. He'd bought into the Wildstar with a huge infusion of capital, in a way that seemed downright suspicious. What did he *really* want? was the question Jess yearned to have answered. Was his magnanimity really a bid to eventually take over the mine? That would have been a scheme worthy of Ashton Burke, and Jess couldn't dismiss the possibility as blithely as everyone else seemed to be doing.

She tried to warn her father of the danger, but Riley merely brushed off her concerns.

"I can't believe you actually let Devlin waltz in and take control of our mine," Jess finally exclaimed in frustration.

"He didn't take control. He didn't want it."

"It's close enough to make no difference. How could you let him talk you into it?"

"He's not a man to take no for an answer, Jess."

"That's exactly my point. He's no different than Burke when it comes to wanting his way. How do we know Devlin's not only out for himself? How do we know we're not being taken in? That we can trust him?"

"Because my instincts say so."

Jess couldn't buy that; Riley's instincts had been wrong before. "Then why did he spend so much money on the Wildstar when there's so little profit in it for him?"

Her father gave her a long look. "He did it for you, Jess."

She blinked, startled. "What do you mean, for me?" she asked.

"Do you really think any man in his right mind would sink a fortune into a low-grade mine that's not likely to pay out his investment just on a lark? No, he wanted to help you, and giving me the money to start over seemed the best way. He probably figured you would appreciate what he did instead of doubting his intentions."

Jess stared. "I don't believe it," she said finally. "Why would Devlin want to do anything for me?"

Riley was silent for a minute, his mouth pursed as if debating how much more to say. "Well, maybe that wasn't his only reason. After getting caught in that cave, he was riled enough at Burke to want to get even. And being part owner gave him the legal clout to take on Burke."

That sounded much more like the truth, Jess decided. Like Burke, Devlin would doubtless hate having his will crossed by anybody.

But even if he wasn't like Burke, even if she was wrong about Devlin, even if he didn't have any ulterior motives and wasn't trying to take over their mine, it still stuck in her craw having to suffer his patronage. Until now, she and Riley had always made it on their own, without any help from anyone—in fact, with active opposition and sometimes with pretty poor luck. Having to admit they needed Devlin didn't go down easy. And his apparent success in making Burke back off when they'd failed was only one more bitter pill to swallow.

That afternoon, the pill got so large Jess nearly choked on it. The Wildstar miners discovered a vein of silver ore in the lower level of Riley's mine, a vein so rich that it nearly went off the assayer's scale.

Clem came racing into the boardinghouse kitchen to tell Jessica the fabulous news, waving his felt hat in the air and whooping like a painted Indian.

"We're rich, Jessie! We're goddamned rich!"

Before she could do more than look up, the wiry mule skinner had picked her up by the waist and was whirling her around and around.

"Lord have mercy, what's goin' on?" Flo exclaimed, seeing all the excitement. "You been hittin' the bottle again, Clem Haverty?"

"Not hardly, woman! Riley made his big strike! We done found a lode!"

It was a long moment before he calmed down enough to make sense, and even then he was almost breathing too hard to tell them what had happened and his words all ran together.

"Riley found this crack in the low tunnel, see, and we set a charge, and you could see it was a vein, and Riley said 'Holy shit,' beg pardon, Jessie, but it was the damnedest sight you ever seen, all that ore what looked like pure silver! We done our own testin', but the numbers came out plumb crazy, I mean who would believe nine hundred a ton? I thought Riley was funnin' me, but we took some ore down to the assay office an' they said it was for real, more'n nine hundred ounces to the ton, and it goes on like forever! Hallelujah, we're richhhhhhhh!"

Just about then Riley came limping through the back door, a big grin on his weary face. When Jess asked, "Is it really true?" in an awed tone, her father laughed and held out his arms. His bear hug was full of love and triumph and completely ignored the still-painful wound in his back, although Jess tried to tell him to be careful.

Riley wasn't having any of it. This day was the culmination of a lifetime of searching for that elusive lode, and he declared he wasn't going to spoil it by playing the invalid.

At Riley's request, Jess broke out the decanter of currant wine that she kept for special occasions and the bottle of good rye whiskey she kept hidden from Clem, and poured glasses all around.

Riley raised his glass for a toast, meeting his daughter's eyes. "I only wish your ma could have been here. That's my only regret."

A bittersweet ache caught at Jess's throat. Riley missed Jenny Ann even more than she did, and all the silver in the world couldn't make up for her loss.

They drank to Jenny Ann Sommers—which made them all somber—and to the future of the Wildstar mine—which made them all light-headed with excitement—and then sat around the long pine-board table in the communal dining room and planned the expansion of the mine. Riley drew a layout of the tunnels on the writing paper Jess had fetched.

"We'll start a new drift there," he said, pointing, "and follow the vein back. From the looks of it, we may have trouble smelting the ore around here—got too much silver for the rock—but we can ship it down to Denver."

"All that purty silver," Clem said reverently.

Riley grinned. "I'm still not sure I believe it. Of course, the first thing we have do is hire a surveyor. We've got to make sure we have the rights to mine that lode, though as best as I can tell, it starts on our claim."

Adjacent to the Wildstar, Riley sketched in the outline

of Burke's Lady J mine. "We don't want to get in a legal
tiff with Burke over this and have it tied up in court so we
can't mine—" He broke off suddenly, seeing what he'd
drawn. "I'll be damned."

They all stared at the rough pencil marks that showed a
Lady J tunnel running smack into the vein Riley had discovered. It wasn't an accurate rendering, certainly, but it
raised the suspicions of every person sitting at the table,
even Flo, whose extent of knowledge about mining was
only that it resulted in hungry men.

"That low-down, two-timin' skunk," Clem growled.
"That's why Burke was so hot to get his hands on the
Wildstar. He found our lode!"

Riley nodded slowly. "Look's like it. What do you bet
they've been mining our vein?"

"I ain't betting those odds," the mule skinner snorted.

Suddenly Riley started to chuckle.

"What's so funny?" Jess asked indignantly, her anger at
Burke obscuring her ability to see the remotest humor in
this situation.

"Maybe this is what books call poetic justice," her father said. "The only reason we found the lode was because
of that crack in the wall. And that crack wasn't there last
week. I know every inch of that lower tunnel and I'd stake
my life on it. The blast that Burke's hirelings set off—
the one that almost killed you, Jess—must've shook
something loose."

She forced a smile. It would indeed be ironic if the fabulous strike was the result of Burke's foul play; if by trying to coerce them to give up the Wildstar, the silver king
had actually hastened the discovery of the vein that would
set them up in riches for life.

"Have you told Devlin?" Flo interjected.

Jess stiffened at the very mention of the name, and her
father gave her a sharp glance.

"He knows," Riley answered. "We sent somebody over
to the Diamond Dust to fetch him down to the assay office. He said if everything turns out the way we hope, he's
going to take us all out to celebrate."

"Not me," Clem declared adamantly. "I ain't gonna put on no fancy suit."

Flo hit him on the arm. "You will, too, you old coot, and you'll take a bath and put on some o' that sweet-smellin' shaving cologne, even if you won't get rid of that rats' nest you call a beard."

Jess didn't add her own declaration—that she wasn't going, either. Not for all the silver in the state of Colorado would she spoil this day for her father by reminding him of her estrangement with Devlin. This day was Riley's triumph, the fulfillment of a dream ... *if* it didn't fade away like a mirage when a survey was done, if it was really and truly *real*.

But this strike didn't make up for what Devlin had done, not by a long shot. She still wasn't willing to absolve him from having hidden motives regarding the mine.

Come to think of it, it did seem a bit odd that he had bought a large share of the Wildstar just before the vein had been discovered. It was almost as if he'd known about the silver being there. . . .

Jess frowned as she tried to form a mental picture of the tunnel the night of the explosion. Devlin had left her in order to find some water, she remembered, and he'd taken a long time to return. She'd even called out to him, asking if anything was wrong, which he'd denied. *Had he been inspecting a crack in the rock wall?*

A score of troubling thoughts assaulted her at once. Had Devlin discovered the rich silver vein then? Was *that* the real reason he had forked over such a huge sum for an interest in the Wildstar? Because he knew they would soon be hauling out ore worth many times that amount?

It made all too much sense.

A raw, scorching anger started to build inside Jess, along with a stabbing anguish that Devlin might have betrayed them so callously.

She didn't mention a word to her father about her suspicions, though. He was so blinded by gratitude, by Devlin's charm and money, he wouldn't have believed her any more readily now than he had earlier.

Instead, she waited until her father and Clem had left for the mine before she grabbed a bonnet and her reticule, which held the two-hundred-and-fifty-dollar salary that Devlin had refused and the extra money he had tried to throw in her face. Then she snapped out an excuse to Flo about having business to attend to and stormed out of the boardinghouse.

All the way to Devlin's hotel, Jess dredged up every single grievance she had against him, the latest being his possible concealment of the silver lode in the Wildstar. His combined transgressions were enough to whip her fury into a white-hot pitch. By the time she arrived at the Diamond Dust, inquired in the lobby for Devlin's room number, and endured the shocked stares of the clerk behind the counter, Jess was so mad she was breathing smoke. Muttering a thank-you for the information, she turned and nearly collided with Ashton Burke.

At her involuntary gasp, the Englishman reached out to steady her, his golden eyebrows raised in an expression that showed surprise and perhaps a hint of disdain. "Are you lost, Miss Sommers? May I be of assistance?"

Burke had a right to ask such questions, Jess remembered as she regained her balance. He was the hotel's owner, after all. She was the one who had no business being here, since no lady would visit a gentleman's hotel room alone. It was apparent from Burke's snide smile that he'd heard her ask for Mr. Devlin's room number.

Refusing to be discomfited or sidetracked from her purpose, though, Jess glared up at him. "No, Mr. Burke, I am not lost—and I hardly think I must account for my presence here to you. This is a public hotel, is it not?"

With that, she turned and made her way through the wide doors at the rear of the lobby and down the corridor, smarting from the humiliation of being discovered in such a position by her arch enemy, Ashton Burke, but not enough to forget her reason for coming here or her contention with Devlin.

Her fury had returned in full measure by the time she'd marched up the stairs and along the hall to his room.

Rather than knock, she pounded on the door with her fist. She hadn't even planned what she would say to Devlin if he was in, other than to ask if he had known about the silver vein before he'd made that lavish contribution to Riley's future.

She had raised her arm to hammer a second time when the door swung open on a masculine curse.

"What the hell . . .?"

Jessica's fist arrested in mid flight, six inches from Devlin's shoulder.

He had discarded his coat and vest, and his finely ruffled linen shirt was partially open, revealing the dark hair covering his muscular chest. Her heart did a flip-flop—she couldn't help it. He still had more masculine appeal than any man she'd ever known—and she was still half in love with him, no matter what he'd done, or how degenerate his character, or how hard she'd tried to forget him.

There was the barest tinge of surprise in his smoke-hued eyes at finding her at his door. She supposed he must be growing accustomed to her showing up in places no lady would ever willingly go.

"What is it?" he asked sharply, whether from annoyance or concern she couldn't tell.

"I should like to speak to you," Jess replied through gritted teeth.

Devlin raised a dark eyebrow, regarding her narrowly. He hesitated a long moment before stepping back with a sweeping gesture of his arm, inviting her to enter. Jess took three steps inside and stopped cold. The room was occupied. By a woman. A beautiful, sultry, lushly shaped woman.

She had raven-black hair and wore a blue silk afternoon gown that must have cost more than most miners made in a week. Her face was skillfully painted to show her features to best advantage, although she was sitting in the shadows, well back from the revealing sunlight streaming in the window.

The owner of the feather boa, was Jess's first intuitive thought. She couldn't believe the fierceness of the ache

that twisted in her chest at the idea of Devlin with this . . .
this . . . woman. At least the bed was made this time,
though, even if the velvet counterpane was rumpled with
the imprint of a human body . . . or two. Jess tore her
stricken gaze away from that objectionable piece of furniture as Devlin spoke.

"This is Lena Thorpe," he said, his tone cool, unapolo-
getic. "Lena works at the saloon next door and deals a
wicked game of faro. Lena, Miss Jessica Sommers."

After a moment's pause, the woman issued a polite
"How d' you do?"

Jessica managed a stiff reply, all the while feeling a devastating hurt at Devlin for introducing her to one of his
soiled doves. He was flaunting his relationship, Jess was
sure.

"I should like to speak to you," she repeated unsteadily,
turning to Devil. "*Alone*, if I may."

"Lena, love, will you give us a minute?"

"Sure, sugar." The beautiful dealer rose gracefully from
her chair and glided across the room, passing Jess in a fra-
grant cloud of expensive perfume. She paused beside Devlin, giving him a sultry smile. "You know where to find
me if you want me."

Quite deliberately, he reached up to brush back a raven
tendril that had fallen over Lena's ear. The caress lingered
far longer than necessary, Jess thought wretchedly. Devlin
had once touched *her* like that.

Keeping her eyes averted to hide her hurt, she waited
until the door shut behind the woman. She was twisting
the strings of her reticule together uncontrollably as Devlin
turned to her.

He leaned back against the door, crossing his arms over
his chest. Jess couldn't help but follow the arrogant movement, her gaze riveted on the bare flesh exposed by his
open shirt. Her lips had once tasted that naked skin covered with dark spirals of hair, had once explored the sleek
contours and powerful male musculature.

"Like what you see?" he drawled softly.

Jessica flushed a delicate crimson. "No . . . I mean . . ." She stumbled over the lie and fell silent.

"I could take off my clothes this time . . . *and* yours."

She drew a sharp breath. He was deliberately trying to disconcert her, and he was succeeding. She'd totally lost whatever composure she'd come here with, while the memories of her and Devlin doing shocking, intimate things together wouldn't leave her mind.

"The bed here is a lot larger than the one we used the other day."

"I didn't come here in order to go to bed with you!" Jess declared, her voice unnaturally high.

"Then to what do I owe the honor of this visit?" Uncrossing his arms, he pushed himself away from the door and moved toward her, his gray eyes locking with hers.

She shouldn't have come here like this, Jess thought wildly. Not when she had to face him alone. She couldn't trust herself alone with this man. Ten minutes ago she had been livid with him, and now she couldn't even think straight, not with him looking at her like that, as if he'd relish undressing her and taking his time making slow, hot love to her.

He stopped when he was almost touching her—far too close for her comfort—but Jess was determined not to give ground.

"Why'd you come here, sweetheart? Because you couldn't keep away?"

The suggestion that she found him irresistible grated on her nerves, and she tried to muster a scathing tone. "Do you honestly expect every woman to come panting after you?"

"Honestly?" His beautiful smile was charm itself. "I'd have to say that has been my experience, yes."

Jess drew in a ragged breath, feeling a sharp ache in her chest. She had little doubt he was telling the truth about his effect on woman.

He reached up to touch a forefinger to her lower lip, sensually, provocatively. "Do I disturb you, angel?"

"N-no . . ." she managed to stammer, trying not to flinch.

"No? Then why are you so hot and bothered?"

He was doing the same thing he'd done three days before, twisting her words and thoughts and feelings around till she didn't know up from down, right from wrong, truth from fiction. In a minute he'd have her quivering with longing.

His finger erotically stroked her lower lip, dipping just inside.

"No, don't . . ."

"That's what you said the last time, but you didn't mean it then, either."

"Devlin, stop it!" She heard the panic in her voice and hated herself for it. She couldn't let him do this to her.

Taking a step back, she drew herself up to her fullest height and said in her most formidable finishing school manner, "I did *not* come here to be assaulted, *Mr.* Devlin. I only want to talk to you."

"A pity," he murmured. To her vast relief, though, he turned away. "I'm all for accommodating a lady." He gestured toward a chair. "Please sit down."

Jess would rather not have taken the same seat his fancy woman had vacated, but she masked her hurt and sat down, perching on the edge and clutching her reticule in her lap. She wished it were a shotgun; she would have felt safer. Warily she watched Devlin.

He walked over to the bureau, where the liquor decanters sat. The golden sunlight streamed in the window and glinted off his sable hair. "Would you care for a drink?"

"No, thank you. I told you I don't drink spirits."

"Ah, yes. Saint Jessica."

"That isn't fair."

He glanced at her, a quick flash of gray, intensely cool in the warm light.

"I don't make my boarders or anyone else follow my rules outside my boardinghouse," Jess said in her own defense.

Not trusting himself to reply, Devlin poured himself

three fingers of whiskey and drank one of them in a single swallow, feeling the mellow fire burn all the way down to his stomach.

It didn't rid him of the sour taste in his mouth over his own boorish behavior. His fondling of Lena a few moments ago had been entirely deliberate. He'd purposefully flaunted his association with the faro dealer in a crude attempt to make Jessica jealous, to demonstrate what she was giving up by spurning him. It had been a petty gesture, unworthy of her, or of him. Primitive, base, and crude.

But more and more these days, his urges toward Jessica were degenerating into the primitive and base. The desire slamming through his body just now proved it. His condition, Devlin knew, had a good deal to do with certain memories that wouldn't go away. Jess clinging to him during a long dark night. Jess panting beneath him, meeting his every thrust with a fierceness all her own. Jess eager and giving, as passionate in her loving as she was in her anger. Too vividly he remembered the silkiness of her lustrous tawny hair, the velvet smoothness of her skin, the supple responsiveness of her body. The simple joy of holding her afterward.

Yet he also remembered the accusations she'd thrown at him the other day, and how she'd ordered him from her house. Her rejection had shot his male pride all to hell, but the hurt went far deeper than wounded pride. He'd felt *betrayed*. Jess had trusted him so little that she'd convicted him of treachery on the flimsiest of evidence.

Sure, he hadn't been entirely honest about his wealth, but he'd had good reason, wanting to protect himself from the kind of mercenary females he'd known all his life. Could he be faulted for trying to keep his heart from being savaged again? Ever since his fiancée had sliced up his heart, he'd sworn never again to let himself be used by a woman. Jess had used him, every bit as much as he'd used her, and then she'd accused him of being in league with that bastard Burke.

Devlin clenched his teeth. He hadn't felt pain that sharp

in ten years. He wanted Jess to acknowledge how wrong she'd been about him, but he wasn't sure even an apology would make up for her lack of faith.

Trying unsuccessfully to repress both memories and urges, Devlin ambled over to the bed and sat down with his back to the headboard, where he'd been when Jessica had interrupted. If she'd come here to apologize, he was willing to listen ... but he wouldn't make it easy for her.

Drawing one leg up, he rested his arm on his knee, the crystal glass dangling from his fingers. "I suppose you'll eventually get around to telling me why you're here?"

Jess regarded Devlin as if she'd never seen him before. How could she ever have believed he was a mere gambler? He had *always* looked like the kind of man who knew about power and wealth, how to get it and how to keep it. She had little doubt that he could be every bit as ruthless as Burke in getting what he wanted. Just now Devlin was lounging on the bed like a lazing wolf, alert yet perfectly at ease. But beneath the relaxed, almost lazy demeanor was a frame of coiled steel, the kind of hardness that could only be earned by physical exertion, by labor and sweat and strife. Who *was* this beautiful man who had crept into her heart and left it wounded and aching?

Realizing that she was staring again, Jessica shook herself and tried to marshal her scattered thoughts. "I only have one question," she began finally. "Did you find the lode in the Wildstar before you talked Riley into selling to you?"

Devlin stared at her for a long moment, before his eyelids drooped in insolent reply. "Let me see if I have this straight. You hunted me down here to accuse me of finding the silver lode in the mine and defrauding your father?"

His tone had turned chill, his eyes cold and diamond-hard, but Jess wouldn't let herself look away. The truth was too important to her. "The night we were trapped, you took a long time checking out the lower tunnel."

"You're giving me more credit than I deserve," Devlin said in a voice that was dangerous for its very calmness.

"That night I was concerned about a few more important things, if I recall—like staying alive. If there was a vein of silver showing down there, I sure as hell didn't recognize it."

"You found something in that tunnel, I'm sure of it."

"I found a crack in the wall. It was letting in a stream of air that I hoped would save our lives. I didn't tell you about it because I didn't want to raise your hopes."

Jessica's expression turned to anguished pleading. "Then why did you give Riley so much money for the mine? What were you trying to buy? The whole claim wasn't worth half that much, and Riley said he only sold you a minority interest."

Devlin found himself gripping the glass in his hand until the delicate crystal threatened to shatter. He'd told himself he wouldn't lose control with Jessica ever again. He could have hurt her a few days ago when he'd taken her so forcefully, when he'd been lost in the mindless pleasure her body could give him, the fierce joy of making love to her. But her latest accusation savaged his hard-won discipline and filled him with a cold rage.

"It would be just the kind of mercenary thing Burke would do," Jess added uncertainly, as if to justify her suspicions.

Devlin's wintry eyes impaled her. "Will you," he said in a deadly voice, "get it through your beautiful head that I am *not* Ashton Burke?"

Jessica nearly recoiled at the fierceness of the expression on his face.

"My motivation at the time," Devlin added icily, "was purely unselfish. Your father needed money to repair the mine and was too proud to take it. And being a partner in the Wildstar gave me the necessary leverage against Burke to threaten him with a lawsuit. I had absolutely *no* expectation of ever seeing the kind of return I usually get on my investments. And I certainly didn't expect to make a strike of this magnitude. Before you showed up just now, I'd already decided to let Riley buy back my interest at the same price as soon as he can afford it. I would have told him this afternoon, but I wanted to wait until the strike was verified and we could be sure Burke wasn't going to try anything else to sabotage the mine."

Jess stared incredulously. Devlin was willing to sell back his share without taking a profit? Surely he couldn't be serious about making such a generous offer. "You don't . . . really mean it? About letting Riley have the Wildstar back?"

His mouth tightened in a thin line. "Yes, dammit, I really mean it. I told you before I don't need the money."

Jessica bit her lip hard. Was it possible that maybe she might have been mistaken about Devlin's intentions? Her heart, so bitter and mistrustful, began to lighten. "I thought . . . I mean . . . you see . . ."

"I know, you told me. You thought I was trying to steal from your father. I'm a thief now, as well as a liar and a traitor. Saint Jess has tried and convicted me."

She didn't know how to answer him, since that was precisely what she had thought. Even clear across the room, she could feel his simmering fury, yet she couldn't really blame him for being angry at her. She *had* convicted him, even if deep in her heart she had prayed she was mistaken. She rose to her feet, her fingers making shreds of the strings to her reticule. "Devlin . . . I . . ."

She was about to tell him she was sorry for jumping to conclusions when his drawling comment stopped her.

"On second thought, maybe you were right. I suppose I did lie to you after all. My motives for offering to help your father weren't entirely unselfish. I also did it to appease my conscience." Devlin's mouth twisted. "Buying into the Wildstar was the best way I knew to make amends for what happened between us the other night in the mine. I felt guilty as hell about taking your virginity, and I thought I owed you something."

His stinging admission had the devastating effect he wanted: Jessica went white.

She moved toward him slowly, as if drawn to him against her will. "You gave us that money to alleviate your *guilt*?" She reached his side and stood staring down at him. "You were paying me for my services like any whore?"

Put that bluntly, it sounded cold and cruel, Devlin realized, yet it was partly true, and he was a trifle too enraged at the moment to be his usual charming self, or to couch the truth in softer terms. Besides, he was fed up with Jess always seeing his actions in the worst possible light.

"If that was what I was doing, darlin', then you have to be the most expensive whore I've ever had the pleasure of bedding."

Her white face grew even paler, if that were possible. "You bastard. . . ." Her voice was low and raw.

"What's wrong, sweetheart? Don't you think your virginity is worth fifty thousand?"

She slapped him then, *hard,* as tears sprang to her eyes, blurring her vision. In reaction, he caught her wrist in a tight grip.

"You . . . you . . ." Jess sputtered, furious. "I can't think of a word bad enough to describe you!" Nearly shaking with fury and pain, she struggled to free her arm.

Wisely, for his own well-being, Devlin wouldn't let go. He thought about pulling her down on the bed with him, like he had the last time they'd fought, but decided it would only end with him feeling more guilt than he did now.

"I'm surprised at your tactics, angel," he retorted instead. "You should have played on my sense of honor and tried to wrangle a marriage proposal out of me—but then you never have behaved the way a normal woman would."

It was a good thing he had hold of both her wrists by then, or she would have scratched his eyes out.

"I wouldn't marry you if you had a million trillion dollars!" Jess shrieked. "You couldn't pay me enough to take a man like you for a husband! Oh, I despise you! One of these days you and your ilk are going to learn you can't buy *people*! Especially me!"

Jerking free of his hold, she fumbled in her reticule for an instant and pulled out a wad of bills, which she threw in Devlin's face with all her might. "That's your salary! I don't care if you burn it or eat it or give it to that . . . that *woman* who was here. Just keep away from me!"

This time Jessica was the one who stormed out and slammed the door.

Sinking back on the bed, Devlin stared after her, his jaw muscles clenched, his left cheek still stinging from her slap.

He couldn't believe what had just happened. He couldn't believe she had actually waltzed in here and accused him of trying to bilk her father out of his newfound wealth. He couldn't believe how much her accusations *hurt*. The only thing he was certain of was that Jess was crazy. Loco. Stark, raving unhinged. At least when it came to anyone who bore the slightest resemblance to Ashton Burke.

She had this obsessive hatred for wealth and the men who owned that wealth. It was an issue she saw in stark black and white, with absolutely no shades of gray; if you were wealthy, you were—what was it she'd called him the other day—manipulative and heartless? She considered rich men totally beneath contempt.

But then, Devlin reflected reluctantly, didn't he have a similar prejudice? Hadn't he always viewed women in a similarly bad light, lumping them together with his one-time fiancée and his mother? The women in his life had been takers, only out for themselves. In his cynical view, women were apt to do far more for money than for blood or love.

He couldn't say that about Jessica Sommers. She truly did care for her father. Everything she'd done for the past three weeks, every desperate and dangerous action she'd taken, had been for Riley's sake. She'd tried her best to protect him from Burke's spitefulness and greed. In fact, her fierce loyalty was something Devlin had actually envied. He wanted Jess to be that loyal to him. He wanted her to trust him—

Realizing how laughable that wish was, Devlin ran a hand raggedly down his face. Her belief in him was so shallow that it had crumbled at the first test. Just as his fiancée's had ten years ago.

He was willing to admit that Riley's hellcat daughter wasn't the kind of mercenary woman his fiancée had been. But that Jessica could think *him* cold and mercenary— Devlin swore with a viciousness that did nothing to satisfy the blow she'd dealt to his pride or his heart, and tossed off the rest of the whiskey in his glass with complete disregard for its quality. The very notion that she wanted nothing to do with him because he *was* rich frankly stunned him. He'd never been spurned because he *had* money.

He remembered her latest accusation and cursed again. Goddammit, but she could set him off faster than any woman he knew. And that was a good deal of the problem. Every time he got close to Jessica lately, he wound up wanting to throttle her or make love to her or both.

Perhaps he should have taken Lena up on her offer, after all, when she'd wanted to spend the afternoon soothing him in bed. She could have satisfied his body and left him too wrung out to lust after a tawny-haired spitfire who made his blood boil with fury and desire. The trouble was that after making love to Jessica, the thought of sex with any other woman, even someone as sensual and as skilled as Lena, not only held no appeal, it was actually distasteful. Absurd, when one considered that Jess was a virtual novice at pleasing a man. Even more absurd after all the infuriating accusations she'd thrown at his head.

It bewildered him, the strength of his desire for her. He'd had dozens of women as beautiful as Jessica. He'd had women far more sophisticated and certainly more feminine. Women who, for all their calculation and greed, had known how to satisfy a man, not rip his character and integrity to shreds with unjustified accusations. Yet he didn't want any of those other women. He wanted Jessica Sommers.

Devlin raked a hand through his dark hair in frustration. Maybe he was the one who was loco. Maybe he ought to have Doc Wheeler examine his head—or other more critical parts of his anatomy.

He wanted Jessica Sommers.

He wanted her in his bed, in his arms, but it went much further than mere lust. On some deep, primitive, emotional level, he wanted to be wanted by that woman. He wanted her to *need* him. Not for his wealth, not for whatever help or material possessions he could provide her, not for the physical pleasure he could give her body, but solely for himself. Him. Man to woman.

He wanted her to need him. He wanted her to believe in him. He wanted her to trust him enough to *know*, despite whatever appearances to the contrary, that he would never have betrayed her the way she'd accused him of doing.

And he intended to succeed. If there was one thing he had in common with Ashton Burke, it was that he knew how to get what he wanted.

Keep away from you, angel? Not on your life. You're going to eat your words, sweet Jessie.

Devlin's gray eyes glinted in anticipation.

He *always* won when he put his mind to it. And he wanted Jessica Sommers.

Chapter 15

"You don't want to go?" Riley asked his daughter in surprise as they sat at the kitchen table finishing dinner. It was Sunday afternoon, several days after she'd stormed out of Devlin's hotel room. "Why not? I thought you'd like a chance to drive down to Georgetown and eat at a fancy restaurant and have somebody else cook for a change."

"I just would rather not, that's all."

"But it's supposed to be a celebration. Even Clem's going."

They were discussing Devlin's invitation for Wednesday night; he'd offered to take them out to celebrate their good fortune. The fabulously rich strike in the Wildstar had proved to be real. The survey team had ruled that the apex of the vein was located on the Wildstar claim, and their findings were as reliable as any could be, given the uncertainties of underground mining. Ashton Burke hadn't challenged the claim. In fact, they hadn't heard a peep out of Burke since Devlin had threatened him. Riley was more convinced than ever that Burke's Lady J miners had actually been mining Wildstar silver.

"I accepted Garrett's invitation to dinner for all of us, Jess. What am I supposed to tell him if you don't come?"

Jess ground her teeth at the familiar use of Devlin's first name; her father had become far too cozy with that low-down womanizing snake for her peace of mind. "You can tell him I took sick."

"You haven't been sick in years."

"I will be Wednesday night."

Riley stared.

Uncomfortable with her father's scrutiny, Jess jumped up from the table and began clearing the dinner dishes.

"What's come over you lately, Jess? Ever since the mine cave you've been as jumpy as a cat."

"Nothing. I'm fine." She lifted the pot of scalding water she'd left heating on the stove and poured it into the sink.

"Then how come you're so steamed at Devlin all of a sudden? You used to like the fellow."

"That was before I knew what kind of man he is."

"What kind of man is he? What'd he do that's got you so all-fired upset?"

She couldn't possibly tell her father all the reasons she wanted nothing to do with Devlin. Glancing over her shoulder as she tied on her apron, she hedged. "For one thing, he's so damnably arrogant I could spit."

Riley's eyebrows shot up, and Jess knew it was because she'd sworn in his presence. She *never* swore. She felt it incumbent on her to follow her own rules that she'd set up for her boarders.

"That's no reason not to go celebrate," Riley said slowly. "I'd like you to go with us, Jess." He gave her a coaxing smile. "You can buy you a pretty new dress and get all fancied up—"

"My own dresses aren't good enough to be worn in his company, is that it? He's too rich to be seen with us the way we are?" She shoved a skillet under the water, heedless of the good china plates and her usual order of washing.

"I didn't say that. You know I don't give a hoot about things like that. But we owe him a lot, after everything he's done for us."

I thought I owed you. The memory of Devlin's biting words brought an ache to her throat. She'd lost her heart to him, but he'd tried to buy her off with fifty thousand dollars. *What's wrong? Don't you think your virginity is worth fifty thousand?* He'd paid a huge sum for something she'd given freely, willingly—and only proved without a doubt that he and Burke were cut from the same cloth.

"I thought you liked Devlin," her father pressed.

"Well, I don't. I want nothing more to do with that pompous male popinjay."

"Why not? You've got to give me a better reason than just because he's rich."

"It isn't only that." She searched her mind for an excuse her father would accept. "He has a fancy woman."

"How do you know?"

"Because I saw her in Devlin's hotel room."

"You— *What?* When?"

She felt a blush rise to her cheeks. "When I went there the other day."

"You went to Devlin's hotel room? Bold as brass? Confound it, Jess, your ma would have had a fit!"

At her father's shock, Jess felt like squirming, especially when she thought of what Riley's reaction would be if he knew the entire truth about her and Devlin, that she done more than merely visit his hotel room. "I only wanted to ask him what he knew about the lode in the Wildstar. . . . And that *woman* was there."

Riley took a sip of coffee, mulling over her answer. "Sounds like you're a mite jealous."

"I am not!" Jess denied hotly. "I couldn't care less what tarts he keeps!"

"Then why are you shouting?"

When Jess didn't answer, Riley shook his head. "A man like that always has a fancy piece or two."

"Or two!" She went rigid as she thought of Devlin fooling around with *two* fallen angels like Lena Thorpe. "You mean to tell me you *approve* of such despicable behavior?"

"I don't know that it's so despicable. There's no law that says a man can't enjoy himself before he settles down."

"Well, there should be! And Devlin ought to be run out of town!"

"Seems to me you've got some pretty powerful feelings for that fella."

Jess went to work on the pots and pans with a vengeance. Her father watched for a while, before he said finally, gently, "Seems to me you're in love with him, Jess."

The skillet made a big splash in the sink as it slipped from her fingers. Jess spun around, looking frantic. "I am not! I hardly know the man. He only came to town a few weeks ago!"

Riley eyed his daughter sympathetically. "I didn't have to know your ma long before I was sure I was in love."

"Yes, but ... everybody was in love with Mama."

"Seems like all the females around here are in love with Devlin. Just look at Flo, acting all starry-eyed."

"Flo doesn't have a lick of sense sometimes. And I'm not in love with him." She was determined *not* to be in love with Devlin. She was one woman who wouldn't fall for his manipulative charm—even if it killed her.

"Did he make you an improper proposal?" she heard her father ask.

How should she answer that? She didn't want to lie. And yet to be perfectly truthful, Devlin actually had done little more than steal some kisses from her. *She'd* been the one to offer the improper proposal. "No," she mumbled.

"Funny. A man like that, I would have expected him to. Fact is, I'd be downright surprised if he didn't."

Her eyes widened; her father grinned ruefully. "I was a young man myself once. I just hope you know better than to listen to those sweet-talking bucks."

She knew better. She just hadn't acted on her knowledge, to her infinite regret now. Her mother had often warned her about certain kinds of men. They talked smooth and soft, but in the end, they only wanted one thing from a woman—and it wasn't love and a family and a future. Devlin was like that. He didn't want those permanent things. He didn't want her either—

"I'd like you to go Wednesday night, Jess. Will you do it for me?"

She swallowed the tightness in her throat. Put that way, how could she refuse?

Nodding mutely, Jess turned back around and tried to salvage the dishes from the mess she'd made in the sink, but her tormented thoughts wouldn't leave her alone. She was in love with Devlin, even her father had noticed it. She'd only been lying to herself by denying it.

She was in love with Devlin.

And the hopelessness of that love left her so terribly vulnerable.

At exactly six o'clock on Wednesday evening, the elegant hired carriage drew up before the Sommerses' small house and a gentleman stepped down.

Flo was watching impatiently through the parlor window, where they'd all gathered to await Devlin's arrival. "He's here! Oh, my . . . doesn't he look fine!"

Hating herself for her uncontrollable interest, Jess joined Flo at the window and peered out. The sight nearly took her breath away; Devlin was simply striking in black and white—black cutaway evening coat, white waistcoat, white bow tie, white gloves, and tall black opera hat. Even at a distance, his air of elegance and superiority was evident, while the stark hues only intensified his male magnetism.

"Lordy, isn't this gonna be fun?" Flo chirped.

Neither Clem, tugging on his restrictive tie, nor Jess, feeling acutely self-conscious in her three-year-old gown, were inclined to agree. Her high-collared black bombazine with the blond lace trim had always been adequate for church socials and an occasional concert, but it couldn't compare with Devlin's attire for sophistication. Yet her gown was the least of her concerns. Her cheeks burned as she recalled what had occurred the last time Devlin had been in this house. She also remembered demanding that he never darken her door again, yet here he was, merely a week later, strolling up the walk as arrogant as you please.

Riley met him at the front door and ushered him into the crowded little parlor. Jess felt her heartbeat quicken at his entrance. He had no right to look so handsome and de-sirable. His presence seemed larger than life, overwhelm-ing. And then his eyes locked with hers. Time seemed to stand still as amber clashed with gray. For a breathless moment, Jess felt as if she were the only one in the room . . . the only woman in the world.

But then Devlin had that ability, she remembered bit-terly. To make every woman, no matter what her age or appearance or social standing, feel special, feel wanted. She knew exactly how special she was to him. She was worth fifty thousand dollars—which was only pocket change to him. *I spend more each year on my horses.* How much did he spend on his women?

The ache in her heart intensified at the thought, and only grew worse when Devlin smiled his devastating smile that took in the entire company.

"Ladies." He bowed formally with an ease that made the gesture seem perfectly natural in the little parlor. "How lovely you both look."

Just as naturally, he took Flo's hand and carried it to his lips. The widow went pink and looked as flustered as Jess had ever seen her. Jess, on the other hand, clutched her own hands together and backed up a step, afraid that Dev-lin would try to work his suave charm on her.

He noticed her gesture, and the sudden mocking amuse-ment that entered his eyes told her very clearly that he knew what she was afraid of.

Jess swore silently at herself. He was so damnedly con-fident of his practiced power over women—and with good cause. She had meant to be cool and aloof toward him, but already Devlin had her on the defensive.

When he turned to speak to Clem, Flo leaned over to whisper in Jess's ear, "Gracious, doesn't that gorgeous fella have fine manners?"

"Fine manners don't make a fine man," Jess snapped back in a waspish tone.

Her defensiveness only increased, for a minute later Devlin offered her his arm to escort her out to the carriage. A glance of appeal at her father only received a stern frown, and Jess knew she was trapped. She couldn't refuse Devlin's offer without appearing incredibly rude. Gritting her teeth, she took his arm. She had promised her father she would get through this evening, and she would do it, even if she ground her teeth down to mere nubs.

Devlin tucked her fingers in the crook of his elbow and covered them with a gloved hand—far too possessively for Jess's peace of mind. She endured his touch, though, not about to give him cause to question her ability to conduct herself as a woman should.

As he walked her to the street, she even forced herself to say politely, if falsely, "I trust you have been well, Mr. Devlin?"

"Indeed, Miss Sommers. I enjoy the best of health."

"How unfortunate," Jess muttered under her breath.

The corner of his mouth kicked up in amusement, indicating he had heard her nasty remark. "I trust *you* have been well," he retorted in a low silken voice. "You didn't suffer any ill effects from our little tussle in bed the other day?"

At the reminder of her shameful behavior, Jess colored fiercely and glanced wildly over her shoulder to see if her father had overheard. She was vastly relieved to see that Flo was holding both Riley's and Clem's attention.

Determined not to be provoked, she took a deep breath and tried again. "I thought you would have left town by now."

"I'm devastated to disappoint you, angel, but I intend to stick around for a while longer. I *never* leave unfinished business."

They had reached the street by then, and he paused to look down at her, his gaze so unwavering that it startled her. His look seemed to imply that *she* was his unfinished business. There was something in his eyes that was both a promise and a threat. A dangerous threat. Dangerous and intimate. Jessica felt her heart lurch in confusion and alarm. Was he planning some kind of revenge in return for the accusations she'd made against him? His slow half

smile gave her no clue. With a bland expression of benev-
olence and generosity, he handed her into the carriage.

The vehicle was an expensive landau, with gold-etched
door panels and maroon leather seat coverings. Devlin
gave the ladies the forward-facing seats, intending for the
gentlemen to take the opposite ones. Clem, however, stubbornly climbed up beside the young driver Devlin had
hired for the evening and took over the reins, declaring no
wet-behind-the-ears kid was going to handle a team while
he was around.

The two-mile drive to Georgetown was generally pleasant. The landau's top had been dropped in deference to the
unusual warmth of the September evening, letting the pas-
sengers enjoy the blue sky and golden mountain air. Under
normal circumstances Jess would have relished such an
outing. This part of Clear Creek Canyon was unspoiled by
mining works and provided some of the grandest scenery
in the district.

The narrow road followed the twists and turns of the
canyon, running alongside the rushing, boulder-strewn
stream, whose banks were lined with willows and alders.
Great walls of rock flanked the road, rising almost straight
up. The surrounding mountains were clad with green ponderosa pines, as well as aspens and mountain maples that
were just starting to turn brilliant gold and red in a prelude
to fall.

Jess was relieved she wasn't sharing her seat with Devlin, yet having him directly across from her was almost
worse. She suffered his scrutiny in annoyance and bewilderment. She couldn't dismiss the intensity and awareness
in his eyes, the speculation. His shrewd gray eyes were
measuring her, as if he were mentally undressing her and
then regowning her in something far more feminine and
revealing.

Twilight was begining to fall as they reached Georgetown. They drove along quiet, prosperous streets, beneath
golden aspens and leafy cottonwoods, passing pretty clapboard houses with picket fences, and attractive Victorian

mansions built in the Queen Anne and Gothic Revival styles, where the recognized pillars of society lived.

Georgetown boasted several fine hotels and restaurants, but Devlin was taking them to the finest—the Hotel de Paris, which was renowned for its elegant decor, superb food, and excellent wines. When they arrived at the hotel and were shown to their table in the dining room, she could almost understand Devlin's earlier scrutiny of her attire. All the other ladies there wore evening gowns that left the shoulders bare and set off the tasteful jewelry at their throats and ears. Jessica suddenly felt dowdy in comparison. She should have done as her father had suggested, she decided, and bought a new outfit, even if it sent her into bankruptcy.

To her dismay she found herself seated next to Devlin, who, as host, claimed the head of the table. The owner and chef himself, Louis Dupuy, came out to greet Devlin personally. Jess listened in surprise as Devlin spoke in French. When he had introduced his guests and Monsieur Dupuy had gone off to prepare what he promised would be a fabulous meal, Clem gave Devlin a narrow-eyed stare.

"How'd you learn to talk that la-dee-da Frenchy jawin'?"

Devlin smiled easily. "My esteemed father insisted on a gentleman's education for his only son. It's come in handy a time or two in my business dealings."

He might have said more, but Flo interrupted in order to threaten Clem. "You behave yourself, Clem Haverty, or you'll be eatin' nothing but greens for the next month."

Clem scowled, but subsided into silence—for about two minutes, until the waiter brought the champagne. Flo thought that a big treat, but Clem grumbled about wanting some good whiskey instead of this pap that passed for liquor. Flo lit into him then, giving him a blistering lecture on manners and gratitude.

Under the cover of her scolding, Devlin turned to Jess on his right. "I hope the champagne is to your taste, Miss Jess."

His formality irked her. After the intimacies they'd

shared, it seemed absurd that he should revert to calling her "Miss Jess," even though she had been the one to start it. But then, he was only doing it to provoke her, she was sure.

"It's very good," she answered politely. "I suppose you drink champagne all the time?"

"I have it for breakfast occasionally."

He was taunting her about his wealth, Jess decided, her temper rising ten degrees. Only three times in her life had she ever even tasted champagne.

When she didn't reply, Devlin tilted his dark head to one side, giving her the full effect of his lazy smile. "You'll have to become accustomed to champagne, now that you're a wealthy young woman."

"I don't intend to change my habits just because Riley finally made a strike."

"A pity. You could do with some loosening up."

Jess nearly strained the muscles of her jaw, she clenched it so hard. It was all she could do refrain from throwing the rest of the champagne in her glass at Devlin's handsome face.

Dragging her gaze away, she glanced around the dining room. The elegant surroundings brought home more than anything else could the vast difference between her and him. This was Devlin's natural setting. A far, far cry from miners' fare at a communal dining table.

She couldn't keep the bitterness from her tone when she remarked, "If you're used to all this"—she gestured sweepingly at the surrounding elegance—"I guess I should be flattered you condescended to sit at my boarding table."

"It wasn't condescension. Even millionaires have to eat. And you're still the best cook in Colorado."

His compliment didn't mollify her; she knew her simple but hearty meals couldn't possibly compare to the gourmet cuisine they were about to indulge in.

"A shame you can't eat money," Jess muttered.

Devlin's lazy smile never wavered as he sipped his champagne, yet his gaze seemed to sharpen. "What do you have against money, anyway?"

"It's not money I object to. It's what money does to people."

"What does it do?"

"It gives them power that they only misuse."

"And you think everyone who has money misuses power?"

She understood the point he was trying to make, but her chin rose stubbornly. "Everyone I know does."

His eyes gleamed with mocking amusement. "But then, you don't know too many people of wealth."

Jess refused to look away, not forgetting how Devlin had paid her father fifty thousand dollars to ease his conscience. "I know at least one more millionaire than I ever wished to know."

Devlin acknowledged her gibe with a chuckle that was as charming as it was exasperated. "Ah, sweet Jessie, you do know how to cut a man down to size."

It was impossible not to feel the sexual awareness the husky velvet sound of his laughter aroused, but Jess tried to ignore it and returned his gaze, all seriousness. "At least people who work for their living aren't as likely to become corrupted."

"I *do* work for my living. I make money."

"Somehow I don't see making money as doing much to improve a man's character."

"Neither does poverty, necessarily." Reaching for the champagne bottle that had been left cooling in a bucket of ice, he refilled her glass. "And it's not only men who are corrupted by wealth, either. I was fifteen when I learned that lesson. That's when women began chasing me because of who I was . . . or rather, who my father was."

Jessica heard the hard edge of contempt in his tone and bit back the retort that was on her lips. She was frankly shocked by what he had implied—for two reasons. First, it had never occurred to her that someone could actually see great wealth as a liability rather than as a weapon to be wielded. Second, that Devlin could actually believe that was why women chased him. Anyone who looked into his eyes could see that women were drawn to him for a much more basic reason than money and position, or even his stunning good looks. Beyond the aura of wealth and power, beyond the fallen-angel features and the devil smile, was a simple, primal appeal that was as old as Adam and Eve. Some fascinating, elusive quality that made a woman feel warm and alive, that made her want to catch and tame and hold this man in her arms, that simply made her *want*. It was raw, potent, twenty-four-karat masculinity that called to everything feminine and vulnerable in a woman. And even though Devlin had accused *her* of being unfeminine, of not acting the way a normal woman would, in this case she was entirely normal.

Their private conversation was interrupted then by the appearance of the first course—much to Jess's relief mixed with a frustration she tried to ignore. She had forgotten there was anyone else in the room but Devlin. When she caught her father watching her speculatively, she blushed and turned her attention to her food.

They dined on oysters on the half shell, pheasant casserole, venison cutlets, sweetbreads, a julienne of garden vegetables, and several choices of dessert—Peach Charlotte in brandy sauce, petits fours, and apple fritters. Clem refused to eat the oysters and warily eyed everything else but the fritters, which he bolted down like a starved wolf. He did, however, praise the cognac that was served later with coffee. Twice during dinner a violinist came to their table and serenaded the ladies. Jessica flushed, Flo simpered, and Devlin slipped the musician a silver dollar.

They were sipping after-dinner liqueurs when they heard a stir at a nearby table. Ashton Burke had walked in, a lovely lady on his arm—a lady whom Jess recognized as a Georgetown socialite, one Devlin recognized as the type of woman his ex-fiancée had been.

Burke oversaw the seating of his guest and then surprised them all by coming over to their table. Devlin rose politely, and Riley reluctantly followed suit. Clem sat there glowering until Flo kicked him under the table, making him lurch to his feet.

"I wasn't aware you patronized the Hotel de Paris, Mr. Sommers," Burke remarked.

"I wasn't aware you did, either," Riley returned.

The fair-haired Englishman smiled coolly. "I come here frequently after attending the theater. I like to check out the competition. I have similar establishments, you will recall. In fact, perhaps you might join me one evening for dinner. Now that hostilities have ended, we could 'bury the hatchet,' as they say."

Riley looked at him warily, while Jess seethed. Burke was offering no apologies, no admission of guilt for all the trouble he had caused them. It galled her that he should walk away scot-free after nearly committing murder—and looking so unrepentant about it, to boot.

He inclined his head regally, including her in the gesture. "By the way, please accept my congratulations on your strike in the Wildstar."

Clem muttered something profane under his breath, which was cut off by Devlin's dry comment. "I'm gratified you're taking it so well, Mr. Burke."

He gave an elegant shrug. "You know what else they say—win some, lose some. Do enjoy the rest of your evening."

He returned to his own table then, leaving a pall over Devlin's guests.

If the dinner was an ordeal for Jessica, the ride home was worse. Somehow the seating arrangements became switched and Devlin ended up beside her. She could feel the heat and muscular hardness of his thigh, even through their layers of clothing. That, and the casual way he draped his arm across the back of her seat, almost but not quite touching her, unnerved her. Plus the landau's top remained down, leaving the carriage open. The night was quiet and romantic as a crescent moon spilled its pale light over the rocky canyon, transfiguring the hulking mountain peaks around them into immense purple shadows. Jess was grateful for the soft breeze cooling her flushed face, and more grateful still for the way Flo kept up a steady, cheerful stream of conversation.

To Jess's regret, Riley invited them all into the house for a nightcap. Clem refused on the grounds that he had to get out of his "golblamed torture suit," but Devlin stayed nearly an hour—an interminable length.

Her regret was even greater when her father asked her to show Garrett to the door. She caught Devlin's amused expression and bit her lip. Instantly suspicious of anything that pleased him, Jess ushered him into the front hall and handed him his hat, but that was as far as she got. Devlin wouldn't leave.

"Good *night,* Mr. Devlin," she said pointedly, holding the door open. "I trust you won't come here again."

His dark eyebrows rose in a mock dismay. "Such gratitude, Miss Jess."

"I have no reason to be grateful to you," Jess practically hissed. "Your fifty thousand dollars made everything even between us, as you so correctly made clear to me. Now please leave. I don't want you in our house."

Deliberately ignoring her order, Devlin leaned negligently against the wall, looking for all the world as if he were enjoying himself. "But your father invited me to call again. I'd say he approves of me."

"Only because he doesn't know what you did!"

"Shall I tell him?"

"No!" Jess almost yelped the word. She glanced behind her guiltily, but the voices coming from the parlor assured her Flo and Riley hadn't heard. "Good Lord, no."

"Then I think you'd better make it worth my while," Devlin said silkily.

"What? What do you mean?"

"If you want me to keep quiet about our prior relationship, then I suggest you give me something in return."

Clenching her teeth, Jess violently took Devlin by the elbow and nearly pushed him outside. Pulling the door closed behind them, she left them surrounded by darkness. "You cad!" she exploded then, which made Devlin grin, his teeth flashing white in the moonlight.

"So you've said."

"What do you want?"

I want you, lying in my bed, wrapped around me. "A kiss, Miss Jess. Merely a kiss."

"You want me to kiss you after what you've done?" She sounded incredulous.

"I'd rather have you under me," he replied lazily, which made Jess gasp at his frankness, "but tonight I'll settle for a simple kiss."

Jess stared at him. What he was asking was impossible. *Nothing* was simple where this man was concerned, certainly not his kisses. "And then you'll leave?"

"If you really want me to."

His husky, silken rasp, low and sexual and totally arousing, tore through her senses. Jess remained rooted where she stood, unable to move. Devlin reached up to touch her cheek with the back of his hand. He had taken off his gloves, and his fingers were warm, erotic, sending arrows of shivering awareness down her spine. He was going to kiss her, and she was going to do absolutely nothing to stop him.

She watched as his lazy lashes lowered to half shade even lazier eyes. The moon silvered his face, etching his beautiful features with light and shadow, filling her vision. Incredibly, she wanted his kiss.

Yet he didn't oblige at once. His hand slipped behind her neck, lightly cupping, but that was all he did. His hesitation confused her.

Devlin, however, felt no hesitation at all. He was merely savoring the moment, drawing it out to heighten the anticipation. He figured he deserved to indulge himself.

The evening had been sheer hell.

The need to touch her, the need to lower his mouth to Jess's, had driven him half mad the entire time. And now the tightness of his body, the ache in his groin, was a persistent clamor. He wanted her naked beneath him, naked and straining and giving, like she had once been. He wanted her open and trusting, the way she'd been before learning of his vast wealth. At the very least, he wanted her friendship.

It was wishful thinking, he knew. Just now, Jessica

looked as proper and tightlaced and unfriendly as any sour-tempered matron, nothing like the wild, sensual creature he had unleashed in bed an interminable week ago, nor the frightened woman who'd shared the darkest night of his life with him, not even the courageous partner who'd helped him face down two gunmen.

He had hoped she would cool off some by now. He'd endured the past week with impatience and remarkable fortitude, allowing Jess to keep him at arm's length—more than arm's length—while he attempted to understand and come to terms with her deep prejudices. Jessica hated all wealthy men. Unreasonably. Blindly. Period.

Her passionate dislike of Burke, however, at least was based on fact, Devlin realized. And she did have some justification for considering his own actions mercenary. He should never have told her about the fifty thousand being payment for his guilt, even if it was partly true. His primary reason for giving Riley the money was not so mercenary—his desire to make her life easier. Yet she would no more have accepted his generosity on that basis than she would have accepted charity from Burke.

Devlin's own fury at her had abated somewhat in the past week, but his temper had shot up again this evening when Jess had shunned him. She'd made it very clear how much she despised him. He didn't want her to hate him, to look at him as if he were beneath contempt. He wanted Jess to *want* him as much as he did her.

At least she was speaking to him again. He had her father to thank for that—which Devlin had trouble understanding. If she were *his* daughter he wouldn't allow her anywhere near a man like him. Riley couldn't know what had happened between them—that a near stranger had taught his daughter about passion and desire and sexual need. If he had known, instead of pursuing a friendship, he would be hauling out the shotgun Jess was so fond of brandishing.

She wasn't threatening to shoot him now, Devlin reflected with pleasure. She was waiting uncertainly for his kiss, her breathing shallow, her lips parted. He could feel her trembling.

Devlin couldn't help the feeling of triumph that surged through him. She was afraid of what he could do to her, how he could make her feel—which meant she wasn't as indifferent to him as she wanted him to believe. Perhaps she was feeling some of the powerful, conflicting urges that tormented him.

Determined to make her experience every hot, violent sensation of need and desire that was slamming through him, he lowered his head.

His claiming of her mouth was slow and hot and tender, a savoring possession that stroked and caressed. His tongue penetrated her warm interior deeply, with an intimate demand that made very clear his sexual intent. There was absolutely nothing innocent about his embrace, either. He thrust his muscular thigh between hers deliberately, making her feel the hard pressure of his arousal in the front of his trousers. He reached up to cover her breast intentionally, shaping his hand to the lush, corseted curve. When Jess whimpered softly, Devlin felt a flood of intensely male satisfaction. She ached for him, as he did for her.

And there he ended it.

As deliberately as he had begun, he pulled away, leaving her throbbing and unfulfilled, as he was throbbing and unfulfilled.

Lost in a drugged sensuality, Jess opened her eyes and looked up at him in an unfocused daze. His expression was hard and sensual, his silver-smoke eyes dilated with arousal. Raw desire darkened his voice when he spoke.

"Whether you want it or not, angel, you're going to become a woman . . . my woman."

With that, he turned and walked away, leaving Jess to stare after him, her fingers raised to her burning lips.

His declaration didn't make the least bit of sense to Jess. Why Devlin should claim that she was going to become his woman was totally unfathomable to her. Unless her rebuffs had raised his ire to the point of vengeance. Unless she had challenged his inflated self-consequence once too often and he had thrown down the gauntlet. Maybe he was determined to prove his mastery over her. Maybe he wanted to be the one to walk away, to leave her pining after him, spurned and brokenhearted. That would explain his cryptic remark as he had handed her into the carriage. *I never leave unfinished business.*

Whatever his motives, Devlin's threat left Jess confused and worried and, if she were honest with herself, the least bit excited. No matter how he had hurt her before, no matter how mercenary and manipulative he had proven to be, she was woman enough to feel flattered by the pursuit of such a man—even if that pursuit was driven purely by spite. Worse, she was enough in love with Devlin to be grateful for even that crumb of attention.

One thing was clear, in any case. He wasn't going to let her be easily rid of him. The kiss Devlin had given her in the moonlight had told her, emphatically and demonstrably, that he wasn't through with her by any means.

One other thing was clear as well. Her father was bent on matchmaking.

From then on, every chance he got, Riley brought up Devlin's name—first name—in passing conversation, and twice during the latter part of the week he invited Devlin to call. Those evening sessions in the parlor were sheer torment for Jess. Her traitorous father kept making excuses to leave the room, while that scoundrel Devlin sat there and smirked, a triumphant gleam of amusement dancing in his eyes.

She didn't dare order him out, though, or refuse to be present for his visits. Devlin had threatened to tell Riley precisely what had happened when they'd been trapped in the mine together. It was blackmail, pure and simple . . . ungentlemanly and altogether unprincipled. But she wasn't going to take a chance on her father's learning the truth. She didn't want Riley knowing she'd had such terrible judgment as to lose her innocence to this . . . this black-hearted devil.

Saturday night came as a relief. Riley announced that he and Clem were going to spend the evening playing poker at the Diamond Dust Saloon. Riley hadn't indulged in a game in ages, certainly not for such high stakes as the Diamond Dust offered. In fact, he had rarely even been in any of Burke's saloons, calling them too rich for his pockets. But he wasn't above thumbing his nose at Burke now that the battle had been won, Riley told his daughter. That he would be spending Devlin's money until the mine started to show a profit apparently didn't bother him, Jess observed in frustration.

She spent the first part of the quiet evening reading and trying not to dwell on Devlin's perfidy. Having no success, she decided to turn in early.

She was undressing for bed when she heard a noise that seemed to come from out back of the house. Instantly suspicious, Jess bristled. If her father had sent Devlin over in his absence, she would throttle both of them.

Dragging on a robe over her chemise and drawers and shoving her feet into slippers, Jess made her way to the kitchen pantry, where she got down the shotgun. Then she threw open the back door. It was dark outside, with nothing unusual in the night sounds.

"Devlin?" she called uncertainly. She descended the back steps slowly, her eyes scanning the small moonlit yard.

It was nothing she heard that alerted her to the danger; it was more like a sixth sense. Jess whirled just in time to see the dark figure of a man moving toward her, his arm raised, his hand clutching a long object that might have been a piece of firewood. His face was blackened by shadow, but she recognized the man. Hank Purcell, the superintendent of Burke's Lady J mine.

She had no time to wonder what he was doing there in her yard. She didn't even have time to protect herself. His arm descended and pain flashed in her temple. Then everything went black.

Her return to consciousness was slow and confused. She first became aware of the pain in her head ... not too severe but dull and throbbing. Next, that her tongue felt dry and thick against the gag that had been stuffed into her mouth ... highly uncomfortable. Then a smoky, cloying scent ... sickly sweet and overpowering. Finally the low-volume noise ... strange gurgling sounds accompanied by moans and sighs.

Wincing, Jess tried to raise a hand to her aching temple, but to her great bewilderment she found she couldn't. There seemed to be a cord around her wrists ... and her ankles too, if the numb sensation in her feet was any indication.

Disoriented, she opened her eyes. She was lying on some kind of pallet, her head on an Oriental cushion of red-and-black silk. Squinting, she searched the dim, smoke-hazed room. Two dozen other people—mostly men dressed in the rough style of miners—reclined on other pallets and in the tall row of bunks that stood against one wall. A few women, half clad and with painted faces, lay beside the men. All of them were either sprawled in a state of dazed insensibility or occupied in taking long drags from long-stemmed pipes, which sent little clouds of smoke into the air.

This has to be one of the opium dens I've heard about, was Jess's first complete thought. They were smoking opium.

Her initial reaction was curiosity. All her life she had heard about these Chinese dens of iniquity, but she'd never seen one. Nobody she knew frequented these sinful places.

This one was no hovel—but no haven of luxury, either. The room was dark, save for the fitful gleam of the opium lamps. A young Chinese woman who looked much like Mei Lin was moving from pallet to pallet, checking the pipe bowls.

Her second reaction was pity for the young woman. Serving these misguided souls who were lost in the drugging influence of the poppy, perhaps giving her young body to their pleasure like Mei Lin had been forced to do, was one of the most horrible fates Jess could imagine.

Her third reaction was anger as she began to realize

how she must have come to be here. *Hank Purcell,* she remembered witheringly. He had actually hit her, the sneaking coward.

Her fourth reaction was unease, bordering on fear. *What did he intend to do to her?* She had been abducted from her own house, brought here against her will, and now she was bound and nearly naked in an opium den. Her robe was gone and so were her slippers. All she had on was a thin cambric chemise that barely reached her knees—and that, at the moment, was riding up her thighs—and her lace-trimmed underdrawers. With rising panic, she struggled to push down the hem of her chemise, then tested the bonds at her wrists. They wouldn't budge.

Ordering herself to stay calm, Jess let her aching head fall back on the cushion. She had to *think.* How could she get herself out of this fix? She seriously doubted any of the opium-dazed people here would give her any help if she asked for it. Besides, she couldn't even speak with the choking gag crammed in her mouth. Her brain felt so foggy. . . .

The low male chuckle so close beside her startled her. Jerking her head around, Jess looked up to find Hank Purcell grinning down at her.

"Good, you're awake. It'll save me the trouble of bringing you around. Come on, now, we're gonna find you a little more privacy."

Before she could even try to understand what he meant, Purcell had pulled her to her feet and thrown her over his shoulder. The hard bone jammed into her stomach, knocking the breath from her body, while the blood rushed to her head, making her even dizzier.

She tried to fight back, but although she herself was no weakling, his lean, work-honed body was as powerful and unbending as steel. All her struggles were useless. When she did manage to drive her fists into the small of his back, he swore foully and brought the flat of his hand down on her bottom in a stinging slap, a warning for her to desist.

She was seeing spots by the time he carried her down

a dark hall and through a doorway. From what she could tell in her awkward position, they were in a small room lit by a table lamp.

Purcell kicked the door shut behind him and dumped Jess on a pallet much nicer than the one she had just left. This was softer, for one thing, and was covered with red satin sheets. Unlike the other pallet, however, this low bed was surrounded by four-inch-diameter wooden posts protruding from the floor.

Purcell grinned as he began tying her bound wrists to one of the posts above her head. A minute ago, Jess had wondered what they were used for, but it wasn't hard to guess now, or to imagine herself spread-eagled on the pallet. Filled with real fear now, she resumed her struggles with renewed ferocity, yet the result was just as hopeless. In only a few moments he had trussed her up tight, her arms stretched high over her head, tied to one of the posts above, her ankles lashed to another post below. She could only twist helplessly and pant for breath behind the clammy gag. The only thing she could be grateful for was that her feet were still bound together. Purcell couldn't intend to rape her immediately, Jess told herself, or he would have made it easier for himself to get at her.

But if that wasn't why he had brought her here, then what did he want with her?

It seemed he didn't mind telling her. Still grinning, Purcell sat back on his heels and surveyed his efforts. "There, that should do it, Miss Jess. You're gonna be here a while. Nobody's gonna find you for a long time to come. You see, I gave you to Madam Wong. She was right pleased to have a new girl for her crib." He waved his hand at the furnishings. "This is one of Madam's special rooms. And you're gonna get to service all the special customers."

He had given her away? To a Chinese madam? In order to service all the special customers? Jess stared at him in shock and horror.

To her surprise, he loosened the knots behind her head and pulled the gag down. "Don't bother screamin'. It won't do you a lick of good. Nobody pays any mind to what goes on in an opium joint."

Knowing he was right, Jess bit back the scream that had risen to her throat. There would be little use. Instead she carefully flexed her aching jaw. Her tongue was paper-dry and stuck to the roof of her mouth.

"Why?" she rasped when she could manage to speak. "Why are you doing this?"

"For all the grief you and your pa have caused me."

Jess had never realized just how nasty a smile could be. Purcell looked highly pleased with himself.

"I don't think your pa is gonna be too happy to find you gone. It'll be worse when he learns what's happened to you here."

Wishing she could reach Purcell's smirking face with her nails, she gave a fierce tug on the rope, which made his gaze drop to her scantily clad bosom. A speculative gleam flashed in his brown eyes, just before he reached out to pinch her left nipple.

Jess flinched and tried to shrink away in disgust, but she couldn't move more than an inch or two.

"A week or two in a Chink cribhouse like this and you won't be so prissy," Purcell taunted as he deliberately fondled her breast. "You'll be right grateful for a man who ain't all doped up."

She gritted her teeth and tried not to gag.

"You ought to be nice to me, Miss Jess. I could ask Madam Wong to go easy on you, since you're new to this and all."

"You could also go to the devil!" Her tawny eyes flashed fire as she glared at him with impotent rage.

His nasty grin widened. "Too bad I don't have time to see to your training. I'd enjoy bringing you to heel—and it'd make my revenge even sweeter."

Jessica tried to swallow her fear. "Is that what this is about? Revenge? But we didn't do anything to you."

"Oh, yeah, you did. You're the reason Burke fired me."

"What are you talking about? Burke fired you?"

"Last week."

"I don't see how that's our fault."

"*Your* fault mostly. Burke said he didn't care much for my methods. Said the dynamite was bit too rough."

She gasped. "*You* set the charge in the Wildstar?"

"Could be. 'Course I've got more than enough reasons to be riled at you. I didn't much like it when you and that bastard Devlin killed one of my partners."

Trying to comprehend, Jess stared at him. There had been only one man she and Devlin had killed. "Zeke McRoy was your partner?"

Purcell's dark eyebrows drew together in a scowl. "Never mind that. Just you quit talkin' and listen up. I want you to be real clear about what happened between the Lady J and the Wildstar." His eyes narrowed and he seemed to look through her as he continued. "It started about four months ago. We were sinking a new shaft in the Lady J when we cut through a horse and found your pa's claim."

Jess frowned. A "horse" was a wall of bedrock, she knew. What she didn't understand was why Purcell was admitting his complicity in mining another man's claim.

"We dug a crosscut right into the Wildstar," he was saying. "We were stealing right under your pa's nose and he was too stupid to realize it."

"Why are you telling me this?" Jess asked in bewilderment.

"If I'm going down, I'm taking Burke with me. I owe him. I figure your pa won't take too kindly to knowing Burke was swindling him."

"We already guessed that. We just never had any proof Burke was behind the attacks."

"Oh, he was behind 'em, all right. He wanted that silver. Why do you think he was so hot to get his hands on the Wildstar? And then he fired me—" Purcell found his grin again. "The thing is, the joke's on Burke. I don't need his fuckin' job. I have enough money stashed away in the mountains to last a lifetime." He reached for her again. "Now lie still while I put this gag back on you."

Trying futilely to draw back, Jess sent him a hostile glare. "You won't get away with this."

"Who's gonna stop me?"

"I will . . . and Devlin."

He laughed, his expression a taunt. "You'd have to find me first. I'm headin' out of state, just as soon as I pay a little visit to some friends of mine up north."

"We'll find you! Just the way we found Zeke."

Purcell sneered. "Zeke was stupid, flashing his ugly face all over the territory. I should never have hired him."

"But you did. You must be pretty stupid, too."

He looked as if he might hit her, making Jess realize how foolish she'd been to bait him.

"Shut up," he warned. "I don't want to hurt you none. I'll leave that to all those fine bucks who are gonna come in here and show you a good time."

Jess shuddered at his threat, and cringed when he reached for her. When she realized Purcell only meant to gag her, though, she clenched her teeth tightly—and paid for her pitiful resistance. He forced her jaw open so painfully it made her cry out, then he stuffed the gag in her mouth, wrenching her neck as he retied the knots.

Finally, he stood up, his teeth flashing white. "You just lie there and enjoy it, Miss Jess."

He left her alone then. Simply turned and walked out, taking the lamp and shutting the door behind him.

Jess lay there shuddering, relieved that Purcell was gone but terrified by the pitch-blackness he had left behind. It was much like the horrible darkness that had accompanied the mine cave-in. The lack of light frightened her even more than Purcell's threats of sexual assault had, for it brought back that terrible nightmare.

Stop it, Jess! Think!

She bit back a sob and forced herself to take a deep breath. Any minute now she might have to fend off a visit by one of Madam Wong's patrons, and she stood little chance with her hands and feet tied to the posts. She also stood little chance of escape unless she could get loose from her bindings.

With renewed deliberation, she went to work on the cords at her wrists, plucking with her fingers. With her hands stretched above her head, she couldn't use her teeth as she would have liked.

She made no progress whatsoever. The knots resisted her every attempt at untying them. She tried clawing with her nails then, with marginally better results. The rough hemp began to fray after a time.

She didn't know how long she struggled—at least an hour, perhaps—before the door suddenly was flung open.

Jess jumped, and then winced at the bright stream of light flooding the small room. She couldn't make out the menacing figure standing in the doorway, but she was desperately afraid it was one of Madam Wong's special customers.

"Jessica?" The word was a harsh rasp. She knew that voice. It belonged to a man she'd declared she never wanted to see again as long as she lived.

Devlin stepped cautiously into the room, his revolver drawn.

Jess let out her breath on a sob. She had never been so grateful to see anyone in her entire life.

Chapter 16

Because of the darkness, Devlin had to fetch a lamp from the hall. Setting it on the small table just inside the room, he barred the door to prevent anyone else from entering, and knelt beside Jessica. His chiseled features were tight with anger as he loosened the knots of her gag.

"Are you hurt, Jess?" he demanded, going to work on the rope that held her tied to the upper post. The cold fury in his voice made her shiver.

"N-no," she croaked faintly. "Not much."

Devlin swore as he wrestled with the knots. When they finally came loose, Jess didn't wait for him to untie her bound hands or feet but threw herself at his chest with a grateful sob. Immediately she was enfolded in strong, comforting arms.

Devlin held her tightly, his cheek against her hair, his relief so profound at finding her unharmed that he was actually shaking. He could feel Jess trembling as well. She pressed herself fiercely against him, as if she wanted to burrow deep inside him.

"It's okay, sweetheart," he murmured raggedly, soothingly. "It's okay. You can cry."

She shook her head. "I'm too *mad* to cry." Her voice was muffled against his shoulder, but the vehemence of her tone reassured him. Relief surged through Devlin, savage and sweet. He had his stubborn wildcat back. Any other woman who'd endured such an experience would be in deep shock, but not his Jess.

With fervent gratitude, he pressed his lips to her hair, which smelled faintly of opium. He knew he ought to finish untying her and get her out of here, but at the moment she seemed to need, more than rescue, just to be held.

Jess clung to him, soft and pliable, letting his strength renew hers. "How did you find me?" she finally asked.

"I called at your house," Devlin answered thickly. "You weren't at home, so I went to the boardinghouse. Mei Lin met me at the door, frantic because she wasn't sure where to find your father and didn't know what to do. She'd just been given a message for him."

"A message?"

"From the madam here. It seems Madam Wong recognized you and sent for Riley."

"My father's here?" She sounded alarmed. "I don't want him to see me like this."

"He won't," Devlin soothed. "He doesn't even know about it yet. Mei Lin's husband helped me find this place. I showed up here ten minutes ago and threatened to burn this building down if Madam Wong didn't produce you immediately."

Jess shivered. She had no trouble envisioning Devlin getting his way with Madam Wong; he could be devastatingly forceful when he chose. "I don't think it was her fault that I'm here. Hank Purcell is the one to blame. He brought me here and tied me up."

"So Madame Wong said," Devlin returned grimly, recalling the score he had to settle with Purcell. "Thank God she was more interested in earning your father's goodwill than in profiting from your services. She's a good businesswoman. She knew Riley would be grateful for her keeping you unharmed, and her calculation paid off. I intend to reward her well for her trouble."

Jess shuddered, violently this time, as she remembered precisely what depraved "services" Purcell had meant for her. "He *gave* me to that woman," she exclaimed with fresh outrage.

"Shhhhh, angel," Devlin said quietly, stroking her bare arm. "It's over."

His palm was warm and soothing against her skin—which made Jess suddenly realize that she had very little clothing on. Her cheeks flooded with hot color. How humiliating to be found in such a scandalous condition by Devlin, half naked in a den of iniquity, tied to a bed whose purpose was certainly not sleeping. She shouldn't allow him to hold her like this, either, but she didn't want to move. His warmth, his strength, his clean masculine smell were chasing away the horrors of the past hours. She didn't want him to let her go.

Devlin wasn't about to let go, though. He *liked* having Jess cling to him, to need him the way she had during the mine cave. It made up for some of the savage hurt that she'd inflicted so thoroughly on him during the past two weeks, mitigating his ravaged pride and his outraged sense of injustice.

As if she'd had a similar remembrance about the mine disaster, Jess suddenly drew back, her fingers clutching at his waistcoat. "The dynamite! Devlin, it was Purcell. He was the one who set the charge that nearly killed us."

"He told you that?"

"He wouldn't admit it outright, but he didn't deny it, either. And he said that was why Burke fired him. Purcell told me all about stealing ore from the Wildstar. They cut into our lode, which was why Burke wanted our mine."

"We already figured as much."

"But Purcell was behind the dynamite. He tried to murder us! He said it was his revenge for all the grief we caused him. And then he did this." She held up her wrists that were still bound. "Devlin, we have to stop him!"

His hands automatically closed around hers as he studied her flushed, beautiful face, with its wisps of tawny hair falling from their pins. Her expression was set and earnest—and altogether terrifying. Devlin knew that determined look, and he didn't like it in the least. When Jessica got her mind set on something, no one could reason with her.

"*I* have to stop him," he corrected. "You won't have anything to do with it."

"I'm going after him—"

"No, you are *not*, Jess."

"Yes, I am! I'm the one he did this to! And I don't intend to let him get away with it."

"He won't get away with it, I'll see to that. But you're going home."

"I will not!"

Devlin's jaw tightened. With pointed emphasis, he glanced down at her bonds. "I haven't untied you yet. And I won't unless I have your promise to let me handle Purcell alone."

She stared at him incredulously.

"I mean it, Jess. I'll leave you here where you can stay out of trouble."

"You wouldn't!"

No, he wouldn't. He couldn't leave her to the doubtful mercy of Madam Wong and her lusty customers. But he wasn't about to weaken his hand by admitting it. "You're not setting foot out of this room without giving me your word," Devlin said firmly.

Her expression turned mutinous. "I'm not giving you anything."

"Jessica, be reasonable. You can trust me to take care of Purcell."

She stiffened at his mention of the word *trust*, suddenly remembering all the grievances she had against Devlin. "How dare you talk to me about trust after the way you lied to me and used me? I'd sooner trust a . . . a flea-manged polecat!"

She had chosen the wrong response. All the savage anger that Devlin had harbored against her for the past two weeks, all the resentment and indignation and wounded pride, came flooding back in a solid rush. Without stopping to reconsider, he reached for the rope behind her, the one still attached to the upper post, and pressed Jessica back down on the pallet.

She gasped as she realized his intent. "What are you doing!" She tried to sit up again, but Devlin had threaded the rope around her wrist bonds and was securing them tightly. He was actually tying her up! Jess jerked at the rope with impotent rage. "You can't do this to me, you . . . you devil!"

"I'm doing it." His tone was grim. "If you want me to stop, you'll give me your word to stay out of this."

Refusing to yield to his coercion, she tried a different tack. "Devlin, Purcell will get away if we don't go after him right now! He already has more than an hour's head start."

"He won't get away. I know what he looks like now."

"But you don't understand! He said Zeke McRoy was his partner. He said he had enough money stashed away in the mountains to last a lifetime. You told me once that Zeke took part in those train holdups. What if Purcell was working with him? What if that's how he got all that money, by robbing trains with Zeke's gang?"

Her argument made Devlin pause. "It's possible they were working together."

Seeing him frowning, Jess pressed her point. "I'm *sure* that's what happened. Purcell said that he'd hired Zeke, and I'll bet it was to do more than drive us off our claim. But if we don't follow him now, he's going to get clean away."

Her logic seemed reasonable, except for the "we" part. Devlin shook his head. "You're not going, and that's final."

"But you need me," Jess insisted. "What if Purcell has gone to meet up with his gang? He said he planned to leave the state, but first he had to visit some friends up north. What if they're outlaws? You can't face all of them alone."

"I'll take the marshal with me."

"That lily-livered chicken won't help you. I can—"

"We've had this same conversation once before about Zeke McRoy, but this time I'm not budging, Jess. You *aren't* going."

She set her jaw mulishly. "You can't stop me."

Grinding his teeth in frustration, Devlin stared down at her. He needed to be riding after Purcell, but just now driving some sense into Jess was even more important to him. He wasn't about to let her go chasing about the countryside and possibly get herself killed. If Purcell really was part of the outlaw gang, he wouldn't hesitate to harm Jess simply because she was a woman. Just look at her current predicament.

Besides, Devlin thought grimly, he had a few other bones to pick with Jessica Sommers just now. And he doubted he would ever have a better opportunity. He was alone with her, without her father or Flo hovering around, without any interference at all. Mr. Kwan was standing down the hall as guard and would alert him to any trouble.

Devlin narrowed his eyes as he gazed at Jess speculatively. What he was considering wasn't playing fair, certainly, but then fairness hadn't gotten him anywhere with Jess. Extraordinary measures were called for.

A hard smile touched his lips. He was going to have it out with her right now. Before she left here, Jess was going to learn a few basic truths about herself—and him.

He reached up and pulled a pin from her hair.

Jess looked at him in alarm. "What are you doing?" she exclaimed, trying to twist her head away.

"I'm taking your hair down. I want to see how it looks spread across a pillow when I make love to you."

"Wh-what? You c-can't be serious," she stammered. "You can't mean to . . . to . . ."

"Love you? Indeed I do."

As the pins came loose one by one, her hair fell about her shoulders in gleaming cascades. With the devotion of a connoisseur, Devlin smoothed the long tawny tresses over the red-and-black satin pillow.

"Beautiful," he murmured, his voice thick and husky.

His preoccupation with her hair made Jess more furious than his arrogant demands had. She squirmed fiercely. "Devlin, if you dare touch me, I'll shoot you, I swear I will!"

He smiled that devilish, infuriating smile that was so achingly familiar. "No, you won't, angel. You aren't as tough as you let on. You're a responsive, sensuous woman beneath all that stubbornness."

"You can't do this to me!"

"I think I can."

"I'm warning you, I'll scream—"

"It won't do you any good. Madam Wong won't interfere, not after I promised her a huge sum for leading me to you."

"That's despicable, buying her off with your filthy money!"

"No, it's just smart business. She did me a good turn, and I reciprocated."

Jess would have retorted, except that Devlin had bent over her and was untying the cord that shackled her feet to the lower post. She held her breath, hoping that he had changed his mind and was going to release her entirely.

But her hope was wasted. He freed her legs, removing even the bonds around her ankles, but he left her arms pinioned over her head. Looking smug, he stretched out beside her on the silken sheets, not touching yet near enough for her to feel the warmth of his body.

"Damn you, Devlin. . . ."

"Call me Garrett."

"I won't . . . you *snake!*"

"You don't seem very appreciative, my sweet ingrate. After I went to such trouble to rescue you, I expect at least a proper thank-you. Thank me properly, Jessica. . . ."

His hand entwined in her tousled mane. Dipping his dark head, he kissed her softly, barely, teasingly.

When he drew back slightly, Jess glared at him helplessly. It infuriated her that he was enjoying having her at his mercy. In fact, he looked as if he *relished* it. "Devlin . . . don't . . ." she pleaded through gritted teeth.

"You don't want me to make love to you?" A half smile swaggered into one corner of his mouth as he smoothed one hand up the inside of her thigh. "You'll understand if I don't believe your protests." He bent to whisper seductively in her ear. "You go wild every time I touch you. You turn into a tigress in bed. . . ."

Even as he spoke, he moved his hand higher, beneath the hem of her chemise, along her hipbone to stroke the velvet of her bare belly. Every muscle in Jess's body tightened at his intimate caress. "D-Devlin ... I swear ... I'll hate you ... for this."

"No, you won't." Withdrawing his hand, he began working loose the row of small buttons on her chemise. In only a moment her full creamy breasts spilled out to him.

His hot gaze lingered on the lush sight. "You have the loveliest breasts. . . ."

He probably said that to every woman he undressed, Jess thought with dazed fury.

As if he couldn't restrain himself, Devlin reached up to cup a pale globe, his palm molding the generous fullness. She closed her eyes, clenching her teeth against the erotic sensations his delicate touch aroused. "You ... lecherous ... beast. . . ."

He chuckled brazenly. "I think you like my lechery, sweeting." Purposefully, he put his lean forefinger into his mouth and wet it. Reaching out, he brushed her left nipple, drawing a slow circular pattern around the pink aureole. Jess gasped at the sharp pleasure that raced through her body.

"I think you like me touching you. And before I'm done with you, you're going to admit it." Each low sensuous word stroked her. "You need me, Jessica ... and by the time I'm through with you, you're going to *know* you need me."

It should have startled her, the determination in his voice. He meant to prove his sexual prowess, his mastery over her. It should have shocked and disturbed her. He wasn't going to stop; he intended to make love to her in a squalid opium den, regardless of her wishes or the moral bankruptcy of preying on a helpless, captive female.

She gave one last frantic tug on the rope that bound her arms overhead. She was lying half-naked and completely vulnerable to him, yet the sense of being powerless was at the same time sensuously exciting.

"Just lie still, sweetheart," Devlin ordered softly, his eyes heated with desire.

The sultry look in his depthless gray gaze was a promise of pleasure. The slow movement of his hand against her silky, shivering flesh was a foreshadowing of the care he meant to take with her.

Her full trembling breasts blossomed beneath his touch, at his gentle stroking. Jess could do nothing to prevent it. With a knowing smile, Devlin bent to her mouth, giving her light, provocative, indulgent kisses that drew the breath from her body, while his fingers played over her breasts. His arousing hand roamed at will, leaving a trail of delicate flame wherever he touched her. The nipples of her breasts were now tingling points of sensation.

Leaving them, he worked leisurely downward, over her tight, flat belly, the curve of her hip, her woman's mound.

"Devlin . . ." Jess wanted to move away from him, from his brazen caresses, but against her will, she wound up straining her hips helplessly *toward* him, wishing he would ease the sudden powerful ache that was throbbing between her thighs.

"Hush, sweetheart, I know what you want."

And it seemed that he did. His dexterous fingers seemed to know just where the most sensitive spots on her body were. Jess's breath faltered as his fingers teased between her legs. Devlin smiled a little at the heated moisture that was there to greet him, a smile which deepened when he caught the look she was giving him. Her amber eyes were filled with a sensual, reluctant pleasure that told him, more than words, the seductive effect he was having on her.

His skillful fingers continued toying with her . . . slowly, erotically . . . until her breath grew heavy and her legs parted of their own accord. Jess tilted her head back in surrender. Her pride was gone, seared away by the heat of his caresses.

His thumb brushed aside the folds of her drawers to touch the core of her need, to ply it to heated wanting, while he watched the passion play on her beautiful face. Her hips began to lift and then fall, repeatedly, the rhythm imploring—which he allowed for a time. Then, with gentle deliberation, he sheathed his fingers in her pulsing warmth.

Jess let out a soft keening moan that turned Devlin's blood hot.

Ruthlessly he stroked her until she thrashed and whimpered, until with shuddering spasms, the first shattering release swept through her, brutal and scalding in its intensity.

Devlin's eyes gleamed with male satisfaction as he bent to kiss the corner of her mouth. Jess lay there shaken and spent, hardly aware what he was doing.

"Don't fall asleep on me, angel. We aren't nearly finished."

Startled, she looked up to see the lazy fire in his eyes as he moved over over her and knelt between her legs.

There was nothing lazy or easy, though, about his assault when he kissed her lips again. When his tongue plunged deep and hot into her wanting mouth. Or when he broke off to brush the column of her throat with heated, nibbling caresses. Or when he took her aching nipples into his mouth to lave and suck them.

Moving his lips downward, he ran warm hands beneath her hips and gently squeezed her buttocks. Lifting her up, he bent to her, his mouth nuzzling through the thin fabric of her drawers, a gesture that sent Jessica into gasping shock.

"Devlin—stop! What . . . are . . . you—?" She wanted to reach down to him, to make him stop his scandalous action, but her arms were still pinned securely above her head.

Not answering, he pressed his mouth right up against her, searching out her heated, weeping flesh. Jess thought she might die from the sensual bliss. He was nibbling at the core of her, stroking her with his tongue, finding her most sheltered secrets.

"You . . . *can't!*" The word was almost a shriek.

"I can, love." He punctuated his answer with soft, wicked kisses, nipping softly, tasting her to his ruthless satisfaction.

She trembled under his stunning, erotic assault. She couldn't believe this was truly happening, that his dark head was between her burning thighs, giving her the most exquisite pleasure she had ever known. His mouth was like magic, tender and demanding, dictating the actions of her body, silencing the protests of her reason. Her senses sang in wanton harmony as he compelled her surrender.

He tasted and lapped at her, his lips and tongue claiming her female essence, plundering her with tender savagery. The yielding, primitive scent of her made his groin grind, and strengthened his determination to search out the secrets of her body. Heedless of her soft pleas, he gripped her bottom with his strong hands and held her up to him, giving him complete access, making the anguished pleasure inescapable.

"So sweet . . ." he murmured hoarsely, his tongue thrusting into her moist warmth.

Her reaction was everything he could have hoped for. She was writhing wildly now, breathing in sharp little gasps, reduced to primitive, pagan need. His lips wet with her dew, Devlin raised his head and looked along the length of her. Her back was arched, her lush, ripe breasts jutting proud and bare with the thrusting motion she made.

He could have sent her over the edge. He could have given her the ecstasy she was sobbing for. Yet he held back, watching her, savoring his power.

His hesitation was not what Jess wanted. Not when she was in such agony. Such sweet, tumultuous agony. She had reached a point of shuddering, throbbing need, and yet he wouldn't give her the shattering fulfillment she craved.

"Say it, Jess," he whispered hoarsely.

With her senses so dazed, she could make little sense of his demand. "Wh-what?"

"Say you need me."

Confusion assaulted her. He was making her confession the price of completion?

"Say it, or I'll leave you aching like this. You need me to make love to you, you need me to rescue you from this place, you need me to stop Purcell from getting away. You *need* me."

Fury and frustration swept through her, so fiercely that she wanted to scream at him. And yet she had no choice. She *did* need him.

"*Say it,* Jessica."

"Yes, I need you. . . . Devlin, please!"

"Garrett."

"Yes, Garrett . . . *please.*"

Her breathless, keening plea was more demand than surrender, but it satisfied him. His eyes a hot, liquid smoke, he freed his swollen, thick erection from his trousers and, lowering himself to cover her body, thrust deep inside her.

The sweet force of his invasion made her gasp, yet she wrapped her legs about his powerful hips and moaned at the delight of sheathing him. The glorious melding of his flesh with hers was a pleasure too fierce to be borne. Seconds later, she cried out in savage release and stiffened as hard racking shudders convulsed her, as wave after wave of violent, blinding ecstasy ripped through her.

The fiery pagan climax caught Devlin in its clutches. The wild creature bucking beneath him with such abandon made his body explode, and he poured himself into her endlessly, his own harsh cry joining hers.

Neither of them were sure how much time passed before their senses returned and their breathing settled down to something resembling normal. They lay cuddled together, his body around hers, the lamplight playing over their strengthless forms.

Finally Devlin roused himself to reach up and untie the cords over her head. When Jess gave a soft moan at the rush of feeling that flowed into her fingers, he brought her hands to his lips, brushing the red-marked skin at her wrists with feather-light, penitent kisses. She didn't even open her eyes. Tenderly, Devlin gathered her boneless body into his arms and nuzzled her ear. "The next time I intend to take off both our clothes."

Limp and languid from his caresses, Jess couldn't form a protest. She should be furious with him, she knew, but she couldn't summon the energy. Devlin had won this latest battle, yet she wouldn't call herself the loser. In fact, she could barely remember what they had been fighting about. She could almost fall asleep. . . .

He couldn't even get a response out of her when his hand strayed up to fondle her bare breast. "But that will have to wait," he said reluctantly. "Right now I'm going to take you home and then find your father. And then I'm going after Purcell. Alone. *You're* going to stay put."

Slowly, Jess opened her eyes. The heavy sexuality that had brought them together hung in the air, resonating between them.

"And you won't give me any arguments," Devlin added firmly.

She remembered then what they had been fighting about. His blackmail.

"No, I won't give you any arguments," she answered in a subdued voice.

His burning look surveyed her flushed face, her kiss-swollen mouth, and he smiled, his eyes filled with latent tenderness and triumph.

Jessica allowed him his moment of glory. She clamped her teeth together and forced back the heated accusation that was on the tip of her tongue, consoling herself by reflecting that Devlin's victory was only temporary. She was merely being wise, appearing to surrender while she was still at his mercy.

Yet she wasn't beaten, by any means. What Devlin saw as capitulation, she saw merely as tactical retreat.

Chapter 17

He cradled her in his arms on their ride back. Despite the urgency of going after Purcell, Devlin tenderly put Jess to bed—which included making her drink a shot of whiskey to help her sleep. Then, after repeating his order for her to stay put, locking the doors, and posting her Chinese servant in the hall as an armed bodyguard, he went to fetch her father.

The Diamond Dust Saloon was filled with cigar smoke and crowded to overflowing by a more prosperous class of clientele than most mining town saloons could boast, but there was no immediate sign of Riley. Entering the private parlor, Devlin spied the elegant figure of Ashton Burke seated at Lena's faro table, basking in the raven-haired beauty's proprietary smile. A moment later Devlin found Riley playing poker at a rear table and pulled him away.

Riley's face turned a chalky shade of white when he learned that his daughter had been abducted by a vengeful killer and given to the notorious madam of an illicit opium den. Devlin managed to allay some of his alarm, only by swearing that Jess had come to no harm, and that she was at this moment tucked safely in her own bed, asleep. Even so, Devlin had to forcibly restrain Riley from pelting out the door at a run.

"She's all right," Devlin reassured him. "And I left Kwan to watch over her. Right now I could use your help getting my gear together. I intend to ride after Purcell as soon as possible. I promised Jess I would deal with him, and I'd better do it if I want to keep her from going after Purcell herself."

"Kwan's with her, you say?"

"Yes . . . and she should be asleep by now. You won't want to wake her."

"Okay. What do you need me to do?"

They went up to Devlin's hotel room next door, where he changed clothes while Riley gathered up weapons and ammunition. As they worked, Devlin filled Riley in on everything else Jess had learned from Purcell, including her suspicions that Purcell was part of the armed gang that had robbed the Colorado Central.

"Makes sense," Riley commented with a thoughtful frown. "As Burke's mine foreman, he could find out when bullion shipments were going out. 'Course, most of the trains down to Denver from here would have *some* amount of silver."

"Sixty thousand dollars' worth?"

"Mmmm. Maybe not that much." Stuffing several boxes of .44 cartridges into Devlin's saddlebags, Riley changed the subject. "Are you sure it's all that smart to be going after Purcell on your own? If he really is working with that gang, he could be a passel of trouble—more than you could handle on your own."

"I'm hoping to persuade the marshal to ride with me."

"That lily-livered coward?"

"That's what Jess said."

"I better go with you when you talk to him. Maybe he'll listen to me, but I doubt it. Virgil Lockwood has been in Burke's pocket since the last two elections. You might do better to get the Clear Creek County sheriff—darn. You can't. I heard Matt Nash rode over to Blackhawk yesterday."

"I'll go alone if I have to. Purcell isn't going to get away."

Riley nodded and started checking the contents of the bedroll. "I'm right grateful that you talked Jess out of going. It scared the tarnation out of me the last time you two took off."

"It wasn't easy getting her to stay here, I can assure you." Devlin grimaced as he remembered what he'd had to do to extract Jess's promise. "I've never met a woman as stubborn as she is. She's worse than one of Haverty's mules." A wry half smile curved his lips as he pulled on a fresh chambray shirt. "How did you raise a daughter like her anyway?"

There was a pregnant pause. "You telling me you don't care for my Jessie?" Riley asked in a tone that held a hard edge.

At the question, Devlin looked up to find the man studying him intently. Deciding a diplomatic reply was in order, he gave Riley a grin that had been known to charm even irate fathers. "That isn't the case, and you know it. It's just that sometimes she annoys the living daylights out of me."

Riley's expression didn't lighten up. "I'd say the feeling is mutual. What's going on between you two, anyway? You've been at each other's throats like a pair of cats ever since the mine cave."

"I suggest you ask your daughter."

"I did. She wouldn't tell me." He held Devlin's gaze deliberately. "Jess's been acting mighty strange lately. I guess maybe it's because she's in love with you."

Devlin's grin faded abruptly. "Would you mind telling me what makes you think so?" he asked after a moment.

"I know my daughter, Garrett. She's not the same person she was a month ago. She colors up like a tomato whenever she hears your name. And she was actually cussing the other day. That isn't like Jess."

Devlin couldn't stop the sudden pounding of his heart. "That doesn't mean she's in love with me."

"No? She'd never get so riled at somebody she only felt lukewarm toward. She either hates you or loves you, and I don't think it's hate."

"I'm not so sure about that." He grimaced, remembering. "She wasn't exactly overjoyed to learn the size of my bank account. And she considered my purchasing an interest in the Wildstar nothing less than treason. She accused me to my face of knowing about the lode beforehand and trying to swindle you out of your money. That doesn't sound much like love to me."

Riley's mouth curved in a faint grin. "Oh, I didn't say she *likes* being in love with you. Fact is, she's fighting it just as hard as she can. But I kind of hope she loses the battle. I'd be happy to have you as a son-in-law."

Devlin sucked in his breath sharply. "You don't pull your punches, do you?"

"Don't see any reason to. I think you ought to marry her."

A bit stunned and a bit wary, Devlin stood there grim and unmoving, his hands halted in the process of buckling his gun belt. He knew instinctively that what Riley was telling him was true. He'd known too many women not to recognize the signs. Jessica was in love with him. He'd succeeded at least partially in his goal to make her eat her words.

He just didn't know precisely what he intended to do about it.

He didn't much care for being cornered this way by her father, either. But there was no way he could ignore the issue, stated so baldly. Riley wanted him to marry his daughter.

He was mildly surprised when Riley did an about-face and offered him a way out.

"'Course, if you don't love her, that's something else. Jess deserves the love of a good man." Riley began tying the leather thongs of the bedroll. "All I want is for her to be happy, and it wouldn't make her happy to have a husband who didn't love her . . . or who wasn't going to give up his other women and be faithful to her."

"Are you finished?" Devlin asked abruptly, avoiding an answer as he resumed tightening his gun belt. "I need to get going."

Riley didn't look away. "With your gear, I am," he said, implying that he wasn't done with the subject. "You may recall I told you something about my late wife, son. Burke loved Jenny Ann, but he lost her because he wouldn't marry her. So you ought to think about this long and hard—about what's really important in life. You could be the richest man in Colorado, but it won't keep you warm in winter, at least not the kind of warmth that means anything. Your letting Jessie get away could be the biggest mistake of your life."

Refusing to reply, Devlin put on his hat and hefted his rifle. He knew better than most that wealth was cold comfort. For a long, long time he'd been dissatisfied with his life. But until he'd come to Silver Plume, he'd never been so aware of the *emptiness*. He realized something vital was missing—like the love and companionship Riley Sommers shared with his daughter. A relationship that was strong and enduring.

He wanted that kind of relationship in his life, Devlin acknowledged. But his feelings for Jess were intense and complex, and he didn't want to be rushed into sorting them out. Even if he *did* decide to marry Jessica, he intended to go about it slowly. His scars ran deep. He'd been mistaken about a woman's love before, and he wasn't about to set himself up for such a fall again. He wanted to be damn sure that what he felt for her was real, and what she felt for him would last.

When they reached the street, it was near midnight, but the music and revelry coming from the saloons and dance halls along Main Street hadn't diminished in the slightest. They fastened Devlin's saddlebags and bedroll on his horse. Riley had recovered enough from his wound to play poker but not enough to climb into a saddle without pain, so they walked the several blocks through the darkness to his small house, with Devlin leading his mount.

It became immediately clear, however, that Riley wasn't going to let the previous subject die.

"You see, son, I don't want the same thing happening to Jess that happened to her ma. Jess shouldn't have to settle for second-best the way her ma did."

"What do you mean?"

"Jenny Ann wound up with me instead of Burke."

"I doubt if anyone who knows the two of you would consider you second-best to Burke."

"Well, Jenny Ann loved him."

There was pain in his tone even now, Devlin noted. But then it couldn't be easy to stomach your wife loving another man.

"Burke was a damn fool," Riley said with conviction, "for letting her get away. He didn't think she was good enough for him to marry."

Devlin noted the pointed way Jess's father was looking at him. "I assure you," he replied carefully, "the notion that Jess might not be good enough to be my wife never entered my mind."

The moonlight which etched the lines on the older man's forehead showed his concern.

"I realize you only want your daughter's happiness," Devlin added softly, "but you're going to have to let us settle this on our own." He waited for that to sink in. When Riley slowly nodded, Devlin gave a wry smile. "Whatever way it turns out, though, I thank you for your faith in me. It's more than Jess has shown me."

After a moment, Riley sighed. "I just don't want her tied to a loveless marriage."

"I'll do my best to see that doesn't happen," Devlin said solemnly. "That much I can promise you."

In the ensuing silence, Riley seemed lost in his reflections. And when he spoke it was clear he was still dwelling on the past. "It's hell not knowing. Jenny Ann married me instead of Burke, but I never could be sure if she really loved me or if she was just making the best of the situation."

"Why else would she marry you?"

"Because she had to."

"Why, did her father force you two to marry?"

"No, but—"

Riley broke off, and there was another uncomfortable pause. Devlin had the feeling Jess's father wanted to tell him something but didn't know quite how.

"You know," Devlin said slowly, choosing his words

with care, "the first time I saw Jess and Burke together, it surprised me. The similarity in features was remarkable. They have the same color hair . . . the same nose and chin . . . the same determination."

"You noticed that, did you?" Riley replied quietly.

"And something else struck me as odd. Jess calls you by name instead of using 'Papa' or 'Father.' "

There was a long pause. "I always thought you were an observant man. Nobody else ever saw the resemblance. I kept worrying that they would."

"I take it Ashton Burke is. Jess's natural father?"

"Yes."

The answer was so quiet that Devlin could barely hear. He wasn't really surprised to have his suspicions confirmed. What surprised him was Riley's admitting it to him. That kind of honesty implied a great deal of trust. And something else, perhaps? The need for a sympathetic ear? His daughter's parentage wasn't something he could discuss with just anyone. Whatever, Devlin felt touched and honored that Riley had shared such a confidence. And somewhat uncomfortable, as well. He didn't like the idea of knowing such a secret and keeping it from Jess. In the past, he'd held back far more from her than he should have—which was a major bone of contention between them.

"Jess obviously doesn't know," Devlin said pensively.

Riley shook his head. "I never could bring myself to tell her. I thought she might come to hate me if she found out."

"I don't think it would be possible for Jess to hate you."

"I'm not so sure. She never has been able to abide dishonesty. I did try to tell her the night I got shot, but she wouldn't let me talk. And I didn't try very hard afterward. I was afraid once she found out she wouldn't want to be my daughter any longer. I reckon that makes me a coward. I was afraid I'd lose her to Burke."

"There isn't much chance of that. She despises Burke and all he stands for." Devlin gave a sardonic grin. "I should know. Jess has accused me on more than one occasion of being just like him."

His attempt at lightening the conversation fell flat; Riley obviously was still trying to justify his actions to himself, if not to the man beside him.

"Jess is more my daughter than she could ever be Ashton Burke's." It was said fiercely, with a hint of desperation.

"I don't doubt it."

"There was a good reason for keeping it quiet twenty years ago," he tried to explain. "Jenny Ann didn't want anyone to know, *especially* Burke. That's why she married me in the first place, to keep people from finding out and to prevent a scandal—and to give her daughter a name."

"I take it Burke doesn't know, either?"

"There've been a few times that I've been tempted to tell him and watch him squirm. All these years he's been denying his own daughter all the fancy things he thinks are so important. And now this last. . . . He set his hired guns on his own flesh and blood." Riley shook his head. "I don't think even Burke would want to live with that."

Devlin waited a few moments before saying quietly, "You don't think perhaps Jess has the right to make her own decisions?"

"I suppose she does. To be honest, it would be a big relief for her to know. Jenny Ann left it to me to tell her if I wanted to. You think I should?"

By then they had arrived at Riley's home. Devlin hesitated as he tied his horse to the porch rail. He was too involved to answer the question impartially. He had his own reasons for wanting Jess to know she was Burke's natural daughter. Realizing whose blood she shared might shake her up enough to make her reevaluate her fierce prejudices, both against Burke and Devlin himself.

Then again, it might only strengthen them.

It hadn't escaped Devlin that his relationship with Jess wasn't so different from Burke's long-ago relationship with Jess's mother. They both had taken a young woman's innocence and been unwilling to make a commitment to her. Devlin found that a sobering, distasteful realization. Perhaps he had more in common with Burke than he wanted to admit.

One thing was certain, though. Learning such a startling fact about herself at this late date would hurt Jessica profoundly.

"I think you have to decide for yourself," Devlin said finally. "I do know it would be better coming from you than someone else. If there's any chance of her discovering the truth some other way, then you should tell her now."

Riley nodded thoughtfully as he unlocked the front door.

Devlin frowned. The house was dark, even though a half hour ago he'd left a light burning in the hall. And when Riley had lit a lamp, he could see that Mr. Kwan was not at his appointed place.

Worse, neither was Jess. Her bed was empty.

A quick search of the small house gave no clue to her whereabouts. It was clear, however, that both she and her gear were gone.

Only then did Devlin remember precisely how Jess had couched her promise to him. *I won't give you any arguments.* Not "I won't go," or "I'll do as you say."

Venting a choice expletive, Devlin gave her father a look of utterly frustrated rage. Riley appeared worried and bewildered, but Devlin knew very well what had happened.

"Damn her, she's gone after Purcell!"

She couldn't have had much of a head start, Devlin knew, but Jess's pursuit made his own that much more urgent. Thinking of her alone, at night, in the mountains, against a man of Purcell's stamp, was enough to make Devlin's blood run cold.

When he declared his intention of immediately following her, however, Riley replied that he couldn't ride off half-cocked and insisted that he needed help. It would take an entire posse to bring in Purcell if he had hooked up with an outlaw gang. And they needed someone who knew the mountains. A man could hole up for weeks in the hundreds of peaks and canyons north of Silver Plume and never be found. They were banking on Purcell's heading north, since he'd told Jess he meant to visit friends there before leaving the state—probably to recover his stash of stolen money, they figured. North was also where Zeke McRoy had been hiding out, and the most likely direction for Jess to have ridden.

"I'll going with you," Riley announced tersely. "I can shoot and I know the mountains."

"Now who's acting half-cocked?" Devlin retorted. "You can't ride well enough with your back wound. You'll only slow me down."

"I can keep up—"

"No, dammit! You'd be less than useless to me on a long chase. You'd wind up keeling over in the saddle and I'd have to leave you there on the trail. If you think I'd care to face Jess after that, you can think again."

Riley set his jaw. "She's my daughter and I'm going."

Devlin cursed. He'd had this same discussion twice before with Riley's muleheaded daughter, and he was getting a little tired of it. "I'll bring her back safely, Riley. Now, come on. We're wasting precious time with your foolishness."

They argued a bit longer, but Devlin finally persuaded the older man that he hadn't recovered enough to meet the physical demands of a hard ride. Riley, however, still insisted Devlin had to have help. Jointly they concluded that they needed the marshal after all.

While Riley headed to the livery stable to saddle a mount, Devlin quickly rode over to the boardinghouse, where he found Mr. Kwan. Jessica had dismissed him from guard duty, just as Devlin had surmised.

He met up with Riley at the street corner, and they quickly rode the few blocks to Main Street. After very little searching, they found Marshal Lockwood just down from the jail, concluding his rounds, and cornered him as he was about to step off the boardwalk. As Riley had predicted, however, Lockwood had no interest in leaving his comfortable bed to comb the mountains for Riley's wild daughter.

"It's none o' my business if she's gone gunning for Purcell," the marshal hedged, tipping his head back to look up at the two grim-faced men on horseback.

"It *is* your business to uphold law and order!" Riley snapped. "Hank Purcell was the one who blew up my mine. And he was partners with Zeke McRoy in those robberies on the Colorado Central."

Lockwood's eyes narrowed. "What proof do you got?"

"He told Jess about it."

"That's all? You expect me to believe that?"

"My daughter doesn't lie!"

"Well, send Miss Jess down to the jail and I'll question her."

"She's not here, dadblamit! I told you, she's gone after Purcell!"

"And I told *you*, Riley, I'm not gettin' in the middle of any feud between you and Mr. Burke!"

"This has nothing to do with Burke, you stupid fool! My daughter could get killed, and you stand there doing nothing!"

Devlin laid a hand on Riley's arm, wanting to calm him before he had an apoplectic fit. "This isn't getting us anywhere," he said urgently. "I'll do better to hire my own guns."

"You *aren't* gonna take the law into your own hands," the marshal insisted.

"Just watch me," Devlin retorted, his tone grim.

"No," Riley interjected. "There's a better way. Burke is the law around here. If anybody can light a fire under this crowbait"—he gave Lockwood a scornful look—"Burke can. And maybe he also has a notion just where up north Purcell is headed. Purcell worked for him for a good while."

Devlin was skeptical that Ashton Burke would suddenly turn charitable, and said so.

"I'll *make* him help, by God," Riley said through his teeth as he turned his horse.

And so, for the second time that night Devlin found himself entering the Diamond Dust Saloon, looking for someone. Riley was close behind him, hunching his shoulders against the pain in his back.

They found Burke still gaming at Lena's faro table. He appeared highly perturbed at the interruption, but with a grimace acquiesced to their request to speak privately with him. As they left, Lena gave Devlin a probing look, but didn't interfere.

Burke reluctantly led them upstairs to his private office. The room was opulently furnished, as Burke seemed to prefer, but neither of them took the seats they were offered, or accepted a drink.

Burke, however, poured himself a brandy and drank it while Devlin told him briefly, in clipped tones, about Jess's abduction earlier that night, what Purcell had admitted regarding the Lady J's mining ore from the Wildstar, Purcell's alleged connection to Zeke McRoy, their own suspicions about Purcell's having a hand in the train robberies, their trouble with the sheriff, and then finally came to the point. They needed Burke's help in forming a posse to ride after Purcell.

From the faintly contemptuous sneer on his face, Burke obviously wasn't inclined to be cooperative.

"Why the devil should I help?" he said at the conclusion.

"Common decency might do for a start," Devlin replied with sarcasm.

"Because Jess is in danger," Riley added quietly.

"I hardly think that is my concern."

"You sure ought to be concerned about your own daughter."

There was a long pause while Burke digested Riley's words. His expression changed from scorn to a puzzled frown, then utter disbelief. A dozen heartbeats later, the doubt disappeared and comprehension set in. Burke went absolutely white.

"My daugh—?" He choked on the word. The crystal snifter fell from his fingers and shattered on the carpet as he reached blindly for the back of a chair. Staggering over to it, he half fell into the seat. His mouth worked silently, and he couldn't seem to speak or even gather breath.

For a long moment, the noise from the crowd below, muted and distant, was the only sound in the room.

"Dear God . . . Jenny Ann . . ." The harsh rasp was raw with pain. "I didn't know."

"She didn't want you to know," Riley said defensively.

Burke squeezed his eyes shut. "Why? *Why* didn't she tell me?"

"Because you made it clear you would never marry her. You told her you wanted a wife who could move in your social circles, and that darn sure left her out."

"But I would have married her if I'd realized she was carrying my child."

"How was she supposed to know that? All you ever did was lord it over everybody—her included. Jenny Ann didn't want to bear the shame of raising a bastard alone, so she married me. How does that make you feel, Mr. Burke, knowing you threw away the best thing that ever came into your life?"

Devlin had to admire the dignity in Sommers's bearing. Riley obviously felt pain in finally divulging the truth after all these years; the bitter knowledge that his wife had loved this man must have eaten at his soul like acid. And yet his revelations were made with more careful control than Devlin could have managed in the same circumstances.

"No . . ." Burke protested hoarsely. "I loved her."

"You don't know what love is," Riley said quietly. "You never thought about anyone but yourself in your life. I loved Jenny Ann more than you ever could. And I love Jess *more* than if she was my own daughter."

Seeing the anguish contorting Burke's pale face, Devlin could almost feel sympathy for the man. And yet when Burke looked up to glare at Riley, his blue eyes were burning with an emotion that seemed very much like hatred.

"You *knew* all this time. You knew Jessica was mine and you never told me."

"Jessica is *not* yours." Riley's tone finally took on an edge of fury. "You gave up any right to be her father twenty-two years ago, and nothing you've done since has changed that. She hates everything you stand for, and I don't blame her one bit. I raised her to have principles—something you wouldn't recognize if they jumped up and bit you."

"You took my daughter away," Burke muttered. "You turned her against me—"

"No, *you* turned her against you. Good God, you nearly killed her! You tried to take over our mine and blew it to hell with her in it."

Devlin knew the exact moment when Burke made the connection between Riley's angry accusations and the events of a few weeks before; the silver king's stunned, angry look turned to horror.

"Dear God . . ." he rasped again, evidently finally realizing that his machinations had nearly killed his own daughter. He groaned and covered his face with his hands.

Devlin found a kind of grim satisfaction in Burke's dismay. The bastard *should* be horrified by what he'd done. Even if he hadn't given the direct order to dynamite the Wildstar, he'd turned his hired guns loose to terrorize Jessica and her father, with dire results. His ruthless greed had almost cost him dearly. That ruthlessness was also responsible for prejudicing Jess so bitterly against wealthy men—the prime cause of Devlin's own recent battles with her. He held Burke to blame for that, as well.

He watched grimly as Riley stood there clenching his fists at the silver baron. "You didn't deserve to know about her," Riley declared. "And I wouldn't have told you now if it hadn't been necessary. Jess is far too good for you. If she wants to acknowledge you, it'll be her decision. She doesn't know about you yet, and *you* won't be the one to tell her. I will. You'll keep your mouth shut until then, and after—"

"If we don't do something soon," Devlin interrupted quietly, "no one will have the chance to tell her. Burke, we don't have much time. We need to get a posse together and go after her. If she finds Purcell first—I don't even want to think of what might happen. Will you help us or not?"

That seemed to jolt the Englishman. "Yes ... yes, of course I'll help." He stood up, still looking dazed ... as if he'd been poleaxed. "What do you want me to do?"

"Have a word with Lockwood."

"Yes ... certainly." He seemed to gather himself with difficulty. "You'll have your posse in fifteen minutes." It was said with the assurance of a man accustomed to having an army of sycophants at his command. "I can't be sure where Purcell has gone, but I might have an idea. There is a canyon near Middle Park ... I've hunted there—with Purcell, in fact. It would be an ideal location for a hideout. I intend to go with you—" He stopped abruptly and looked at Devlin, obviously realizing the choice was not his to make. "Please?"

Devlin was certain it was one of the few times in Burke's entire life that he'd ever pleaded for anything. Devlin gave Riley a glance, leaving the decision to him. Jessica's father nodded, suddenly looking weary.

"Let's go, then," Devlin said grimly.

It was left to Burke to voice what all three men were thinking. "If Purcell dares hurt my daughter ... I swear I'll rip him apart limb by limb."

Devlin shared the sentiment completely.

Chapter 18

A bullet smashed the rock beside Jess's head, making her flinch. Flattening herself on the ground, she drew a steadying breath. She didn't know how much longer she could hold out. Her ammunition was nearly spent, and her eyes felt gritty from lack of sleep.

Squinting against the bright, early-morning sunshine, she carefully aimed her shotgun but held her fire. She had pinned Purcell and some half dozen other men in the crooked canyon below, but the tangle of growth in the gulch—willows and alders and a few big cottonwoods snarled with patches of wild raspberry—provided them too much cover for her shots to be totally effective. And she couldn't afford to waste a single cartridge.

It had been mostly luck that had allowed her to find Purcell before he could get away. Just after daybreak, she'd seen the smoke from a campfire and spied him down below, harnessing a team to a big ore wagon. When she started shooting, he'd gone to ground with his cohorts in an abandoned mine, some fifty yards up the far slope. She could see the tunnel entrance from where she lay.

Her success surprised Jess a bit. She'd expected them to seek safer ground. Certainly, they could have managed to get away if they'd tried hard enough. But they seemed reluctant to desert the wagon.

The day felt hot already. The sun had burned away the frosty chill of the night and the early-morning mist that had hung over the mountains. Beneath her hat, sweat trickled down her brow—although that could have been caused by tension. Jess wished she could stop for a minute and at least quench her thirst. A clear rushing mountain stream glittered invitingly in the boulder-strewn chasm below, but she couldn't risk leaving her post.

Lifting her gaze, she cast a worried glance above her, trying to judge the time. All around her, lofty granite peaks cloaked in aspens and tall pines stretched upward into a sky of richest blue, where three buzzards swung lazily overhead. She had chosen her position well, with a mountain on each side that would make it difficult for someone to circle around and ambush her from behind. But time and her ammunition were running out.

Where was Devlin? She'd expected him to be hot on her trail. He had planned to ride after Purcell—at least once he'd gotten her safely home. She could use his support just now, even if last night she'd been bound and determined to prove that she *didn't* need him.

Darn it, why hadn't Devlin listened to her when she'd pleaded with him to ride after Purcell at once? Why had he felt the need to be so blasted protective of her and forbid her to go? She could shoot as well as most men, and she could have been a big help to him. Besides, she had her own score to settle with Hank Purcell. After what he'd done to her—both last night's abduction and blowing up the Wildstar—she wanted to see him in jail for a million years. Of course, if she could prove he had robbed the Colorado Central, he might very well hang.

She was almost certain that was his gang down there, and that he'd come to fetch the money he claimed to have stashed away. She would bet her last ten dollars that the ore wagon was filled with stollen silver bullion. Otherwise they would have abandoned it when she'd started shooting.

Jess returned her attention to the sun-splashed canyon below. If Devlin didn't get here soon, she would have to admit defeat, but she wasn't about to draw off until she was down to her last shells. What happened then might be a bit tricky. She would have to get out of there fast if she didn't want them to come after *her*.

And Purcell would likely get away.

The thought made Jess grit her teeth.

That was how Devlin found her five minutes later— holding a half dozen men at bay with the last of her ammunition. He'd heard the gunfire from two ridges away, and rammed his heels into his horse's sides, reaching the scene a dozen yards ahead of the rest of the posse.

Yanking his galloping horse to an abrupt halt, Devlin shucked his Winchester from the scabbard and leaped down from the saddle, just as a bullet whistled past him. He got off a return shot before he threw himself down beside Jess.

"Damn fool woman," Devlin growled through his teeth. "Riley is worried sick about you."

Infinitely grateful for his presence, even despite the despicable, scandalous things he had done to her last night, Jess drank in the sight of him. He was still wearing the same elegantly tailored suit he'd had on the night before, but with his beautiful face stubbled by a night's growth, he looked a lot like an outlaw himself. His gaze was diamond-hard in the sunlight as he gave her a fierce scrutiny.

She lifted her chin stubbornly. "If you'd come with me in the first place, Riley wouldn't have had to worry. We would already have taken Purcell. With your dawdling, he almost got away."

Just then, more than twenty men came galloping up behind them. Jess's eyes narrowed in surprise when she recognized Virgil Lockwood, but she was completely astonished to see Ashton Burke among the marshal's posse. Burke, like Devlin, was dressed for an evening on the town, but he carried a Springfield rifle that had a long range and deadly accuracy. His blue eyes, however, were not searching the canyon for danger; they were riveted on Jess.

Her jaw hardened. "What is *he* doing here?"

"He's here to save your stubborn hide," Devlin retorted

grimly. "Now tell me what's happening. How many are down there?"

"Purcell and six others—" Before she could say more, a volley of gunfire erupted from below.

"Find cover!" the marshal shouted, and immediately everyone scrambled for positions.

Jess went rigid when she realized the man who'd stretched out beside her on her right was Ashton Burke, but there was no time to protest. A hail of bullets struck the rocky slope directly in front of them.

"Dammit, Jess, get the hell out of here!" Devlin yelled as he took aim and fired.

Ignoring his order entirely, she began reloading her shotgun, slipping the last cartridges from her box of shells into the empty chamber to replace those fired.

The ensuing gunfight would likely go down in Colorado history, Jess suspected with no amusement. The crack of rifle fire echoed through the rugged canyon as the desperate men below began a fight for their lives. Those above began picking their targets.

Jess finished reloading and put her weapon to good use, finding it hard to breathe as the burning stench of gunpowder filled the air.

Moments later, a bullet ricocheted off the boulder in front of her while another shot kicked up gravel a few feet away.

"Dammit, Jess!" Devlin seethed. "I told you to get back!"

"Quit cussing at me! And quit telling me what to do! You aren't my keeper!"

Devlin muttered something that she didn't quite catch but that sounded like "I will be."

She might have retorted, but a bullet whizzed through the air a fraction of an inch from her face. A harsh cry sounded beside her.

Burke had taken some lead, she saw with chagrin; he had dropped his rifle and was clutching his left arm.

"Get him out of here," Devlin ordered as he got another shot off.

Jessica would rather have let him bleed to death ... almost. "Don't you dare let Purcell get away," she warned as she flung her shotgun into the grass behind her to free her hands.

"I won't."

Recognizing but not appreciating the irony of helping Ashton Burke, Jess grasped his uninjured arm and helped him slide-scrape backwards over the ground. Burke gritted his teeth at the pain.

By the time they had taken refuge behind a pine tree, out of range, he had lost his fancy hat and sweat dripped down his pale brow. Jess had never seen him at such a disadvantage. She found it really hard to feel much sympathy for this coldhearted, ruthless magnate, though. Burke hadn't shown the least compassion for her father when he'd been shot in the back.

Carefully pushing Burke's elegant coat off his injured shoulder, she ripped open his ruffled shirt and rapidly assessed the severity of the wound. A deep gash scored the outside of his upper arm, and blood was pouring freely from it, but it could have been far worse. He was incredibly lucky the bullet had only pierced the skin and muscle instead of shattering the bones in his shoulder or arm.

Jessica tugged off her bandanna and pressed it hard against the torn flesh of his arm, trying to stop the bleeding. "You'll live," she murmured.

Burke winced, whether from the painful pressure or her unfeeling remark it wasn't clear.

"Th-thank you ..." he gasped, "for ... helping me."

His gratitude surprised her, but she set her jaw. "I'm only doing it for one reason. Unlike you, I don't want a man's death on my conscience."

"Jessica ... I'm sorry. ..."

"It's a bit late for that now, don't you think? My father almost died because of you."

Burke startled her by reaching up to touch her cheek. "You look so much like your mother. ... I never noticed before. ... How could I have been so blind?"

Her brow furrowed in puzzlement. She had the distinct

feeling they were talking about two entirely different things. She'd thought he'd been apologizing for hurting Riley, maybe even for supporting Purcell, but now she wasn't so sure.

Before she could make any sense of it, the sound of gunfire lessened.

"Hold your fire!" she heard Devlin shout.

She was too far away to see what was happening down below in the rocky canyon, but someone else answered her question. "They got a white flag! They want to surrender!"

Devlin's men quit shooting. The resulting silence after all the explosive gunfire seemed deafening. Jess wished she could see.

Pressing Burke's good hand against the bloody bandanna to keep up the pressure, she murmured, "Here, hold this. I'll be back in a minute. You'll be all right till then."

She belly-crawled back to the canyon ridge just as Devlin called out, "Throw up your hands and walk out slowly."

There was another long silence.

Through the sun-dappled tangle of alders and wild raspberry, Jess could see the mouth of the mine tunnel and a glimpse of white. Several figures were making their way down the treacherous trail, hands raised high, the leader waving a flag. Jess had a good idea why they were giving up. The outlaws were trapped and they knew it.

When they reached the bank of the stream and flattened themselves on the ground with hands behind their heads, at Devlin's command, Jess counted six men. "Purcell isn't with them," she whispered to Devlin. "He must still be in the mine."

"Purcell, you, too!" Devlin added after a few moments. "Give yourself up."

"And offer my neck for stretchin'? No way!"

Purcell's distant voice reached her as merely an echo, but the words were clear enough, and not at all encouraging. She saw Devlin draw a bead and fire at the mine entrance in an attempt to force the issue. The rifle report echoed through the canyon.

"Can't we talk this over?" said Purcell.

"I don't bargain with killers."

"I ain't no killer!"

"You robbed the Colorado Central and shot two men to death."

"I had nothing to do with those holdups." Another short pause. "But I know who did it. You promise to let me outa here, and I'll tell you all about it."

Purcell was trying to bargain for his freedom, evidently. Jess hoped Devlin wouldn't believe that scoundrel's claim.

"Tell me now," Devlin retorted.

"They're the ones who pulled 'em off."

"That ain't true!" one of the outlaws on the ground yelled. "Purcell's the one told us when the shipments was going out."

"Why, you dirty double-crosser . . ." someone else exclaimed faintly. Strangely, the voice seemed to come from *inside* the mine.

The sudden explosion of gunfire from the tunnel startled Jess. She and Devlin ducked, but then raised their heads cautiously. The canyon below was silent; the six outlaws on the ground lay unmoving.

"Purcell's dead," the voice in the mine shouted.

Jess stared, wishing she could see inside that black tunnel.

"You must have miscounted," Devlin murmured to her. "Someone else was holding out in the mine with Purcell."

She nodded. Grateful that the ordeal was finally coming to an end, Jess let her head droop wearily.

It was jerked up again when Devlin gripped her shoulder. "I told you to get back," he grated, giving her a grim look that promised a reckoning. "Now do as I say."

Too drained to protest, Jess obeyed. Forcing herself to her feet, she returned to Burke's side.

It was only when she knelt beside him that she realized her forgotten patient wasn't moving. Alarmed, she bent an ear to Burke's chest. The heartbeat was erratic but definite—and a thin stream of air issued from his bloodless lips as he breathed, she saw with relief. Burke had only passed out.

She inspected his wound again. Blood was still welling from the gash, so she tore off the sleeve of his shirt and made a pad, then tied the bandanna around it and his arm. When she'd finished bandaging Burke's wound, she stayed with him, feeling guilty for abandoning him earlier. Resting her chin on her updrawn knees, she closed her eyes. She was so tired she could almost fall asleep sitting right there.

It was nearly a half hour later when Devlin finally came to find her. Jess looked up wearily to see him standing over her, his expression hard.

From the unsmiling look on his face, she could tell he was still angry with her. And he was about to light into her, unless she missed her guess. She sighed heavily. She didn't want to argue with him. She didn't have the strength.

Devlin didn't say a word, however. Without warning, to her complete shock, he reached down and hauled her to her feet. She barely had time to issue a gasp before his lips crashed down on hers in a fierce, punishing kiss.

Taken aback, Jess could only cling to him and accept the bruising pressure of his mouth. There was little evidence in his kiss of the erotic lover of the night before, and yet it still had the power to send her pulse rate soaring.

To her immense regret, his kiss ended almost as suddenly as it began. He didn't let her go, though, but instead dragged her into his arms, his grip so tight it almost crushed her.

"If you *ever* scare me like that again," he rasped in her ear, "I'll beat you black and blue. Do you understand me?"

His harsh, commanding tone held a possessiveness that should have riled her, but Jess could feel only relief that Devlin cared enough to be worried about her. She nodded obediently against his chest. "Is it over?" she murmured contritely.

"Yes." His tone was still gruff. "Purcell's dead. Shot by one of his own men who was holding out with him. The others have been arrested."

"Thank goodness."

Hearing a groan just then, she looked back over her shoulder. On the ground, Burke stirred and flinched, then tried to grab his wounded arm.

Jess pulled out of Devlin's embrace and knelt again beside the injured man. "Be still!" she admonished.

Burke had regained consciousness and was looking at her feverishly. "Jessica . . . my beautiful daughter. . . ."

Jess stiffened.

Devlin froze.

He hoped Jess would consider Burke's mumblings merely the ravings of a wounded man. It was clear Burke wasn't entirely himself. His face was contorted in pain, his blue eyes unfocused.

Burke wet his dry lips. "I have a lot . . . to make up for."

"What are you talking about?" Jess asked, sounding bewildered, wary.

Burke shook himself groggily.

"What did you mean? I'm not your daughter."

He suddenly looked more alert, as if he realized what he'd just revealed. "Nothing. I meant nothing."

"Then why did you say it?" When he didn't answer, Jess's expression turned suspicious. "I don't know what kind of trick you're trying to pull this time, Mr. Burke, but you can just stop it right now."

"I'm not trying to trick you. . . . I wouldn't do that."

"You honestly expect me to swallow that?" she demanded. "You wouldn't hesitate to bilk your own grandmother if you had something to gain. I want to know what you're up to this time."

Grimacing, Burke looked more wounded by her accusation than by his actual injury. "I don't deserve your trust, Jessica . . . I realize that . . . but I'm not trying to hurt you."

"Then why did you say what you did?"

"I . . . don't know."

Devlin had to give Burke partial credit for trying to undo the damage, but Jess was like a dog going after a bone. "What did you mean, darn it?"

He closed his eyes. "You must let Riley tell you."

"Tell me what?"

"Ask him."

"Confound you! You're going to tell me or I swear I'll leave you here for the buzzards!"

Burke's blue eyes flickered to Devlin. "I'm sorry . . . Sommers was right. He should be the one to tell her."

"Tell me what?" Jessica's voice held the high pitch of panic as she surged to her feet.

"She ought to know," Burke said almost pleadingly.

"Know *what*?" Jess cried.

"You . . . are my daughter."

She went stock-still, the color draining from her face. "It isn't true. . . . I don't believe you."

Confusion, denial, pain, all warred for expression on her face.

"It's true," Burke murmured hoarsely. "I fell in love with your mother twenty-two years ago . . . and we made you. I never knew it, though. . . . I only just learned of it last night."

"You're lying." Her voice was raw, anguished.

"No. I would never lie about something like this."

She took an involuntary step backward. It had suddenly become hard for her to breathe. Her head swiveled toward Devlin. "Tell him not to lie."

Devlin swore under his breath, wishing there were some way he could have avoided this, wishing he could have spared her the pain. Jess's look was heartrending, her panic-filled eyes imploring him to deny Burke's claim. But he wasn't going to lie to her. "Riley wanted to be the one to tell you," he said quietly.

She might have been able to disbelieve Burke. She couldn't doubt Devlin.

Terrified, horror-stricken, she backed away from them both, shaking her head frantically. "No . . . *no* . . ."

"Jessica . . ." Burke said pleadingly.

She didn't answer. Blindly turning away, she broke into a run, her stumbling gait painful to watch.

"Jessica!" Burke cried again.

Devlin followed her. He couldn't leave her to face such a shocking revelation alone.

She ran for some time before finally collapsing. When he found her, she was kneeling on a patch of grass, holding her stomach, her forehead nearly touching the ground. Her anguished sobs nearly broke his heart.

Sinking down beside her, Devlin caught her arm and pulled her up, holding her tightly against him. She was shaking violently, but to his surprise she didn't try to pull away. Instead, she clung to him, her face buried against his neck. He simply held her, absorbing her tremors, her pain, feeling the wetness of her tears against his skin.

Jess hardly realized how fiercely she was clutching him. She was aware of little but her own agony, her own need. She needed Devlin to hold her. She felt as if she would shatter in a million pieces if she let go. Her commonplace existence had just exploded like dynamite and sent her entire world careening.

She wasn't Riley's daughter. Everything she had believed in and trusted and lived for had just been blown to smithereens.

It was a long, long moment before her racking sobs lessened—and longer still before she could catch her breath over the stabbing pain in her chest. Only then did Devlin draw back. He didn't release her, though. Instead, he cradled her face in his hands and kissed her . . . her damp eyelids, her pale cheeks, her trembling lips. His tenderness was comforting, compassionate. Intimate, but not sexual. He was offering her solace.

Jess clung to him limply, her rasping breath coming in shallow spurts as she tried to make sense out of her shattered existence. One tormenting thought kept slicing at her, hurting more than all the others.

"Riley . . ." she whispered. "Riley lied to me."

She sounded bewildered, despairing. Devlin hesitated. He knew how obsessively important honesty was to her.

"No, Jess. He didn't lie to you. What he did was spare your mother the scandal and shame she would have faced had the truth come out. He spared you the hurt."

She gazed up at him, her tawny eyes shimmering with tears. "M-my mother . . . she lied to me, too."

"Sometimes there are good reasons for withholding the truth, Jessica."

She sniffed, trying valiantly to swallow the ache in her throat, but losing the battle. Fresh tears spilled over.

Devlin's own gray gaze was gentle, sympathetic, his eyes soft as he brushed her tears away. "Nothing's changed, Jess. Riley still loves you more than life."

"How can he? He's not my father."

"Yes, he is. And you're still his daughter. He thinks of you as his own flesh and blood, no matter what the biological facts are." His thumbs stroked the dampness beneath her eyes. "Riley's given you the kind of love most children never see from their parents." Devlin smiled, a bit sadly. "When I was a boy, I would have done just about anything to have my father cherish me the way Riley does you."

Jess closed her eyes, pressing her face in the curve of his shoulder. His heart beat sure and strong, anchoring her in reality. "I don't . . . think I can bear it."

"Yes, you can." And Devlin knew he spoke the truth. This woman was strong enough to bear any difficulty, even this. She was strong enough to meet any challenge life threw at her. He would lay odds on it—and his gambling instincts had always been uncannily accurate.

"You need to talk to Riley," Devlin said gently.

"He lied to me," Jess repeated, though with less conviction this time. "You don't think that was wrong?"

"Life isn't always black and white, Jess. Goodness and evil aren't always distinct entities. We're all human, Jess. Even Burke."

She shuddered. "He *can't* be my father. I've always hated him. How can I accept him now?"

"You don't have to accept or even acknowledge him, angel. You don't owe Burke a thing. He forfeited any right to your love long ago. But you may find that blood ties are stronger than you think."

He held her away. "Maybe Burke isn't all bad. Maybe he just needs someone to teach him the kind of values Riley taught you." Devlin paused to let that sink in. "If it's any consolation, Burke swears he would have married your mother if he had known."

The muscles in her jaw clenched defiantly. Devlin, remembering his love/hate relationship with his own father, knew better than to press further. She needed time to adjust, to assimilate this shattering revelation. He understood her pain, and wished he could spare her, but she would have to deal with it in her own way, in her own time.

"Well," he said briskly. "That's enough preaching for one morning." Tenderly he tucked an errant lock of hair behind her ear. "You can tell Burke to go to hell, if it will make you feel better."

"You keep forgetting that I don't cuss." Her watery smile, so soft and tremulous, made his heart contract.

He knew then that he loved her. It shouldn't have taken him by surprise. For weeks now he'd been fighting his feelings for her. But this was a quiet conviction that had sneaked up on him. And it rattled him profoundly.

Devlin shook his head silently. How was it possible? Jess had the ability to anger him more than anyone he'd ever met. She could rouse his fury like no one else ever had with her stubbornness and her blind prejudices. But she could also arouse his fiercest protective instincts. The past twelve hours had been sheer hell, thinking of her in Purcell's clutches. He'd never in his life been so shaken.

But *love*?

There was only one answer to that question: Jessica had stolen a large chunk of his heart. He had no doubts on that score.

The question was, what was he going to do about it?

He had always prized softness and femininity in a woman, qualities that Jess would never exhibit in a thousand years. But perhaps he didn't want a soft, feminine woman like he'd always thought. He wanted Jessica to need him, yes, but that didn't mean she had to be molded out of the same cloth as his previous lovers. Most definitely he didn't want her to be like all those other shallow-hearted, greedy socialites in his past.

But did he really want a stubborn, honey-haired fire-brand who challenged him at every turn? *Did he want Jessica for his wife?*

Certainly he wanted her in his bed; he had no doubts about that. Jessica could arouse and excite and satisfy him sexually the way no woman ever had. He knew they would be physically compatible.

That wasn't what he feared.

What concerned him was the strength of her regard. He knew instinctively that Jessica would give her whole heart to the man she loved. But did she love *him* that much? Enough to forsake all others? Would she, unlike his fiancée, have given up a comfortable life to go west with him all those years before? Would she have lived with him in a hovel if that was all he could have provided for her?

She had yet to admit even the smallest affection for him. He had only her father's suspicions to go on.

Was he prepared to risk his heart again on such flimsy evidence?

But what was the alternative? If he didn't marry her, if he left her here and returned to Chicago without her, would he be making the biggest mistake of his life? The kind of mistake Ashton Burke had made and paid dearly for—was still paying dearly for? Riley had warned him not to let real love slip away—

Jess interrupted his troubling contemplations by speaking.

"Devlin, I want to go home ..." She lifted her quivering chin. "To my *father.* I have to talk to Riley."

Forcing aside his own conflicting thoughts, he pressed a soft kiss on her lips. Now was not the proper moment to sort out his future relationship with Jess. She didn't need to deal with anything else but this crisis just now, and he needed to take a good hard look at his feelings for her. Alone, without distractions. "All right, angel. But I'm riding back with you. You don't need to be alone at a time like this."

"Thank you." She hesitated, gazing up at him. "Why are you always so nice to me?"

He gave her the kind of seductive, teasing, heart-stoppingly beautiful grin that couldn't fail to bolster her spirits. "Simple retribution. I want you to be properly repentant for all the terrible things you accused me of. By now you should feel like a lowly worm."

Her mouth trembled with a smile. "I . . . I guess maybe I was wrong about you."

"You *guess*?"

"All right, I *know* I was wrong. I'm sorry."

He dropped a light kiss on her mouth. "Apology accepted. Now, come. Riley's waiting for you at home."

They returned to the canyon rim then. Jess studiously avoided looking at Ashton Burke, but Devlin saw that someone had taken charge of him. The marshal had rounded up all the prisoners as well, so there was nothing remaining for Devlin to do but take Jess home. He collected both her horse and his own, and helped her mount.

They hardly spoke on the long ride back. Devlin hesitated to interrupt the silence, for Jess seemed to need the quietude.

It was well after noon by the time they arrived back in Silver Plume and rode up to the Sommerses' small house. Riley must have been waiting anxiously, for he opened the front door the instant the horses came to a halt. Stepping into the sunlight, he took one long look at Jessica and seemed to shrink. The fear and hurt written on her face proclaimed louder than words that she had learned the truth about her parentage.

Riley stood there awkwardly while she dismounted, looking as uncertain, as vulnerable, as Jess did. They were facing each other before he managed to speak. "Do you hate me, Jessie?"

Her eyes filled abruptly with tears. "I could never hate you."

Her father held out his arms and, after the slightest hesitation, she walked into them, accepting his embrace.

It was a poignant moment, too intimate, too painful, to share with outsiders. Devlin felt like an intruder.

Turning in the saddle, he looked away—up at the rugged mountains that pierced the crisp, blue Colorado sky. This was the moment he should take his leave. There really was no reason for him to stay. His job in Silver Plume was finished; he'd done what he'd come here to do.

They had recovered some of the money and much of the silver bullion that Purcell's gang had stolen. Three of the men had confessed to robbing the Colorado Central and identified the two others who had fired the shots which had killed the engineer and fireman. Purcell hadn't participated directly in the robberies, but he was the brains behind the gang and had provided information about train schedules and bullion shipments.

Devlin took an unsteady breath. He had delivered Jessica safely to her father, so he could leave with a clear conscience. In any case, she needed time to get to know Riley again, time to come to terms with the truth.

Silently he reined back his horse.

Just then Riley lifted his gaze and met Devlin's, over his daughter's head.

Devlin could see the unasked question in the older man's eyes: *Will you be back?*

It was a question Devlin couldn't answer just then.

"Take care of her," he said softly, before he turned his horse and rode away.

Chapter 19

How did one face the fact that the father you'd known all your life wasn't really your father? That was the question Jess wrestled with, waking or sleeping.

Riley's confession upon her return actually filled her with more doubts than it settled. She had talked to him long into the night—about Burke, about her mother, about what had happened twenty-odd years ago. But while Jess understood the logic behind the dissimulation, she still couldn't seem to get a handle on the truth emotionally. Outwardly she seemed unaffected; inwardly she was a mass of jumbled feelings, even though Riley had tried to reassure her.

"It didn't matter that you weren't my kid," he told her more than once. "I loved you like my own flesh and blood . . . maybe more, since it was because of you that your mother married me."

It wasn't that she didn't believe him. She knew Riley still loved her, just like she knew the sun would rise every morning and set every evening. It was just that she seemed suddenly to have lost her identity. She didn't know who she was anymore. She wasn't Riley's daughter, so what did that make her?

It didn't help, either, that Devlin had gone. He had left for Chicago on the afternoon train the same day he'd brought her home. Jess missed him desperately, despite all her grievances against him, even despite the scandalous, infuriating, domineering way he'd treated her the night he'd found her in the opium den. She needed his sympathy, his understanding, and she could have used a good dose of his tenderness and charm, as well. He always seemed to know just the right thing to say to help her through the rough times.

But he wasn't here, and she didn't know if he ever would be.

The thought made her heart ache with longing and dread. His departure had left everything unresolved between them. It felt as if Devlin had taken a part of her with him when he'd gone. Even more absurdly, she felt abandoned.

She didn't have the right to feel that way, Jess knew. Devlin didn't owe her a thing. He hadn't made her any promises. He'd never pretended feeling anything stronger for her than lust. Nor had he ever intimated that he meant to remain in Silver Plume after his business was finished.

Certainly he had never hinted that he was in any danger of falling in love with her. No matter that her father—Abruptly Jess caught herself. No matter that *Riley* would have liked to see a match between them. Even if Devlin were the marrying kind, which he wasn't, he wouldn't want to marry *her*. He'd made that clear enough on several occasions. She wasn't the type of woman who appealed to his masculine ideals. According to him, she was too tough and unfeminine for a woman. Certainly he wouldn't want her for his *wife*. His social standing, his enormous wealth, his physical beauty, his worldliness, all argued against even the possibility.

Of course, if he really loved her, none of those things would matter. Her winning Devlin's love, though, was like wishing on wild stars. She wasn't likely ever to see it come true, not in this lifetime. Especially now that he was gone.

At least she wasn't pregnant. Her monthly courses had come shortly after Devlin's departure, and while one small part of her was disappointed, Jess was mostly relieved. She didn't want to bring a bastard into the world, any more than her mother had wanted to. A child deserved a loving, caring father, and she couldn't give a child that if Devlin wasn't interested.

But if Devlin's absence left her desolate, her new estrangement from Riley was tearing her in two. Riley seemed to take her knowing about her parentage even harder than Jess herself had. Every time he looked at her, she could see the regret and sorrow in his eyes, as if he knew she thought less of him because of it. Jess didn't know how to help him. No matter how many times she told herself it was wrong to blame Riley for deceiving her, she didn't know if she could forgive him. Or her mother, either. Her mother hadn't told her the truth, even when she lay on her deathbed. But it was Riley who had been left to face the consequences.

Jess wished she could feel differently. The awkward reserve, the distance, between her and Riley *hurt*. For the first time in her life, she couldn't be easy with him. The intimacy, the feeling of family they'd always shared, had somehow been shattered.

She didn't even have the usual numbing solace of work to help take her mind off her troubles. During the weeks she'd spent trying to protect the mine from Burke's manipulations, her boardinghouse had suffered, but under Mei Lin's supervision, the Chinese laborers Devlin had hired had vanquished the mountain of cleaning, and Flo had kept up with all the ordering. With everything running so smoothly, Jess felt just a bit superfluous.

Riley told her not to worry about it—in fact, they wouldn't even have to operate the boardinghouse any longer. Once they started seeing a profit from the mine, they would be wealthy enough that they wouldn't need the income her boarders provided. But Jess needed the activity to keep her occupied. She did agree, however, to retain the laborors since Riley asked her to.

She also agreed to be at home when Riley gave Ashton Burke permission to call. To her surprise, Riley not only sanctioned the visit but insisted on it.

"You have to face it sooner or later, Jess," Riley reasoned quietly.

His choice of words was deliberate, Jess realized. He hadn't said, "You have to face Burke," but "You have to face *it*." She could ignore Burke if she chose, but she couldn't ignore the truth just because she didn't like it.

Burke came the following Sunday afternoon. Jess waited tensely as Riley ushered him into the small parlor, not knowing how to act. It seemed that Burke was just as uncomfortable, though, which astonished her. She had never seen the suave, sophisticated Ashton Burke at a loss before.

The atmosphere, which was stiff and constrained, only worsened when Riley excused himself after a few minutes. Jess felt terribly awkward, remaining behind with this stranger who was her father. Oddly, though, Burke seemed content just to *look* at her.

Finally he set down his teacup and cleared his throat. "I truly am sorry, Jessica."

She fought the urge to clench her teeth as she answered quietly, "You expect me to forgive all the things you've done, just because you now say you're *sorry*?"

"Jessica, I never meant to hurt you or your mother."

"But you meant to hurt Riley."

There was a short pause. "Yes. I won't deny that. But I regret it more than I've ever regretted anything in my life." He looked away, as if ashamed to meet her eyes. "My only excuse is that I couldn't forgive him for marrying your mother. Jenny Ann chose him, and for that I hated him."

"There is no excuse for trying to destroy a man as fine as Riley!" Jess replied, her voice low and fierce.

"I know. Believe me, if I had known about you . . ." His voice trailed off lamely.

Jess sat there, squeezing her fists and remembering all the heartless, vicious things this man had done to her father—to *Riley*—as well as to herself. How did you forgive such theft and greed as Burke had shown? How did you forgive attempted murder? How did you forgive such hate? It was all she could do not to shout those questions at him.

Yet she also remembered something Devlin had said about Burke. *Maybe he just needs someone to teach him the kind of values Riley taught you.*

Nothing had ever been truer. Ashton Burke desperately needed to learn such basic values, such simple human decency. Someone should have set him straight long ago.

Jess didn't know if she wanted to attempt the task, though. Or if she was even capable of it. She was guilty of the same kind of hate that Burke was. Hatred of *him*. It wouldn't be easy to give that up after all these years.

Just then he turned his head to look at her again, his blue eyes searching hers. "I know I'm asking a great deal, Jessica, but . . . I should like to become better acquainted with you. I've never had a child before. . . ."

The naked vulnerability on his face shook her. She had never expected Ashton Burke ever to need anything or anyone, and certainly not to admit it. Yet he was laying himself bare before her. And she knew, as certainly as she knew anything, that while he had coveted many things before, he had never wanted anything as much he wanted her respect.

Respect was not something that he could command, though. Even with all his wealth and consequence, Burke was helpless in this situation. It made Jess feel very strange and uncomfortable, knowing she had that kind of power over someone.

"I'm not asking you to accept me as your father," Burke said awkwardly into the silence. "I'm only asking for the chance to get to know you."

Jess met his eyes levelly. "You could never be my father. Riley is my father and always will be."

Even as she said the words, she knew they were right. The truth about her parentage didn't change that elemental fact.

"I would never attempt it," Burke replied solemnly.

There was another long silence. Finally Jess forced a small smile. "There is something you could do for me."

He leaned forward eagerly. "Yes?"

"Would you tell me about my mother?"

The strain in Burke's pale face suddenly faded. He looked like a man who had been given a reprieve from hanging.

"It would be my great pleasure," he said softly.

She found Riley in the kitchen when the visit was over. He was sitting at the table, staring down at his work-worn hands. Without speaking Jess came up behind him.

She felt him stiffen as she bent down and put her arms around his neck, but she pressed her cheek against his weathered one and simply held him.

"Burke's gone," she said finally.

"I figured as much." His tone was low, uncertain. "Did you make peace with him?"

"Not entirely. But it was a good start. I told him he couldn't be my father. That place is already taken."

Riley's hand came up to cover hers.

"I love you, Papa. You'll always be my true father."

"Oh, Jessie. . . ."

There were tears of relief in his eyes when he held her away to look at her.

Jess gave a shaky laugh. "Don't do that, or I'll cry, too."

Riley chuckled and wrapped her in a bear hug. "I'm not about to cry. I have my daughter back."

A thousand miles away in Chicago, Devlin was facing his own father. The length of an impressive dining table separated them, while an elegant silver candelabra almost obscured their view of one another. Devlin had been invited to Sunday dinner.

It was a formal affair, which did little to mitigate the constraint that still lingered between them, but Devlin at least gave his father credit for trying. C.E. quite obviously was exerting himself to make amends for the years of estrangement. In fact, for the past week he had found one excuse after another to secure his son's company.

He'd actually met Devlin's train from Denver. Devlin hadn't expected that courtesy, even though he had cabled ahead, reporting his success in apprehending the outlaw gang. But when he stepped down from his private car, his father was waiting for him.

They stood staring at each other for a long moment before C.E. extended his hand.

"Thank you, son." His tone was low, gruff, as if the admission hurt. "I'm in your debt."

Having his father indebted to him was precisely what Devlin had intended, but the pleasure he'd anticipated somehow fell short. What he wanted now from C.E. was far less petty, far more profound. He wanted the same kind of relationship Jess had with her father. The same kind of love.

It was an impossibility, of course, but they could make a start. Devlin clasped the hand that his father offered to him, firmly, without reticence.

C.E. had driven him home—Devlin's home—in his carriage, and while the conversation had been stilted, before parting they had made arrangements to meet the following afternoon to discuss in more detail Devlin's trip to Colorado.

That meeting had led to other engagements, and culminated in an invitation to dinner at C.E.'s mansion. Exquisitely prepared by a French chef, the meal was a feast fit for a returning prodigal son—an analogy that was not lost on Devlin, to his wry amusement.

The two of them remained at the table, sipping their port, after the dishes had been cleared away by a servant.

"I want to thank you again for all you've done," his father repeated for the third time that week.

"Don't mention it," Devlin responded politely.

"No, no, it meant a great deal to me. And it was a big effort on your part . . . more than a month of your time. I'd like to repay you somehow."

Devlin's fingers tightened on his wineglass. "Some things can't be bought," he said carefully, his tone cool.

"I didn't mean to imply . . . it wasn't money I was thinking of. . . ." His denial was swift, but from the heightened color on his face, Devlin knew very well it was some expensive gift his father had had in mind.

After another moment of silence, C.E. cleared his throat and changed the subject. "Perhaps you would accompany me into the city tomorrow, Garrett. There's a bank I'd like you to look at. It's given me more trouble than it's worth, and I'm thinking of selling."

Devlin raised an eyebrow. "Is there some reason I should?"

"Naturally you'll want to become acquainted with my holdings. You'll need to know all the details when you inherit."

Devlin went very still. The port wine on his tongue suddenly tasted bitter. "You disinherited me ten years ago," he said very slowly.

"No. No, I didn't. I never changed my will. I couldn't bring myself to do it."

Devlin's gray eyes turned wintry. "You merely denied me your affection and companionship all these years."

"I wanted to teach you a lesson."

"Oh, you did that, all right."

"Garrett, I was wrong. . . . I'm sorry."

A dozen seconds ticked by.

"Everything I own—it's still yours, son."

Devlin had to force himself to keep his anger under control. "I don't need," he enunciated clearly, "or want your money. Give it to a charity."

C.E. hesitated, looking frustrated. "If that's how you feel about it. . . ."

"That's how I feel. I won't be in Chicago much longer, in any case. I intend to return to Colorado as soon as I can manage to wrap up some of my business affairs."

C.E.'s heavy brows drew together in a frown. "If I'm not prying, may I ask why?"

"The trial date for Purcell's gang is set for the week after next, and I'd like to be there to testify."

"But you'll be returning afterward?"

"That's doubtful. I have some unfinished business to attend to."

"Ah, I see." But it didn't look as if he did see. Rather,

he looked disappointed. "I thought perhaps . . . we were just coming to know each other again. . . ."

Observing the genuine regret on his father's face, Devlin relented. "It isn't business I can postpone. I intend to be married soon."

"Oh?" C.E.'s tone was startled. "Do I . . . er, know the lady?"

"No. And I doubt you would approve of her. She couldn't come close to meeting your high standards. She doesn't give a damn about wealth or social status." Devlin smiled, as if at a private memory. "She kicked me out of her house when she found out I had money. Threatened to shoot me, in fact."

"Good God."

The look on C.E.'s face was priceless, and it gave Devlin more than a little satisfaction. For ten years he'd wanted to thumb his nose at his father like this.

"She's as different from you as night and day," he added, amused. "Her idea of wealth is a bathtub with hot running water."

"And you want to take this woman to wife?" his father said faintly.

Devlin smiled again, a charming smile that didn't quite reach his eyes. "I'm old enough this time not to need your permission."

"But . . . you've thought this through?"

"I've done nothing *but* think about it for the past week."

"Well, then." It was a helpless little remark, oddly impotent for a man as powerful and accustomed to control as his father.

Sipping his wine, Devlin watched the struggle on his father's face. C.E. was forcibly biting his tongue, obviously trying to hold back the demands he wanted to make.

It was the most Devlin could ask.

"I don't need your permission to marry," he said slowly, "but I'd like your blessing."

There was a long pause while C.E. searched his face. "Are you sure she can make you happy?" he asked at last.

Devlin thought of Jessica, her strength, her stubbornness. He thought of her standing up to Burke in a crowded saloon. Of her pulling a revolver on him the first time he kissed her. Of her trembling in his arms in a darkened mine tunnel. Of her holding Purcell and a half dozen other outlaws at bay. He thought of her wrapping her long legs around him and meeting him thrust for passionate thrust, carrying him to a world of delight and ecstasy he'd found with no other woman but her. He thought of her filling up the emptiness in his life.

No, he didn't know if she could make him happy. All he knew was that his life would be unbearable without her. This past week had more than proved that. He missed her every waking hour, and some when he was sleeping. He missed her fire, her determination . . . her passion, her prejudices. He missed kissing her, missed fighting with her. He missed the challenge of turning her into a sensual, sexually responsive woman.

In short, he couldn't contemplate living his life without her.

He intended to return to Colorado and marry her just as soon as he could settle his most pressing affairs here. Jess might balk at first, he was aware. He hadn't left under the most congenial of terms. But he dismissed the gut-deep fear that she might reject him entirely. He didn't intend to take no for an answer. If Jess wasn't in love with him yet, he would make her fall in love. It was as simple as that.

"As sure as I can be of anything," Devlin answered his father.

"Well then . . . you have my blessing, son."

It was, Devlin thought as he raised his glass, a good enough beginning.

Chapter 20

"**T**hat gorgeous fella's back," Flo announced as she entered the boardinghouse kitchen with an armful of packages from the butcher shop.

Jessica's heart did a double take. "Devlin? He's *here*? In Silver Plume?"

"Doc Wheeler saw him down at the rail station."

"Are you *sure*?"

"I reckon Doc knows enough about anatomy to recognize a gent when he sees one."

"What . . . is he doing back?"

Flo's grin was as broad as a barn door. "Well, I'll give you three guesses and the first two don't count."

Jess's hand stole to her breastbone. Flo was determined to believe Devlin was sweet on her, but she hadn't dared allow herself to hope. It would be devastating to have those hopes shattered. Letting herself dream of romance and love and a future with him—with children and a home—was just setting herself up for a terrible fall. Devlin didn't want those things, any more than he wanted *her*.

For the past two weeks she'd tried to put him out of her mind—which was a bit like trying to pretend she wasn't alive. It was humanly impossible for her lips not to remember Devlin's stunning kisses, for her body to forget his heated, exquisite lovemaking. She couldn't deny, either, that his charm and tenderness, his vital maleness, affected her profoundly, any more than she could claim not to miss his shrewd intelligence and keen understanding. In fact, ever since Devlin had left town, she'd been in pure misery.

She was in love with him, pure and simple. She had to admit it. Even if she hadn't allowed herself to acknowledge the depth of her feelings before now, she couldn't possibly blame the hungry, yearning ache in her heart on anything but love.

Unlike Flo, though, Jess couldn't believe Devlin would return to Colorado just for her. But what else could have brought him back?

"Maybe he just wants to see Riley about his share of the Wildstar," Jess offered lamely, wishing Flo would contradict her.

The widow gave her a disgusted look that was rather heartening. "Lord have mercy, gal, don't you know anything about men?"

Not Devlin's kind of man, she didn't. That had always been the trouble.

That afternoon—the first day of October—was one of the longest Jess had ever endured. Her spirits alternately rose and sank, hope bubbling in her veins like champagne one minute, uncertainty and fear dashing those bubbles the next.

Around two o'clock, she went home to change clothes. If Devlin *had* returned to Colorado for her, as Flo believed, then it was likely he would come to call and Jess wanted to look her absolute best. She donned her Sunday gown—the coffee-striped grenadine with the pearl broach, then sat in the parlor and waited. The seconds ticked away like hours—pure torture on her nerves. Half the time she spent anxiously wondering if Flo could be right, and if so, whether she dared allow herself to hope for a marriage proposal. The other half of the time she spent scolding herself and preparing for the worst. He didn't love her. He didn't want a wife at all, certainly not one with her lack of qualifications. He had only come back to wrap up the loose ends of his business dealings ... the Wildstar and whatever other projects he'd undertaken to make money— his self-professed occupation.

Whatever his intentions, though, Devlin didn't show up. By four o'clock, Jess was a mass of raw anxiety. Five minutes later, she came to a decision. Not only couldn't she stand another minute of suspense, but she couldn't afford to wait any longer. She had supper to fix for her miners. And in a few more hours it would be Saturday night. If the past was anything to judge by, Devlin would likely spend it gambling. Therefore, if she meant to have it out with him, she would have to do it now. She wasn't about to walk into another saloon in order to find him.

With trembling hands, Jess put on her hat and gloves, swept up the parasol that matched her outfit, and walked out the door before she could change her mind.

Although she didn't know where Devlin was staying, she thought it likely he would book a room at the Diamond Dust Hotel, so that was where she headed. Main Street wasn't as chaotic as usual, since the rowdiest evening of the week hadn't yet begun, but the road was still packed with drays and ore wagons.

Jess was a block from the Diamond Dust when she saw him; despite the distance, she was able to pick Devlin out of the crowd. She couldn't mistake the elegant cut of his jacket, the lean-muscled shoulders, the dark silky hair beneath a sleek bowler. Her breath caught in her throat. She thought she had prepared herself to meet him, but she couldn't seem to stop the way her heart clenched with joy at the mere sight of him, or prevent the army of butterflies from turning somersaults in her stomach. She had to force herself to slow down and take a deep breath just to keep from running to his side.

Devlin was driving a single-horse open buggy which was halted before the hotel. Seated on the front seat, he was engaged in conversation with a woman who stood on the boardwalk.

Jess was too busy drinking in the sight of Devlin to pay attention to anyone else at first. But when she was about five yards away, she recognized the ebony-haired woman beside him. Her steps faltered, her heart squeezing in sudden, sharp pain. *Lena.* The faro dealer at the saloon. The same woman who had been in Devlin's bedroom several weeks ago. *The owner of the feather boa.*

Just then, Devlin bent and cupped his hand around Lena's nape, drawing her face up tenderly to brush his lips over hers.

Jess stood frozen, watching in disbelief, in horror.

Devlin drew back with a beautiful smile. "Wish me luck," he said, grinning.

Lena laughed throatily. "I don't think you'll need it, darlin'. You could make a stone melt."

Devlin might have heard the strangled little sound Jess made, for he looked up just then, his gray eyes connecting with her agonized gaze.

Jess took a single step backward in shock, not wanting to face what she had just seen. As Devlin's smile faded, she turned blindly and ran, not caring that she dropped her parasol, not caring that she stumbled over her skirts and nearly fell, merely pushing desperately past a knot of startled men who had just come out of the drugstore.

Behind her Devlin cursed. "Jess!" he shouted. "Jessica, wait!"

"Oh, Lord," Lena breathed.

"Dammit to hell," Devlin muttered in reply. His fingers clenched around the reins, but otherwise he didn't move. The savage pain of seeing Jess run from him held him immobile. Once again she'd believed the worst of him, convicting him without giving him a chance to defend himself.

"Aren't you gonna go after her?" Lena asked.

"No."

"No?" The faro dealer looked at him in puzzlement.

"I'm not running after her. She's jumped to the wrong conclusion about me once too often."

"You want me to tell her it was just a good-bye kiss? That you were on your way to see her and to ask her to marry you?"

"No." Devlin's jaw clenched grimly as he tried to repress the cold fear welling up inside him. Jess couldn't love him very much if she had so little faith in him. Perhaps he'd overestimated his appeal with her. Perhaps he'd been arrogant to think he could make her love him. He couldn't force her love, her trust. But he at least deserved the benefit of the doubt from the woman who was to be his wife. "If she can't learn to trust me on her own, then it won't do any good to push it." He swore again. "Hell, I'm more innocent now than I was about any of her other accusations."

"A lady like her might not see it that way. She's not gonna forgive you for kissing me, even if it *was* innocent."

He thought of the diamond engagement riñg burning a hole in his pocket and shook his head. He was damned if he would run after Jess and beg her forgiveness. She was going to have to come to him this time.

Devlin tore his gaze away from Jess's retreating figure and focused it on the sultry Lena. He smiled again, not pleasantly. "Looks like I won't be getting married any time soon. What about that faro game you suggested?"

Lena eyed him skeptically. "If you're sure, sugar. But I think maybe you're gonna need some of that luck after all."

Jess wept when she got home. She flung herself on her bed and indulged in a storm of tears that released weeks of pent-up grief and uncertainty.

She stayed there all evening, too heartsick to contemplate facing anyone. She hoped Flo would handle getting dinner on the table, because she couldn't move. All she could do was lie there, curled in a ball, and sob.

When Riley came home from the mine, she pleaded illness—which alarmed him considerably until she finally confessed that no, she wasn't sick, it was only that Devlin had come back and she had seen him, but she didn't want to talk about it and would Riley please leave her alone? With an odd mingling of concern and relief on his face, Riley tiptoed from the room and shut the door behind him, leaving Jess to her misery.

She couldn't sleep at all that night. Instead she pounded her pillow and hugged her pain to herself and cursed her stupidity for ever falling in love with that handsome snake. She should have known better than to trust any man who had his kind of wealth and power.

The next morning fury and pride took over. Exhausted but dry-eyed, Jess marched over to the boardinghouse and did battle with chores and dustballs. The first time Flo mentioned Devlin, though, Jess blew up, declaring she didn't want to have anything to do with that two-timing sidewinder, that she didn't even want to hear his name!

It was two days before she was calm enough to tell Flo what had actually happened. They were out back of the boardinghouse, cleaning carpets by beating them with brooms.

"I saw him kiss that *woman* right there on the street!" she gritted out through her teeth as she took her bitter jealousy out on the hapless carpet.

"Maybe there's a simple explanation. Why don't you ask him about it?"

Jess gave another fierce swing, wishing it were Devlin she was hitting. "There's an explanation, all right! He's a lecher. With absolutely no discrimination! He has to try and charm anything in skirts."

"Lord have mercy, gal, you can't expect a man like that to live like a monk."

"I can, too!"

Flo was a bit more practical. "A gorgeous fella like him must have dozens of women runnin' after him. He'd have to be a saint to refuse every one of them."

"That woman wasn't running after him. *He* was kissing *her*, confound it!"

"Well, it's not like he was married. Once he gets hitched he'll settle down."

"How can you possibly believe that?"

"'Cause a man like that only marries for two reasons, money or love. And Devlin sure as shootin' doesn't need the money. If he was to marry you, it'd only be because you got his heart all tied up in knots."

That mollified Jess to only the slightest degree. "He doesn't have a heart," she muttered. "And I don't want to marry him. I don't want anything to do with a man I can't trust out of my sight, one who can't be faithful even before the wedding."

"Listen to yourself, Jess. You're not makin' a lick o' sense. Before the wedding is when a man is supposed to sow his oats."

Jess made a sound that was halfway between a sob and a shriek, and took her fury out on the carpets.

Flo shook her head. "Listen to me, gal. You love him, you better go after him and not leave him to some soiled dove who can only give him the pleasures of the flesh."

"I don't love him! I despise him! Oh, just don't talk to me about him!"

Jess meant it. She only wanted to forget Devlin so she could mend her shattered heart and get on with her life.

Trouble was, nobody would let her forget him. It was impossible not to dwell on her heartbreak when everyone around her seemed determined to remind her of it.

Flo was bad enough. In spite of Jess's expressed wishes, the widow found a way to bring the subject of Devlin into the conversation upwards of ten times a day. But Riley was worse. He rarely mentioned Devlin's name, but his eloquent silences made it very clear he was disappointed in her. Jess began to feel like *she* was at fault for spurning Devlin.

She knew Riley met with him. That became rather obvious when Riley kept leaving various equipment receipts signed with Devlin's bold signature on the kitchen table in plain sight for her to find. Jess knew enough about mining to figure out they were expanding the Wildstar operation big-time, and that Devlin's money was financing it. Even with the mine's vast increase in silver production during the month since the strike, Riley couldn't yet afford on his own to invest in an expensive steam-powered hoist and headframe and all the other tons of hard-rock equipment it would take to bring the Wildstar up to a first-class operation and enable it to compete with the huge consolidated mines.

Jess refused to ask her father about the expansion, though—which only made her feel left out. Until now Riley had always discussed every aspect of his business affairs with her, but this time he was proceeding without her, in league with Devlin. It hurt, knowing that her father was siding with that polecat.

She couldn't understand, either, why Devlin even continued to remain in Colorado. Surely he didn't need to oversee every little detail of the Wildstar enterprise. Riley was more than capable of managing on his own. And Devlin had fulfilled his original purpose for coming to Silver Plume. Three of the train robbers were behind prison bars, while the other three had been sentenced to hang. The aspen leaves turned gaudy gold and began to fall, but even after Devlin testified at the trial, he still didn't return to Chicago.

Jess had been called as a witness at the trial, as well. She'd performed her duty with as much expedience as possible, getting in and out in one afternoon. And yet seeing Devlin again, merely being in the same courtroom with him, was sheer torture. He looked so handsome he took her breath away. In fact, he commanded the attention of everyone in the room, dressed as he was in a superbly tailored wool suit that spelled money, leisure, power.

He didn't make the slightest move to speak to her, or even approach her, though. Certainly he made no attempt to apologize for kissing that *woman*—which was the only way she could have forgiven him.

Her heart aching, Jess tried to ignore him, and yet she was aware of every move Devlin made, every person he spoke to, every occasion when he turned his head in her direction. He watched her sometimes, she knew that. It had been all she could do to sit there in the witness box with Devlin's shrewd gray gaze boring into her.

Her heartache was even harder to bear because she thought that the courtroom might be the last place she ever saw him. Jess braced herself for Devlin's departure afterward. The weather grew cold, bringing chilling frosts and freezing nights. But to her surprise and puzzlement—and relief, if she could bring herself to admit it—when Devlin left town he merely moved to Georgetown, two miles away.

He was staying at the Hotel de Paris, she learned from Flo. A week later she also learned that Devlin had bought a plot of land in Georgetown and was planning on building a fancy house.

"A house?" Jess repeated in shock. "Whatever would he need a house for?"

Flo raised her eyes to the ceiling, as if praying for patience. "For a smart gal, you sure can be thickheaded sometimes, Jess."

"What do you mean?"

"You figure it out. I've already said my piece, and I'm not gonna say one thing more."

Flo didn't keep to her promise to say nothing more in the following weeks, but neither did she explain what she meant. It was left to Jess to puzzle out.

Devlin's actions, however, continued to surprise Jessica. Clem broke the latest news to her one evening after dinner when he was still smarting from the loss of a poker game to Riley. The revelation that Devlin had provided Clem the capital to start his own stock ranch made Jess stare.

"Yep, I'm gonna settle down and raise me some mules, Jessie," Clem explained.

"You're going to quit *mining*?" Jess asked incredulously. She couldn't believe the rugged old-timer whom she'd known since she was a baby would contemplate such a drastic change. Clem was *part* of the Rockies.

"Not quit, perxactly. Just do something on a different end. I'm gettin' too old to be trampin' up and down that mountain, Jessie. And there's big profit to be made in mules. That big-city fella's got it all worked out. Him and me, were gonna be partners."

"You're actually going into business with Devlin? I thought you didn't trust him."

"Aw, he ain't such a bad fella, after all. A bit too purty for my taste, but he knows a good deal when he sees one." Shooting a stream of tobacco juice with bull's-eye precision at the spittoon near his feet, Clem patted his stomach and grinned. "Yep, I'm gonna re-tire and not work so hard."

Jess smiled wryly. "You wouldn't know how to quit working hard."

"Well, you're jest as bad as me. Mebbe you ought to think about easin' off yerself, now that Riley's made his strike. You don't need to keep worryin' about money now. You could shuck the boardinghouse, if'n you wanted to."

"Good heavens, what would I do if I didn't have the boardinghouse to keep me busy?"

Clem eyed her thoughtfully as he tugged on his grizzled beard. "Get yourself hitched, o' course. You ain't getting any younger, you know."

Jess suddenly found a good deal to interest her in her fingers.

"I tell you, Jessie. You don't want to end up like me, with nobody to care for you. With no family or nothin'."

She looked up in distress. "You have somebody to care for you. Riley and I love you. We're your family."

"That ain't what I meant and you know it." Clem held her gaze. "You let that purty fella get away, and you're gonna be sorry. You oughta think about that, Jessie."

With that, Clem climbed to his feet and shuffled out the back door, leaving Jess to brood over what he'd said.

In fact, she did a lot of brooding during the following days, as autumn set in for good and the first snowfall of the season came and went. She found it impossible to do anything else. Devlin stayed on her mind, no matter how desperately she tried to forget him.

And more and more she came to realize she had no support among her family and friends in her campaign to shun him. It even began to seem as if there was a conspiracy against her. Even Ashton Burke managed to mention Devlin.

It was done casually one Sunday afternoon in late October, when Burke was at the Sommers's house. Jess had relented enough to invite him to Sunday dinner with her and Riley.

Having the elegant silver baron dining at her kitchen table seemed incongruous, but he didn't appear to mind that the flatware wasn't made of silver and the yellow-checked tablecloth wasn't lace. In fact, Burke seemed totally content merely to be sharing the time with her. He sat there, relaxed and at ease, sipping his glass of homemade elderberry wine and making pleasant conversation that included Riley as much as Jess, and was obviously designed to disarm.

Jess, too, was growing more at ease with Burke, so much so that she allowed her attention to wander for a minute while her two fathers discussed the state of Colorado politics. It came as a shock to realize the subject had somehow turned to Devlin.

". . . already hired a team of lawyers. He asked for my advice, much to my surprise." Burke made a wry face. "I suggested the best in the state, although I imagine I will come to regret it. Mr. Devlin is all too likely to use them against *me* someday."

"What does Devlin need a team of lawyers for?" Jess found herself asking in spite of herself.

"A simple precaution, my dear. With all the litigation these days, every business venture is a veritable mine field. And since he has relocated his headquarters here, he will need attorneys who know our state law."

"Devlin has moved his headquarters *here*?"

"Several weeks ago. You didn't know?"

"No," Jess said faintly.

"Well, I doubt he will have much difficulty settling in. He can buy and sell stocks here almost as easily as in Chicago, now that telegraphs and telephones have made communication so easy. I have invited Mr. Devlin to use my telephone, in fact, until his is operational."

Jess looked at Riley, only to find him watching her. Suddenly restless, she jumped up to clear away the dishes and bring the cherry pie to the table.

"Did I say something wrong?" Burke asked into the silence.

"Jess hasn't done much talking to Devlin lately," Riley responded evenly.

Burke tactfully refrained from commenting. "Did you receive the invitation I sent you for next week, Jessica?" he said, changing the subject.

"Yes, thank you." Carefully saying nothing more, she began to cut pie wedges. Three days ago a gold-embossed card had been hand-delivered by one of Ashton Burke's fancy footmen, inviting her and Riley to the evening party Burke was giving Monday after next.

The idea of attending one of Burke's society functions didn't much appeal to Jess, although she was reluctant to hurt his feelings by telling him so. He had been trying so hard to make up for his past failures that she felt almost obliged to be nice to him.

In fact, to her surprise she'd begun to see Burke in a different light. Just as Devlin had suggested, Ashton Burke wasn't all bad. The fact that he'd loved her mother and regretted not marrying her made his subsequent actions, though not forgivable, at least more understandable.

"There will be dancing and supper," Burke said encouragingly. "And perhaps a few hands of cards. I should be honored if you would attend. And Riley, as well, naturally."

"Well, we'll see," Riley replied.

Jess was grateful to her father for sparing her the necessity of answering, for she had just thought of another reason she didn't want to attend Burke's party. As cozy as he and Devlin had apparently become, Devlin might very well be there. And she just didn't know if she had the strength to face him. Her wounds were too raw.

In fact, she didn't know if they would ever heal. For the past month, she'd prayed that Devlin would just leave town and get out of her life so she could begin to recover. But now it looked as if he truly was here to stay.

Could she bear it, knowing he was so close and yet so far away?

That night, after Burke had long gone, after she and Riley had shared a cold supper and the dishes had been put away, Jess found herself pondering that question for the hundredth time. Too restless to sleep, she draped a shawl over her shoulders and went outside to sit on the back step.

The fall air was crisp and frosty, the ebony sky diamond-studded with thousands of stars which looked close enough to touch. Jess couldn't enjoy the beautiful night, though. She was hurting too much.

Resting her forehead on her updrawn knees, she silently cursed Garrett Devlin. "Wherever you are," she muttered, "I hope you're *half* as miserable as I am."

Ten minutes later the kitchen door creaked open behind her, accompanied by a spill of lanternlight. It was followed by Riley's gentle voice stealing out to meet her.

"You okay, Jess?"

"No," she mumbled truthfully.

There was a long, concerned silence.

"You want me to fetch the doc?"

Jess gave a choked laugh. "I don't think Doc Wheeler could fix what's wrong with me."

Without replying, Riley came out to join her, shutting the door behind him and enfolding them again in darkness. Settling himself beside her on the top step, he found her hand and entwined her fingers with his rough, calloused ones. Jess felt immensely comforted. Riley might not be her blood father, but she'd never felt closer to him.

It was some time before he finally spoke, but he didn't give her the sympathetic condolences Jess had hoped to hear.

"Don't you think you're being a bit hard on him?" Riley asked.

It took a second for her to realize he was taking Devlin's side. She took a deep breath, trying to control her indignation. "*I'm* being hard?"

"Judging a man guilty without even giving him a chance to explain. . . . Seems to me that isn't quite fair, Jess."

Her chin came up. "And just what did Devlin tell you?"

"Climb down off your high horse; he didn't say a thing. Flo told me what happened."

"And you think it wasn't important? That I should just forget I ever saw him kissing that *woman*?"

"I didn't say that. Maybe it was important and maybe it wasn't. What I do know is that nobody ever solved their problems by not talking about them. I also know that ever since you brought Devlin home, you've been mighty quick to believe the worst about him. And you've been wrong before."

"Maybe so," Jess admitted grudgingly, "but I'm not wrong now. I know what I saw."

Her father gave her a searching look in the darkness. "You absolutely sure you're not being a bit unreasonable?"

She wasn't sure about anything anymore, except that she wanted to bury her face in her lap and cry. Swallowing the sudden lump in her throat, she maintained her defensiveness. "I don't think I'm being the least unreasonable. What would you do if you had found Mama kissing another man?"

Evidently it was the wrong thing to say, for Riley stiffened. "I'd marry her," he said quietly.

The subdued bitterness in his tone made Jess realize she had struck a raw nerve. She bit her lip, not wanting to hurt Riley more, yet needing to know. "Mama wasn't . . . unfaithful to you, was she?"

He gave a slow, deep sigh. "Not that I ever knew, except maybe in her heart. She never did get over losing Burke."

"He told me a little about her," Jess said quietly. "He said he loved her but he didn't realize it till it was too late."

"She should have married him. She would have been better off with him than me."

"No, how can you say that?"

"Jenny Ann never came right out and told me, but I always knew she regretted marrying me. I couldn't give her the nice things Burke could. . . . I couldn't even give her a child."

"I don't believe that was the way she saw it."

"She never loved me. Not like she did Burke."

Jess shook her head. Riley might believe that, but deep down, she knew differently. Since she'd fallen hopelessly in love with Devlin, she'd become a lot more sensitive to things like that. She knew now how her mother had felt loving Ashton Burke. And yet all the precious memories she had of her mother couldn't be wrong. Jenny Ann's feelings for Riley had been deep and abiding. That kind of love had been far stronger than the infatuation she'd once felt for Ashton Burke.

"The way Mama loved you was a lot better than the way she loved Burke," Jess declared with conviction. "She knew you were the better man."

"Well, maybe," Riley said after a long moment. "Thing is, Jess, I don't want to see you end up with the same regrets as your ma did. Remember that wild star she used to talk about? A star's darn hard to get a hold of, just like love. And if you do catch it, you better not let go."

Jess fell silent. She'd always known her mother was referring to Ashton Burke with that analogy, but she'd never given it the same interpretation Riley did. "I thought Mama meant that you shouldn't spend your life wishing for something you could never have. And more than that . . . I think maybe she was talking about Burke himself. She was saying that he's just like a wild star—all flash and no substance."

"Garrett Devlin has substance. You knew it the first time you laid eyes on him. You never would have brought him home, otherwise."

She couldn't argue with that. Devlin had proven over and over again that he wasn't the same kind of man as Ashton Burke, even if he was rich and powerful.

"I think you ought to go catch yourself that wild star," Riley said softly.

"But . . . what if Devlin doesn't want to be caught?"

"He wants to, Jess."

"How can you tell?"

"He came back here, didn't he? Why else would he move out to Colorado unless he meant to settle down?"

"Maybe he figures he can make more money here than in Chicago."

"Maybe he figures money isn't as important as the love of a good woman."

That comment stumped Jess momentarily.

"He isn't like all those other rich fellows around here, Jess, only out for himself. He's a fair man and a straight shooter. And I think you know it."

"I suppose so," she admitted grudgingly. Devlin might be filthy rich, but he hadn't used his wealth to crush the little people who got in his way. In fact, he'd helped Riley get back on his feet again and risked his life to go head-to-head with Burke. And he'd fulfilled one of Clem's dreams, staking him to a mule ranch. Those weren't the acts of a selfish, greedy, manipulative man.

"I also think you ought to give him a chance to explain what happened," Riley said after a minute.

"You really think he plans to settle down?"

"Yep. And if he does, he's gonna need a wife. You would be a good choice."

Jess felt her heartbeat quicken with hope, but she shook her head. Devlin wouldn't want an unsophisticated, unworldly, unfeminine Westerner like her for a wife. "He wouldn't want to marry me."

"Well, I think he would. To tell the truth, I think he's already made up his mind. He's just waiting for you to make up yours. If you love him, then you ought to try and work things out."

"That isn't the question," Jess replied dejectedly. "I do love him . . . so much it hurts. The question is, does he love me?"

"I reckon you better find out."

She didn't know what to say. She'd had her hopes raised before, only to have them crushed by that faro dealer she'd seen Devlin kissing. But if it was true, that Devlin really did love her, then maybe she'd been mistaken about him again. Maybe he'd had a reason for kissing that woman on the street. Maybe she *had* overreacted. And maybe she'd ruined her chances to have a future with him, after all the times she'd accused him of things he hadn't done.

"What am I going to do?" she asked finally.

"I think you should go to that party Burke invited you to. Devlin's likely to be there, and you can talk to him about what happened."

Jess shuddered. Ashton Burke embraced the best and most highly respected element of society. "I would just be out of place there."

"No, you won't. You can hold your own with the best of 'em. You buy yourself a fancy new dress, and you'll be the prettiest girl there. If Devlin isn't in love with you, he will be when he sees you."

Still Jess hesitated. She didn't want to go there alone and face Devlin all by herself. She couldn't bear it if he turned away.

"Will you come with me?" she asked her father in a small voice.

Riley smiled in the darkness and patted her hand. "Sure, I'll come with you. If you need me, Jess, I'll always be there."

Chapter 21

Her party gown was a creation of emerald-green silk and ecru lace that lovingly caressed her figure and left more of her bosom bare than Jess had ever before exposed in public. The low décolletage, off-the-shoulder and ornamented by a deep lace fichu, graced a cuirasse bodice and puffed, elbow-length sleeves. The lace underskirt fell in straight pleats, while the emerald faille overskirt gathered behind in a full bustle and ended in a train decorated with flounces and ruching.

Jess felt positively indecent, but Flo insisted she looked beautiful and entirely appropriate for the occasion. The cheval mirror tended to agree. Eying herself critically, Jessica saw an elegant young woman richly gowned, her tawny hair swept up, with fringed bangs and curling tendrils at the temples. Kid gloves and a fan completed the ensemble.

Jess couldn't deny her guilt over the expense, though. The gown had taken the dressmaker the entire week to sew, and had cost a fortune. She also couldn't deny that she was as nervous as she'd ever been in her life. The army of butterflies had taken refuge in her stomach again, and she was quaking like the proverbial aspen. She'd staked her whole future on this one meeting with Devlin, and the suspense was driving her mad.

At least Clem helped to ease her fears.

"Jumpin' Jehoshaphat!" the wizened mule skinner exclaimed when Jess finally emerged from her room, where

she and Flo had been closeted all afternoon. He'd come
over from the boardinghouse specifically to see her off,
and now all he could do was gape. "You're gonna set that
big-city fella on his ears, Jessie, that's fer shore."

Flo beamed, her grin wide and smug. "She does look
grand, doesn't she?"

Riley—all dressed up himself in a tailcoat and tall opera
hat—kissed his daughter on the cheek and held out his
arm with a proud chuckle.

Riley had hired a carriage for the occasion, but as they
made the short drive to Georgetown, Jess was grateful for
the velvet mantle that protected her shoulders against the
chill of early November. Fallen aspen leaves swirled
around the hem of her gown as Riley helped her down
from the carriage. He gave her another encouraging smile,
but all Jess could manage was a quivering one in return.

They were met by a butler who took her wrap and
showed them into a large chamber that appeared to be a
cross between a ballroom and a drawing room. An orchestra played quietly in one corner, competing with a buzz of
polite conversation. A crowd of some fifty people were already gathered there, all superbly dressed in swallow-
tailed coats or evening dresses. Jess didn't feel so out of
place for the elegant evening.

Ashton Burke must have been watching for them, for he
came up to Jess almost at once and took her hand. "Welcome, my dear. I'm delighted you could come. I have
several people I want you to meet."

Looking every inch the proud papa—although not divulging a word about their relationship—Burke escorted
Jessica and Riley around the room, introducing them as ri-
val mine owners to the kind of rich, high-powered men
Jess had always despised. There were several capitalists
from Denver who had ridden the train up for the occasion
with their wives, a railroad magnate from Kansas City, a
silver baron from neighboring Leadville, a state senator,
and two mayors.

Jess was listening politely to one of the Denver capitalists and looking surreptitiously around for Devlin when

she finally saw him. Her heart took on a suddenly erratic rhythm, while her breath ebbed away. He looked positively magnificent in a black cutaway evening coat and white silk bow tie that subtly declared his wealth and authority.

He had one shoulder propped negligently against a wall, and had hooked a thumb in the pocket of his white, single-breasted waistcoat. A half dozen ladies had gathered around him, obviously vying for his attention. And no wonder, Jess thought with a surge of bitter jealousy. Devlin exuded raw masculinity and power, an aura as potent and alluring as catnip to a cat.

He was watching her, Jess realized with sudden surprise. When she met his eyes, though, he deliberately dropped his gaze, moving it slowly over her, down the expanse of emerald silk and lifting again to fasten on the low neckline of her gown. His intense scrutiny made her feel as if he were caressing her naked breasts.

Jess felt the color rise to her cheeks. Her nipples had tightened in direct response to his perusal, while a flare of heat had suddenly gathered between her thighs.

As if he knew precisely the effect he was having on her, Devlin smiled. Not the charming, seductive grin he had perfected to an art. This one was cool, aloof, and more than a little arrogant. When she stared, he inclined his head at her briefly, almost insolently, in recognition. Jess's heart sank. Devlin didn't look at all as if he were in love with her. In fact, he looked downright disinterested. She heard the Denver capitalist say something to her, but she could no more have responded than she could have moved one of the Rocky Mountains.

The next half hour was pure torture for Jess; she was nervous, restless, anxious, and scared. When a waiter proffered a tray loaded with glasses of champagne, she accepted one and drained it more quickly than was wise. The fizzing wine gave her false courage and filled her with the desire to do something wild and reckless. By the time Ashton Burke found her again, she had regained a measure of bravado.

"I should be honored if you would help open the dancing. Oh, not with me," Burke said with a smile when she started to take his arm. "I fear etiquette demands I partner the plump Mrs. Greely. I have someone else in mind for you."

He took her elbow and lead her straight to the crowd gathered around Devlin. Jess almost balked when she realized what Burke intended, but her pride kept her from pulling away. That and the knowledge that if she and Devlin were going to have a reconciliation, it would be up to her.

His unsmiling features gave her no encouragement as he stared coolly down at her.

"Mr. Devlin, my I present a lovely partner for the waltz?" Burke asked.

She thought for a minute that he might refuse, but instead Devlin inclined his head. "It would be my pleasure."

Burke left them alone then, and an awkward silence descended between them. When Devlin politely offered his arm to lead her out onto the floor, Jess nervously took it. She felt a muscle jump beneath her touch, which heartened her a bit; maybe Devlin wasn't as unaffected by her as he pretended.

Other couples began gathering around them in preparation for the dance, but Jess scarcely noticed as they stood waiting for the music to begin. She was only aware of the stunningly handsome man beside her who was treating her like a stranger.

Gazing up into wood-smoke gray eyes, she falteringly began her rehearsed speech. "Riley says that maybe . . . that he thinks . . . I may have judged you too harshly."

"Indeed?"

His tone was curt, cool, unforgiving. She swallowed. Devlin wasn't making this the least bit easy for her. "He also said . . . I should talk to you about it."

Devlin's penetrating gaze stabbed her. "Is this an apology?"

"No. Yes . . . I mean . . . I just wanted you to know . . . if you have anything to say about what happened, I'll listen."

He pressed his lips together in a tight line. "That's very generous of you, Miss Jess, but I have nothing to say."

The orchestra struck up the chords of a waltz, but neither she nor Devlin moved.

"You aren't going to tell me why you were kissing her?" Jess asked in a trembling voice.

"That depends." He eyed her coolly. "If you've already made up your mind about me, there's no point in discussing it."

"No . . . I haven't made up my mind."

There was a long moment of silence while Devlin seemed to deliberate her answer. His gray eyes were shadowed with emotion, but it wasn't anger she saw in them now. Oddly, it was vulnerability and a certain wariness.

Suddenly he grasped her hand and turned on his heel, pulling a startled Jess behind him.

Ignoring the curious looks of the guests and servants alike, he led her through the whirling dancers, off the crowded floor, out of the room, and along the hall. Finally he pushed her into a large, dimly lit chamber that looked like a library.

Trying to catch her breath, Jess turned in time to see Devlin rotating the key in the lock. Facing her, he crossed his arms over his chest and leaned back against the door.

Devlin's stance was more an effort at control than belligerence, though. The fear running through him was palpable. The interminable weeks of frustration and uncertainty while he'd waited for Jess to make up her mind about him had culminated in this single moment, when his future, his entire chance at happiness, would likely be decided.

Yet nearly as strong as fear was desire. After weeks of denial, the mere sight of Jess had made his blood hot. That gown she was wearing showed a provocative amount of her splendid figure. Her naked, scented shoulders, the hint of luxurious cleavage, the knowledge that the layers of skirts hid a pair of long silken legs, all were driving him crazy. He'd grown hard just watching her.

"If you expect me," Devlin managed to say evenly, "to

discuss my reasons for what happened, you're going to have to tell what set you off that last time."

"I should think that would be obvious."

"Tell me anyway."

He was going to make her humble her pride, Jess realized. "Well, I . . . I was jealous."

The tightness in Devlin's features visibly relaxed. "Why?"

"Well . . ." Unable to meet his gaze any longer, Jess looked down at the floor and began twisting her fingers together. "I just didn't want you kissing her, that's all."

"Why?"

He wasn't going to give up, evidently, until she confessed. Jess took a deep breath. "Because . . ." Her voice dropped to a miserable whisper. "Because . . . I love you."

Until she'd said the words, Devlin hadn't realized how desperately he'd needed them, wanted them. The cold fear inside him dissipated. His heart seemed to swell and melt with tenderness all at the same time. And yet he didn't intend to let Jess off the hook quite so easily. "Say it louder, angel. I couldn't hear you."

Lifting her chin, Jessica suddenly glared at him. "I love you, all right? And I couldn't stand seeing you kiss that *woman*. It *hurt*. I thought that if you were kissing her, you couldn't possibly care for me."

"Did you ever stop to consider how you hurt me every time you accused me of having base motives?"

"Well, I'm sorry. I was wrong, I admit it! Now are you satisfied?"

Devlin cocked his head. "No."

Jess looked at him in frustration. "What do you want from me, a pint of blood?"

"Your trust would be adequate, darlin'," Devlin said wryly.

"I . . . I trust you."

"Then you believe me when I say the kiss I gave Lena was entirely innocent?"

"I . . ." Jess couldn't bring herself to swallow that much. "It didn't look that way to me."

"That's what trust is, Jessica. Believing in someone on faith, even if all the evidence points to the contrary."

Having no defense, she remained miserably silent. It was true, she hadn't trusted Devlin. She'd always assumed the worst about him, never even giving him the benefit of the doubt.

"I see I'm going to have to teach you the difference between kisses of passion and kisses of friendship," Devlin said finally.

Pushing himself from the door, he strode toward her. There was little gentleness in his fingers when he gripped her upper arms and pulled her against him. His lips, when they descended, were hot and fierce, his tongue thrusting and hard. His sensual assault sent Jess's senses reeling.

His withdrawal was just as abrupt. "That's how I kiss a woman I want. The chaste peck I gave Lena meant absolutely nothing."

"You w-want me?" Jess asked, shaking.

"More than I've ever wanted anything in my life," Devlin said solemnly.

"That's ... all she is to you? A friend?"

"That's all."

Jess closed her eyes as a vast relief swept through her. Weakly she leaned against Devlin, burying her nose in the curve of his shoulder. He smelled clean and masculine, with a hint of citrus shaving cologne.

"I thought you didn't want me," she murmured.

Devlin gave a sharp laugh as he rested his chin on her tawny hair. "You stubborn, infuriating hellcat. How could you possibly think that? I haven't been able to keep my hands off you since we met."

"That isn't true. For the past month you haven't even spoken to me, much less touched me."

"Which is your fault entirely. If you hadn't jumped to the wrong conclusion again, we could have been enjoying each other all this time. Instead, you caused us both misery."

She lifted her head to give him a searching look. "Were you really miserable?"

The corner of his mouth kicked up in amusement as, in reply, he took her hand and guided it to the stiff bulge in his trousers. "As miserable as a man can get."

"Oh," Jessica said, color rising to her cheeks.

Still smiling, Devlin bent to kiss her bare throat. Jess's blood temperature shot up an instant ten degrees. His seductive touch vividly reminded her of how much she had missed him, how much she had ached for him to do just this to her. When his mouth moved lower, to her bosom, and his tongue shot out to trace hot little circles on the swells of her breasts, Jess's knees nearly buckled beneath her. "D-Devlin . . ." she moaned.

"Damn, but I'd like to find a bed."

"Me . . . too."

His chuckle was a breathy rasp against her skin. "Didn't anyone ever tell you you're not supposed to go to bed with a man who isn't your husband, Miss Jess?"

"My mother told me . . . but she didn't even take her own advice."

"If it weren't for the throng of guests on the other side of this door, I'd take you right here. You've never made love standing up."

Her passion-hazed eyes widened in surprise as he lifted his head. "Can you really do it that way?"

His seductive smile was wickedness itself. "There are countless ways, angel, and I want to show you every one."

Her heart tumbled over itself at his remark. "Oh, Devlin."

"Call me Garrett. And stop looking at me that way, sweetheart. My control is tenuous enough as it is without your beautiful eyes begging me to bury myself inside you."

"You . . . think I have beautiful eyes?"

"God, yes. And you look gorgeous in that gown. The only thing I'd like better than seeing you in that gown is seeing you out of it. But I suppose I'll have to restrain myself. A score of people saw us leave, and your reputation is already on shaky ground. If I were to do what I'd *like* to do to you, I'd no doubt have to deal with both Riley and Burke—and *two* irate fathers are a little more than I want to tackle at once. One of them is going to come looking for you any minute now, I expect. And in any case, you and I need to get a few things straight first."

"Like what?"

"Like where we go from here."

"Riley says"—Jess hesitated shyly—"that you're thinking about . . . settling down."

"Does he? Riley's a smart man."

Jess suddenly grew interested in the top button of Devlin's waistcoat. "He said . . . maybe you might want a wife."

"That's a distinct possibility. But I doubt you would be interested in the position." When Jess raised her anxious gaze to his, Devlin cocked an eyebrow. "You'd have to take me as your husband then, and I could never manage to measure up to your standards. No man could. They're damn near sainthood."

His tone was teasing, but his expression was entirely serious; Jess didn't know whether to be relieved or distraught. "I don't want a saint for a husband," she mumbled.

"Well, then, there's the matter of my bank account. First I was too poor for you. Then I was too rich."

Squirming, Jess could barely meet his penetrating gaze. "I never objected to your being poor. It's just that I thought you were a good-for-nothing gambler."

"So now I'm a good-for-nothing moneybags." His eyes narrowed. "You've got to get over this obsessive idea that rich men are all alike, Jessica. We're not—any more than all poor men are alike."

"I know that . . . now."

"And if you'd think about it, you would realize it isn't power and wealth you object to, but the *misuse* of power and wealth."

"I know. I have thought about it, Devl—Garrett. I admit that I might have misjudged you—"

"You *might* have?"

"All right, I did misjudge you. Just because you're wealthy doesn't mean you're like Burke."

"Thank you," Devlin said dryly.

"No, I mean it. You aren't anything like him."

"In one respect, I am. I make money for a living. If you can't accept that, then we have a problem. I don't see any need for me to slave away at manual labor for a mere pittance."

"I can accept it."

"And you're going to learn to trust me?"

"Yes," Jess said in a small voice.

He put a finger under her chin, keeping her from avoiding his gaze. "I want your promise. I don't care what the situation is, if I do something you don't like, you talk to me first before you go off half-cocked. Do we have a deal?"

"Yes ... yes, I promise."

He smiled then and bent his head, giving her a kiss that held such tenderness it nearly shattered her soul. Jess clung to him for support, even after their lips had parted.

"Oh, Garrett ... I do love you so."

"I'm glad you finally admitted it, sweetheart." Holding her gaze, he moved his hands to lightly frame her face, his thumbs tracing delicate circles along her cheekbones. "And since you have, I don't mind telling you that the feeling is entirely mutual."

Jess's heart seemed to stand still. "You ... mean it? You love me?"

"I mean it, sweetheart. I've been waiting for a damned month—"

His words were nearly drowned out when a tremendous commotion sounded from outside in the hall. Both Devlin and Jess wanted to ignore the intrusion, but the shouts didn't die down, and the sound of running feet seemed ominous.

Reluctantly Devlin pulled away. "We'd better see what's going on."

Jess could have screamed in frustration at the untimely interruption. She ached to know what Devlin had been about to tell her. He'd said he wanted her, that—incredulously—he even loved her. But did that mean he wanted her enough to marry her? Enough to overlook her shortcomings and the awful way she'd treated him in the past? Enough to give up that Lena woman as his mistress? Or did he merely want her as a replacement for Lena in his bed?

But all her anxious questions would have to wait, Jess realized when Devlin had turned the key in the lock and opened the door to the hall. Men and women in evening attire were frantically rushing past.

Above the din, though, Jess could make out what one man was yelling.

"Fire! Fire! The Plume is burning! Silver Plume's on fire."

Chapter 22

By the time Jessica and Devlin managed to push their way through the crowd and out the front door, they could hear a fire bell ringing, giving the alarm. Up the canyon, in the distance, a faint glow lit up the night sky.

"Dear God," Jess breathed. She started to tremble, but it had nothing to do with the chill breeze attacking her bare shoulders.

"It looks bad," Riley added fearfully as he came up behind her. "We've got to get home, Jessie."

"We have to find a carriage first," Devlin responded grimly.

He dragged off his coat and threw it around Jess's shoulders, then grabbed her hand and pulled her along through the frantic crowd. People were running in six different directions, searching for loved ones and transportation amid the tangle of horses and vehicles that had suddenly packed the residential street.

The terror that the shouted word "Fire!" struck in the hearts of Westerners was well earned, Jess knew. Most towns lacked the adequate resources to fight a blaze of any magnitude. And while Georgetown had its own volunteer fire department and an efficient waterworks, Silver Plume had only one major source of water—Clear Creek—and no equipment to speak of. Bucket brigades would have to battle the blaze until the Georgetown fire companies, with their hand-drawn carts and lengths of fire hose, could make it up the hill to help.

347

With the ominous glow on the horizon, however, Jess was deathly afraid that Georgetown's rescue would be too late.

Thankfully, Devlin managed to appropriate a carriage quickly—a closed brougham that doubtless belonged to one of Burke's guests. He shoved Jess and her father inside and climbed up in the driver's seat, taking the reins from an astonished groom. Just as he started to whip up the pair of bays, though, Ashton Burke came running toward them.

"I'm accompanying you!" Burke shouted, and grabbed for the door.

Devlin waited only long enough for Burke to climb inside before springing the horses.

Jess hung on tightly as the carriage lurched and swayed, while her lips move in a fervent litany, "Please, please, please . . ." Across from her, Burke sat in grim silence. Next to her, Riley leaned out the window, watching the rocky canyon wall streak past. It was highly dangerous, racing through the darkness along the narrow road in the wake of dozens of other vehicles, but Jess had faith that Devlin would get them through in one piece.

He slowed only when Silver Plume was in sight. From the carriage window, Jess could see the conflagration in the east end of town. It was roaring out of control through the densely packed wood-frame commercial district. Already the acrid smoke and heat were so intense she almost choked.

"What shall we do?" Jess asked her father anxiously, wondering if they should try to save any of their belongings from their home or boardinghouse.

"Better try to stop the fire first," Riley answered brusquely. "We won't have time to save much anyway if it gets as far as our place. And about the only thing that can't be replaced are the pictures of your ma. I won't let anything happen to those."

Burke, wincing at the reference to Jenny Ann, leaped down from the carriage. Riley and Jess followed with Devlin, heading toward the fire. When they reached Main

Street, they could see that a line of men had formed to haul leather buckets from the creek, but dozens of others milled about helplessly. Taking charge, Burke began shouting orders and organizing the stragglers into another line.

Jess would have pitched in, but Devlin stopped her.

"You help with the women and children! Get them out of here and keep them calm."

Wishing she could do more, Jess nodded obediently and caught the hand of a sobbing boy, leading him to a safer place down the street.

She spent the next five desperate hours corralling children and wetting down blankets and doctoring burns, but mostly she prayed. Her prayers went unanswered. The flames blazed higher as the mountain winds swept through the valley, fanning the fires and negating the most determined efforts of Silver Plume's residents and even the well-trained volunteer firemen of Georgetown's fire department. Building after building along Main Street went up in a whoosh of sparks. Burke's Diamond Dust Hotel and Saloon, which lay directly in the path of the flames, were two of the first to go.

Jess felt a pang of regret for all the beautiful furnishings that were incinerated, but as Riley had said, belongings could be replaced; people couldn't. Her real fear was for Flo and Clem and her boarders and the hundreds of other friends she had known all her life.

For the most part, though, the townspeople managed to flee to safety. Jess saw hundreds of dazed victims of the fire trudge past her, lugging valuables. Others packed the crowded thoroughfare, merely staring in shock as the Plume burned down around them. Once she spied Clem fighting the fire, his shouted curses reaching her even over the crackling roar of the flames. And just past midnight, Flo joined her. Calm and motherly, Flo provided Jess the inspiration to keep on and even managed to dredge a strangled laugh from her in the midst of the hellish nightmare.

A knot of women and children had gathered at the little

Catholic church to pray, but Flo scolded them into action, pointing to the church.

"Those walls may be made of stone, but that roof is pure tinder. And the Good Lord sure as shootin' would rather you get up off your knees and get to work at a time like this!"

As a group, the women began carrying water to throw on the church roof. Trouble was, the cisterns in back of the adjacent buildings held too little water to make any difference in a blaze like this. They gave it their best effort, though, Jess included. Too afraid to be tired, too tired to be afraid, she kept swinging buckets. Her throat and nostrils ached from the stinging smoke, while her palms blistered from the leather handles.

And all the while the dreaded flames kept crawling closer, engulfing everything in their path, driving the firefighters back.

Finally the heat and smoke became too intense to bear. The lines of men fell back, sweeping the women behind them.

Incredibly, though, just as the fire began licking at the stone wall of the little church, the wind miraculously shifted. Jess and everyone else held their breaths as the greedy flames curled back on themselves. Minute after minute they watched, but the devastation seemed to have faltered. The firefighters continued the battle with bucket and hoses, and actually appeared to be winning.

It was nearly dawn by the time they could declare victory, though—if such destruction could be called victory. Three blocks of the town had been razed, and most of the business district lay in smoldering ruins. All the saloons, dance halls, hotels, stores, shops, and offices—everything that had been the lifeblood of Silver Plume was gone.

A few lanterns appeared then to illuminate the terrible scene. Groups of weary, soot-covered men searched in the smoking debris for burning coals, extinguishing any remaining flames. The women made coffee and passed out mugs with forced smiles. Some of the townspeople simply sank to their knees where they stood, their stricken, defeated expressions showing more clearly than words what wreckage the fire had made of their lives.

Jess felt immeasurably lucky and somewhat guilty. Their house and boardinghouse had been spared, but many had lost their livelihood and hundreds of miners and their families were now homeless.

And at least one person had died. At dawn, the charred remains of a body was found among the ashes of the building that had been Patrick Barrett's saloon.

"Poor bastard," Jess heard somebody say. "Patty was too young to die . . . if that's him."

Jess shivered in the cold dawn air. Reminded forcefully of how fragile life was in this rugged country, she worriedly searched the crowds for Devlin and Riley. She found her father resting on the boardwalk with Clem, while Flo hovered over them. Both men were exhausted but unhurt, but there was no sign of Devlin.

Two minutes later, though, she spied his tall form moving through the throng. Picking up her now-ruined skirts, Jess ran to meet him, and with a glad cry flung her arms around his neck.

"Devlin—Garrett . . . I was so worried about you. . . ." Her breathless comment was muffled against his throat.

"I'm all right, angel," he said huskily. "What about you?" He held her away tenderly, searching her face, emotion bright and intense in his smoky eyes.

"I'm fine." Jess regarded Devlin anxiously in return. In the chill gray light of dawn, his face was lined with fatigue and grime, but he had never looked more handsome to her, never had been more beloved.

His thoughts must have been running along the same track, for he smiled tiredly, a slow, seductive curving of lips that made her heart race. "I remember being interrupted last night," he murmured before bending his head, covering her mouth urgently with his.

He kissed her long and hard, in plain sight of half the occupants of Silver Plume. It was a strangely poignant kiss—fervent triumph mingled with intense relief, a celebration of life and victory, of a hard-fought battle won.

And delivered with enough passion to warm her all over, despite the frosty morning air. Jess's limbs were weak, her heart pounding, by the time Devlin finally allowed her up for air. And then he stole her breath away again with his murmured admission.

"I love you, you stubborn hellcat, but if you don't stop kissing me like that, I'll make you a fallen woman right here on the street."

"Would you say that again? Just so I'm sure I heard right?"

"I'll make you a fallen woman right here—"

"No, not that part! The part about you loving me."

"I love you, angel." He reached up and brushed her cheek with the back of his knuckles. "More than I ever thought it was possible to love anyone."

Jess's eyes absurdly filled with tears. "Are you *sure*, Garrett? You could have any woman you wanted. In fact, you've probably *had* any woman you wanted—"

"There've been others in my past, Jessica, I won't deny it. But you'll be the only one in my future."

She felt like crying, she was so happy—in spite of the devastation around her. "You aren't going to kiss that . . . Lena anymore?"

"I don't have any plans to, certainly. But if I should, you're going to listen to my side of the story before you jump to any conclusions, right?"

"Yes."

Devlin's arm tightened about her waist. "Actually, you had no reason to be jealous of Lena, especially not that day. She was congratulating me on my upcoming marriage when you saw us. I was on my way to propose to you."

Jess stared. "You really were going to propose to me?"

"I had the ring in my pocket."

"Oh, Garrett . . . I'm sorry."

"You should be."

He started to kiss her again, but just before their lips met, he saw a scowling Riley beckoning at them from across the way.

Draping a protective arm around her shoulders, Devlin

led a dazed Jess through the crowd to her father's side. Riley gave them both a weary, stern-eyed glance, then held a finger to his lips and gestured toward a knot of men several yards away.

Jess had difficulty dragging her thoughts away from the passionate kiss Devlin had given her in order to focus on what was happening.

A group had gathered around Ashton Burke and appeared to be listening intently. How Burke managed to look so elegant and wealthy with his formal attire covered with soot, his face blackened, his tawny gold hair thoroughly disheveled, and one burned hand wrapped in a makeshift bandage, she would never know.

"Buildings can be rebuilt," he was saying emphatically in his upperclass British accent.

"With what?" someone muttered. "We ain't got your kind of money. We ain't got nothin' left."

The dismay and defeat on the weary faces of the merchants and householders had turned to hostility. Jess understood their anger. The fire had leveled nearly half the town and most of east Main Street had been destroyed, and yet Burke was acting as if the devastation was merely a minor setback.

"I intend to make a donation to start rebuilding the town. A hundred thousand dollars for our city councilmen to do with as they see fit."

A murmur of shock rippled through the crowd at Burke's announcement. Jess most of all could hardly believe her ears. Was this Ashton Burke making such a generous offer? The greedy, money-hungry, manipulative silver baron who had made Riley's life hell for the past twenty-odd years?

Just then Burke turned and searched the faces of the crowd. When he caught Jessica's astonished gaze, his blue eyes softened. The quizzical smile he gave her held uncertainty, almost as if he were seeking her approval.

"Because of this town, I have achieved great prosperity over the years," he said directly to Jessica. "I believe it is time I gave something back."

Jess felt the warm moisture of tears blur her vision as she smiled at the man who was her blood father. She could not have asked for any more positive proof that he was trying to change his ways for her sake. Ashton Burke valued wealth above all else. Moreover, he'd probably sustained greater losses from the fire than any other single individual. To donate such a huge sum to the less fortunate spoke volumes about his transformation.

He was still the consummate businessman, though.

"And I issue a challenge to the consolidated mine owners in the district to match my offer," Burke added in a loud voice.

"I'll match it," Devlin said at once, which made Jess tighten her arm about his waist in gratitude.

She wasn't surprised by such generosity from Devlin, but it frankly astounded her to hear at least three more voices in the crowd volunteering to match Burke's hundred-thousand-dollar offer. And she suspected that more would follow suit once a fund was actually started.

"Good," Devlin murmured in her ear. "There's no need for the town to be *too* grateful to Burke."

Jess gave him an amused nod, and then became distracted by the arousing way Devlin was nibbling on her earlobe. When she caught sight of the scowl on Riley's face, however, she drew back sedately, willing her heart to settle down.

Burke was speaking to the crowd again. "We shall start over. The council can float a bond issue to finance a waterworks and better fire protection. And instead of wood, we should build with brick. If we begin immediately, we can have a good start before winter sets in."

"That's all well and good," a miner said grimly, "but where are we gonna live till then? Where are our kids and wives gonna sleep? How are they gonna eat?"

Clem piped up in answer. "If it's all right with Jessie, Homer, your Mollie and kids can have my room at the boardinghouse. It won't hurt me none to camp out in a tent like in the olden days. It ain't winter by a long chalk."

"Of course it's all right with me," Jess agreed. "And if

all my other boarders would be as generous as Clem, we'd have room for fifteen or so families. We could also take two or three more at our home, if they don't mind a little crowding."

That was the signal for everyone to start talking at once, with those more fortunate townspeople volunteering to put up the homeless in their houses. Tired but satisfied, Jess leaned her head against Devlin's shoulder, reveling in his warmth.

His hand came up tenderly to brush a wisp of honey-blond hair back from her cheek. "I'm jealous, angel," he murmured. "You've arranged accommodations for everyone else in town, but you didn't once think about me."

Jess gave him a puzzled look. "You already have a place to stay in Georgetown in a hotel, don't you?"

"Not one that's adequate for my needs."

"What do you mean?"

His slow grin was positively wicked. "I suggest you give up your bed here and sleep with me in Georgetown. My room at the Hotel de Paris is large enough for the both of us. And it would be the charitable thing to do—provide more space for the needy families of Silver Plume."

A throat being cleared beside them made Jess start guiltily. She looked up to find Riley pinning Devlin with an intense stare.

"No daughter of mine," her father said emphatically, hands on hips, "is going to any hotel with a man who isn't her husband."

Jess turned a delicate shade of pink. "Riley, he was only teasing."

"No, I wasn't." Devlin bent and pressed a kiss at her temple, staying there long enough to whisper in her ear, "If you think I'm sleeping alone after the month of celibacy you've put me through, hellcat, you'd better think again."

Clem shuffled up just then. "You two finally gonna get hitched?"

Jessica's embarrassed color wouldn't recede. "I . . . don't know. Garrett hasn't asked me to marry him."

Devlin's mouth curved in a wry grin. "I think perhaps I'd better. Riley looks like he might fetch his shotgun any minute."

"Always knew you were a smart man, son," Riley observed pleasantly, crossing his arms over his chest and looking prepared to wait all day if need be.

"Would it be too much to ask for you to accord us a moment of privacy?"

"There he goes again," Clem muttered, "talking fancy."

Flo, with a disgusted look, grabbed the ornery mule skinner by his grizzled beard. "Come on, you old coot. Don't you know when you aren't wanted?" Ignoring Clem's yelp of pain, she hustled the two older men a short distance away, leaving Devlin and Jess alone in the crowd.

Not wasting any time, he turned Jess to face him, locking his arms loosely about her waist and gazing down at her with a laughing gleam in his gray eyes. "Miss Jess, sweetheart, will you do me the honor of becoming my wife before your father takes it into his head to deprive me of some vital part of my anatomy?"

Unable to make light of so serious a subject, though, Jess searched his face anxiously. "Are you sure, Garrett? Marriage is what you really want?"

The amusement in his eyes softened, while the tender look he gave her went a long way toward chasing away Jessica's doubt. "That's what I really want," he said huskily. "I want you for my wife, Jess. I want to have children with you and build a life together. I want to fall asleep with you in my bed and wake up with you in my arms. Starting today."

"Today?" she echoed, startled.

"Today, this very morning. I'm not going to risk another misunderstanding before I have my ring on your finger."

"But . . . there's just been a fire—"

"We ought to be able to arrange a ceremony, even with all this chaos."

"But . . . so soon? People will talk if we get married in such a rush."

"Let them talk. Besides, I don't consider it a rush. It's

been a whole damn month of torture for me. And the fire will actually give us a good excuse for a hasty wedding. All those homeless families need a place to stay."

Still she hesitated.

"Do you really see any reason to put if off?" Devlin demanded, his tone only half teasing.

Jess looked down at her ruined gown, which twelve hours ago had been beautiful. The emerald silk and delicate lace were stained by soot and water, and reeked with the stench of smoke. "You want to get married with me looking like this?"

"I want to marry you any way I can get you," he assured her. "Do you really care what gown you're wearing?"

Lifting her gaze to his, she gave him a smile as brilliant as the sun that was just rising over the mountains. "I don't care."

"Good." His voice dropped to a seductive whisper. "Because I can think of at least one very pressing reason to hasten the wedding." He drew her closer, making Jess intimately aware of the painful state of arousal he was enduring. A blush flooded her cheeks for the third time that morning, and only deepened when Devlin added huskily, "No more kisses for you, angel, until we're alone. We oughtn't scandalize these good people any more than we already have."

Reluctantly dragging her yearning gaze away from Devlin's beautiful mouth, Jess looked around her to find dozens of people watching them with varying stages of curiosity, shock, and good-natured amusement.

Devlin chuckled when her blush deepened. "We have only one thing left to settle," he added. "What kind of house do you want?"

"What?" Jess asked, still a bit dazed.

"You told me it would be nice to have a fine house in Georgetown, so I'm building you one. I couldn't start construction without your approval, though. I've had several different architectural plans drawn up, but if you don't like any of those, you can choose something else. All the designs have three bathrooms and a boiler to provide hot running water."

"Three bathrooms—" Jess stared at him. "You were mighty certain of me if you were going off building me a house, weren't you?"

Devlin grinned his sexy grin. "I was certain of *me,* sweetheart, not you. I'm good at winning, remember? I wasn't going to chase after you, but I sure as hell didn't intend to let you get away, either. I figured you'd come around sooner or later. At least I hoped to God you would."

When Jess shook her head, he planted a teasing kiss on her nose. "You don't even know when you're licked, angel."

"But *three* bathrooms? I don't know if I want *that* fine a house." She remembered Burke's opulent drawing room and library. "Burke's kind of place would be too fine for me."

"Nothing would be too fine for you, but if you don't care for it, you don't have to have it. I'll build you a log cabin, if you like."

She gave him a tremulous smile. "It doesn't matter about the house. I just want you."

"I know. That's why I love you." He reached up and tucked an errant tendril behind her ear. "I used to think that all women were mercenary, that wealth and position were all that mattered to them. But you proved otherwise. I'd love you for that if for no other reason. Now, come. We have a wedding to arrange."

Determinedly Devlin released Jess and took her hand, leading her over to where her father waited with Clem and Flo.

"We're gonna get hitched," he announced, mimicking Clem's Western drawl. "This morning, if you can find us a Justice of the Peace."

Clem slapped his knee in glee and shouted "Hot damn!" while Flo grabbed Jess and gave her a hug that threatened to crush her ribs.

Riley waited his turn to enfold her in a loving embrace.

There were tears in his eyes when he held her away. "I just want you to be happy, Jess."

"I know," she said with a watery laugh. "And I will be. Garrett says he loves me."

He nodded in satisfaction. "Are you going to ask Burke to the wedding?"

"You wouldn't mind?"

"No . . . not if I get to give you away."

"Of course you do," Jess said, startled that Riley could possibly think she would consider any other alternative. "Burke can be a witness, if he likes." She glanced up at her future husband. "Is that okay with you?" she asked uncertainly.

His lips curving in an impatient smile, Devlin slipped a possessive arm about her waist. "Anything you want, angel—as long as you make it happen within the next half hour. I won't vouch for my control any longer than that. If you aren't my wife in the next thirty minutes, I'll just have to carry you off."

"Then I guess," Jessica said with a pleased smile of her own, "we'd better go find that Justice of the Peace."

Chapter 23

J essica made a beautiful bride, even with her gown be-
draggled and soot-stained. She carried a bouquet of
white hothouse roses which Ashton Burke had insisted on
having fetched from Georgetown. Around her shoulders
she wore her mantle of green velvet that she'd left at his
home. Her tawny hair, smoothed and rearranged into its
previous elegant coiffure by Flo's motherly fingers,
gleamed golden in the early-morning sunshine. Her com-
plexion, scrubbed virginally clean in the privacy of Doc
Wheeler's office, held a radiance that only a woman in
love could exhibit.

Devlin made a magnificent groom, or so all the ladies
thought. His formal black tailcoat enhanced his dark, stunning looks and leanly muscled physique, and hid most of
the grime on his white shirt and waistcoat, which were
blackened beyond salvage. The disreputable stubble shadowing his jaw lent him an edge of danger that was highly
potent, while his expression held the unmistakable possessiveness that a man in love showed toward the woman he
had claimed for his bride. Married and unmarried females
alike sighed with envy, while the mothers present warned
their innocent daughters to quit gawking.

The ceremony took place in the middle of Main Street,
surrounded by the majesty of the Rockies, with a cool blue
Colorado sky providing a canopy overhead. Half the occupants of Silver Plume looked on, most of them grateful at
finding some joy in the midst of disaster. Both of Jessica's

proud fathers watched the proceedings with their hearts in their eyes, going so far as to slap each other on the back when the justice pronounced the couple married and said, "You may kiss the bride."

Those were the words Devlin had been waiting for, for what seemed like a lifetime. "Finally," he murmured.

He took Jess in his arms, gazing down at her with a powerful tenderness he couldn't possibly hide. He'd returned to Colorado more than a month ago with every intention of making Jessica his wife. She wasn't the kind of woman, however, to meekly fall in with plans not of her own making. In fact, she was just stubborn enough to deliberately overset his ambitions on general principle—and determined enough to hold on to her convictions, even if it meant losing the things she held dear. Oddly enough, though, that was one of the things Devlin loved most about her. That she had principles she fiercely believed in, principles that meant more to her than wealth or power or comfort, even more than love. It was his misfortune that Jess also had a blind spot a mile wide. Until she'd sorted out her feelings for him, all he'd been able to do was wait . . . and pace . . . and pull out his hair . . . and pray.

Now, it was all over. Now, with the delay and uncertainty at an end, he could breathe again.

"You gonna kiss her or what?" Clem complained, interrupting his reflections.

Devlin grinned and obediently bent his head to seal their vows. He felt Jess's mouth warm and trembling under his own. It was all he could do to force himself to pull back and turn her over to her family and friends for their congratulations.

The celebration afterward was more elaborate than Devlin could find patience for. Burke had sent to Georgetown for several dozen cases of champagne, and ordered beer all around from a nearby saloon that was still standing, so the gathering turned into a holiday, with the town commemorating not only the marriage of one of its own, but the victory over the fire and the new future of Silver Plume, which would be rebuilt out of the ashes.

Devlin cursed under his breath when someone brought out a fiddle and the crowd spontaneously began dancing in the street. He watched jealously as a laughing and radiant Jess was passed from miner to miner—some of whom had known her since childhood—for a whirl. And yet he clamped down on his urge to tear her away from their good-natured embraces. In his haste to tie Jessica to him, he hadn't allowed her the kind of wedding most young women dreamed of. The least he could do was let her enjoy this moment.

It was nearly an hour later before he managed to get close enough to slip an arm around her waist. Jess, looking up at her new husband, felt her heart catch at the bright, warm light moving in his eyes.

"If you're sorry we couldn't manage a church wedding," Devlin said in her ear, "we can do this again properly in a week or two."

Smiling joyfully, Jess shook her head. "I'm not in the least sorry. This is much better than a stuffy ceremony in a church."

Devlin's guilt faded. "At least we'll have something to tell our grandchildren. . . . We were married the day Silver Plume burned down."

At his reference to grandchildren, a warm glow kindled inside her. "I never figured you would want a family."

"I expect there are still some things you don't know about me, angel"—his mouth curved seductively—"but I intend to take great pleasure helping you find out."

"You really want children? You told me once that you didn't."

"Only because I never found the right woman until now."

Jess's amber eyes still held a hint of uncertainty as she gazed up at him. "Oh, Garrett, are you sure I'm the right woman for you?"

"Damn sure. I'll show you just how right if I ever get you alone. Do you think we could make our excuses and get out of here? We still have a marriage to consummate."

Jess blushed and nodded mutely, excitement and shivering anticipation making her limbs suddenly weak.

They made their farewells amid a chorus of bawdy comments and good wishes. Jess hugged everyone, Burke included, Riley the hardest of all, and finally allowed Devlin to help her into the closed carriage.

When he had joined her, though, Flo poked her head inside. "I'll send some of your things down to the hotel, Jess."

"Fine," Devlin answered for his wife, "but that's all we need anyone to do for us. I don't care if the rest of the town burns down. Don't bother us for a week."

Flo grinned broadly and winked at a blushing Jess. "Lordy, that gorgeous fella is a man after my own heart."

Returning the widow's grin, Devlin pulled the door shut, determined to whisk his bride away before anyone else could corner her. He rapped firmly on the roof, signaling the driver to leave, and draped an arm around Jess's shoulders, pulling her into the curve of his body as the vehicle lurched forward.

After the noise of the crowd, the quiet within the carriage seemed almost intimidating to Jess. Weariness and tension suddenly assaulting her, she lay her head gratefully against Devlin's shoulder. She felt light-headed from lack of sleep and filled with fear. A fear different from the kind she'd endured during the fire, but just as intense. She was petrified that she wouldn't live up to Devlin's expectations as either wife or lover.

He must have sensed something was wrong, though, for his lips brushed her hair in a comforting kiss. "You okay, angel?"

"No," Jess answered truthfully. "I'm so nervous I'm shaking."

"Why are you nervous?"

"I guess because I've never had a husband before."

"That's understandable. I'm a touch nervous myself."

"You?" She sounded skeptical.

"I've never had a wife before, either." His tone held an

undertone of teasing laughter. "I think I could grow to like it."

"You really are nervous?"

"I wouldn't lie to you, Jess," he said more seriously. "I hope you finally realize that."

"I do."

"Good." Grasping her hand, he linked their fingers together, creating a physical bond. "Yes, I really am nervous. Getting married isn't a responsibility a man can take lightly. Nor is losing his bachelorhood. But this is nothing compared to what I went through the past month. It scared the devil out of me, waiting for you to decide whether I was worthy of you or not. I spent the entire time pacing the floor and wondering if you loved me enough to come to me. I had hoped . . . prayed . . ." Entirely serious now, he put a finger under her chin, tilting her face up to his, and gazed at her solemnly. "I knew what I wanted was you, Jess. I didn't know, though, if you wanted me."

"Oh, Garrett, I did want you, I do . . . more than anything. I love you so much. . . . I just couldn't believe you could ever love me. I'm still not sure I'm not dreaming."

"Believe it, angel."

"Tell me again, Garrett, please?"

"I love you, sweetheart, never doubt it. I love you, I love you, I love you. . . ."

His whispered endearments broke off as his lips came down on hers hungrily. Jess responded with heartfelt eagerness, twining her fingers in his hair and opening to his thrusting, searching tongue. The heat that rose between them was suddenly scalding in its intensity. The small whimper of longing that Jess made deep in her throat was echoed in the primitive groan Devlin gave before he abruptly held her away and inhaled a harsh breath.

"Lord, woman, what you do to me. . . . But I'm not going to start our marriage by taking you on a hard carriage seat."

"I wouldn't mind," Jess said shyly, not daring to meet his hot eyes.

His husky chuckle rasped against her temple. "That's

one of the things I love most about you. But I have something much more comfortable in mind."

They shared a state of half painful, half delicious sexual
arousal until the carriage drew to a halt before the Hotel de
Paris. Then Jess, on her best behavior, made a great show
of allowing Devlin to help her down from the carriage,
offering her hand to him regally, in her most formal finishing school manner.

When Devlin raised a quizzical eyebrow, Jess commented pointedly, "I know how to be feminine when I
want to be."

"I think you should forget I ever said that."

"How can I forget? You've told me often I enough I
don't know how to be a normal woman."

His smile was pure sensuality. "Well, I was wrong.
You've always been an armful of woman, Miss Jess, almost more woman than I can handle."

He wouldn't take her hand, though. Instead he slipped
one arm around her waist, the other behind her knees, and
scooped her into his arms, making Jess gasp.

"Tradition," Devlin teased, and carried her over the
threshold of the hotel's front door.

The proprietor came to greet them at once, his mouth
creased in a welcoming smile. He didn't appear to be at all
surprised or alarmed to see a young lady being carried into
his hotel.

"All ready, Louis?"

"Indeed, Monsieur Devlin. Everything is as you ordered. Shall I aid you and madame?"

"Thank you, no, we can manage. Would you see that no
one disturbs us?"

"But of course, m'sieur. And may I wish you and madame every happiness?"

Devlin responded with a satisfied smile. "You certainly
may."

Without further ceremony, he carried his bride past the
registration desk, through a wide door, down a hall, and up
a flight of stairs. Jess, with her arms around his neck,

peered up at Devlin. "What did he mean, everything is ready?"

"I rented the floor for a week so we wouldn't have to contend with any other guests."

"The entire floor?" Jess echoed, aghast.

"You object to my being alone with you?"

"No. . . . Only, it's so decadent."

"Not decadent. Smart. I intend to have you all to myself for a while."

He paused before a door marked "12," and asked Jess to open it. She did, and as he carried her inside, she glanced around curiously. The spacious room was as elegantly decorated as the floor below, with a large walnut-framed bed and matching rockers of the same gleaming dark wood. The Wilton-weave carpet boasted a rose pattern, while white lace curtains adorned the windows. On the bureau sat a silver tray loaded with covered dishes, and a bottle of wine had been left to cool in a silver bucket.

To Jess's surprise, a large copper tub stood in the far corner. It didn't appear to be part of the usual decor, and there was steam rising from the water. Obviously, their arrival had been expected and every effort made to ensure their comfort.

"How did you possibly have time to arrange all this?" Jess asked in awe.

"I planned it long before this. I only had to send Louis a message this morning, and he took care of the rest. We can honeymoon in a real Paris hotel later, if you like, but this will have to do for now."

"Do? Garrett, this is more than enough." Shaking her head, Jess gave him a concerned glance. "You didn't have to go to so much trouble for me."

"But I wanted to, angel. You deserve to be pampered a little."

"A little? This is a *lot* to me. This is heaven."

Devlin gazed down at her with a wicked grin. "Not yet, but I promise it will be."

He set Jess on her feet, facing him, but kept his arms wrapped around her waist. "The way I see it, Mrs. Devlin, you have four choices of what to do first ... eat, sleep, bathe, or make love. Which do you favor?"

The warm light in his eyes left no doubt as to which choice he would prefer. Jess felt a knot of pure excitement curl in the pit of her stomach.

"Well ... I know what I'd *like* to do first, but I suppose it would be wiser to take a bath. My clothes and hair still reek of smoke."

"True," Devlin said agreeably. He rubbed his whiskered jaw. "And I should shave if you don't want to be scraped raw by tomorrow morning. Fortunately, bathing and making love aren't mutually exclusive."

"You mean at the same time?" The shock in her tone made him chuckle, a low, rich sound of pleasure.

"Exactly, angel. I intend to give you a bath you won't forget."

The vivid color that rose to his young bride's cheeks charmed him. Determined not to let it fade, Devlin reached for the ribbon ties of her mantle. "Why don't we start by getting undressed? I have yet to see you entirely without clothes."

Her breathing suddenly growing shallow, Jess could only gaze mutely at him. He drew her wrap off her shoulders and tossed it haphazardly on the floor near the door. Then he began removing her numerous hairpins one by one. When her mane of honey-gold hair at last came tumbling down about her shoulders, Devlin threaded his fingers reverently through the thick mass and gave Jess a tantalizing, all-too-brief kiss.

Her other garments came next. He took a long while, though, pausing to place a kiss on each inch of flesh he exposed. Becoming impatient with his tormenting slowness, Jess tried to help, but Devlin stopped her. "This is my pleasure," he stated firmly.

Finally, though, only her shift remained. Slowly he tugged on the straps. Her bodice fell away and her bare, trembling breasts spilled out.

Devlin audibly sucked in his breath.

The room wasn't at all chilly, warmed as it was by the

hotel's central furnace, and yet Jess shivered as eyes of heated gray roamed over her, touching her intimately, their admiration unmistakable. She felt alive and radiantly female—and very much wanted.

To her surprise—and regret—all he did was look. And when he removed the undergarment entirely and she finally stood shyly naked before him, he merely lifted her in his arms and carried her to the tub, lowering her carefully into the hot water.

Her regret fading, Jess gave a sigh of pure unadulterated pleasure. "This really is heaven," she murmured, which brought an indulgent chuckle from her husband.

"It doesn't take much to please you."

Scooping up a handful of bath salts from the jar that sat beside the tub, he sprinkled the crystals over the water, then swirled it with his fingers. Jess leaned her head back and closed her eyes, savoring the warmth of the silky water, feeling her tiredness seep away. "I could get addicted to this."

"Good," Devlin replied, straightening and turning away.

She kept her eyes shut while Devlin popped the cork on the bottle of champagne, only opening them again when he handed her a full glass and a plate of flaky croissants filed with thin slices of ham and dripping with melted cheese. He fed her a bite, then took one himself, before stepping back to remove his own clothing.

"This is so decadent," she repeated lazily, letting the bubbly wine roll around on her tongue.

His mouth lifted on an indolent grin as he pulled off his soot-streaked shirt. "If I have my way, you'll learn to fully enjoy decadence, Mrs. Devlin."

Mrs. Devlin. Devlin's wife. She still wasn't sure she could believe it. After all the accusations she'd made against him, after all the times she'd mistrusted him and doubted him, he still professed to love her. She'd never imagined she would be lucky enough to win the love of a man like him. It was impossible, but somehow she'd done it. She'd caught her own unreachable wild star.

Fully aware of her good fortune, she glanced over at

him. Devlin had stripped off his clothing and was standing at the washstand, lathering his stubbled jaw, his right side toward her.

She tried not to stare, but the display of rippling muscles in his arms and shoulders held her gaze like a magnet. He stood there, entirely naked, in broad daylight, without the least sign of self-consciousness or embarrassment—just like the first time she had seen him, his naked torso framed by his hotel window. But this time she had a right to watch.

Heat rising to her cheeks, she took in the beauty of the man who was now her husband ... the hard, sleek body, the potent masculinity. He was her dream lover, handsome, magnificent.

Hesitantly, with increasing boldness, she let her gaze drop lower, to fasten on the swollen shaft at his groin. He was fully aroused, his splendid erection blatant, powerful, beautifully formed. The sight of that masculine flesh that could give such wild, wild pleasure sent Jessica's pulse rate soaring, while the thought of having that rigid fullness thrusting inside her, filling her, made her hot all over.

Suddenly becoming aware of her lustful thoughts, she swallowed the rest of her croissant and resumed her bath, soaping herself all over. A bottle of shampoo scented with lemon sat beside the tub, and she used it to wash her hair.

She had just finished ducking her head under the water to rinse out the suds when Devlin carried a pitcher of fresh warm water over to her. Having him so near, so naked, had a devastating effect on her senses. She couldn't seem to move. And he was watching her, his eyes filled with an intimate fire. She submitted to his lazy scrutiny with a shiver of excitement.

He knelt beside the tub and slowly poured the contents of the pitcher over her hair, his fingers kneading the remaining soap from her wet tresses, gently plying her scalp. Jess closed her eyes, nearly melting at his tenderness.

His magical fingers drifted across her face and throat and shoulders, then lower, to cup and fondle her bare sts. She drew a sharp breath and came totally awake, her lashes lifting.

"I get to finish washing you." He gave her a slow smile that held so much sexual charm it made her tremble. "You neglected a few spots," he explained, his thumbs making lazy circles over the sensitive buds.

Jess clenched her teeth, wondering how long she could bear such sweet torment, but Devlin remained unhurried, taking his time, his fingers smoothing, skimming over the slick wet flesh. Finally, he scooped up a handful of water and let it dribble over her breasts. Then, his hands curling around her upper arms, holding her still, he leaned forward.

She inhaled a sharp breath as he captured a tight, hurting nipple and drew it into his mouth, sending a streak of heat arrowing straight to the feminine hollow between her thighs, and dredging a hushed moan from her throat. Helplessly, Jess arched her back, letting him have his way.

His tongue swirled and lapped, tasting, teasing, tormenting her nipples till they throbbed with a pleasure so intense it was almost painful. Jess was softly panting by the time he finally drew back and got to his feet.

"Stand up, sweetheart, will you?"

She didn't know if it was possible. Weakly, Jess unfolded her long legs and tried to stand, clutching at him for support. When she started to step from the tub, though, Devlin forestalled her.

"No, stay. You're not even halfway finished, love."

Her eyes widened as he stepped into the tub and settled himself in her place. Then turning Jess so that she faced away from him, he drew her down, her back to him, her hips cradled by his hard thighs. The position was a bit cramped, and the higher water level lapped at the tub's rim, but Jess couldn't find the slightest desire to protest. She lay back obediently, resting her head in the curve of her husband's shoulder.

"I wanted to do this two months ago," Devlin said in her ear, in a voice that was velvet-smooth and husky. "Every time I took a bath at your house, I'd think of you in the water with me and get hard."

"Really, you did? You'd think of me?"

"Every time. And get hard." He wrapped an arm around her waist and pulled her bottom closer, very deliberately letting her feel precisely what he meant. "See what you do to me, sweet?"

Jess could hardly breathe, let alone give him a reply. He was moving his hips against her softly, stroking the velvet-sheathed hardness of his arousal against her buttocks. "But . . . you didn't want . . . to make love to me that first time when we were trapped in the Wildstar," she managed to get out.

"You're wrong, angel. I wanted you so much I hurt with it." His hand moved up to cup the swelling weight of her breast, making Jess tense.

"Then why . . . did you make me beg you?"

"Because, love, I was trying to be a gentleman. Where I come from, a man doesn't seduce a young lady he doesn't plan to marry." As if to apologize, his other hand glided downward over her body, his lean fingers spreading to stroke her taut, flat belly.

"You didn't want . . . to marry me. . . ."

"Not at first. I didn't want to marry anyone." His fingers reached lower, to tangle in the wet curls between her thighs; every muscle in her body tightened. "But I changed my mind when I realized how much I loved you. Just relax, sweetheart. I'm going to show you how to really enjoy a bath."

Relax? That was physically impossible, Jess thought, and so was further speech. Any ability she might have had for a coherent conversation fled as Devlin pressed against the moist cleft, withdrew slightly, and pressed again.

Her hips arched at his sensual caress, and her damp quivering thighs opened to him. Immediately, his fingers thrust inside her, stroking, sliding, moving in a slow, bewitching rhythm, leisurely plying the swollen, aching folds of her flesh.

He ignored the soft, keening moans she gave, the fingers of one hand massaging the slick hot satin flesh between her thighs to his ruthless satisfaction; the other hand stroking her jutting breasts, pulling and caressing her nipples, the hard thumb pressing and releasing; his tongue swirling around the shell of her ear, thrusting within, mimicking what his magical fingers were doing elsewhere.

Jess writhed in abandoned surrender; she couldn't stop. She whimpered Devlin's name on a strangled moan, but that only made him quicken his rhythm as he stroked her to climax.

He smiled in satisfaction as the trembling, sexually aroused woman he held came apart in his arms. Her lush body jerked in liquid, mindless shudders, splashing bathwater all over the elegant carpet, but Devlin simply tightened his hold, not letting her go, delighting in the passion that flushed her skin and made her breathing harsh.

The tremors of her body faded away slowly. Limp, pliant, satiated, Jess lay there languorously, unmoving. The racking pleasure had exhausted her.

"Jess?"

"Mmmm?"

"Are you going to sleep on me?"

"No . . . just taking a rest."

His lips curved in a molasses-slow, contented smile. "Think you could find the energy to give your husband a bath?"

Husband, she thought with a blissful glow of happiness that warmed her all over. Her eyelashes fluttered open.

Unhurriedly, he turned her over to face him, spreading her knees on either side of his hips to straddle his thighs. Not surprisingly, the hot, hungry look in his smoky gray eyes made Jess's tiredness vanish, her body come alive again.

The silky hair on his chest abraded her sensitive breasts as she sat up. She could feel the stiffness of his powerful shaft against her stomach, hard and long and ready.

"Garrett? Do you want me to . . ." She blushed at the question she couldn't bring herself to ask.

"Not yet. I want this to last. Wash my hair first," he commanded softly.

Her senses humming with anticipation, Jess obeyed. She made it into a ritual: slowly soaping his hair . . . sensually massaging his scalp with her fingers . . . meticulously rinsing away the suds . . . attending Devlin with the same devotion he had shown her. All the while she sat astride him brazenly, in nearly the most intimate way possible, with his heavy shaft brushing tantalizingly against her femininity every time she made the slightest movement. The scent of lemon surrounded her, blending with intense sexual awareness to caress and arouse her senses to a fever pitch.

His muscles coiled and rippled under her hands as she carried her ministrations further, to include his shoulders and arms and chest. It was a joy, being able to touch Devlin freely this way, to run her hands over his sleek skin, the hard contours of his body. And yet all she began to think about was whether he would put an end to the hot restless longing that was swelling again inside her, when he would ease the throbbing ache between her thighs.

Unable to bear it any longer, she let her hands move lower to skim tentatively over his taut abdomen . . . to encircle the thick, rigid fullness that was taunting her with the promise of fulfillment.

Devlin's entire body clenched, and he gave a low groan that vibrated with pleasure—but still he did nothing to hasten the moment.

"Garrett . . . please . . . I want you. . . ."

His hands came to her hips then. In a single powerful motion, he raised her up and held her poised over his jutting arousal.

Then, his bright, hot eyes holding hers intently, he lowered her slowly upon his rigid, throbbing length, his entry sensual, tormenting, exquisite as he pulled her down and around him.

Jess exhaled a shuddering breath, her eyes closing in ecstasy.

His body completely still, Devlin held her there, impaled on his erection, filling her but not allowing her fulfillment. A tremor quivered through Jess, resonating outward, upward, from her very center, moving with aching intensity throughout her entire body. Helplessly, she shuddered and rocked against him.

"No . . . easy, take it slow, angel." His fingers tightened on her hips, staying her motion with a strength that only màde her desire sharper. "We have all the time in the world." He leaned back, closing his eyes, his face tightening as if in pain. "Oh, God, this is so good. . . ."

Jess agreed with all her heart, and yet his demand that she go slowly was impossible to obey. Clinging to Devlin, she shut her eyes and tried to stop the quivering explosion she felt building inside her, but it was like trying to hold back one of the devastating flash floods that swept down the Rocky Mountain canyons in a storm. The torrent of desire was too strong, her need too savage.

"Garrett . . . !" His name on her lips was a gasped plea. Her muscles clenched around him involuntarily, gripping the hard, pulsing length of him.

His hands clamped down hard on her hips, trying to hold back, but he was losing his maddening control, she could feel it. His fading willpower gave her a fierce sensation of triumph, of joy.

With a final effort at restraint, his strong hands gripped her buttocks, holding her close as he swelled upward into her lush heat. But it was the beginning of the end for Jess. She rode him helplessly as he moved, unable to contain the frenzied passion that swept through her in a tremendous rush.

"*Jess.*" The word, a harsh sound ripped from deep inside him, mingled with her keening, incoherent cry. The sweet, tearing burst of light and heat shuddering through her had caught Devlin in its power.

He shut his eyes against the wild delirium, the incredible, staggering pleasure, as he arched deep into her. Nothing in his previous, vast carnal experience had prepared him for the impossible ecstasy he felt at this moment, at the wild, flame-hot consummation of his marriage to the woman he loved. He never wanted it to end.

The explosive climax did end, of course; it was physically impossible to maintain such a shattering peak of desire at such a fierce intensity. And yet long after Jess had collapsed in his arms, melting around him, their harsh breaths mingling, the pleasure remained, a slow, pulsing golden glow that surrounded him with warmth.

Some long while later—neither of them could have said when—sanity returned. Jess was lying draped over him like a rug, her face buried in the curve of his throat, while Devlin lay quietly beneath her, his head thrown back, his eyes closed.

When she started to stir, though, his fingers tightened on her hips. "No . . . hold still. I want to feel you around me."

The water had grown cold and she was half asleep before Devlin finally allowed her to move. He lifted Jess to her feet and lovingly dried her off, then carried her to the bed.

"Garrett, was it all right?" she asked as he tucked her in.

"Was what all right, sweet?"

"Making love to me?"

The tenderness that entered his eyes reassured her. "It was far better than all right, Jess. It was . . ." Settling one hip on the mattress beside her, he searched for a word that could adequately describe the fierce feelings that had flowed through him when he'd taken her the first time as her husband. The shattering climax had been heightened, intensified, nearly tearing him apart. This woman—his wife, the woman he loved—had touched a part of him that he'd never known existed.

"It was exquisite," he said simply, honestly.

"But . . . I don't have any experience."

"You gave me something I consider far more precious, Jess . . . your love. That more than makes up for any technical skill you might lack." With a gentle solemnity, Devlin's hand came up to trace the delicate outline of her jaw. "Do you know what I used to dream about? That someday I would have a woman like you to love me as loyally as you loved your father. To stick by me through thick and thin, to cherish me for myself, not the size of my bank account."

Her gaze softening with love, Jess turned her face to press her lips to his palm. "I'll stick by you, Garrett, with or without your bank account."

"I don't doubt that in the slightest, angel. You're a special kind of woman."

He leaned down to press a chaste kiss on her forehead, but instead of joining her in bed, he stood up.

Drowsily, her eyebrows drew together in a frown. "Are you going somewhere?"

"No. I just want to lower the window shades."

Efficiently, he took care of the task, shutting out the bright fall sunshine and cloaking the hotel room in semi-darkness. Just as he was about to return to the bed, however, a quiet knock sounded on the door.

Biting back an oath, Devlin pulled on a dressing gown, then strode impatiently to the door and yanked it open just a crack.

"My excuses, m'sieur," Louis Dupuy said, "but a telegram has come for you. I thought you would wish to see it, since it is marked 'urgent.' "

"Thank you, Louis."

Accepting the telegram, Devlin shut the door and began to read.

No longer sleepy, Jess sat up in bed, clutching the covers to her breasts. "Is something wrong?"

"No," Devlin said dryly. "It's just my father demanding attention, as usual. I had Clem wire him about our marriage, and this is his answer. C.E. welcomes you into the Devlin family, by the way."

Devlin returned to the bed and handed her the telegram. As he shrugged out of his dressing gown, Jess tried to read in the dim light. It was indeed the senior Devlin's polite congratulations on his son's marriage and, surprisingly, a warmly worded welcome to Jessica. But there was an additional cryptic message at the end that read, "Will send marble tub next week. Stop. Signed, C.E."

"What does this mean, 'Will send marble tub'?" Jess

asked as Devlin climbed into bed beside her and arranged the covers over them both.

"My father intends to give us a bathtub for a wedding present."

"A bathtub?"

"I told him you had a fetish for hot water and bath salts."

"You told your father I wanted a *bathtub*? Good Lord, what will he think of me?"

"Correction, angel." Facing her, Devlin draped his arm possessively over her rib cage, beneath her breasts. "I told him *we* wanted a bathtub—and that was all we wanted from him. And truthfully, I don't give a damn what he thinks of you. You married *me*, not the Devlin family."

His grim tone told Jess very clearly she had struck a nerve. "It sounds like you don't much care for your father."

Devlin gave a soft grunt of agreement. "He's a manipulative bastard who could run circles around Burke. You'd like him as little as you like Burke."

"I don't dislike Burke so much anymore. I can't forgive everything he's done, but it's hard to hold the past against him when he's trying to change. Besides, if it weren't for him, I would never have known you. It was because of Burke that I hired you."

Devlin's mouth curved in a smile. Sliding down a bit farther, he pressed his naked body closer and nuzzled his lips in the curve of her throat. "I suppose I can't be too upset with my father, either. He was the reason I came to Silver Plume."

"Oh. In that case, I think I could kiss him."

Devlin tensed at her comment. "Don't you dare even *think* about it."

Jess was curious. "Would you be jealous?"

In answer, Devlin raised his head and gave her a hard kiss. "I'll tell you about my father and his women, sometime. But not now. We have better things to do." Slipping his hand between their bodies, he ran his palm provocatively down the silken length of her thigh, then slowly up again, to press suggestively against the threshold of her femininity.

"Aren't . . . you sleepy yet?" she murmured breathlessly, surprised at his stamina. He had been up all night, battling a raging fire.

The tender light in Devlin's eyes was a potent mingling of amusement and hunger. "Exhausted, but I don't feel it. Do you?"

"No," Jess answered honestly, distracted by his bold fingers.

"Good. We can sleep later. At the moment I intend to convince you just how much I want you."

With a love-dazed smile, Jessica threaded her arms around her handsome husband's neck and drew his head down. "I think I may need a lot of convincing. You've told me more than once than I'm stubborn."

Devlin's low, sensual chuckle whispered tantalizingly against her lips. "It will be my pleasure, Mrs. Devlin."